OTHER WORK
MCGOLDR
MCGOLDRICK

MW00623137

Writing as

MAY MCGOLDRICK
JAN COFFEY AND NIK JAMES

MAY MCGOLDRICK NOVELS

A Midsummer Wedding

The Thistle and the Rose

Angel of Skye (Macpherson Trilogy Book 1)

Heart of Gold (Book 2)

Beauty of the Mist (Book 3)

Macpherson Trilogy (Box Set)

The Intended

Flame

Tess and the Highlander

The Dreamer (Highland Treasure Trilogy Book 1)

The Enchantress (Book 2)

The Firebrand (Book 3)

Highland Treasure Trilogy Box Set

Much Ado About Highlanders (Scottish Relic Trilogy Book 1)

Taming the Highlander (Book 2)

Tempest in the Highlands (Book 3)

Scottish Relic Trilogy Box Set

Arsenic and Old Armor

The Promise (Pennington Family)

The Rebel

Secret Vows Box Set

Borrowed Dreams (Scottish Dream Trilogy Book 1)

Captured Dreams (Book 2)

Dreams of Destiny (Book 3)

Scottish Dream Trilogy Box Set

Romancing the Scot

It Happened in the Highlands

Sweet Home Highland Christmas

Sleepless in Scotland

Dearest Millie

How to Ditch a Duke

A Prince in the Pantry

Highland Crown (Royal Highlander Series Book 1)

Highland Jewel (Book 2)

Highland Sword (Book 3)

Ghost of the Thames

Thanksgiving in Connecticut

Made in Heaven

Marriage of Minds: Collaborative Writing *(Nonfiction)*

Step Write Up: Writing Exercises for 21st Century *(Nonfiction)*

NIK JAMES NOVELS

Caleb Marlowe Westerns

High Country Justice

Bullets and Silver

The Winter Road

Silver Trail Christmas

JAN COFFEY NOVELS

Trust Me Once

Twice Burned

Triple Threat

Fourth Victim

Five in a Row

Silent Waters

Cross Wired

The Janus Effect

The Puppet Master

Blind Eye

Road Kill

Mercy

When the Mirror Cracks

Tropical Kiss

Aquarian

Omid's Shadow

JANE AUSTEN CANNOT MARRY!

MAY MCGOLDRICK

JAN COFFEY

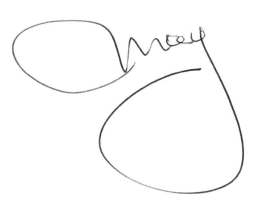

2022

MERRY CHRISTMAS, Emily!

WISHING you PEACE, HEALTH,

Nile & Jim & THERESA

Thank you for choosing *Jane Austen* Cannot *Marry!* In the event that you appreciate this book, please consider sharing the good word(s) by leaving a review, or connect with the authors.

Cover by Dar Albert, WickedSmartDesigns.com

"There could have been no two hearts so open, no tastes so similar, no feelings so in unison..."

— JANE AUSTEN, *PERSUASION*

Village of Hythe, on the English Channel
April 12, 1811

NADINE GLANCED across the cobbled road at the fog hanging like a cloud around the flickering lamp outside the White Hart Tavern. The deep voices of men singing a sea chanty inside spilled out onto the narrow street.

The tavern nestled amid the cluster of shops and homes that lined the High Street. The main thoroughfare ran east and west, and the shoreline lay a quarter mile to the south. The road followed one of the natural terraces of hills that rose steadily to the north, where the land eventually leveled out into farms and pastures all the way to Canterbury. Below the High Street, at the bottom of the hill, a new military canal was nearly finished, and beyond it, fishing huts and small cottages dotted the land along the beach and the edges of a great marsh.

Regardless of its similarity to a thousand other English towns, the village of Hythe was special.

Twice a day, the eastbound coach came through. And it was here in Hythe, four days from now, that Jane Austen would disembark on her way to London. Jane Austen, who was on her way to prepare her first novel, *Sense and Sensibility*, for publication. Jane Austen, who was destined to have her writing touch generations of people.

Nadine pulled the hood of her cloak tight against the damp chill of the night breeze. The strap of the bag she carried under the cloak was digging into her shoulder, but she didn't dare adjust it.

"You're saying that Captain Gordon arrived just before dark?"

"Aye, ma'am. Right before our supper." The young footman glanced from the coin she'd given him to the tavern door, his destination before she waylaid him.

"How long does he plan to stay?"

"No telling. But he's on leave, and one of the upstairs maids says the mistress expects him to be at Hythe for a fortnight, at least."

Nadine was relieved that Gordon had finally arrived. She'd called at Churchill House two days ago and again yesterday, asking for him. Any more visits and she'd risk arousing suspicion.

"Is your mistress expecting any other company this weekend?"

"Not that I know, ma'am."

"Any planned excursions by the captain...say, for tomorrow?"

"No word on that, ma'am."

Nadine's attention shifted to an elderly woman being pulled along by a squat, one-eyed dog. Since arriving in Hythe, she'd seen the pair numerous times. The woman always cast suspicious looks in her direction, and the dog never passed without growling at her and straining at his leash.

She stepped back into the shadows of the building, hoping they'd pass by without noticing her.

"Anything else you'll be needing, ma'am."

"No. Thank you. I'll be calling on your mistress and the captain tomorrow."

The footman tipped his bicorn hat and crossed the road to the tavern, tossing the coin in the air as he walked.

The muffled sound of church bells tolling nine came out of the fog. Nadine glanced down the road toward the Swan, the coaching inn where she was staying. It was only a few doors away from the tavern, but it might as well have been in Ireland, for what she could make of it through the darkness and the fog. Even the lamp hanging by the arched entry to the inner yard and stables was invisible.

Nadine was tired, but the thought of having to walk past the grim-faced innkeeper and his suspicious glares made her cringe. When she'd taken the room, her smile had been met with a frown. Her pleasant greeting answered with a snarl. And tipping him a few extra coins had made no difference in the hospitality.

Even though providing shelter to strangers was his stock-in-trade, the innkeeper was not exactly hospitable to her, a woman alone. And she'd learned not to ask for a plate to be sent up. The cold meat and fetid greens and stale buns she'd been served the night of her arrival had tested the strength of her stomach.

Nadine adjusted the strap of the bag beneath her cloak. She had one more stop to make before facing the innkeeper and the discomforts of the Swan.

She stepped out of the shadows.

"Who are you?"

Nadine jumped, not realizing that the villager and her dog were waiting for her. It took a moment for her to find her courage and her voice.

"I could ask the same of you. Why are you following me?"

The older woman's frown was fierce. "You're not from here, and you talk funny. What's that accent? Are you a Frenchie?"

"No," Nadine replied firmly. "I'm just a traveler passing through Hythe."

She looked down warily at the dog. He was pulling at his lead and baring his teeth only inches from the hem of her cloak.

Animals usually liked her. Strangers generally trusted her, with the innkeeper being one of the few exceptions to the rule. Nadine had often been told she had a warm and friendly demeanor. But she also knew that the British were big on introductions and propriety. A woman, traveling on her own with no male figure or chaperone, was suspicious.

"But you're *not* passing through." The voice rose, and a bony finger pointed accusingly at Nadine's chest. "You've been here since Tuesday, and don't try to deny it."

It wasn't her imagination. The busybody *was* following her. Nadine thought of the warnings she'd received before arriving in this village. The war with the French was on everyone's mind, and there had been rumors that an invasion could happen along the coast at any time. Because of that, the locals were fearful, and strangers were suspect.

"Yes, you're correct. I've been here since Tuesday for a family matter."

"Without your husband?"

The memory of the dark brown eyes of the man who'd asked Nadine to be his wife flashed in her brain. Regardless of how much time went by, Xander was always with her. What had been said and done between them was still alive within her. In some ways, it was as if she'd never walked away. Never left him standing at the altar.

"You are married, aren't you?"

"Yes, I am."

"Then, where is he?"

Nadine wished Xander would simply show up. But that was an impossible dream.

"My husband's not with me."

"Where is he?"

"He is in London. He'll soon join me."

"Your children?"

A lump grew in her throat. A normal, healthy woman in a loving relationship could dream of such things. A child. A future. Not her.

"Well, out with it? Where are your children?"

"I have none."

"You're *old* enough to have a dozen."

If the woman only knew Nadine's real age. Centuries separated her future birth from today's date. In a biological sense, though, she was thirty-five.

"What's your name? Introduce yourself at once."

"My name is Nadine Finley. And you are?"

"Elizabeth Hole. Daughter of the late James Hole, a fishmonger with premises right here in the High Street. My mother was a Lydd. And they were both born in Hythe, as were their parents and every generation back to the day of the Conqueror. Not that I need to be telling you this, but St Leonard's, up there...?" She waved a hand up the hill. "I was christened in that church, not a dozen steps from where my family's bones are stored in the ossuary. So, I'm *from* here, and there are no Finleys living in Hythe. In short, Miss Finley—or whoever you are—you're lying."

That was quite an introduction. She was tempted to do the same thing. She could certainly fabricate an ancestry to satisfy this inquisitor.

The dog gave a sharp bark and a growl. Nadine sent a guarded look at the snarling animal, wondering if those sharp teeth were about to clamp onto her leg.

"I didn't say I was visiting my *own* family." She took a step back. "And I'll thank you to keep your little Cyclops away from my ankle."

"Never mind about Kai." She picked up the dog and tucked him under her arm. "Why are you here? Explain yourself and be quick about it."

Nadine wasn't about to tell Elizabeth Hole her business. She certainly wasn't going to mention Captain Gordon or the Honorable Margaret Deedes, the sister he was visiting. If this one went running up to Churchill House, the plans could be ruined. The last thing Nadine needed was to have the captain refuse to speak with her.

"You are correct that I arrived on Tuesday. And it is my intention to leave on the coach Saturday...or at the latest on Monday." She hoped sooner. She didn't want to cut it too close, and Monday would be cutting it close. "So, if you'll pardon me..."

Nadine stepped around the shrew. Almost simultaneously, the door of the tavern opened, and three uniformed coast guardsmen staggered out. The trio, clearly drunk, linked arms and marched unsteadily off into the darkness, singing as they went.

Nadine followed, listening to the low growling recede behind her. When she was a few doors down from the White Hart, she looked over her shoulder and was relieved to see the woman and her canine companion had disappeared. Elizabeth Hole had apparently given up the chase for tonight, but Nadine was certain that wasn't the last she'd be seeing of her.

Keeping to the shadows and walking quickly, she passed the Swan and then turned down the hill. In a few moments, she reached the canal and crossed the new bridge. Down here, the fog was thicker, and the smell of salt air and fish mixed with woodsmoke. None of the tradesmen's shops were open, given the hour, and only a few of the cottages she passed showed a light in the windows.

The darkness and stillness were a bit unnerving. Nadine preferred cities to villages and the countryside. Safety in numbers. Situations like this always left her with the acid taste of vulnerability in her mouth. But where she was sent and what assignment she was given had never been her choice to make.

And she'd had some very unsavory assignments. Russia in 1917, as the Bolshevik revolutionaries stormed the Winter Palace. Egypt in 48 BC, as Caesar's troops burned Alexandria and the great library there. The Yucatan in 1562, as Spanish priests and soldiers destroyed Mayan books.

But she always succeeded in finishing the task she was given. She had to. This was her life, the path she'd been forced to take.

She moved along the rutted road that led toward the shoreline. The silence of the neighborhood was broken only once by the sound of men laughing and quarreling outside a public house down one of the side streets.

Nadine judged, from the directions she'd received, that she was getting close to her destination. She turned her head at the sound of footsteps behind her. She could see nothing through the fog. To be safe, she slipped into the deep shadows beside a shack and waited.

Her hand slid inside the bag, and her fingers wrapped around the weapon she carried. It was small, lipstick-sized, but it was powerful enough to stun a good-sized man.

Seconds ticked by. The footsteps stopped a few doors up. A low cough. She heard mud being scraped from the soles of boots. A knock, a murmured greeting from a man, and a woman's voice asking him in. A moment later, the door closed, leaving Nadine alone once more.

She stepped out of the shadows and continued down the lane. Another turn and she spied her destination.

The place was little more than a black blur of walls and thatched roof, huddled between a low hill and a neighbor's cottage. Nadine made her way stealthily through a large kitchen garden filled with rows of seedlings. Through a gap in the shutters of a window, Nadine could make out the flickering light from a fireplace. Deirdre was up late.

She went to the door and knocked softly.

The sound of footsteps inside was followed by an uncertain voice. "Who is it?"

"It's Nadine."

The door opened, and the young woman peered outside toward

the lane before pulling her in and closing the door. "I can't believe it. You're here."

"I told you I'd come."

Nadine glanced past her for the person she'd come to see. Deirdre's son, Andrew.

Across the room, the toddler was sleeping on the bed he shared with his mother.

"How is he doing?"

"Been sleeping soundly since supper. And that's a blessing."

"Coughing?"

"None tonight."

"Fever?"

"He had a good appetite, and his face is cool to my touch."

Relieved, Nadine looked around her. The cottage was small, but snug enough against the early spring chill. Above the fire, a pot hung from a long arm. A steaming kettle sat on the hearthstones. Near the fireplace, a cloth was draped over a tray of bread loaves that were rising. A variety of herbs were strung together, hanging down from the low rafters.

A table with three chairs sat by the shuttered window, and plates and cups were arranged neatly on shelves above a sideboard. A large pile of sewing had been stacked on a small cot. A wardrobe, a low wooden chest, a washstand, and the bed where Andrew slept comprised the rest of the cottage's furnishings.

Deirdre covered the window with a blanket. "They were here, looking for you. I was afraid they'd already found you."

"Who was here?"

"The coast guardsmen."

"Why? What did they say?"

"They wanted to know about the stranger...the woman with the French accent who was seen at the market the other day, asking questions."

Damn. She'd arrived in Hythe on Tuesday, the town's market day. And she *had* spoken to a few vendors, trying to find her bearings.

"I don't have a French accent," Nadine said defensively, knowing the authorities were on the lookout for Napoleon's spies.

"Well, you talk different."

"I don't. I speak English. The same as you."

"No, you don't. You talk different."

She could stand there all night and argue. But what was the point? Compared to the locals, she did have an accent. But it definitely wasn't French.

"What did you tell them?"

She shrugged. "That I saw you at the market, but not since."

"Why did they come here?"

"Someone saw us talking, I suppose." Deirdre shook her head. "Hythe is a village. People are on the lookout. Ears are pressed against the walls. Everyone knows everyone else's business. I've lived here my whole life, but my mother had Irish blood. So, I've been the center of attention since my husband left. And far more than I like, let me tell you."

Deirdre's husband had been hauled off by a press gang to 'volunteer' in the British fleet eight months ago, and she hadn't heard from him since.

At the market, Nadine had only struck up a conversation with Deirdre because of Andrew. Walking along the stalls, she'd felt a tug on her skirt and looked down to find a youngster, perhaps two or three years of age, staring up at her. Red hair, the face of a cherub, and a head that seemed too big for the small, thin body.

"Lost," he'd said to her.

"Are you lost?" Nadine had asked.

"No. You."

She'd crouched down, and the boy's green eyes locked with hers. The intensity of the stare was unsettling. It was like he saw through her, knew she didn't belong in that marketplace, in that period.

"Who do you belong to?" she'd asked. "Where are your parents?"

He cupped her face with small hands, and that's when she noticed he was feverish, burning.

"Here you are. I've been looking for you everywhere." A woman appeared and lifted the boy into her arms. He started coughing. He couldn't catch his breath.

Shaking herself free of the memory, Nadine's eyes focused on the sleeping form of the toddler. "Can I listen to him breathe? Are you sure there's no fever?"

"See for yourself." Deirdre motioned to her son.

Walking toward him, Nadine smiled at the red hair standing up straight as porcupine needles on the pillow. He looked pale in the flickering firelight. Even so, she could hear no more wheezing when she put her ear to his chest.

Deirdre stood beside her. "Your magic potion worked."

"Not magic," Nadine replied, a bit sharper than she intended. She didn't know whether they were still burning witches in Hythe. "Only medicine."

"Better medicine than anything I've ever seen." Deirdre sat on the edge of the bed and tucked the blanket around her son. "My mother-in-law brought the doctor here yesterday, still thinking my Andrew was fighting to breathe. He was going to bleed my poor lad."

"What did you do?"

"I told them my prayers had been answered. That he was mending. I sent them away."

"You did the right thing."

"I know I did. I have a good sense of these things. For people too. I know who to trust and not to trust. I trusted you, didn't I?"

Andrew had trusted her first. He'd been the one who found her. Got her attention.

Nadine recalled her conversation with Deirdre at the market. She'd asked about Andrew's symptoms and how long he'd been suffering from them. Deirdre had asked suspiciously if Nadine had some training with a doctor.

—*Some. And better training than the doctors in this village.*

—*I don't trust them at all. I lost Andrew's older brother to the same cough when he was a wee babe.*

—*I can help him. Will you trust me?*

After a dozen more questions, the woman had decided that Nadine would not give her son anything that would hurt him or make his condition worse.

"His lungs seem clear."

"I did as you said. Whenever he gets coughing, I put the drops you gave me into a bowl with the boiling water and hold his head over the steam. It works right away."

Nadine put a hand on the boy's forehead to check for the fever herself. It was cool.

"I told you. He's cool to my touch. But I finished the pills you gave me."

Nadine pulled back her cloak. Reaching into the leather bag that hung from her shoulder, she drew out a small round tin and handed it to Deirdre.

"This is the rest of what I have. Give it to him twice a day. Morning and night."

The mother took the tin. "What happens after? Will the fever come back?"

"Not right away. Maybe never. The cough might come back, but you know what to do if it does. And he might outgrow it. Some people do." And some don't, regardless of medical advances.

Nadine glanced around the cottage, counting a dozen things that could be the trigger for the child's asthma attacks. She'd lied when she said she had some medical training. She was no doctor. Her knowledge came from personal experience. The supplies she carried were for her own use, in case of an emergency. Her asthma was stress induced and she still had her inhaler in her bag and that was enough.

She pressed her hand to Andrew's forehead one more time. The boy smiled in his sleep and murmured something. Emotions welled up inside Nadine, and she wondered if she'd ever see him or his mother again. She'd lost count of all the people, like these two—like Xander— that she'd had to walk away from in her life.

"I need to be going."

Deirdre put her hand on Nadine's arm. "When are you leaving Hythe?"

"Hopefully, as soon as tomorrow, if I can convince Captain Gordon to escort me to Portsmouth." She'd given herself until Monday, she told herself for the hundredth time, but that was absolutely the latest.

"He's come to the village?"

"Yes, he arrived today."

Deirdre glanced at her child and back at Nadine. "Will you ever come back?"

"I really don't know. Maybe. Maybe not." The two stood and headed for the door. "By the way, do you know an elderly woman named Elizabeth Hole?"

"Everyone knows her. And she makes it her business to know everyone in Hythe." Deirdre pretended to shudder. "Don't tell me you've crossed her?"

"No, but she's also made it her business to follow me."

"That's not good. Not good at all. She's trouble. A nuisance of a woman. I'd keep my distance from her if I were you."

"I'll do my best."

"And I'd do the same in dealing with the coast guard. They won't deal kindly with you once they hear your French accent."

"It's not..." Nadine stopped, realizing she was being teased.

"Whatever you say." The woman smiled and the two hugged. "I don't know where you came from, Nadine Finley. But I thank the Lord that our paths crossed."

"Good luck to you, Deirdre." She cast one last look at the sleeping child. "Give Andrew a hug for me."

Slipping out of the cottage, she went up the lane in the direction of the coaching inn. Her plans for the next few days were tentative, at best. The simplest solution would be for the captain to believe her story and leave with her for the navy town of Portsmouth. She shook her head in the darkness. If they didn't go right away, however, so many complications could arise.

When Nadine reached the canal, she spotted a pair of armed coast guardsmen patrolling the far bank. They didn't appear to be on high alert, though. As they strolled along the canal, one of them was keeping the other entertained with some story. Still, she waited until the fog and darkness had swallowed them up before she hurried across the bridge and climbed the hill toward the High Street.

She reached the corner, stopped, and drew back a step. Directly in front of the Swan, an agitated Elizabeth Hole was bending the ear of a well-dressed gentleman and two tired-looking coast guardsmen. Whatever she was saying, she halted abruptly when her little dog swung around and began barking and snarling in Nadine's direction.

Damn that mutt.

"That's her. It must be."

As they all turned to look, Nadine spun on her heel and went back down the hill. Reaching the corner of the first building, she turned into the alley behind it.

Shouts and the sound of running followed her. She considered her options, which were few. She couldn't afford to be caught and questioned by the authorities. She had to evade them at all costs.

Her heart pounded in her chest. Her breath was getting heavy.

The alley was pitch black, and Nadine's shoulder scraped a wall as the lane doglegged slightly. Staying on her feet, she hurried along. The sound of Kai's barking was getting closer. They were right behind her and coming hard.

Ahead, a faint light from an upper-story window brightened the way enough for her to realize she'd come to a dead end. There was no way out.

"Damn it."

On her right, the back door to a shop was flanked by stacks of wood planks. She darted toward them and tried the door. No luck. Barred on the inside.

Her chest tightened some more. She was beginning to wheeze. She was horrified to think she was about to deal with a full-blown asthma attack.

Her pursuers were getting closer. Looking around her, Nadine spied three long wooden boxes leaning on an angle against the back wall of the shop.

Not just boxes, she realized. Coffins.

"There's no way out of this alley." Elizabeth Hole's voice rang out over the others. "She has nowhere to go. Arrest her!"

Nadine lifted the lid of one of the coffins. Covering her mouth to hush a cough, she stepped into the box and pulled the lid shut.

Elkhorn, Colorado
April 12, 2022

VISIBILITY WAS ZERO.

The heavy snow Xander had driven through after leaving Denver late this afternoon was history, at least for the moment. It was a barrage of sleet that now battered the pickup, and the gusting wind was strong enough to knock over an eighteen-wheeler. The wipers were icing up badly, and the blasting heat couldn't keep the windshield from fogging.

As Xander leaned forward to clear a spot to see through, a bolt of lightning split the darkening sky just ahead.

Spring in the Rockies. Gotta love it.

"Still there?" Ken's voice crackled through the speaker on the steering wheel. The cell reception along this stretch was always shaky, and the storm wasn't helping any.

"Yeah. Give me a minute."

After a year of living up on this mountain, Xander knew the curve ahead was a dangerous one. The service road had only an eyelash of a shoulder, having been carved out of a ledge of rock two miles high.

He eased up on the gas pedal, but not enough. The gut-tightening slide across the pavement was the last thing he wanted right now. He steered into the skid, aware of the drop beyond the invisible river churning through the deep gorge below. If he hit the brakes, they wouldn't find his picked-over carcass until July or August.

"Come on, baby. Grab. Grab. Grab."

For what felt like an eternity, he continued to slide closer to the edge. Finally, the tires hit the narrow, graveled shoulder, lurched and found some traction.

"Did I lose you?"

"Almost." He glanced out his window at the swirling clouds beyond the ledge. "I'm still here."

"Donna is saying I shouldn't be chirping at you while you're driving."

"Your wife is right."

"Well, maybe. But she's also delusional enough to think you'll call us back."

"I'll call you back."

"When? Next week? You've already ignored three texts and two voicemails."

That was true. Xander *had* ignored them. He knew what they were about. But there was no point admitting it to Ken.

"I've been out straight in Denver. One meeting after the other. Come over for a beer, and I'll tell you about it."

"Not tonight. This storm could get bad."

"Oh? No kidding?" Xander considered stopping and knocking the ice off his wipers.

"Don't hang up. We're not done talking about Saturday."

"Saturday? What's Saturday?"

"Don't joke. I *need* you, buddy."

For a baby shower. Ken and his wife Donna wanted him to tend the bar at their house while two dozen women 'oohed and ahhed' over diapers and miniature clothing. No thanks.

"You don't need me. You can handle it fine by yourself."

"I can't manage the barbecue and the bar at the same time."

"Barbecue in April? What happens if it snows?"

"She's put up with being pregnant for all these months, so I get her what she wants." Ken's voice softened, and Xander knew his friend was really talking to his wife.

"As well you should."

"Glad you agree. Most of Donna's friends like their booze. I need your help. *We* need your help."

Xander knew perfectly well what was going on. Donna was match-making. Lately, she'd been searching high and low for the right girl-friend-preferably-wife candidate for him. He had no doubt their last-minute 'Oh, the bartender canceled on us' line had nothing to do with a shortage of help and everything to do with Donna's plotting.

"I'll find you a bartender." Xander figured he could stop at any bar in Elkhorn, put a big enough tip on the table, and someone would jump at doing the four-hour job.

"I don't want you to find us a bartender. I want *you* here."

"What's Donna up to?"

"Nothing. This was my idea."

"Baby shower." Xander snorted. "You're throwing a baby shower for your wife and her girlfriends. Her single, available girlfriends, I'm guessing."

"Don't be paranoid." Long pause. "Why are you surprised that the people closest to you actually care about you and want you around? *We* want you to be part of the important moments in our life."

He knew what was coming next. Ken was about to pull the 'best friend' card.

"Is it too much to ask a favor of my best friend?"

"There it is, you fucker."

Xander and Ken grew up together, went to college together, started a company together, made their first million together, and almost got married the same weekend. A couple of years ago. In Vegas. Since then, Ken's marriage to Donna had been solid. Xander's marriage remained in the 'almost' category. He *almost* got married.

Then, everything changed for him and for the world.

Six months later, with the Covid pandemic wreaking havoc across the world, they sold their company, packed their bags, and left New York. Ken and Donna settled in a neighborhood of large, beautiful homes on the outskirts of Elkhorn, Colorado, a former silver boom town at the foot of this very mountain. Xander had wanted a view and, more importantly, he wanted privacy. So, he bought some land and a house up near a peak the locals called Devil's Claw.

Ken was happy with marriage and retirement. Aside from learning to fish and ski, he was even starting to dabble with writing fiction.

Xander, on the other hand, was restless. He'd already begun looking for involvement in another start-up.

"Nice way to talk to a highly sensitive and probably hormonal father-to-be. Not only am I your best friend, I'm also your *only* friend. And even that's a little iffy."

Xander scoffed, but it was pretty much true.

"Seriously, you're family. We want you to be part of the day."

Ken was cornering him at a vulnerable moment. The four-day conference at the convention center and the hotel had left him bone tired. And the two-hour drive from Denver had taken him five hours due to the weather and an accident on the state highway. And this icy road wasn't helping.

Neither he nor Ken had any siblings. They'd been like brothers since childhood. They *were* family.

An array of lightning exploded brilliantly across the sky, and then the frozen rain began to fall even harder.

"Are you still thinking?"

"Trying. If you'd shut up."

As he slowed the vehicle to a crawl, Xander thought of what his friend was asking him to do. Other than patching the now snow-and-ice-covered roof of the tumbledown garage, he had nothing going on this weekend. And if the weather kept up like this, he might not want to work outdoors, anyway.

Hell, being charming and pouring mimosas and mixing a Bloody Mary or two was certainly no trouble. And Xander also knew how to say no when he wanted to. He'd been doing a lot of that lately. He wasn't ready for a relationship. Not a serious one. Especially not with one of Donna's friends.

He cracked his window to help the defroster clear at least some of the icy smear from the windshield. The sleet sounded like machine gun fire on the roof and windows. He considered pulling over and waiting out the worst of the storm. But with his luck, he'd probably take a direct hit from one of these lightning strikes. Crazy, lightning in a winter storm. Who knew?

"Say something. I need to know you aren't plunging down the side of that mountain right now. 'Cuz then I'll really have to find another bartender."

"Fine. I'll do it. I'll come to the baby shower. But you'll owe me."

"You bet, bro. I'll be the best man at your wedding. I'll be the bartender at your wife's baby shower. I'll be—"

Xander punched the button to end the call. He didn't want to think about weddings and babies. He had no desire to dwell on how, at age thirty-eight, the only time he'd been tempted to tie the knot was with a woman that he'd met only three days before. The same one who skipped the wedding and disappeared while Xander stood like a fool in front of an Elvis impersonator with Ken and Donna ready to serve as witnesses.

She stood him up.

Stood. Him. Up.

Sex was easy. Relationships were complicated. And marriage? She hadn't even known him long enough to realize that he was a workaholic. And that he sucked at relationships.

Well, something caused her to wise up.

A blast of wind shook the pickup. Trying to keep his hands relaxed on the wheel, he forced himself to think about the offer he had on the table in Denver. Another project. Another business.

This time, he didn't have to put any of his own money down. The tech investors and the trio of engineers wanted him to run the operation as CEO. They were offering Xander a partnership because of his reputation for handling pressure. He'd taken an idea to market before and cashed in big time. He'd turned coal into diamonds, figuratively speaking.

He told them he'd get back to them.

Was he ready to come out of retirement already? Was he that bored?

A hard gust of sleet swept across the gleaming pavement. Xander flashed on his high beams and saw the reflection of the eyes. Immediately, a massive shape loomed in the car's path.

He slowed the truck to a crawl.

An elk the size of the Statue of Liberty was right in the middle of the road. It just stood there, gazing at him. The animal had a chest like a Clydesdale. Its neck was covered with a thick mane of dark fur. And the beast had a rack of antlers at least six feet wide, splaying out in all directions like spiders' legs.

"Jeez," Xander breathed, a thrill coursing down his spine.

He stopped the vehicle.

"Hello, big fellow."

Never in his life had he seen anything as magnificent as this.

"Nice to finally meet you."

At the outfitter's store down in Elkhorn, the locals had been arguing about a legendary giant elk. A few fellows claimed to have seen him. They called him the 'Spider Bull' because of the spread of the antlers. Hunters had been searching him out for years, but the elk was too smart for them. One skeptic grouched that the animal was nothing more than a myth that the guides had invented to sell hunting trips.

"And yet, here you are. King of the Mountain."

Xander sat transfixed, feeling his heart pounding in his chest. He had no intention of shortening this moment.

"And don't you worry. I won't say a word to anybody about seeing you up here."

The elk turned and faced the pickup. The sleet, mixed with snow, glistened on the animal's broad muzzle.

The two of them gazed at each other.

"I can do this all night. How about you?"

The elk pawed at the icy pavement.

Fingers of lightning streaked across the sky, and Xander saw something in the road beyond the animal.

"What've you got there?"

Suddenly, the elk raised his head and let out a noise like Xander had never heard before. It started off like a low growl and rose in pitch and intensity, deep and resonant.

"Holy..." He froze when the elk took a step toward the pickup.

For an electrifying moment, Xander thought he was going to charge. Then, with an unhurried air, the animal turned and walked slowly off the road. When he reached the tree line, he leaped effortlessly up the hill and disappeared into the night.

"Wow," Xander murmured. His heart was pounding like a steel drum in a subway.

He'd spent most of his adult life in crowded New York City and its environs. He'd never lived anywhere far from the sounds of traffic and people. And yet, here he was, surrounded by acres of wilderness so remote and rugged that one could travel much of it only on foot or horseback.

Ken and Donna gave him a hard time for becoming such a hermit, but since settling here, Xander loved losing himself for a day or a week amid these mountain forests and peaks, where the only signs of people were the trail, the random signpost, and maybe the odd shack or abandoned mine. Living here, he'd gained a new sense of the world and his place in it, along with a new appreciation for soft beds and working toilets.

He stared up the hill where the Spider Bull had disappeared. Taking another deep breath, he gave his pulse time to slow. This was one special moment.

Lightning flashed again, illuminating the night. Xander put the vehicle in drive, pulled up closer, and stared. Rocks and ice had tumbled down the hillside onto the pavement, partially obstructing his path. But that wasn't the problem.

Directly ahead of him, a wooden box lay diagonally across the road, blocking the way.

"What the hell?"

He studied the thing. About two feet high, two feet across, and six feet long.

Man, if that box didn't look like a coffin.

3

LEANING ON THE STEERING WHEEL, he stared at the box that was keeping him from a hot shower, a warm bed, and ten solid hours of sleep.

"You don't belong there."

Other than Xander and the occasional lost tourist, the service road was used mostly by the Forest Service. A week ago, during a hike into the State Forest, he'd come upon a ranger directing a group of volunteers who were starting to dismantle an old mining cabin. They'd dated the log structure to the gold rush days of the 1850s or 60s.

Hard living was the first thing that came to Xander's mind when he saw that abandoned cabin. No indoor plumbing and no electricity. Just a dirt floor and gaps in the walls that wouldn't have done much to keep a person from freezing during the long, cold Colorado winters.

They planned to preserve as much of the cabin as possible, truck it down to Elkhorn along this road, and piece it back together.

"To protect a relic of Colorado history." That was how one of the volunteers put it.

Xander had paid very little attention to history growing up. In fact, he'd ignored it as much as he could. The same went for literature. The only reading he was drawn to involved some puzzle or game. He was a left-brain person. Analytical. A math guy. That was who he was, and he was perfectly comfortable with it.

His almost wife-to-be had been the complete opposite.

Even though their time together had been brief, he'd learned that she loved books. Novels. Poetry. She couldn't understand how it was that he couldn't name a single book he'd read in the past year. Past two years. Five years.

Then he'd given her a lecture on the importance of numbers.

Math wasn't subjective. Every question had a clear answer. You were either right or wrong. There were no gray areas. Empirical evidence was supreme.

Xander recalled telling her, "Data is king. Imagine the number of problems that could be prevented if everything was based on objective data rather than emotions."

She showed him how she felt about his opinion. She left him standing in the chapel with his 'data' swinging in the breeze.

The arcing windshield wipers scattered the memories, and he focused on the coffin-shaped box that had been dumped on the road. Whoever lost it was probably home right now, sitting in front of a warm fire.

"Let's go, Xander," he muttered. "Nobody's going to move that thing for you."

Pulling on his coat and hat, he stepped out of the truck. The freezing rain stung his face. The wind blasted him sideways as he approached. He definitely could see it falling off the back of one of the preservation group's trucks.

With all the close attention they'd been giving to every possible artifact in that cabin, someone would be looking for this crate sooner or later. All he had to do was to push it to the side of the road and they'd come back for it.

Another bolt of lightning exploded overhead, and the sleet changed to hail in an instant.

Xander stopped in his tracks. Marbled-sized balls of ice pounded him.

The box was hexagonal. It *was* a damn coffin. Hail bounced off the top of it.

He approached tentatively. New wood. Unstained. But still, the possibility of old bones rattling around in there made him cringe.

Just then, a few basketball-sized boulders and a yard of gravel and

nching down onto the edge of the road, firing up his
..n.

kay, let's do this before we get buried here."

He positioned himself at one end of the coffin. Heaving and shoving at the same time, he got it moving. Wood scraped on wet tar as he swung one end closer to the shoulder. He straightened up and started for the other end, but stopped dead and jumped back a step. Something moved inside.

"What the..."

The hackles on his neck rose as three sharp knocks came from inside the casket. Then a few more.

He stared at the box in disbelief as the top lifted an inch. It wasn't nailed down!

So many horror movies started just like this, immediately followed by a character doing something stupid and becoming Victim Number One.

A coffin in the middle of nowhere. There was something inside, trying to get out. What do you do?

Get the hell out of here.

The top lifted again, but instead of sprinting for his car, Xander suddenly found himself sitting on the box, holding the top down.

Not what he'd planned.

"Great. Now what, genius?"

Taking the phone out of his pocket, he checked for cell service. Not one fucking bar. He glanced at his truck. The windshield wipers were slapping back and forth double time.

The hail had turned to sleet again, but it was coming down just as hard. If he could make it back to the pickup, it would be ridiculous— never mind dangerous—to turn around and go all the way down the mountain to Elkhorn.

He felt some thumping against his butt through the wood and glanced down at the box. There had to be some perfectly reasonable explanation for this situation. Hell, it could be an animal in there. Right, some animal had crawled into a casket in the middle of nowhere and then pulled a heavy top over itself. Okay, maybe not that.

But maybe someone had put an animal in there and...

"Help!" A woman's voice.

So much for that theory.

Xander stood up, yanked the top off, and tossed it to the side.

He stood frozen for a moment, unable to believe his eyes. It *was* a woman, and she was struggling. As soon as the lid was off, she sat up, coughing violently, and trying like hell to catch her breath.

"What...? How...? What are you doing in there? How did you get here?"

Her focus was on her next breath and not on his questions. The headlights gleamed off her dark hair, which was braided and pinned on top of her head. He crouched down, trying to think of how he could help her.

Her body was shaking from the raspy bark of her coughing. She was taking in the air but couldn't expel it. He recognized the problem. The wheezing between the ragged breaths was a giveaway.

"You're having an asthma attack. Do you have an inhaler?"

She nodded and her fingers grabbed for the edges of the box. He took her by the elbow and helped her to her feet.

His body was blocking the truck's headlights, and she stood in his shadow. He could see she was wearing a heavy woolen cloak over what appeared to be a period dress. Xander wondered if she was part of a reenactment group. Or maybe someone was shooting a movie up here. He'd seen *The Revenant*. He knew they made movies in all kinds of conditions.

But how did she end up in this predicament?

Struggling with a button at her throat, she finally managed to unfasten the cloak. He caught it as she whipped it off her shoulders. The freezing rain began to soak her dress. A leather bag hung from her shoulder, but her fingers couldn't get it open. The racking coughs sounded painful, and she was beginning to wobble a little.

"Let me help you."

She peeled the bag off her shoulder and handed it to him.

The bag was handmade, of the same antique style as the dress. No sooner had he undone the tie at the top than she snatched it away from him and shoved her hand into the bag, rummaging around.

"I know what an inhaler looks like," he told her. "Maybe I can find it for you."

As the hail turned back into freezing rain, she turned her back to Xander and bent over her precious bag, still coughing and wheezing.

He shook his head. "You know, there's nothing in there that I'd want."

She ignored him and kept searching. All he could do was wait.

His mother suffered from asthma. He recalled a few midnight trips to the emergency room, his father driving like a maniac, and Xander looking on helplessly from the back seat of the family car.

Well, whoever she was and however she'd ended up in this situation, he wasn't about to leave her here. He figured his plans for tonight had just been revised. Storm or no storm, he needed to get her down to Elkhorn. Someone had to be looking for her.

A couple of things fell out of the bag into the box she was still standing in. She paid no attention to them, still searching for her medicine. From what he could hear, she was really struggling to breathe. Xander felt the urge to breathe for her.

"I know what you're dealing with," he told her. "We're over ten thousand feet above the sea level. Your oxygen level is dropping. Let me help you find the inhaler."

As he reached for the bag, she pulled a small object out and brought it to her mouth. She took a couple of quick breaths.

The dispenser was much more compact than the inhalers his mother had lying around the house. And it seemed to work faster. She coughed once, and then her breathing immediately began to slow down and clear.

Her face remained in his shadow as she stuffed the dispenser back into the bag.

"I have to get the name of that medicine. I was sure we'd be racing down this mountain to get you to a hospital."

She looked up quickly, and the bag slipped out of her hands into the casket.

"Do you have any cell reception?" he asked. "I don't have any here. You probably want to get hold of someone and let them know you're safe."

She wasn't responding. Just staring. Maybe she was in shock. Maybe she had a concussion from when the casket hit the pavement.

He stepped to the side to let the headlights shine on her face. He wanted to get a better look at her.

Words, questions, his entire train of thought escaped him in an instant.

No. It wasn't possible. He had to be imagining this.

The large brown eyes were fixed on his face. "Xander?"

Standing there, dressed in some period custom with the freezing rain streaming down her face, was his *almost* wife.

"Nadine? Nadine Finley?"

✤ 4 ✤

ONE DAY, she was there.

The next, she wasn't.

After she disappeared, Xander went crazy trying to find her. With every passing hour, he'd grown more and more sick with worry.

None of it made sense. There was no reservation under her name at the hotel, despite what she'd told him about where she was staying. No 'Nadine Finley' that looked familiar showed up in his Internet and social media searches. Some eyewitnesses had seen the two of them together, but no one could offer anything about where she'd come from or where she'd gone.

Nadine told him she'd come to Vegas for a bachelorette party for a girlfriend. But in the three days they were together, Xander never saw any friends. Not that there was an opportunity. They had spent almost every minute together. He'd barely thought about it at the time. But when she was gone, he had no other names to trace.

He was worried enough that he'd gone to the cops to file a missing person report.

—*My girlfriend of three days has disappeared.*

—*I don't think she gave me her real name.*

—*She also lied about being from Philadelphia.*

—*I suspect she may not have been completely honest about her job and her family too. At least, I can't confirm any of what she told me.*

26

—*No, I don't have a picture of her. She said she didn't like having pictures taken.*

—*No, I didn't give her access to my credit cards.*

Their final response, *You're in Vegas, pal.*

A waste of time.

Xander wiped the rain off his face and stared at the woman shivering in front of him.

"Are you real?"

As she took the cloak from him, her fingers brushed against his. They were ice cold. She pulled the woolen garment around her shoulders. "What do you think?"

"What are you doing here?" He pointed to the coffin. "In this?"

She glanced around her at the road and the dark, wooded hills. It was as if she were seeing it for the first time.

"You disappear from Vegas, and then I find you here in Colorado. What's going on?"

She climbed out of the casket, walked unsteadily to the ledge, looked down, and quickly stepped back. He remembered she was afraid of heights. At least, that was what she'd told him.

As she came back to him, his gaze fixed on the droplets of rain glistening on her face. The cheekbones, the eyes, the nose. Classic beauty. She didn't look any different than when he last saw her.

"Nadine," he said sharply, trying to get her attention.

Her eyes returned to his.

"Is that even your real name?"

"Of course, it is. I wouldn't lie to you about my name."

"Really? You lied to me about everything else."

"Could we *not* have this conversation right now? It would be nice to get out of this miserable weather."

He stared at her. Their personal history aside, what had just happened was mindboggling. If it weren't for the elk, Xander wouldn't have slowed down and probably would have hit that box. She'd have been crushed under his tires. Or the box, with Nadine in it, would have tumbled down the side of the mountain.

He shook off the morbid thought.

For the life of him, he couldn't fathom why she, or anyone, would climb into a coffin. And how did she end up on this road? His mind raced through a few scenarios.

Someone could have put her in that box...but they didn't nail down the top.

She could have been drugged and put in there...but she was standing here, clear-eyed.

Maybe she *did* climb in of her own volition, but for what reason? And as screwy as that sounded, wouldn't she try to get out when the box fell off the truck?

No vehicle had passed him going in the direction of the state road and Elkhorn. That meant she had to be lying there for a while. Unless the truck had been heading up the mountain, but he hadn't seen any...

"Xander?"

Her voice brought him around. She was standing there, shivering. She was soaked, and the cloak wasn't enough to keep her warm.

"Can we get out of here, please?"

"Where do you want to go?"

"Wherever you're going."

Xander wasn't much of a gambler. He didn't like the house advantage casinos had over players. He didn't go to Vegas for fun. He was there for two reasons. A three-day tech conference. And Ken and Donna were coming at the end of the week to tie the knot. He was supposed to stand up as best man.

He remembered the day he met Nadine like it was yesterday.

The penny slots were as much of a contribution he was willing to make to the Luxor Casino. The two dollars and fifty-five cents he'd lost so far wasn't making much of a dent in the hundred-dollar chip the conference welcoming committee had put in each gift bag. Having registered a couple of hours ago, Xander was killing time until they opened the Meet-and-Greet cocktail hour. With one eye on the video poker game he was playing and the other on the registration desk, he was considering stretching his legs and wandering out by the pool.

He spotted her the first time she walked past him. It was her eyes and mouth that caught his attention. She had the look of that gorgeous Iranian actress from *Body of Lies*. Golshifteh Farahani. Her face turned heads. Then he realized she was dressed for the ski slopes, not the desert. Winter coat, winter hat, boots, and gloves. But he brushed off her choice of clothes. After all, it was February, and people descended on Vegas from all over the country. He watched her disappear across the crowded gaming room.

Ten minutes later, she came into his line of vision again. The hat and gloves were off. The winter coat was tucked under one arm. She stopped to ask directions from someone who worked at the casino. This time, as she passed, their eyes met. Was it his imagination or had her gaze lingered for a moment? Damn, but she was beautiful.

He didn't believe in instant attraction. At least, it had never happened to him. And he wasn't about chasing women, either. Because of his money or his looks, they usually came on to him. But as she moved past Xander, he found himself hoping that they were there for the same conference.

The third time, he was watching for her. And then, there she was, moving through the crowd. He grabbed his jacket and stood up.

She stopped near him and shifted the coat from one arm to the other.

"Need help?" he asked.

"This place is a damn puzzle. I've stopped and asked directions a dozen times, but they just send me around in circles." She motioned to the security fixtures on the ceiling. "I think those bastards up there are having fun watching me do laps."

"Maybe I can help." He grabbed a cocktail napkin off the nearest table and proceeded to draw a map. "You're here. These are the elevators you just passed...and the exit doors to the Strip are here."

She moved closer. She bent her face over his arm to see. Her soft brown hair brushed against his chin, and Xander smelled her perfume. Intoxicating.

"By the way, I'm Xander Nouri."

When she smiled up at him with her deep brown eyes, he was a lost man.

"Nadine. Nadine Finley." She took the napkin out of his hand, crumpled it, and put it on a nearby tray. "Maybe you can show me the way."

"Sure. Where to?"

She paused for only a heartbeat. "Wherever you're going."

༼ 5 ༽

THE HOT SHOWER in Xander's house felt like heaven, and as the water ran over her body, Nadine thought through what had just happened. And about the risks of being a Scribe Guardian.

Life as a Scribe Guardian wasn't a matter of choice for Nadine. It was a matter of survival.

In her world, people were divided into two groups. Those who went about their daily lives in the present, and a select few who traveled, as a profession, back and forth through time. What she did was top secret and necessary, but it was hardly the safest of occupations.

These quantum commuters, of whom Nadine was one, had long ago been organized into concise divisions.

The Assassins. The Bodyguards. The Scribe Guardians. And others.

Everyone who traveled received extensive screening and even more extensive training. Nadine was thoroughly prepared for the missions she was given to complete. She knew exactly what to do and what not to do. She was well-versed in the regulations. And she was skilled in extricating herself from dangerous situations if something went wrong.

So, with the coast guardsmen closing in on her in that alley in Hythe, the protocol was clear. She needed to shift just enough of a block of time so that the people chasing her would lose interest when she was nowhere to be found. Then, having made the short quantum

30

leap—a couple of hours or half a day—she could still complete the task she'd been sent back to do.

Nadine's assignment was to travel to Regency England to stop Jane Austen from meeting Captain Charles Gordon. If she failed this mission, the fledgling author would never get to London. She'd never reach her brother Henry's house, who was to serve as her literary agent. She'd never work with the printer for most of May to get her first book ready for the presses. And once the novel, *Sense and Sensibility,* was ready for printing, she'd never go back to Chawton with the expressed intention of revising her manuscript *First Impressions* into what would eventually be published as *Pride and Prejudice.* In short, it would be a disaster for the world of literature.

The instructions were simple: Jane Austen cannot marry.

Nadine's strategy was to convince Captain Gordon to escort her to Plymouth at the request of her 'father', an admiral who was actually known to the captain. She needed Gordon to be far from Hythe on Tuesday.

No one in the village knew it, but this storm would intensify and produce the worst downpours in decades. Raging waters of a swollen river would wash out a section of the coach road toward Canterbury, forcing Jane to spend Tuesday night in Hythe. While waiting for the roads to open, she would accidentally reconnect with the naval captain, a former friend. Jane and Gordon had previously met—and felt the stirrings of love—when Jane was in Sidmouth ten years prior.

This was the risk of time travel. Another quantum commuter had created a slight change in history. The ricochet effect was reaching Jane and the captain, and the Scribe Guardians couldn't rely on history to self-correct.

Nadine had to keep Austen and Gordon apart. That way, the two would not fall in love all over again, and literary history would remain intact.

Something had gone wrong, however. She'd never intended to travel from 1811 England to 21st-century Colorado. Her mind had played a trick on her, or perhaps it was just that her focus had been off. But somewhere in her subconscious, a parallel thought regarding another potential marriage had bulled its way to the surface. Destiny had separated Jane Austen and Charles Gordon years earlier, and destiny had also kept Nadine from marrying Xander Nouri on that warm February day in Las Vegas.

During the three days she had with Xander, they'd been like two charged atoms, and the pull between them was undeniable. Never before had she experienced such passion, such an immediate bond with another human being.

At the same time, she came from the future and had only been in Xander's time for a specific mission. She couldn't explain who she was or where she came from or what she knew. He wouldn't have believed her.

Even so, Nadine had tried to fool herself, agreeing to marry him. And all the while, she knew that what they had couldn't last.

She'd thought of Xander many times since the day she left. Whenever she jumped the gyre loops of history into his lifetime. Whenever she imagined seeing him in a crowd. But never had her raw feelings for him interfered with her task at hand. Until now.

Every quantum commuter had instrumentation to assist them in their time travel jumps, but those were intended for novices. Nadine was an experienced traveler, and her thoughts were enough to initiate the transfer.

It had to be the intensity of her memories of Xander and her feelings for him—surfacing at the moment of the jump—that caused the distortion. Hours had become centuries. She'd gone from Hythe to Colorado. And in doing so, Nadine had somehow managed to bring the casket along with her. Another first in her experience.

She flattened a hand against the shower tiles and let the hot water pound on her head and back. Every transfer through time was hard on the body. The longer the jump, the more severe the reaction and the longer the recovery time.

The freezing cold weather didn't help, either, as it slowed her molecular recompositing. And the asthma attack complicated the situation as well. She didn't know how long she must have lain in that box before Xander found her.

What year was this exactly? She needed to look at a calendar and refigure her schedule. The trouble was that another transfer was impossible for at least three days. That was the minimum time her cells needed before they could take another beating.

At the time of the jump, there were four days left before Jane's arrival at Hythe. Nadine was cutting it close, but there would still be time to correct the history if she kept to a tight schedule.

Shutting off the water, she took a towel from the heated rack and wrapped it around herself. She'd missed hot water, scented soap, and soft towels while she was back in 1811.

Her nineteenth-century clothing was hanging on the back of the door. Everything was still damp. She held the dress to her nose and immediately drew back at the smell of the wet wool. She'd need to wash the clothes before she went back.

She also had to figure out a way to take that coffin with her. It was the little hiccups such as this—a piece of furniture out of place, a coat left behind, a photo of a time traveler carrying an instrument of technology from the future—that tilted the gyre and changed history.

On the mountain road, she'd helped load the box into the back of his truck, bringing on a moment of lightheadedness from exerting herself so soon after the transfer. At least, the coffin was now under cover. Xander had pulled his pickup into a separate building he used as a garage.

She opened the bathroom door a crack and listened to the rattle and bang of pots and pans. He didn't sound happy.

Nadine was totally unaware of the mistake she'd made until she recognized Xander on the road.

The full beard was different. But other than that, he didn't look much older than she remembered. Six feet tall, broad-shouldered. Lean and muscular. He had dark eyes and wavy hair courtesy of his Iranian ancestors, and his face was drop-dead handsome.

She wondered how his life had changed since they last met. Did he have a wife? Children? A girlfriend? What did he do with the company he and his friend had started?

At least, he remembered her name. But did he ever think of her? Had he forgiven her for walking out on him?

Probably not the smartest things to ask, she decided.

Xander had respected her wishes once they got inside his truck. He hadn't asked a single question, and they'd driven along in silence.

The ride here had taken only a few minutes, but in that time, they passed no houses. No neighbors or signs of life for as far as she could see.

He'd turned off the paved mountain road and driven up a long driveway before pulling into an open area, where motion-sensor flood-lights had come on, illuminating two buildings.

The spacious two-story structure was made of timber and stone and shingle, and half of the second floor had walls of glass, which she guessed would provide a view of the valley and the mountains. He drove past it to the separate garage beyond some tall fir trees.

The remote mountain retreat was exactly the kind of place Xander had spoken of when he'd talked about the future they could have together. At the time, he was working and living in Manhattan, but he had dreams of getting out of the city. And the life he described had been enticing.

Almost without intending to, she'd told him that was what she wanted too, all the while knowing it was a life she could never have. She came from the future. Her life was a pendulum, swinging back and forth in time. Where she'd be next week, or next month, or next year wasn't for her to decide.

Xander had parked the pickup in the garage and ushered her through the snow to his house. Entering through a ground-floor door-way, they'd gone up a flight of stairs to an open great room. From there, he'd directed her into a wide hallway on the right and into a bathroom, pointing out a guest bedroom across the way.

Hearing him in a distant part of the house, Nadine grabbed her clothes from behind the door and stepped out of the bathroom. Down the hallway to her right, the door of what appeared to be a master suite stood open. To her left, the hallway led back to the great room.

She crossed into the bedroom and closed the door, hoping there were dry clothes she could wear. Spending time with Xander while dressed only in a towel was not the best idea.

The guest bedroom was pristine, a very masculine-looking room. Earth tones on painted wood panel walls. A single queen bed, a dresser, an upholstered chair with a lamp, and a desk and chair. Framed photographs of mountains on the walls. The sheets and blankets and pillows were stylishly attractive, like a nice hotel from this time period. She guessed he must have a housekeeper who came and saw to those things. Large windows were covered with quilted shades.

There was no hint of feminine input evident in the decor. No other personal photos, no books, nothing that indicated what kind of people stayed with him, or what kinds of friends, if any, visited.

She hung her wet clothes and the bag in the empty closet. He'd taken her muddy shoes and wet cloak from her when they entered the house.

A long sleeve t-shirt, a sweatshirt, sweatpants, and a pair of thick woolen socks had been laid out on the bed. They all belonged to Xander, she guessed, as they looked to be his size. She pressed the sweatshirt against her face, and the memories of their time together flooded back.

Damn it.

"Dinner will be ready in five," he called from the kitchen. He'd been listening for when she came out of the bathroom.

The sweatpants were baggy, but she cinched the waist tie tight. She could have worn the t-shirt as a dress, so she tucked it in. The sweatshirt hung off one shoulder. No underwear, but this was definitely more comfortable than the corset she'd been wearing.

Taking a peek at her reflection in the mirror hanging inside the door, she twisted her long, wet hair and pushed it behind her. She'd need to find an elastic she could tie it with. Her face was pale. What she needed right now were fluids, food, and sleep.

As Nadine opened the bedroom door, a cell phone rang, and Xander answered. She stood still, listening to the conversation.

"No. I got in okay." Pause. "There was a rock and ice slide a couple of miles down the road. Yeah. I got around it."

She stood in the doorway, staring at the bathroom door and waiting for Xander to tell whoever he was speaking to about his find.

"No. I'm good. Nothing's wrong." Pause. "I'll make it on Saturday. No sweat."

Saturday. What day was today? What year?

She padded silently along the gleaming wood floor and stopped at the entrance to the large, high-ceilinged living room. Sometime after she disappeared inside the bathroom, he'd turned on every light.

Flames crackled in a stone fireplace. Pocket blinds covered floor-to-ceiling windows on both the front and back walls of the house. Sofas and comfortable-looking upholstered chairs were grouped together and handsome Persian carpets covered wide floorboards.

On her left, the stairs they'd used led down to a ground floor. On her right, a dining area and a wooden desk where some papers and mail had been tossed. She moved in that direction. Mail had dates. She had to locate herself in time exactly.

Xander was moving around in the kitchen, working on dinner beyond a high breakfast counter.

She waited, listening.

"Just tired. Gotta go."

He ended the call without giving her away. He was a good man.

She quickly sifted through the mail until she found a date on a letter. April. 2022. She'd left Hythe on April 12th, 1811. The day stayed the same. Today...tonight had to be the 12th of April.

Three days. She had to convince him to keep her for three days. But would he let her stay after what she'd done to him before? She doubted it. But what if she told him the truth? There was nothing in the volumes of regulations and instructions that said she couldn't, though it was highly discouraged. Being covert preserved the status quo and kept the peace. People didn't do well with something they hadn't experienced—like time travel, which most would presume to be a hoax.

She might have to try it with Xander. After all, he was smarter than almost anyone she'd met in her travels.

Nadine needed shelter. A place to survive for three days. Then, she'd still have one day left to stop Jane Austin from falling in love and ruining the love affair so many readers had with Regency-era literature.

Just three days.

❧ 6 ❧

WHILE XANDER WAS TALKING on the phone, he finished putting away the groceries and eyed the late-night meal he was in the middle of preparing. He hadn't expected to be bringing home company, so he was glad he had meat and fresh produce to feed her. The delivery service had stocked the bear-proof food locker by the downstairs door while he was gone.

Steak sandwiches and salad. That was what they were having for dinner.

Xander ended the call with Ken and went back to cutting tomatoes for the salad.

Regardless of how close they were, he wasn't going to say a word to his friend about finding Nadine on that road. Not yet. Not until he had some answers. A lot of answers.

He hadn't pressured her to explain anything, even though he was burning to know what the fuck was going on with her. He'd waited a long time to ask her about Las Vegas and her disappearance off the face of the planet. Still, he could almost excuse her decision not to show up at the chapel. After all, they'd only known each other for three days. They'd been caught up in the heat of the moment. Well, *he* had.

But what about tonight? Appearing out of nowhere in a snow-storm and only a mile from his house? In a casket, for God's sake, and dressed as she was? And why didn't she want to call someone right away? Let them know about her whereabouts. That she was okay. None of it made any sense.

Okay, he was still angry that she hadn't at least said something before vanishing two years ago. Or called or texted him afterward to say she was okay. Didn't she realize how worried he'd be? So far tonight, he'd kept his cool. After all, Xander was the master of repressed emotions. He was the product of his upbringing. His father, an Iranian immigrant, was the master's master in that department.

Hakim Nouri had been a great father. Still was. He'd had a good career working as an engineer for the same company for thirty-plus years before retiring. He was a good husband to Xander's mother. Linda had been an American exchange student in France when the two of them met in Lyon. Love at first sight, they always said. They settled in Brooklyn to raise their son. And Hakim never tired of lecturing Xander on what he called his secrets for survival in this country. Sad, but he never got over the feeling that among these people he was a foreigner and an outsider.

Never show them you're vulnerable, my son.

Xander grabbed another tomato to cut.

You're sad? Man up. Scared? Don't show it.

Cut. Cut. Cut. The tomatoes went into the salad bowl.

Frustrated? Deal with it. No one cares.

He grabbed another cucumber and started chopping it.

Never complain; never explain. Your feelings and opinions don't matter.

Cut. Cut. Cut.

Angry? Stifle it. If you express it, they'll label you as that angry Middle Eastern guy.

"Mom, you're a saint," Xander muttered, reaching for more lettuce.

He stopped. The salad bowl was already overflowing onto the counter.

"No wonder I'm so good at relationships," he muttered wryly under his breath. Never mind that he was getting an ulcer.

Putting the knife and the cutting board into the sink, he stared out the kitchen window. On moonlit nights, he could see Devil's Claw from here, but not tonight. The icy mix had given way to heavy snow.

"It smells amazing in here."

He turned around and took a step to the breakfast bar that

opened onto the dining area and the great room. She was standing by his desk.

Her curves were invisible inside the baggy sweatshirt and sweat-pants. No makeup. Her hair was wet and tucked behind her ear. She looked fucking incredible.

He recalled her standing by the window in his hotel room in Vegas, wearing nothing but one of his t-shirts. She had a scar high on her right hip. A small moon-shaped birthmark between her breasts. She'd been short on clothes then too. The airline had lost her suitcase. If they hadn't, he would have paid them to lose it.

Don't do it, Xander, he thought, pushing the image aside. *Don't even think about it.*

He picked up the salad bowl and moved it to the counter, adding to the barrier between them.

He'd turned on every light in the house while she was in the shower. He didn't want 'romantic'. No getting lost in her smell, in the soft tones of her voice. No ending up having sex on the counter or against the wall or in the shower or in his bed.

A burning log popped in the fireplace in the other room, cutting into his train of thought. Okay, he'd lit the fire, but it wasn't romantic. It was a necessity. The temperature would drop below zero tonight. True, he had a heating system that could keep the Reykjavík Ritz-Carlton cozy, but you couldn't be too careful.

"Are you hungry?"

"Famished."

Her fingers trailed across the surface of the desk as she came toward him. A week's worth of advertisements and magazines and unimportant mail sat unopened there. He'd refinished that desk himself. A hobby he'd picked up after moving to Colorado. It was surprising how much extra time he had, now that he wasn't glued to his computer 24/7.

"Do you still eat meat?"

"I do."

"Because I was going to say, if you didn't, there's plenty of salad."

"I'll have them both." She approached the counter. "The shower felt nice. Great pressure. And warm water."

"Did you have to splash around in an icy stream to wash up at the...wherever it was you were?"

"Not quite that bad. But close." She looked past him. "How can I help?"

The placemats and cutlery were already on the table. The steak was staying warm in the pan, and the rolls were in the oven. Xander pulled them out and started assembling the sandwiches.

He shot a glance at her. "You could start by explaining a few things. Actually, a lot of things."

She took the salad bowl from the counter to the table. "How did you make out with Covid? Did you catch it?"

Xander waved a roll in her direction. "I'm not interested in talking about the pandemic. What I want to know is—"

"Think I could get a glass of water?"

He stared at her. She'd rolled up her sleeves and was going back and forth between the table and the counter. Moving salt and paper shakers. Folding a pair of napkins. Busy work.

"Nadine." He waited until she stopped and faced him. He noticed how pale she was. "Do you want something stronger?"

"No. Just water."

Xander filled two glasses from the refrigerator door and set them on the counter in front of her.

She drank down her entire glass. He watched her throat move. This close, she looked thinner than a couple of years ago. He wondered if she'd been sick.

"Mind if I help myself to some more?"

"Of course not. Go ahead."

She emptied his glass into hers and drank that one too, before coming around the counter into the kitchen and heading for the fridge.

As Nadine started to go by him, the baggy sweats caught on a drawer handle. Her woolen sock slipped on the tile floor. Xander reached out, getting an arm around her. The glass hit his foot on the way down and rolled away across the floor. Her hands pressed against his chest to steady herself.

Despite his good intentions about keeping his distance, he found both of his arms wrapped around her. She clutched the back of his flannel shirt, her face against his chest.

He could have let her go, but instead, he held her. Xander had wanted to do this from the moment he saw who it was standing in that box in the road.

Everything felt right. In his mind, time slipped. They were back in Vegas, in his hotel room, holding each other. Xander was asking her to marry him. And she was about to say yes.

That day, he'd given no thought whatsoever to tomorrow or the days after. Where they were going to live. And what about her job? She'd claimed she was a librarian. If he'd met a librarian as beautiful and sexy as Nadine when he was younger, maybe he wouldn't have grown up avoiding books.

And there had been other important questions. Things like how he was going to tell his parents. And how *her* family would react to what they'd done. Family opinions mattered in the culture he'd grown up in.

In the end, it didn't matter.

And once she'd gone missing and he'd come to accept that she really was gone, the idiocy of what they'd almost done became so obvious. They were strangers.

She didn't feel like a stranger to him now, though.

Xander released her and let his hands drop to his side as questions he'd been carrying around bore down on him. Logic poked at the romance trying to take possession of him again.

He needed answers. Now.

"Tell me about tonight. How did you end up on that road?"

She pushed away from him, stepped back, and leaned against the counter. He did the same against the opposite counter, crossing his arms over his chest. He didn't want to reach for her again.

"Did someone put you in that casket?"

"No, I got into that box myself."

"How did that casket end up on the road? Did it fall out of some-one's truck?"

"No. I managed that by myself."

"So, you drove it there yourself and pushed it out of the back of a truck?"

"There was no truck."

"Helicopter?"

"No."

"Horse-drawn wagon? Following a procession of other actors? That would explain the outfit."

"No, it wasn't as complicated as that."

"Not complicated, she says." He tried to gauge her expression, wondering if she was teasing him. Her face was serious. "Casket. Road. You inside of it. How about if I stop guessing and you just explain?"

She stared at him for a few heartbeats before she spoke again. "Okay. You deserve the truth."

"Thank you for that. Yes, I do."

"But..."

"But?"

"But you won't believe me."

"Do you know what I went through after you disappeared? How worried I was? How many doors I kicked down, trying to make sure that nothing bad had happened to you?"

"I can imagine."

"Okay, then. Shoot."

"I'm telling you, Xander. You won't believe me."

"Do you realize you haven't said a thing yet? You've explained nothing. But you're already making excuses."

"The truth..." She gestured vaguely. "You'll think I've lost my mind."

"*Have* you lost your mind?"

"No, of course not."

He ran a frustrated hand through his hair, then bent down and picked up the glass from the floor and put it in the sink. He took a clean one out of the cabinet and filled it with water before handing it to her. "Whatever you tell me, it can't be worse than what I've imagined."

She drank the water and walked again toward the fridge, making sure her clothes got caught on nothing.

"I need to eat something first. Then we can get back to this."

Get back to this? There was no *this*. She hadn't said a thing. Still, his Iranian hospitality genes kicked in. He was a damn poor host for not feeding her first. His upbringing again superseded common sense.

"Sure." He cut the sandwiches in half, picked up the plates, and headed for the table. "Hungry. Thirsty. Pale as a ghost. How long were you in that box anyway?"

She followed him out of the kitchen, carrying the water glasses. "Two hundred eleven years."

"Funny."

"I told you."

They sat down, and he watched her dive into the food right away. She really *was* hungry.

"Two hundred eleven years since you drank water. Two hundred eleven years since you last ate. What was the year...1811?"

"Such a relief you're good with math." She spoke with her mouth full. "And yes, you're getting the hang of it."

"And where are they putting this reenactment on? In Elkhorn? Denver?"

"It's not a reenactment."

"Movie, then."

"Not a movie."

"Are you an actress?" He'd believe that.

She paused, staring at the last bite of the sandwich in her hand. "I have acted before."

"Stage? Movies? Television?"

"In life."

"With me? With us?"

Her head tilted to the side, and her gaze lifted to his. She gave a small shake of her head.

"I need to hear the words."

"The days we shared together were real. No acting. What I said to you then was the truth."

"All of it?"

"All the parts that mattered."

Xander still had no answers, but the sincerity in the way she spoke threw him.

"And you're doing the same thing now? I mean, about telling the truth?"

"I'll do better now. I'll tell you all of it, but I still think—"

"That I won't believe you," he cut in, feeling his frustration building.

Her attention turned back to her plate, and she put the last of the sandwich in her mouth and nodded. "I'm certain of it."

"Can I make you another sandwich?"

"No. I always do this...eat and drink too much and too quickly after a transfer. Then I end up sick to my stomach. I'm trying to do better tonight." Even as she spoke, though, she piled salad onto her plate.

"Transfer?" He pushed his plate away and placed his elbows on the table. "Do librarians get transferred?"

"Not a job transfer. Being here is my own doing. I screwed up."

"You've really lost me." Everything coming out of her mouth was vague and unexpected. She was weaving an unsolvable diophantine equation. He was a math guy. He was good at solving problems. But in this case, there were too many variables. There was no way to solve it. Nothing was getting clearer. "How did you screw up? What does that even mean?"

She sat back and pressed the side of her stomach. "I was running away from some people who were chasing after me. I climbed into that box to hide. The problem was, my mind was on you. On us."

Xander considered himself a reasonably intelligent man, but he couldn't make head nor tail of what she was telling him.

"People were chasing you," he repeated, grasping for some semblance of understanding. "Was it the police? Were they chasing you two years ago too? Is that why you ran? Are you a criminal?"

"No, I'm not a criminal." She gestured to his plate. "Are you going to eat that?"

He pushed his plate across the table. She hadn't touched her salad.

"Do you work for some government agency? Are you some kind of spy? Or is this a witness protection thing?"

"You watch too many movies." She picked up a half sandwich and bit into it.

Spies weren't supposed to admit what they did. Or people in witness protection, either. Thinking of her as one of them made more sense than anything else. She didn't exist on the Internet. People were chasing after her. She was hiding in a box in the middle of nowhere. Maybe Nadine Finley wasn't even her real name.

"Okay, since we're playing twenty questions, I'd really like to know the answer to this one."

She paused with the food halfway to her mouth.

"Are you married?"

Her gaze locked on his, and he saw tenderness there.

"No, Xander. I'm not married. Never have been. And I never imagined I ever would be...until you."

Fuck. She knew how to get to him. He stood up. He had to hold her.

Nadine, too, was on her feet in an instant.

He reached out for her. "Listen, I—"

"Stop! I'm going to be sick."

Turning on her heel, she ran for the bathroom.

❧ 7 ❧

NADINE AWOKE with her head nestled between two thick pillows. The rest of her was wrapped in the duvet.

Although she'd always been successful in finishing her assignments, her record of actual quantum jumps wasn't *perfectly* pristine. There was the occasion when she found herself lying in a Parisian sewer. And there were other instances. A Scandinavian cow barn, a California gold rush brothel. Once, she'd become conscious with a Mexican desert sun beating down on her and a half-circle of buzzards eyeing her hungrily.

This was infinitely better. She felt like a very pampered mummy.

Even so, last night had been a rough one. Three times, she'd gone running for the bathroom. Each time, Xander had shown up at the door, wearing boxer shorts and a t-shirt, wanting to take her to the hospital or at least hold her hair back as she clung to the toilet. She'd refused, begging him to go back to bed. She'd been through this before. She knew what was wrong with her. A long jump and a sudden excess of liquids and food never meshed well. Ideally, she had to pace herself, allowing her body to adjust. She knew this from experience, but the body didn't always obey what the brain told it to do.

Getting involved with Xander in Las Vegas had been further proof of that mind/body disconnect.

Pushing the pillows and covers aside, Nadine sat up in the bed. After her last trip to the bathroom, she'd opened the bedroom blinds.

Now, outside the window, she could see blue sky and the tops of trees pushed by a breeze.

She glanced at the bedside clock. 1:20.

Surprised, she leaned over to get a closer look. "Seriously?"

Momentary panic hit her. Time was precious, and she needed to know how much of it she'd slept away.

Jumping out of bed, she pulled open the drawers of the desk, looking for a calendar of some kind. Nothing. This was a tech guy's house. Of course, he wouldn't have a physical calendar lying around. But she found paper and a pen in one of the drawers. That would have to do.

She sketched a grid of a calendar, marking the day she'd left Hythe and the day of Jane Austen's future arrival there. Once again, she reminded herself of the rules. Dates remained constant, but the day of the week changed, depending on the year. Right now, she needed to keep track of the number of days.

The soonest she could travel back to 1811 would be the night before Jane's arrival. And once Nadine got to Hythe, she'd need to act quickly. She had to make Captain Gordon believe in the urgency of her request and then rush him out of the village in the middle of a howling storm. She had to get him away before Austen's coach arrived.

There'd been too much on her mind last night to fully grasp how tight the schedule would be, but she could see it now.

Nadine slid the makeshift calendar into the desk drawer and pulled on the sweatshirt and sweatpants. She'd slept in Xander's t-shirt and socks last night, and she wondered if she could last in these same clothes until it was time to go back.

Hunger pangs pulled at her insides.

The house was quiet when she hurried from the bedroom to the bathroom. Stealing a look at her reflection in the mirror, Nadine was relieved to see some color had come back into her face, although the lack of makeup made her feel naked. Next to the sink, there was a bag sporting a pharmacy logo. It wasn't there last night. In it, she found a new toothbrush, toothpaste, a brush, and some hair bands. There was even a travel kit with an assortment of toiletry items.

She looked in the direction of the door and back at the supplies again, imagining Xander running to the store for her this morning. He'd done the same thing for her in Las Vegas when she showed up at the right time but at the wrong location. He went to the store to get things she was missing. Her commute should have taken her to a ski resort in Lake Tahoe, but she'd ended up in Vegas.

As she tore open the package of the toothbrush, her mind turned to all the questions that had gone unanswered last night. He was a good person. A great one. The best man she'd ever met in her entire life. And he certainly needed to be treated better than she'd treated him before.

A few minutes later, she padded out into the great room.

"Good morning," she said loudly. "Or should I say, good afternoon?"

No answer.

"Xander?" she called down the staircase.

Nothing.

They hadn't had an opportunity to talk about what he was up to these days. Colorado was a long way from New York City, where his company was based. Did he still have it? If so, this was a long commute. She knew quite a bit about what happened during the Covid pandemic. A great many workers had gone remote. Was he one of them?

Not that she had any right to ask these questions, considering the fact that her entire existence was a mystery to him.

Nadine stopped in the center of the large, open room. Her breath caught in her chest. The blinds that had covered the floor-to-ceiling walls of glass were now open. The view was truly dazzling. Looking out the front windows of the house, she let her eyes wander over the snowy landscape. The driveway leading away from the house had been plowed. Overnight, several feet of snow had fallen, judging from the depth of the cuts.

"Quite a spot you found for yourself, Xander. I'm glad."

In the distance, a wide valley had been carved into the mountains by some primeval river. The wide ribbon of water still wound past rocky bluffs and tall, snow-covered firs. Faint mists rose above the sparkling, tumultuous current.

Turning around, she looked out the glass beyond the dining table. In that direction, the land rose in glittering waves of green and white to rocky summits above the tree line. Together, the peaks looked like a great hand holding up the deep blue sky.

Sadness gripped her insides. She knew what was to come. In fifty years, the sky would no longer be blue.

In her finite lifetime, as a thirty-five-year-old in the year 2078, Nadine couldn't swim in a lake or put her feet in the ocean. She couldn't touch snow, walk in the rain, or see a wild animal...outside of a virtual zoo. Nature, as historians recorded it, no longer existed in the form she was looking at.

There had been warnings. Plenty of them. And humankind had done its best to save the earth's climate. But by the time they got serious about it, they were too late. The anticipated consequences had followed...and quickly.

The rising temperatures caused more melting of the ice caps, ocean currents had changed course, severely altering climates. Lakes and rivers evaporated, followed by larger and more violent storms. Acid rains contaminated land and ocean, sickening broad populations. When something came down from above, everyone ran for cover.

As dangerous as her profession was, being a quantum commuter was the only way Nadine had an opportunity to experience Nature as it had been intended. And here she was again, standing before an absolute masterpiece of creation.

An ember popped in the fireplace behind the metal screen, drawing her eye. It was then that she spotted the bookcase near it.

"Well, what do you know?"

She hadn't seen it last night, and she now stopped to peruse the shelves. Nonfiction titles on furniture building. A stack of magazines. Self-help books. Memoirs and biographies of business titans. *Meditations by Marcus Aurelius*, Sun Tzu's *The Art of War*, Machiavelli's *The Prince*. She touched the spine of an oversized volume of the *Shahnameh*, the Iranian Book of Kings. A collection of poetry by Rumi. Another collection by the poet Hafez.

Below them was an entire shelf of adventure, thriller, and mystery novels. Nadine smiled as she ran her fingers over the row of western-themed books. Novels by Louis L'Amour, Zane Grey, Larry McMurtry, Leslie Marmon Silko, N. Scott Momaday. Others by Nik James, Patrick deWitt, Winston Groom, David Nix, Jeff Mariotte. And below them, an interesting assortment of classics. *Jane Eyre*, *Bleak House*, *Canterbury Tales*, the *Complete Works of Shakespeare*, *Don Quixote*,

Remains of the Day, Things Fall Apart, Lord of the Flies, Zen and the Art of Motorcycle Maintenance, and others.

Every shelf contained titles she'd talked about in Las Vegas. Nadine recalled how she'd told him that no household was complete without a bookcase.

She eyed two that held particular interest for her. *Pride and Prejudice* and *Persuasion.*

"So, Miss Austen made the cut."

She pulled the latter off the shelf and paged through it. "You're still a novelist, Jane."

Satisfied, Nadine put the volume back on the shelf just as a clump of snow slid off the roof and dropped past the window.

The outdoors was calling to her.

How long had it been since she breathed in clean mountain air? How long since she felt the crunch of snow beneath her feet? She had to get outside.

At one end of the great room, a sliding glass door led out onto what looked like a very large deck. Next to the door, she looked over a rack with several pairs of boots and a collection of coats hanging from hooks. Xander had hung her cloak there last night.

"Yes!" she exclaimed. "We're doing this."

Deciding that the nineteenth-century cloak was insufficient for the cold and the snow, she grabbed one of Xander's coats. The boots were four or five sizes too big, but it didn't matter. She pulled on a pair and laced them up as tightly as she could. She wasn't planning on going far. Zipping up the down jacket, she opened the sliding glass and went out.

The air was crisp and cold and clean and smelled of the pine and spruce forest that surrounded Xander's house. The breeze was light, and she stood in snow up to her knees and took a few deep breaths. God, she loved this.

A fire pit stood in the center of the porch, surrounded by a half-dozen chairs. A table and chairs for eating outside ran along one railing. The furniture was covered with canvas, and snow was piled up on everything. Several fir trees grew up against the porch, and ice crystals glistened on overhanging branches.

She moved toward a railing that faced out toward the back of Xander's property. The porch decking was slippery from a coating of ice under the powdery snow. She scooped snow off the top rail with her bare hands, relishing the feel of it on her skin. Forming it into a ball, she threw it far out into the field of snow. She moved to a corner of the deck, where a towering spruce tree rose high above her. She leaned against the railing and gazed at the distant peaks.

Despite the cold air, the sun felt warm, and Nadine raised her face to the sky. Closing her eyes, she thought that this was perhaps the most perfect of places. It was heaven.

Right then, a bit of snow dropped from a branch above her, and she opened her eyes just as sharp claws latched onto her upturned face.

8

XANDER JERKED his head in the direction of the scream.

"Nadine?"

The sound came from the porch on the far side of the house.

He'd been on the garage roof for less than an hour, shoveling it off before stripping old shingles. Half sliding, half scrambling, he hurried across the slippery incline toward the ladder.

Nadine was continuing to scream. She was fighting something. But what?

Bear? God knows there were plenty on this mountain. Since buying this house, Xander had come face-to-face with several while out hiking. The black bears in the Rockies were not the docile creatures that went through dumpsters back East. And despite yesterday's storm, they were surfacing from hibernation. And they were hungry. The locals had already reported attacks.

Mountain lion? He'd heard mountain lions screaming at night and early in the morning, He'd seen their large four-toed paw prints with the M-shaped heel pad in snow and mud. Once, there'd been tracks going right across the clearing in the back of his house.

Coyotes? They came around all the time. Their yapping barks were as common as the sound of sirens in Manhattan.

He finally reached the ladder. Swinging over the top, he started down.

Xander heard no predator's growls, but Nadine could be fighting off any of them. No deer or elk or moose was likely to climb the steps to the porch, but he'd seen a bear pressing his face against the glass this past September.

The screams continued. "*NO!* Get away!"

"Go inside!" he yelled, realizing she wouldn't hear him over the noise she was making.

He jumped the last half dozen rungs and landed in a snowbank.

"Get away! Get *AWAY!*" she shrieked.

Pulling the hammer from his tool belt, Xander plowed through the snow toward the house. He started for the steps leading directly up to the porch and then realized he didn't want to corner the animal that was up there. Veering toward the ground floor entry, he yanked open the door and leaped up the inside stairs three at a time.

Even though he'd found her alone on the mountain road last night, Xander didn't have a sense that Nadine had much experience in the wild. Two years ago in Vegas, she'd claimed that she was born and raised in Philly. A city girl. True or not, it didn't matter. Around here, even the residents were cautious when dealing with wildlife. And occasionally running into some four-footed threat was pretty much unavoidable.

He saw Nadine through the glass as soon as he reached the top of the stairs. She had her back to him, and she was twisting and turning. Yelling the entire time, she was waving her arms and backing along the railing.

But there was no bear, no cougar, no coyote. Nothing threatening on the porch that he could see.

He slid open the door and went out. "Nadine?"

"Help me!" Sheer panic. "Get this thing away from me."

"What thing?" He moved across the slippery, snow-covered surface.

She spun, landed on her behind with a thud, and screamed again.

"There." Crab-walking backward through the snow, she stared at the closest covered chair. "He went under there."

No large predator was going to fit under that chair. And the few snakes that lived this high in the mountains wouldn't appear for a couple of months, at least.

Xander crouched down and spotted the assailant.

Two small, brown eyes peered out at him. A nut was clutched in the furry jaws.

"Didn't I tell you not to show your face around here?" He looked over his shoulder at Nadine. "You're lucky to be alive."

"Oh, my God."

"And you, monster, are smart to be hiding under there. You're in *so* much trouble."

She scrambled to her feet and approached, looking over his shoulder. "He jumped on my head, my face, tried to get inside my coat. He was trying to bite me."

He glanced up at her. "They go right for the jugular."

Her hands shot to her throat. "Did he scratch me? Did he bite me?"

There were no marks on her face or neck that he could see, but he couldn't help himself. He stood up, yanked off a glove, and ran his fingers down her cheek. There were a couple of small, slightly red bumps where he guessed the animal must have landed on her. Her unbroken skin was as soft as he remembered. He stared at her lips, so close.

He stepped back and looked up at the spruce branch hanging over the balcony. "I've warned him repeatedly, but he keeps coming around. Still, I don't think he meant to attack you."

"Is he poisonous?"

"Chipmunks?"

"Are they?"

"I'm sure they'll bite and scratch if they're cornered. But poisonous? No. Dangerous? I doubt he has a rap sheet." He gestured toward the chair. "Look for yourself."

She crouched down. "That thing is a rat."

"No, he isn't."

"A rat," she repeated.

"Don't go around name-calling. He's a chipmunk. There's a difference."

"There's *no* difference. It's a rat."

"Haven't you ever seen a chipmunk?"

"No. But I know all about rats."

"You've *never* seen a chipmunk?"

"Rats carry plague. They can be rabid."

"We're talking about two different things. This animal is harmless."

"Did you know that rats caused the Black Death?" She wasn't listening to him.

"You're going to give me a history lesson now, aren't you?"

"During the Middle Ages, *millions* of people died along the Silk Road because of this thing." Her hands flew in the air as she delivered her lecture. "More than a *third* of the people in Western Europe were wiped out in the first years of the epidemic. All because of this filthy rodent."

"This guy is still a chipmunk. He's not a rat."

"Bubonic plague, hantavirus, leptospirosis, lymphocytic choriomeningitis, tularemia, salmonella. Do you want me to go on?"

"That's some serious research, right there. But my client still pleads 'Not Guilty' to causing any kind of plague. Look how small and timid he is."

"That's because he's young. Wait until he gets older."

"He probably just fell out of that tree by accident."

"It was intentional. He planned it."

The chipmunk darted away across the surface of the snow, leaping onto the railing and then onto a tree branch.

"There. He's gone. Probably tired of being slandered."

"Good." Nadine shuddered.

The two of them were still crouched in the snow. Nadine was glaring at where her attacker had disappeared, clearly expecting a return. Xander stole a glance at the breaths escaping her parted lips and forced himself to stand up. He offered her a hand, and she took it.

"Well, that was certainly a good workout for me, running up here."

"Sorry. I was pretty loud, wasn't I?" She didn't wait for him to answer and pointed to the hammer he still carried like a weapon in one hand. "What did you think you were going to find up here?"

He slid the hammer into his toolbelt. "Could have been anything. A bear, maybe. Or even a mountain lion."

"Roaming around free?"

He burst out laughing. She had a way of saying things so deadpan, as if she'd never heard of such a possibility. She was the same way in Vegas.

"Are there many of them left around here?"

"I doubt the last census did a head count."

She punched him in the bicep. "I'm serious."

"These are the Rocky Mountains. There's a lot of wilderness out here. You don't know much about Colorado, do you?"

"My first visit here." Her gaze stayed glued to the landscape beyond the porch. "Are they dangerous?"

"Some of them can be, in certain situations."

"I mean, rats carry diseases. That's bad enough. But bears and mountain lions are large carnivores. They *eat* other mammals. Even people."

"Intelligent people don't put themselves in harm's way. Of course, there are always a few knuckleheads."

She turned to him. "Have you seen any?"

"Seen any what? Knuckleheads?"

"Bears? Lions? Any other animal but a rat?"

"I've seen bears right on this porch, pressing their noses right there." He motioned to the glass.

Instantly, her face changed, and a smile bloomed on her lips. Her eyes sparkled with excitement. "Do you think I can see one?"

Always surprising. "You were scared of a chipmunk a minute ago, but now you want to see a bear?"

"I'd love to."

"I'll fire off an invitation. But they're not great at reading their texts. We might have to wait until they come around on trash day."

"When is that?"

"Monday morning."

A frown creased her brow, and she stared at the mountains and valley.

"Will you still be around then?"

She shot a quick look at him and then averted her glance. That was no answer. Or maybe it was.

"You live in a beautiful place, Xander. It suits you."

He stared at her profile. It could have suited *them*.

Xander had enough money that he never had to worry about working another day in his life. During the past couple of years, there'd been too many moments when he'd imagined what his life would have been like if Nadine had stayed. If they'd married. If they'd moved up here together.

Shit. Shit. Shit. He had to stop. This was a dead end, and he was barreling toward a stone wall at full speed.

She turned to face him. "About last night, I want you to know how sorry I am about waking you up every time I got sick."

"No worries," Xander replied. But he had been worried about her. Between an asthma attack on the road and her heaving her guts in the bathroom, he'd questioned his decision not to take her to the nearest hospital as soon he found her. "How's your stomach today?"

"It may have already started munching on my liver." She looked in through the wall of glass toward the kitchen and then back at him.

"So, you think you can eat something? I mean, after that close encounter with Colorado's most dangerous wildlife?"

"I thought you'd never ask."

As they went inside, Xander got a better look at her. She definitely looked healthier now than she did last night. Maybe it was the cold air outside. Or her battle with the killer chipmunk. Whatever it was, she had more color in her face.

"And thanks for running to the store for me."

"Happy to do it. The roads were clear."

He unbuckled his tool belt as she shrugged out of his coat. He took it from her and hung it on the hook next to his. Watching her slip out of his deep-snow hiking boots was entertaining. The Kenetreks were monstrous next to her small feet. She picked up the boots and placed them on the rack.

"By the way, is there someone you need to call or email or text? Won't somebody want to know you're okay?"

"No."

"No?"

She shook her head. "There's no point. They won't get any messages."

"No calls. No emails. No texts."

"No."

"Why not?" He followed her into the kitchen. "And who are *they*?"

"She. My boss. It's not possible to get a message to her. But she really wouldn't care anyway, even if I could. She just wants the job done."

Two years ago, she claimed to be a librarian. He had no clue what she did now. "What about your family? The parents that I couldn't find, no matter how hard I tried. There must be someone who'll be worried about you."

"No one." She stopped, one hand on the fridge door. "Okay if I help myself?"

"Make yourself at home."

She began rummaging through the fridge. "I know it's afternoon, but can I make us some eggs?"

"Go right ahead."

"Still like your eggs over easy?"

"Yeah, I do." Xander was surprised that she remembered. "I'll take care of the toast."

They started the meal preparations, often working side-by-side. He showed her where he kept the frying pans and the dishes, while he put the English muffins in the toaster and set out placemats and cutlery. He started coffee, then poured two glasses of juice and carried them to the table.

He was so aware of her. Hyper aware. Every brush of their shoulders, every touch as they reached for a utensil in a drawer, their very proximity stirred memories he'd been trying to forget. The hints of red in her brown hair. The freckle on her neck, just below her delicately shaped ear. The longer, tapered fingers. He tried to focus on his tasks, eventually standing over the toaster and staring at the browning muffins.

As she cut up fruit onto the plates, she asked him about his company and why he was in Colorado. He explained it all to her.

"During and after Covid, the number of people turning to online shopping exploded."

"But your company made games, didn't it?"

"We 'gamified' product browsing or purchasing. We took an everyday activity that could have become repetitive and onerous for a majority of consumers and used our expertise in gaming to make it into something much more interesting."

Xander mentioned some famous accounts they'd worked on. The blank expression on her face said she had never shopped on those websites.

"When the pandemic was going full swing, we were approached by a major financial player who wanted to buy our company. And New

York City was not the place to be during Covid. So, Ken and I decided to sell and move to Colorado."

As they talked, he was beginning to feel as if she'd never gone out of his life. She made comments about the house. Without apparent guile or agenda, she complimented him on the smallest things. And she had the same wry sense of humor that he'd found so appealing in Vegas. She was so comfortable in her skin, and Xander couldn't help but feel that himself.

He'd hooked up with a few women over the years, but he'd never felt the same chemistry that he had with Nadine. That was what made it all worse. He thought he'd never see her again. Never feel this easy sense of connection.

"These eggs." She held two of them up to the light of the window. "Are they real?"

"Drop them and you'll find out."

"Where I come from, the genetics people have gotten so good at replicating this stuff that it's hard to tell them apart. But I love real eggs."

"Replicating them, huh? Well, these are organic. Cage-free. You're in Colorado. I can send a text and find out the name of the chicken that laid them. They're real."

She smiled and broke them one by one into the pan.

Where I come from, the genetics people have gotten so good at replicating this stuff...

Okay. Where the hell *did* she come from? What was she doing here? How did she end up a mile from his house? In a box in the road?

Xander asked himself why he couldn't enjoy these moments with her without the pressure of getting answers. Outside, she'd pretty much told him that she wouldn't be here on Monday.

"How long are you planning to stay?"

"Till the night of the 15th, if you'll have me. That's Friday, isn't it?"

"Only two days away."

"If I won't be inconveniencing you."

"It's fine." He was not built to let things hang. "But let me get this straight. You're not going to answer any more questions, are you? Or if you do, they won't be honest answers, anyway. So why bother asking? Is that it?"

"Is that okay?"

"No, that's not okay. But I won't kick you out."

She turned off the stove and faced him. "So, you really want the truth."

He stared at her. "Of course, I want the truth."

"As strange as it might sound?"

"Try me."

"I tried last night."

"Never mind last night. Start from the beginning."

"All right." She pointed the spatula toward the dining table. "I'll bring in the eggs and tell you everything."

Xander wondered what she was going to come up with now. He poured two mugs of coffee and took what he could to the table. She brought their plates in and sat across from him. They ate in silence for a couple of moments, and then she laid down her fork.

"I'm a Scribe Guardian."

"Is that a library job? You told me you're a librarian."

"In a way. But our libraries aren't like yours. And in my job, we don't lend books. We protect them."

What did he know about libraries? Not much. The last time he'd been in one was when he was still in college. There was a sunny second-floor alcove that had been a good place to nap.

"So, you work in the rare books department of a research library?"

"No. We...I *protect* literature. I make sure that books that are supposed to be written are able to *get* written."

She was already losing him, but he stayed quiet.

"And sometimes, I manage situations so that authors and specific works find and keep their place in the literary canon. Am I making sense?"

"Not really. I'm a math guy."

"But you have a bookcase now, I see. My work has involved a few of those authors."

He smiled, happy that she'd noticed it. "Okay. Then give me examples of your work. And talk my language."

"*Moby Dick* and *Le Morte d'Arthur.*"

He wasn't about to admit that he'd only read the Cliff Notes of the first one and never heard of the second. Xander gazed at her as she tucked a tendril of brown hair behind her ear. He forced himself to pay attention.

"Did you know that *Moby Dick* was almost lost to literature?"

Was that a good thing or a bad thing? He decided to say nothing.

"When Herman Melville wrote *Moby Dick*, it wasn't exactly a best seller. In fact, by the time he died in 1891, his publishers here and in England had managed to sell only about 3200 copies. And for the next thirty years after that, only a few scholars and intellectuals showed any interest in him. He and that book were pretty much forgotten."

"Unfortunately, they weren't forgotten. I even had to read it."

"Exactly." She smiled. "Did you ever hear of a woman named Bess Meredyth?"

"No." He motioned to his desk. "Should I get a pen and paper and take notes? I feel a quiz coming on."

"No quizzes." Nadine shook her head and sipped her coffee. "Bess Meredyth was an actress and a screenwriter in Hollywood going back to the silent film era. Very prolific and highly respected. She was even one of the founders of the Academy of Motion Picture Arts and Sciences."

"What does she have to do with *Moby Dick*?"

"Everything. Back in 1926, she was looking for a good story for the actor John Barrymore, who was a huge star then. Bess got hold of a copy of *Moby Dick*, read it, and thought it would be perfect. She wrote a screenplay of it, got Barrymore excited, and they made the movie."

He wasn't going to say so, but he'd never seen the movie, either.

"That movie was such a huge hit that suddenly people started reading the novel. Almost immediately, the book was hailed as an American classic, and it's been that way ever since."

Xander eyed her. Her eyes shone; her face was flushed with excitement. "Interesting story. But what did you have to do with it?"

"I'll get to that in a minute." She picked up her coffee mug and waved it at him. "First, do you know how it happened that the stories of King Arthur and his Knights of the Round Table were written down?"

"You're definitely asking the wrong person."

"Ready for a little history lesson?"

"I'm all ears."

"Sir Thomas Malory was an English knight back in the 1400s. He was a thief and a murderer. He even led a revolt against King Edward the Fourth."

"Did Bess Meredyth write a movie about it?"

"No. But listen to this. The revolt failed, and Sir Thomas was thrown in prison for a couple of years. While he was cooling his heels in jail, he wrote a bunch of stories about knights and ladies and magicians and the quest for the Holy Grail."

"I've heard of King Arthur."

"But Malory almost didn't write the stories."

"Why?"

"Because he nearly got released from prison before he had the chance to write them. The king was about to let him out. But the mistress of the Archbishop of Canterbury got word to the king that Malory had sworn to lead another rebellion. So, he stayed in prison, where he wrote *Le Morte d'Arthur*."

"And this also has something to do with your job?"

"I told you. I'm a Scribe Guardian. It's my job to make sure literary works like those either come into existence or continue to be read."

"I'm confused."

"What I'm about to tell you isn't going to help much."

"Give it a shot."

"*Moby Dick*. It was a rainy night in Los Angeles. January 1926. I was drinking with Bess Meredyth in a speakeasy on Sunset Boulevard. I was the one who told her about *Moby Dick*."

"*You* told her. In 1926."

She smiled. "And in 1468, I was the one who told the archbishop's mistress about Thomas Malory's intention of leading another rebellion."

Xander said nothing for a moment, not sure if he should laugh or call for an ambulance. Nadine appeared to be completely serious. Which would mean she was out of her mind.

No. Maybe she was a writer. Writers had to have active imaginations, he assumed. Or she could be an actor. That would explain the way she was dressed last night. He'd heard of actors who really got into...what was it called...method acting. Actors like Robert De Niro. Angelina Jolie.

She leaned forward and lowered her voice. "It's my job to travel through time and make sure certain works of fiction are written or preserved. I come from the future, Xander."

Laughter burst out of him. It was a minute before he realized she wasn't joining in. Her straight face didn't change.

"Where is this being filmed?"

"Filmed?"

"There has to be a script." He leaned forward, facing her. She was certainly beautiful enough to be in movies. "The more I think of it, it makes sense. You give me a name that's not yours. Actors do that all the time. They don't want to be found. You're off the grid. And this also explains how I found you last night. Where are they shooting this movie? It must be somewhere around here."

"I'm *not* an actress. What I told you is *not* from a movie." She held his hand, looking into his eyes. "A few days ago, I made the quantum commute to the year 1811. My assignment was to make sure Jane Austen never connects with an old flame and marries him. There was a mix-up, which landed me here."

"A mix-up."

"I was being chased by some coast guardsmen."

She was good. Really good at whatever role she'd just slid into. "Does the Coast Guard have a station in Colorado? I don't recall any lighthouses—"

"Hythe, England. I jumped from there to here. From then to now."

"That's a great story, Nadine. And you deserve every penny they're paying you."

She scoffed and pulled her hands off the table. "Okay. I told you that you wouldn't believe me."

It was disappointing that she wouldn't trust him with something like that, with the truth about what she did. They had history. He'd hoped she knew she could trust him.

"I understand. It's a hard thing to wrap your head around."

Now she was being patronizing.

"Yeah. Well, I'm more of a 'seeing is believing' guy these days. I believe in things I can put my hands on. Solid things. Like that." He pointed to the shelves of books. "I'm so glad you noticed it. I built the bookcase myself."

"It's very nice. And I love your selection of books. You're a reader now?"

"A reader? No. Those books are just for decoration."

"Decoration?"

"Yeah, I haven't read any of them. Too many words."

She sat back and crossed her arms, smiling.

"I picked the books for the color of the spines, but I'm thinking about replacing them with all leather bindings. That would add more style to the place. Don't you think?"

"Leather."

"I hear they can be a good investment too. Especially if you keep them in pristine condition. By not...well..."

"By not reading them?"

"Exactly."

Before she could say anything more, the sound of the door opening downstairs drew their attention.

She pushed her chair back, looking alarmed.

A moment later, Ken appeared at the top of the stairs.

❦ 9 ❦

NADINE FOUGHT the impulse to run. She didn't want to see anyone else. She had to minimize her interactions with people in this time period. Disappearing into the guest bedroom and locking the door was out of the question, however. She'd already been spotted. There was no escaping.

"Ken." Xander got to his feet. "What are you doing here?"

So, this was Ken. The situation was getting worse by the moment.

"I dropped you a text before coming over." The man never took his eyes off her. "But when you didn't answer, I figured you were working on the roof."

Ken was clean-shaven, olive-skinned, tall, and wiry. And he had the perfect haircut for an accountant or a lawyer. From what Xander had told her, Ken was the number cruncher and the finance man behind their start-up.

"I had no idea you had company."

Xander looked over his shoulder at her. "This is Ken Sola. My old partner. Remember me telling you about him?"

She tried to muster a smile and a nod. She remembered. Ken and his fiancée Donna were supposed to get married the same week she'd been in Vegas. And the couple was lined up to serve as their witnesses at the wedding chapel. Along with Elvis.

"Are you going to introduce me?" the newcomer asked.

She didn't wait. "Nadine. Nadine Finley."

She stood up, immediately remembering she was wearing Xander's clothes. Ken gave her the once over, and his look told her that he noticed.

Then her name registered with him. His mouth opened and closed like a fish out of water before the words spilled out.

"No way. Nadine? As in...*Vegas* Nadine?" He glanced at Xander, who nodded. Ken looked back at her. "So, you're real, after all."

"Of course, she's real," Xander snapped. "You doubted me?"

Ignoring the question, Ken strolled to the table. "Please, sit. I've been dying to meet you." He didn't wait for an invitation and pulled out a chair for himself. "When did you arrive?"

Whatever deal she'd made with Xander about telling the truth did not apply here. She sat down. "Last night. Late."

"I didn't see another car in the driveway."

"I didn't drive. My flight was canceled at...at..."

"Denver," Xander finished for her, collecting their plates off the table. "She called me, and I asked her to take an Uber out. And here she is."

She sent a grateful look at him. Their eyes met and locked.

"You're lucky you found someone to come out here in that weather. How long are you staying?"

"Being pretty nosey, aren't you, pal?" Xander replied for her.

He snorted at his friend's comment. "I mean, hopefully, you'll be here through the weekend."

"A couple of days at the most. *Not* through the weekend."

Ken's brow furrowed. "And you two have had each other's phone numbers since Vegas?"

"I had his," Nadine offered, watching Xander as he went into the kitchen and picked up his phone. For years, she'd been honing the skills required for her profession. Assuming false identities and making up stories about her life had become almost second nature now.

"And this is the first time you've connected since—?"

"Hey! Just found your text," Xander cut in. "You want to borrow my gas grill? What's wrong with yours?"

"I need two for Saturday."

"It's stored in the garage. Did you bring your pickup?"

"Uh, yeah."

"Good. Come on, I'll help you load it."

"The grill can wait." Ken's cell phone rang, and he immediately answered it. "Hey, hon. What's wrong? Are you in labor?"

Nadine grabbed her mug and went to the coffee maker.

"Yeah." Pause. "I'll pick some up on the way home. But wait...wait. You won't believe who's here at Xander's place right now." Ken stood up and moved toward the fireplace, speaking in a low tone with his wife.

Nadine stood next to Xander. "I should have introduced myself under some other name. Not made a connection to our past."

"You do that often?"

"Every time I jump to a new period, a different country, I try to fit in. This trip, though, I stayed as me, Nadine Finley."

"And where and when was that trip?"

"I told you before. Hythe, 1811."

He smiled, like she'd just repeated a joke. "Don't share any of these stories with Ken. He's gullible. Not like me."

"Trust me. I won't."

She'd been honest with Xander, but she was done trying to convince him. She was no magician. She couldn't snap her fingers, disappear and reappear like it was a party trick. He was clearly taking everything she'd said with a grain of salt. And she didn't blame him. The reality of time travel was still decades off. Even in her own time, unless you were recruited into the program, people knew nothing about it.

"I'm sorry about him showing up like this." He motioned toward his friend. "Ken and Donna are good people, and I consider them family. But..."

"But?"

"Now that they know you're here, there'll be no getting rid of them. She'll want to meet you."

Right on cue, Ken appeared at the entrance to the kitchen, holding the phone to his ear.

"Option one, Donna will order some takeout and drive up here so we all can have dinner together."

"You're going to have your wife, eight months pregnant, drive on these dangerous roads?" Xander asked. "What's wrong with you?"

"I won't. That's why we're going with option two."

"And that is?"

"You two are coming to our house for dinner."

Nadine tapped Xander on the arm. "Why don't you go? I'll stay here."

A voice crackled through Ken's phone, and he listened for a moment.

"No, we don't care about having dinner with Xander. We see him all the time. You're the one Donna is excited to meet. If you don't come, we'll get together here."

"I didn't invite you," Xander protested.

"As if that matters. We're coming. And I have my own key."

"She's eight months pregnant?" Nadine asked.

"Not eight months. Thirty-six weeks," Ken answered. "The baby can come any time. And yes, I agree. It would be dangerous to have her drive up here, so far away from the hospital."

"How about if we take a rain check?" Xander asked. "Nadine and I have other plans for tonight."

He put his arm around her waist and pulled her close to his side. Her stomach twisted deliciously, and she leaned into him. She didn't have to pretend.

Donna's voice came through the phone, loud and clear. "They can have sex later."

Nadine buried her face against Xander's chest for a moment to hide her smile. Damn it, he smelled good.

Ken listened to his wife and then held the phone out to Nadine. "Would you mind hearing what my very pregnant and bordering on hysterical wife has to say?"

"I heard that, Ken," the voice said.

Nadine stared at the outstretched hand and understood her options. Zero. She'd already put Xander in a very awkward position with his friends. She couldn't lie and say she had a flight to catch. There was no place else to go and wait out the days she had left here.

She looked into Xander's face. "Is that okay with you?"

"He has no vote," Ken said.

"Do you want to have dinner with them?" Xander asked.

"They're your friends. And it sounds like we don't have a choice."

"No, we don't."

She took the phone from Ken. "Hi, Donna. This is Nadine. We'd love to come over for dinner. What can we bring?"

❧ 10 ❧

ASIDE FROM THE obvious concern about the million and one questions she'd be asked regarding Las Vegas and why she ran away and where she's been since then, there were a few minor complications in going to Xander's friends' house for dinner.

Namely, what to wear.

They were expected for dinner at five because Donna was an early-to-bed person at this point in her pregnancy. That left Nadine with less than two hours to get ready.

There was no way she could go in her Regency garb. And wearing Xander's clothes was out of the question. She also had no money from this time period, and she doubted that stores in Colorado would accept British pounds and shillings from 1811. Scribe Guardians traveled well equipped to handle the job at hand for any period in history, but jumping gyre loops and landing in the year 2022 was Nadine's mistake. Until she went back, she was a fish out of water.

As soon as Ken left, she raised the subject. "You wouldn't by any chance have any clothing that a female friend...or your mother...might have left here. Something I can borrow?"

"I moved here during Covid. I've gone East a number of times to visit my parents, but they haven't come out here yet." He picked up his keys. "Let's go. I'm taking you shopping."

"I don't have any money."

"I'm taking you shopping," he repeated.

She knew from Vegas that money was a sensitive subject with Xander. He was a bear when it came to anyone else paying for anything, and there was no arguing with him. The man was generous to a fault, and he'd gotten downright insulted when she tried to pay for dinner one night. Sort of quaintly old-fashioned. Even in this time when he was living.

"Go get ready."

Getting ready consisted of running into the bathroom and fretting over the washed-out face staring back at her from the mirror.

As she tried to do something with her hair, the question Xander hadn't answered weighed on her mind. When she'd mentioned a female friend or a girlfriend, he glossed over it. It wasn't possible that a guy this special was unattached. He had to have gotten involved in other relationships since their time in Las Vegas.

She was only here for two more days, though. She really had no right to ask.

Nadine focused on clothes. Her cloak was functional, but the shoes weren't. Still, they were better than wearing Xander's size fourteen boots. Maybe she could find something in the town he'd called Elkhorn.

Not ten minutes later, they were winding along the serpentine mountain road. Looking out her window, she felt her stomach muscles tighten as she stared past the two-foot-high bank of snow at the ledge and the valley far below. Xander pointed out where he'd come upon a huge elk and the coffin. She could see debris from the rockslide had been bulldozed to the side of the road along with the snow.

Nadine still had serious questions about her arrival. Back in Hythe, her mind had been on Xander, that was clear. But why had she ended up where she did? Why not arrive at his house? On that snow-covered porch? In his garage? Or in Las Vegas, where she'd seen him last, for that matter?

Apparently, she was so eager to be with him that her subconscious had controlled the jump. Whatever it was, she'd unwittingly broken every quantum travel protocol in the books.

"By the way, I'm not done asking how you ended up here."

He was reading her mind.

"I was just thinking the exact same thing." She turned in her seat, studying his profile.

The curve of his ear fascinated her. She recalled tracing it as they lay in bed. His lips were firm and the skin surprisingly soft. Under the full beard he now wore, he had a scar near the cleft of his chin. He'd told her it was from a bicycle accident when he was six. Her gaze went to his hands wrapped around the wheel. Those fingers had made her body sing.

He tore his eyes from the road for a second. His gaze brushed over her face.

She remembered awakening to the half-light of the desert dawn brightening their room in the Las Vegas hotel. How quickly the tenderness turned to hunger between them, and the lovemaking began.

"Why here? Why those clothes? What happened if I wasn't driving up this road?"

Thank goodness he wasn't reading her mind at this very moment.

"You could have been swiped clean by the snowplows."

"I already told you how I got here, but you didn't believe me."

"And when you go?" he asked. "Do you climb in that same box and go *poof*? Disappear?"

"That's the plan."

A smile lifted a corner of his lips. "Donna will drag it out of you. She's brutal."

"You're dealing with a professional here."

"Professional actor?"

"Professional Scribe Guardian." She turned and focused her gaze on the mountains across the deep gorge. She didn't want to see his reaction.

They rode in relative silence until they reached the center of the town. On a main road called Silver Street, Xander parked his truck in front of a glass-fronted establishment.

"This is where we're shopping?" she asked, looking at the gleaming storefront.

"Sure. It has nice clothes, I hear."

The store appeared to have taken over an old movie theater and transformed it. The marquee above the shining brass doors extended out over the wide sidewalk. The vibrant and colorful window dressings shouted class and upscale offerings. Highlighted by gold and silver foil, the brilliant spring colors nearly burst through the huge glass windows. The displays included everything from women's apparel and accessories to home furniture and décor. From the look of it, she had a pretty good idea of how expensive things would be inside. Marketing certainly hadn't changed much from Xander's time to her own.

The clothes in the window displays were beautiful, but she was only here for two more days, she reminded herself. Whatever she bought now would be left behind.

"Can I borrow your phone for a minute?"

He handed it to her. "Finally, you have someone to call?"

"I wish. Your telecommunications network is not *that* good." She half turned away from him and did a couple of quick searches before handing the phone back. "I'm ready."

"You know I'm a tech guy. Now I have your search history."

"Don't bother. You'll find out soon enough."

Together, they walked into the store. Two young women approached them, gave Nadine a quick look, and then turned their smiling faces on Xander. They knew him by name. Naturally.

She recognized some of the home décor was similar to the furniture she'd seen at his house.

Leaving him with the sales associates, she moved to the clothing racks and checked the price tags on a few sweaters and slacks before going back to where she could catch Xander's eye. She motioned toward the street and walked out.

Waiting on the sidewalk, she took a deep breath of the crisp, fresh air. Elkhorn was charming. It had the look and feel of an old West town that had enjoyed a boom when silver and gold were being dug out of the surrounding hills.

Across the street, a large granite building had a carved stone inscription, identifying it as the H. D. PATTERSON COURTHOUSE 1881. And a few doors away, a cowboy bar and restaurant called THE BELLE looked very authentic.

Xander came out almost immediately. "How come you left? They're closing in half an hour. I thought you agreed to pick up a few things."

"I did agree."

"And I'm paying."

"And you're paying." She linked his arm with hers and headed toward the store she'd found in her search. "Right this way."

An OPEN sign hung slightly askew inside the door of a thrift shop down a side street.

"No, you're not shopping here."

"Yes, I am."

He took Nadine's hand and tried to stop her, but she pushed the door open anyway.

"Do you know how much water is used to process textiles? And don't get me started on the pollution, greenhouse gas emissions, and landfills."

"I see a lecture coming."

"Take a guess how much water is used to make *one* single shirt?"

He shook his head and smiled as he followed her inside the store.

"Seven hundred gallons. Enough water for one person to drink for nine hundred days."

"Deny it all you want; you're a research librarian, through and through."

Twenty minutes later, Nadine was finished with her shopping and looking at herself in the mirror in the store's tiny fitting room. A pair of cowboy boots, comfortable jeans, and a deep green knitted top—all of which cost a fraction of one sweater at the first store. She picked up the other two shirts Xander had forced her to take and pushed aside the privacy curtain.

His gaze told her that she'd made good choices.

Walking back to the pickup truck, Nadine stopped in front of a flower shop that was about to close.

"One more thing," she said to him. "If you don't mind. I'd hate to meet Donna empty-handed."

"Of course." As they went in, Xander pointed out the plaque by the door. "This used to be the sheriff's office, back in the day."

"They've found a much better use for it now."

"Based on the town's history they have online, I'd say they put it to good use back then too. Elkhorn was a wild and lawless place, apparently. The gunfighter Caleb Marlowe himself once spent some time in this jail."

"Wow!" Nadine had no idea who Caleb Marlowe was, but she smiled and headed for the bouquets.

As Xander drove through the town, Nadine took in the mix of new and old. Some of the downtown side streets had seen better days, but renovations were going on everywhere she looked. And on one tree-lined avenue a few blocks off Main Street, more than a dozen Victorian mansions were a reminder of the town's most prosperous era.

Xander noticed her looking at the stately homes. "A lot of fortunes were made in silver mining here. Made and lost. They say Elkhorn had more millionaires per capita than New York at one time."

She thought about her experiences during the gold rush in California. Saving a youthful Mark Twain—at the time, still Sam Clemens—from a deadly brawl over cards and whisky in a mining camp near San Francisco was a story for another day, however.

Darkness was gathering quickly as the pickup climbed into the hills above the town. They passed several neighborhoods, filled with upscale homes. After going by a snow-covered golf course, Xander steered through some handsome stone pillars into one of those developments. The houses she could see out her window were large and well-lit, and most were situated at the end of long, curving driveways. A great deal of timber and stone and glass went into them.

She thought about Xander's friends. "Before we get there, can you tell me a little about Donna?"

"Sure. What do you want to know?"

"Anything. Something. How old is she? What does she do? What kind of people does she associate with?" A couple of years ago in Las Vegas, Nadine had heard much about Xander's partner, but nothing much about Ken's then-fiancée.

"She's thirty-seven. The two of them have been together since college, but they only got married the week you and I met."

She hoped none of them would dwell on Vegas tonight.

"Ken and I have known each other since we were kids, but Donna wasn't from New York. I think she was raised in Georgia or Tennessee. One of those Southern states."

"Know anything about her family?"

"Both of her parents died before I met her. I don't know what happened. She never talks about it. She had some kind of chronic illness as a child. Another topic that she never brings up. At least, not with me. I do think she's sort of a hypochondriac. Or at least, she worries about her health a lot."

"She probably has a good reason for it," Nadine thought of her own situation and how different her life would have been if she were healthy. No recruitment into the Scribe Guardians. No traveling through the past, facing danger with each mission. On the other hand, she wouldn't be here now if she were healthy. "Did I hear you correctly? This is her first pregnancy?"

"Third." Xander turned onto a long driveway. "She got pregnant twice before they got married and both times had a miscarriage in the first trimester."

They hadn't met yet, but Nadine's heart still went out to the other woman. "That's so sad."

She looked ahead at the house as they approached it. Partially hidden from the road, it had a similar style to the others in the neighborhood. From the outside, it looked perfect, but Nadine recalled an old saying she'd read recently by a Persian writer. *If someone's life looks perfect, you don't know them well enough.*

"I know that going full term in this pregnancy has been a major deal for them."

"I'm sure. Does Donna have a good support group here in Elkhorn?"

"She doesn't have any brothers or sisters. No family that comes around or that I've ever met. But she volunteers at the library, at the historical society, at the elementary school, and probably at more places than I know. That's where all her friends come from. Still, I don't think she's known any of them too long. We're all new to the area. So, as far as support, I don't really know. She has Ken."

When Nadine was younger, she had a few friends. But those days were gone. She had no one she could call or check on or get together with since she'd been recruited as a Scribe Guardian. It was impossible for her to keep a relationship intact. Other people could plan their own lives. They knew they had a tomorrow, a next week, a year from now. They had calendars and could tick the days off. Her life lay in the past.

To them, she was there one day and then gone from their lives the next. And there was always a possibility that she'd never return.

"Donna is abrupt, though. Tough. She either likes you or she doesn't. And you'll know it."

Nadine guessed Donna wouldn't like her. After all, Nadine stood their friend up at the altar.

"She studied law and practiced it in New York. Even though she hasn't bothered to sit for the bar exam in Colorado, I'd be ready for a serious cross-examination tonight, if I were you."

Every time Nadine made a quantum leap, she faced that.

Xander's hand brushed against hers. "Are you ready to tell the truth?"

"I've already told you the truth, but you didn't believe me."

"I mean the *real* truth."

Nadine stared at the sprawling, multi-level house ahead. Ken opened the front door, having spotted them in the driveway.

"Don't worry, I can handle this."

PREGNANT.

As Ken had said earlier, *very* pregnant.

That wasn't the only way to describe the ginger-haired, bronze-skinned woman who waited inside the door. Donna was gorgeous. She wore a flattering faun-colored tunic sweater over black leggings. Plush brown slippers came almost to the knee. She made late-stage pregnancy look both chic and comfortable.

The foyer of the Solas' house struck Nadine in the same way, stylishly informal. Rough-hewn beams supported high, sloped ceilings. Beyond the grey slate flooring laid out in a semi-circle by the door, wide wooden floorboards the color of dark honey led past a stairway that curved upward to the second floor. A timber-framed archway led into the rest of the house.

Ken opened the door to a coatroom, and Nadine espied a rack filled with boots and shoes, an assortment of coats on hangers.

Warm and cozy, the entrance exuded a feeling of homeyness and welcome. But as Xander helped her off with her coat, she realized that the jury was still out with their hostess, who was silently appraising her. Nadine handed her the bouquet.

"These are lovely." Donna passed the flowers to her husband.

"Thank you so much for inviting me over to your home."

"How could I pass up the opportunity of meeting the runaway bride?" Her voice had the attractive honeyed accent of the American South, but there was a hint of accusation there too.

Nadine pushed aside her earlier hope that tonight wouldn't be focused on the past. Before she could respond, however, she was pulled into a warm hug. The belly within the bulky sweater was solid between them, and she was shocked to feel a solid kick. Nadine drew a sharp breath, and her hold on the other woman tightened. Emotions sprang up from nowhere and everywhere, and she fought the unexpected pooling of tears in her eyes.

"I'm glad you came. And, just so you know, that was not the greeting I'd intended."

"The hug or the words?" Nadine teased.

"Both," she smiled. "Please, please don't be offended by anything I say. My feelings are all over the place these days. The filter is gone, and words just tumble out of me."

"This is something new?" Xander teased.

"Quiet, you." Donna scowled as he followed Ken beyond the archway into the house.

She took Nadine by the shoulders and scanned her face. She wasn't shy about looking.

"You're prettier than I imagined."

"Thank you."

Her eyes lingered on the wet cheeks. "And more sensitive."

Nadine quickly wiped the stray tears from her face and motioned toward Donna's pregnant belly. "I don't remember the last time I got a group hug."

"I'm a little impulsive these days."

"And candid in your appraisals."

"Yeah. Well, I do surprise myself with the things that come out of my mouth."

"That's perfectly okay."

"Why, because I'm pregnant?"

Nadine laughed. "No. Because I value honesty."

"Really? From what I hear, you weren't too honest with Xander when you two met."

Talk about direct. She'd been warned. The questioning *was* going to be serious. "I couldn't be, at the time."

"Why is that?"

"The two of us were caught up in the moment. Everything was moving too fast. I got scared."

"Get real, woman. Scared of Xander? The man's a teddy bear."

"I wasn't scared of *him*. I was scared of myself. I was just getting out of a difficult relationship. There was no way I could jump into a new one. And Xander was already talking about *forever*."

An eyebrow arched and eyes the color of dark chocolate stared at her with such intensity that Nadine was sure Donna was looking into her soul. She waited for the next question. Instead, she got a verdict.

"I get it. He can be intense. When he decides what he wants, he goes after it." She touched Nadine's sleeve. "By the way, I love this sweater. Where did you get it?"

"In the thrift shop downtown."

The brow arched again, this time in surprise. "Which one?"

"I don't remember the name. It's off Silver Street, if that helps." She named the intersection.

"I know the place. I was in there last week. Didn't see this, or I would have grabbed it myself."

"You can still have it." Nadine thought of how soon she'd be leaving. "Loan me an old t-shirt, and I'll give it to you now."

"I was just joking about buying it for myself. It'd never fit. Look at this belly." She cradled her stomach like a basketball. "I'm the size of Detroit."

"Not for too long. And this color will look great on you."

"I'm not going to take your sweater."

"I want you to have it." She gestured toward the door. "I have a change of clothes in the car. I'll just run out and—"

Donna took hold of Nadine's arm. "You're not going anywhere. I'll borrow it when I need it. Deal?"

Tonight would be the last time she'd see Xander's friends, but there was no point in saying so. "Deal."

Donna steered her past the staircase. "I like you."

"And why is that?"

"You're not what I expected. It's the openness, I guess."

Now, Nadine felt bad. "I like you too."

Donna's directness was refreshing. In some ways, she reminded her of Deirdre, the woman she'd left behind in 1811.

"Do you want the twenty-five-cent tour of the house?"

"I'd love it."

"The nursery will be reserved for the dollar tour, though."

Nadine grinned and patted the pocket of her jeans. "Are you collecting up front?"

"Nah. Your credit is good with me. But I'll show you the downstairs first. It takes me a while to work my way up there."

The two women went into a large open area, and Donna chatted as she pointed out the house's features. To the right, beyond a dining table already set for four, Nadine took in a kitchen with chestnut-colored cabinets, a large island, and dark granite counters that provided ample workspace. On one wall, beneath a sloping copper hood sat a restaurant-sized range.

Her hostess led her past the dining table into the sitting area, sectioned off by sofas and chairs. The two men stood by a stone fireplace. The entire space was well-lit. The floors were covered with colorful rugs bearing Native American designs. In one corner, boxes wrapped with baby-themed papers and decorated with bows and ribbons sat on a table. Nadine recalled there was to be a baby shower held here this coming Saturday.

A log fire crackled on the hearth, warming the room. As in Xander's house, large windows faced out onto what Nadine was sure were views of the mountains. The furniture looked comfortable and well-used.

Donna noticed her looking at the furniture. "We were apartment dwellers back in New York. Most of what we had, we left behind. When we got here, I decided to buy everything used. Some of it had to be refinished and reupholstered, and Ken and I worked together on a number of these pieces."

"I love it. Everything has its own history."

"Exactly right." Donna smiled and touched the sleeve of Nadine's sweater. "Somehow, I'm not surprised that you'd appreciate it."

It was easy to imagine why Xander felt so strongly about his friends. They were down to earth. Their house felt like a real home. And they treated him like family.

"Dinner gets delivered in half an hour," Ken announced, glancing at his watch. "What do you want to drink, Nadine? A glass of wine?"

"I'm fine for now. Just water for me with dinner, thanks."

"You boys get yourselves a drink."

"Oh, I was planning on it," Ken laughed, heading to the fridge.

Donna patted Nadine's arm. "It's hard for me to sit, stand, or lie down right now. I need to waddle. Want to waddle with me to the nursery?"

"Love to."

Beyond the kitchen, a back stairway led to the upper floor. At a landing halfway up, Donna stopped to catch her breath. "What do you do, Nadine?"

"I'm a library consultant."

"That's what Xander told us...after you two parted ways in Vegas."

Nadine tried to not imagine what else Xander would have told them about her. But she couldn't help but wonder if it was good or bad.

"What does a library consultant do, exactly?"

Nadine knew her response well. Before becoming a Scribe Guardian, that was what she actually did, though the specifics were far different because of how libraries functioned in the future. "I travel from assignment to assignment. Keep moving, wherever they need me."

"Doing what?"

"Organizational work, mainly. Towns or businesses hire me if they want to set up a new library or improve the collection they already have."

"I love libraries. I volunteer at the local one in Elkhorn. Of course, I perform only highly skilled functions...like putting books back on the shelf. And nothing goes on the bottom shelf on my shift. The knees don't bend that far. Well, not if I want to get back up." She smiled. "What do you do, specifically?"

"I do all kinds of stuff. That's what keeps the job interesting. But I have special training in the preservation of old manuscripts."

"That's fascinating. You're talking about the books and papers that end up in museums?"

"Sometimes."

They made their way upstairs. A guest bedroom. A master bedroom suite. She looked at each room with interest. A home like this—a place where she could go back to every day—was a foreign concept to her. Nadine didn't spend enough time in her apartment to justify the expense.

"So, where do these jobs take you? East Coast? West Coast? Out of the country?"

"Wherever the good offers come from. I'm independent. I work project to project. I move around. I do one job and then move to the next one."

"That must be hard on relationships."

"My home is on the road. Relationships? Like with Xander?" She held Donna's gaze. "Yes, it's very difficult."

"How about your parents? Your family? Get to see them often?"

"My parents are both gone. They died when I was young."

In talking with Donna, it was easy to mix fragments of the truth—parts of her past—with the fiction she needed to fabricate. One reason why she was recruited as a Scribe Guardian by the organization was that she had no family.

Another reason? She was dying.

What do you do when you have no tomorrow? You go back in time and live in the past. But not everyone in 2078 had the same opportunity. Only the ones raised by the state. The ones with all the medical and DNA records locked in the government's system. She'd been matched with the job before she was told a word about it.

"How old were you when you lost them?" Donna asked.

"Twelve. They died in a highway accident." Not only them, of course. And not exactly a highway, the way Donna understood the term. Over eight hundred people died when the automated transportation system malfunctioned. It was a disaster.

"Shit."

"It was a long time ago," Nadine said.

"I lost my father when I was twelve. My mom died the week I turned sixteen."

"I'm sorry." Nadine put a hand on Donna's arm. They were standing outside of the nursery. "That's tough."

"You know how it is. You've gone through it yourself."

Nadine followed Donna into the baby's room. Cozy and rustic, like the rest of the house, with light wood tones and pale green hues. Above the white crib, large framed prints of light green ferns. A comfortable armchair had been positioned by one of the windows, and white chests of drawers and a matching changing table completed the furnishings.

She turned slowly around, taking in everything. A baby was going to move into this room within weeks. A precious living and breathing being. The same one who'd kicked her in greeting. Again, another wave of emotions ran through her. What would be like to be a mother? To deliver a child? To hold them, change their dirty diapers, feed and talk to them? To nurture them as they grew?

These were experiences she would never have. She wasn't even allowed to dream of them. She turned away from Donna and focused on the wall decorations.

"This is absolutely beautiful." She motioned to bunnies and deer and trees stenciled around the tops. "Did you do those yourself?"

"My husband would have killed me if he found me on a ladder. Ken did all of it."

Nadine smiled appreciatively. "Do you know the baby's gender?"

Donna walked to the crib and shook loose a receiving blanket draped over the end.

In a split second, the smile disappeared, and the air became tense. Nadine wondered if she'd asked the wrong question. She watched Donna's hands as she refolded the blanket meticulously and put it back where she'd found it.

"Ken and I have waited so long and tried so many times that we didn't want to know."

"It doesn't matter at all, though, does it?" Nadine asked, in what she hoped was a bright tone. "I can see you right now, sitting in that chair, cuddling your baby."

"I hope so. Or at least that's my plan. But I don't have much to say about it, do I?"

Nadine saw tears welling up in Donna's eyes, and she rushed to her side. "What's wrong?"

"It's our last chance. And if something goes wrong now..."

Nadine imagined last-minute jitters were independent of time and circumstances. "You're almost there."

"That's what I keep telling myself."

"Everything is going to be great. You've carried this healthy baby full term. Xander drove by the hospital where you're going to deliver. It's only a couple of miles away."

In Nadine's future time, carrying a child full term in the uterus was unheard of. With the widespread decline in fertility, population growth hovered around zero, so no one was allowed to reach the point where Donna was now. If a woman decided against full ectogenesis— gestation happening completely outside a human body from conception to birth—she still delivered early and had the infant come to term in the state's prenatal care units.

Tears escaped and ran down Donna's face.

"Hey!" Nadine wrapped her arms around her. "What's wrong?"

"Everything's wrong."

"What do you mean?"

"I mean...I mean I won't be around to see my baby's first steps. I won't see the first day of kindergarten. Or take pictures before the prom. Or go on college visits..." A strangled sound escaped Donna's throat. She pulled away and walked to the window.

Nadine searched in panic for some tissues and found a box by the changing table. She took it to her. "Do you want to talk about it?"

"I lost both my parents to cancer. I'm scared because I had breast cancer when I was twenty-eight. Back then, I told the doctors to go to hell when they recommended genetic testing. I knew what it would mean if anything came out positive." She blew her nose in a tissue, wiped at the tears. "Take everything out. Never have children."

"You did what was best for *you*. And look at you now. Healthy. Ready to deliver your baby."

She shook her head. "There *is* something wrong now."

Nadine glanced at the doorway, recalling how cheerful Ken was at Xander's house and downstairs. He didn't act like a panicked father-to-be.

"He doesn't know. I can't tell him. Not now. Not before the baby comes."

"What is it that he doesn't know?"

"That the breast cancer might be back."

Nadine's heart dropped into her stomach. They'd just met, but the concern she felt for this woman was as if they'd known each other for decades. She knew what it felt like to have dreams shattered. To never be able to plan for tomorrow.

"Might be? So, you aren't sure yet?"

"My gut tells me it's back. My doctor agrees." She reached under her arm and touched what was there. "I'm going for a biopsy tomorrow. Then we know for sure."

"They're going to biopsy before the baby comes?"

"Yes. I asked for it. I can't live with this thing sitting under my arm, where I touch it, feel it, think about it all the time. I have to know." She pulled more tissues out of the box and wiped her eyes. "And I can't tell Ken. Not at this stage. I can't pass on my worry to him. He's as solid as a rock. But he turns into mush when something goes wrong with me. One of us has to stay strong. Be here for this baby."

Nadine had been told of her own fate during a virtual tele-med visit. She'd been all alone. No one to hold her, console her. No shoulder to cry on.

"Who's going with you if Ken isn't doing it?"

Donna shook her head.

"You can't do this alone. Maybe one of your friends?"

"That's the trouble with being new to an area. I've met quite a few people. But real friends? People who know what I've gone through before this? Who know the reason why I'm terrified? None."

"Would you like me to go with you?" Nadine heard herself ask.

Donna's gaze lifted, and she saw the glimmer of hope in the brown eyes. "Would you do that for me?"

"Of course, I will."

🥀 12 🥀

INCREDIBLE, how quickly these two women connected, Xander thought as they drove home.

Before dinner was over, Nadine and Donna were practically finishing up each other's sentences. Smiling at what seemed like private jokes. Each defending the other in the table banter. They acted like there was a lifetime of understanding between them. The two of them seemed to be as tight as he and Ken were. And *their* friendship had been forged in the fires of more than three decades.

Xander's mother would say these two had "old souls."

He was glad of it, of course. But what he *didn't* particularly like was that they were planning on spending the day together tomorrow. And that was cutting into his own time with Nadine.

As they pulled into his garage, Xander asked her if she'd consider changing her plans and staying through the weekend. Then, she could be there for Donna's baby shower. Considering everything tonight, he thought maybe she'd agree.

"No, I have to go on Friday."

Her answer was abrupt and disappointing. Xander stopped himself from asking why, as he was sure whatever answer she gave him wouldn't be satisfying. Her stories were farfetched, and he was in no mood for it.

They climbed the steps to the kitchen door. "What do you two have planned for tomorrow?"

"Donna has a couple of appointments in the morning. Then, some shopping for 'thank you' gifts and game prizes for the baby shower. I don't really know what else she's got on her schedule for the rest of the day."

Inside, he hung up their coats.

"You really don't mind driving me down to Elkhorn in the morning?"

"No problem at all." He'd take every minute he had left with her, and the way things were going, commuting back and forth to Elkhorn looked to be a big portion of those minutes.

"But it'll be early. She wants me at their house at eight."

"I'm an early riser."

He tried to imagine what kind of appointments Donna might have that early. Ken seemed surprised when the two women announced that they were spending the day together. And no, the men weren't invited to join them.

"When should I pick you up? Afternoon? Before dinner?"

"I have no idea. Can I call you?"

"You don't have a phone."

"Donna will have one."

He turned on the lights in the kitchen and the living room on his way to the fireplace. Crouching in front of it, he stacked up some logs and kindling. It was already past eleven, but Xander hoped she'd stay up so they could talk for a while. Dinner and the visit had stretched out much longer than he'd hoped. He felt like they'd covered every topic under the sun, from history, politics, and law, to parenting and even to engineering. There was an ease in the way Nadine moved through conversations. Everything she said showed her vast knowledge of almost every topic. She was smart, compassionate, and interesting.

"Thank you for introducing me to Ken and Donna. I have a much better understanding of your connection to them now."

"They're family to me. They're home away from my New York family. It was nice to see how well you and Donna hit it off."

"I was surprised how much we have in common."

He held a lit match to the kindling. When it caught, he glanced over his shoulder at her. She was standing next to the bookcase, perusing the volumes. After years of being around Ken and his wife, he congratulated himself on knowing a lot about Donna. But Nadine? He wished he knew more about her.

"What do you have in common?"

There was a pause. "We're both stubborn. Loners. Independent. We're vulnerable, in our own way, but we hide it well."

Two words stuck out for him. *Loners. Vulnerable.*

"We both had, well, unsettled childhoods. Now, we surround ourselves with people, but it's not easy for us to trust them. Neither of us has too many real friends."

Unsettled childhood. In Vegas, she'd thrown him a few hints about her family. But none of them had proved helpful when he tried to find her. In the end, he thought she'd made up everything.

"You told her you were getting out of a difficult relationship when you and I met."

"You were listening?"

"I didn't have any choice. You two were still in the foyer, and I was worried that Donna would put you back out on the street."

She smiled, pulled a book off the shelf, and hugged it to her chest.

"Yeah, I had a few worries myself, right then."

"So, was it the truth about the boyfriend?"

"No, I made that up."

How quickly he'd come to suspect much of what she said. He pushed to his feet and put the fire screen in front of the logs. "Then why? What was it about me that scared you?"

"Are we going to talk about that again?"

"Again? I've never gotten a straight answer. So, yes. And now is as good a time as any." He rubbed the back of his neck, forcing himself to stay where he was. He didn't want to go to her. Crowd her. "Help me out here, Nadine. I'm not trying to put pressure on you. But I'd really like to know. Did I come on too strong? Did I misread the signals? I honestly thought you felt the same way about me that I felt about you. Was I—?"

"It wasn't you," she interrupted.

"Then what?"

"For three days, I lost my mind. I allowed myself to dream. But then, reality returned."

"And what was this reality?"

"That we could never be."

"And why was that?"

"Because we're from two separate times."

"East Coast, West Coast? There are only twenty-four time zones across the globe. Relationships survive that all the time."

"Not time zones. Times. I don't exist in the year 2022."

She was back to her story world. He hoped she wouldn't spot his disbelief, but she did.

"You're rolling your eyes again. But know this. You can search all you want; you cannot find me."

"You're not giving me enough credit. I could find you if I wanted to."

Her smile was gentle. Confident. "It's not possible. You couldn't find me two years ago, and you wouldn't be able to find me now. That's because there is no record of me to find."

"There must be a logical explanation for that. People delete themselves off the Internet all the time. Is that what you've done? How about what you've told me? Is there another name?"

"No. Nadine Finley is my real name. It's what I go by."

He didn't believe it. "You're real. You're standing in front of me. And that means you exist. Somehow, some way, there *has* to be a way to find you."

"You can't find me, Xander, because I haven't been born yet."

"Nadine—"

"I'm done explaining. You'll just have to believe me." She held out the book she'd taken off the shelf. "Mind if I take this to bed? For tonight?"

"Can you take that book to bed? What do you think?"

"Your answer is yes?"

"Yes. Of course, yes. Do you remember the conversations we had in Vegas?"

"I do."

"Then you should realize that the shelves of that bookcase are filled with books *you* mentioned." He motioned toward the wall. "Those prints are the work of Paul Cezanne. I only got them because you lectured me about the post-Impressionist era."

Her eyes widened as she stared at the framed works.

"And the middle shelf in the first kitchen cabinet. It's packed with dark chocolate and double-stuffed Oreos, even though I never eat them myself. And I always keep a bottle of Sauvignon Blanc in the fridge, even though I'm a beer drinker." He waved a hand at the space around him. "Everything in here. The furniture, the walls, everything. Do you remember saying you like the calm of earth tones? And saying you love seeing snow? Watching it fall while you sit inside, in front of a roaring fire?"

"I remember," she said softly. "I remember every conversation we had."

"Then you must see that this house is a product of my time with you."

She walked toward him. He didn't move.

"I see it now."

"I didn't want to forgive you, Nadine, but I didn't want to forget you, either. Those few days meant a lot to me."

She pressed her hand against his chest. Only a breath of air separated them. "Those days meant a lot to me, too, Xander. You meant...and you continue to mean a lot to me."

This close, her scent, her eyes, her lips drew him in. Xander kissed her, and she kissed him back. Their lips molded together, and memories poured back in. But the kiss ended as quickly as it started. Nadine stepped back.

"You matter to me, Xander. You matter a lot. And I wish that someday you'll be able to believe that. I hope you'll be able to understand that I've been telling you the truth all along. But you probably never will."

Her eyes welled up as her fingers softly touched his lips. Then, without another word, she turned and walked away.

🙊 13 🙉

NADINE WAS TOLD that the clinic where Donna drove them had different waiting rooms, depending on what the patient was there for. Oncology, Breast Surgery, Imaging, Radiation.

She was only allowed to accompany her new friend as far as the main reception area. Not long after they arrived, a nurse escorted Donna in. That was seventy-six minutes ago.

Where she waited was a large, bright space with picture windows, comfortable chairs, and health-related magazines. People came through the door from the parking lot at a steady pace, going directly to the glass-fronted counter and checking in. As they turned to find seats, every one of them cast discreet looks around the room at the others who were waiting.

On a wall-mounted TV, two people chattered away. But no one paid any attention to the screen.

Waiting was hell. Nadine moved to a chair where she could see a clock mounted behind the receptionist. When he wasn't greeting arriving patients, the balding young man spent most of his time tapping away at a computer.

Time was moving slowly, and Nadine tried to not stare at the rack of flyers and pamphlets that each focused on a different form of cancer. She picked up a magazine promising better health through exercise, and paged through it, keeping her eye on the door where Donna had disappeared.

In her own future time, there were no office visits to doctors. No waiting in rooms like this. One spoke to a specialist, not in person, but via transmitted hologram. Tests were done in mobile units that arrived in front of the patient's building at appointment times. You only went to a hospital for a specific procedure or severe illness. Medical professionals had come to realize that waiting was a potent agent of anxiety, frustration, and hopelessness.

Nadine looked around at the dozen people who were currently sitting in the reception room. Some, she guessed, were friends and family. Others were waiting to be called into what she imagined as a honeycomb of rooms filled with machines and tables and worker bees. Almost all eyes turned to the door in unison any time an aide appeared to call the next patient, or someone came out.

Across from her, a very pale elderly woman wearing a knitted cap grasped the hand of the old man beside her. "I don't feel good."

He patted her hand and walked to the water cooler, returning in a moment with a cone-shaped cup of water for her.

A nurse came out, drawing all eyes. When she called for "Linda," two women stood up at the same time. A third also approached from a window on the far side of the waiting room.

"This happens every time I come here," the person sitting to Nadine's right said to her. "Too many Lindas live in Elkhorn, I guess."

Nadine glanced over at her. Probably in her sixties, she was wearing a 1920s flapper style, black-and-white turban and a long woolen coat. Dark, alert eyes watched the entire proceeding with interest as the nurse tried to clarify the confusion.

"I assume you're not a Linda," Nadine commented.

"No, I'm Jo."

"Nadine."

"First time here?"

"Yes. You could tell?"

"I'm a regular. I've seen almost everyone in this room before. Even those I haven't, I can tell you why they're here."

Jo had arrived long after Nadine. "Why do you think I'm here?"

"Helping a friend. Holding her hand. Moral support."

"What makes you think I'm not family?"

She smiled. "Personal experience and prejudice, I suppose. I don't feel too warmly about anyone in my family. So, when I see someone like you, looking genuinely worried, it makes me think you must be a good friend."

Nadine already liked Jo. And her mind lingered on the words, 'good friend'. This morning, when Xander dropped Nadine off, Donna had come out the front door and thrown her arms around her. They'd held each other for a long moment, to Ken's and Xander's obvious surprise.

"Aren't you going to ask me why I'm here? If I'm a regular, I mean?"

"Is it okay to ask? I didn't want to pry."

"Of course, it's okay. In general, I've found women are open about talking to other women. And most cancer patients, I'd say, like sharing their stories. Need it, maybe. Isolation can be a killer too."

Nadine took a second look at Jo's turban.

"Yes. Chemo. I have my head shaved. And this is my fourth time, fighting this."

Chemo was no longer a method of treatment in the future. Individual immunotherapies and more accurately targeted therapies were used. Side effects—like nausea and losing one's hair—were no longer an issue.

"How are you doing, this time?"

"Physically, I'll know better after today's appointment." A defiant smile creased Jo's face. "Mentally and emotionally, I'm good. I'll be fine."

Nadine wished she could bottle the woman's pluckiness and pass it on to Donna. "How do you do it? Your attitude is a marvel."

"Way back, during my second round with this, something shifted inside me. I stopped asking, 'Why me?' Instead, I thought, 'Why *not* me?' After all, I'm no different from anyone else. Illness and tragedy can happen to anybody. There's no real rhyme or reason to it. It just happens."

Nadine knew that some people got more than their fair share of bad things in life. Or this was what they thought, at least.

"We all die eventually. Some of us sooner, some later. Life isn't about what happens to you, but more about how you deal with it," Jo asserted, straightening her turban. "And accepting what's gotten thrown at you is the first step in dealing with the situation."

"In your case, situations. You're truly a warrior."

"I said 'fight' before, but I don't really like the battle terminology. Call me a *thriver* instead."

"You're a true thriver."

"Thank you. But don't let this face fool you." Jo smiled. "The initial shock gets you every time. But I'm quicker now at getting myself together. After that, it's just, *Okay, what can I do to fix it*."

The door to the treatment rooms opened, and a nurse stepped out, glancing at the folder in her hand. "Jo?"

At the same time, Donna came out, and Nadine stood up when she saw her.

Jo and Donna paused as they passed by each other in the middle of the waiting area.

"Hi, hon. You okay?" the older woman asked.

"I've had better mornings."

"You'll get there. And I think I hear this little one inside of you, growling with hunger."

"You're right." Donna touched her round belly. "We're both starved."

Jo disappeared through the door, and Nadine helped her friend put on her coat. She already knew that Donna wouldn't have any results right away, so she figured there was no point in asking.

"What are your activity limits today?" she asked as they turned toward the door. "Is skiing too strenuous? We can always go bungee jumping and follow it up with wine tasting."

"The woman after my own heart." Donna tried to button the front of the coat but gave up. "Snowshoeing and cross-country skiing will be excellent. And why bother with wine? I say we go straight for the tequila shooters."

They left the clinic, and Donna stopped on the sidewalk. She lifted her face to the sky, and a few tears escaped and fell on her cheeks.

Nadine took her hand. "Listen. You've had the biopsy. Now, wait for the results. One foot in front of the other. Appreciate that baby growing inside of you. And before he or she decides to make an entrance into this crazy world, let's live and live and live. What do you say?"

Donna took a tissue out of her pocket and wiped her face. "I knew you were the right person to come with me today."

14

AFTER DROPPING Nadine off with Donna, Xander had a cup of coffee with Ken and drove back up the mountain.

Based on the weather app, today would be his only chance to work on the garage roof for the next few days. The weather forecasters were keeping an eye on an area of low pressure coming from the direction of the Pacific Northwest. The Rockies was going to get hit with intense snowfall before the storm tracked into the Northern Plains. It looked like blizzard conditions from central Colorado up into Minnesota. The exact timing was still up in the air, though they were leaning toward Friday.

Hearing the weather report, a few scenarios immediately ran through Xander's mind.

What if this blizzard hit and Nadine wouldn't be able to leave? He suspected that she needed to be dropped off somewhere. Airport? Train station? Bus stop? She said she didn't have her wallet on her, so she wouldn't be able to rent a car. And she'd said nothing about anyone else picking her up.

That cheered him up a little, but only momentarily.

Earlier, on the drive down the mountain to Elkhorn, he and Nadine had not discussed what would happen once she left. Xander had no clue if he'd ever see her again. Hell, did she even *want* to see him again?

He knew it would hurt when she left. He already missed her. Still, he wasn't going to pressure her to stay or even set up some way that they could connect again. Not if she didn't want to.

He'd been an open book with her. She, on the other hand, was locked down tight. And some of the things that came out of her mouth were, frankly, bat shit crazy.

For the first time since he'd moved here, the house seemed empty and silent. He stared at her coffee mug, all rinsed and ready, next to his by the sink. Vegas started with sex and ended with him losing his mind. This visit...he didn't know how to describe this visit. The kiss last night, certainly, was more confusing than anything.

"The roof, pal. Get to it." He couldn't stand around lollygagging all day. Thinking about this was getting him nowhere.

Zipping up his vest and pulling on his boots, Xander went out to the garage.

Yesterday morning, he'd moved the coffin from the back of his truck onto a couple of two-by-fours on the floor by his workbench.

Coming out to Colorado and having a shitload of free time had triggered an interest in woodworking. He found he enjoyed the feel of working with his hands. And he had a good teacher. A semi-retired cabinetmaker. The guy had a shop down by the railroad tracks, and he'd been happy for the extra money. The bookcase, a couple of side tables, and a small chest that Xander had built were up in the house. As they worked, the craftsman had rambled on constantly about wood and the history of furniture building, but Xander wasn't keen on his lectures. He was there to build things.

Crouching by the coffin now, he ran his hands over the surface of the sides and top. The planks had been hand-planed and the joints nicely dovetailed. He'd practiced making joints like that, and it took a lot of skill to do it well. There wasn't a nail used in this thing as far as he could tell. This box had gotten more attention to detail than a lot of fine furniture getting built these days.

He had no idea if Nadine was taking it back with her. She'd made no mention of it. She hadn't even given it a second glance since she arrived. Maybe he'd offer to keep it for her, though it would look a little weird, a coffin in his garage.

Xander thought of the historical society restoration people down in Elkhorn. Maybe they could tell him more about it. He touched the wood again and his mind drifted to Nadine's claim of coming from

England in the 1800s. The old-fashioned dress. It still hung in the closet of the guestroom.

Regardless of what she said, the only rational explanation for all this was that she was an actor.

He lifted the top of the coffin off and looked inside.

Two things in a corner of the box caught his eye. "What's this?"

Xander stood up and switched on the shop light over his bench to get a better look.

They both easily fit in his palm. One was a very lightweight metal tube about two inches long and a half inch in diameter. Pewter or something. No markings on it. No seams. The inside of the tube was blocked at both ends. It was about the size of a Chap Stick, but he couldn't see any way to get it open.

He tapped it on the bench, thinking maybe it'd pop open. Nothing. He slid a small screwdriver into one end and then the other.

"Don't damage it," he muttered.

He didn't know who it belonged to. Was it Nadine's? Was it there before she climbed inside the box?

He glanced inside the coffin again, thinking it might be part of something else. Nothing more in there.

The second piece looked like a kid's toy. A wooden whistle...or a musical instrument. About three inches long, an inch wide, and a half-inch thick. And it only had two finger holes. When Xander held it up to the light again, he could see through it, end to end. Blowing into it produced no sound at all, though. When he looked closely, he realized it wasn't real wood. It was some kind of hard plastic made to look like wood.

The two pieces didn't belong to each other. That he was sure of.

Xander recalled Nadine rummaging through her bag on the dark road and coming up with her inhaler. Maybe they fell out then. Maybe she knew what they were. He'd have to ask her.

Gadgets were his thing. But these two items? He shook his head.

"You got me."

Dropping them into his vest pocket, he strapped on his tool belt. The roof was waiting.

❧ 15 ❧

"I'm afraid of heights."

"We'll barely be above the trees."

"Small consolation when the gondola cable gives out."

The list of fears Nadine had collected over the years as a time traveler was long. Torture and extreme executions ranked high on the list. Being burned alive; or hanged, drawn, and quartered were simply not that appealing. Rats and bubonic plague weren't in the plus column for the past either, along with the barbarity of medical procedures prior to anesthesia. There were other things too.

And then there was her innate acrophobia. She hated the near-panic feeling of anxiety that gripped her whenever she was high in the air.

"The cable won't give out. And seriously, we'll be, like, thirty feet up."

"You said you haven't been on this deathtrap yet," she reminded Donna.

"I've seen videos online."

"I could quote you historical statistics about the dangers of—"

"And the hillsides are covered in soft, fluffy snow."

"With boulders underneath." A fifty-foot drop was a fifty-foot drop. The human body wasn't designed to survive that kind of fall. "They don't call this the Rockies for nothing, you know."

Donna laughed, obviously not sharing Nadine's concerns.

After leaving the clinic, they'd had breakfast at a quaint little pancake place where they were served by a grouchy, white-haired waitress who must have been working there since the silver boom days. "Local color," Donna whispered.

After that, the two had spent the rest of the morning meandering through town, stopping in at the dollar store, the bakery, the flower shop, and several other places that caught Donna's interest.

In their travels, Nadine learned that the baby shower on Saturday wasn't being arranged for Donna by her new friends. Apparently, the people she'd met since moving to Elkhorn were expecting a party, though. And no one was lending a hand. Donna and Ken were doing the work themselves, with some assistance from Xander.

Nadine wished her circumstances were different. She would have gladly stuck around to help. But that was out of the question. She had to get back to Hythe before Jane Austen arrived on the coach.

It was past noon by the time they finished the errands. Instead of going home, however, Donna was now insisting that they have lunch at a restaurant at the top of a rather ominous-looking mountain peak. And it appeared the only way to get there was to ride up to 11,000 feet in a tiny gondola, dangling no doubt from a fraying wire.

"Can't we drive?"

"No. The service road is closed to the general public for the winter, and I know they won't open it until June." Donna patted her on the knee. "It's okay. I'll hold your hand."

"I'm pretty hungry now." Nadine pointed at a restaurant they were passing. "Look at that steakhouse. A lot of cars parked in front too, so it must be good. Why don't we go there?"

"Already eaten there. Ken loves his steak. Trust me, where we're going is worth a small case of the jitters."

"Easy for you to say."

Nadine's profession required that she be prepared for any situation. She had trained herself to deal with her fear of heights. For the most part, anyway. Gradual exposure to extreme situations, if possible. Deep breathing. Meditative relaxation. Still, if given the choice, she'd stay away from ledges, not fly, and avoid glass elevators on skyscraper exteriors. She just didn't need to put herself through that. Jumping the gyre loops of time was hard enough.

No, she was definitely not looking forward to riding in some plastic bubble suspended God knows *how* many feet off the ground...no matter what Donna saw on YouTube.

"If this restaurant is so good, why haven't you and Ken gone there yet?"

"They had a change of ownership before we moved to Colorado. Then it was closed for Covid, and they did a big renovation. The place is just reopening."

"I've got a great idea. How about if you two go? You could make a date out of it. Very memorable, I'm sure."

"We won't have time before the baby comes." The dark eyes left the road and met Nadine's for a brief second. The face was serious. "It's hard not obsessing about the biopsy. Every time my phone rings, I think it's the doctor. The whole thing is alarming *and* depressing. I could really use the distraction right now. Please?"

How could she say no? Donna was thirty-six weeks pregnant and in need of a friend. And Nadine couldn't even hang around long enough to help her with the party. More importantly, she wouldn't be around when her friend got the results of the biopsy. Having lunch with her—regardless of how scary the ride up would be—was the least she could do.

"Okay. But the food better be good. And I mean *really* good."

A few minutes later, Donna pulled into the parking lot. The gondola cable ran up the mountain for about a hundred miles before disappearing behind a ridge. And the lot was practically empty.

"No one's here. Maybe they're not open," Nadine suggested hopefully

"It's open. A flyer I got in the mail said they're doing a 'soft opening' for the restaurant this week. There's a large lodge that is still being renovated, but that won't be ready for guests until this summer, at least."

Nadine took a deep breath to loosen the knot in her stomach and tried to focus on relaxing her already clenched back and shoulder muscles. "Okay. Let's do this before I run all the way back to Xander's house."

At a glass window, they got their tickets from a bored-looking girl with purple hair who kept eyeing Donna's belly. They were the only riders on a gondola built for four, and the lanky, pimple-faced teenager who was working as the attendant looked high to Nadine. Still, he politely held the gondola door for them.

"How long is this ride?" she asked him.

Startled by the question, he squinched his face up tight. "Uh. Eight minutes. Yeah. Eight minutes."

"Ever have any accidents? Breakdowns? Gondolas jumping the cable and tumbling the twelve miles to the bottom?"

He had to bear down on that one. "Uh. Nope. Not that I know of."

"Have you been doing this job long?"

Nadine ignored the sharp jab from Donna.

"Uh, yeah." He nodded. "Since Monday."

"All right, then. I feel much more confident. Lay on, Macduff."

"Actually, it's Jared." He pointed to his name tag.

"Thanks. I'll keep that in mind."

The door clicked shut, and Jared pushed the rocking gondola a few feet along a track until it reached a point where the moving cable engaged it with a jerk. And off they went.

Nadine focused on her breathing again. The gondola was really nothing more than a clear plastic bubble with four seats facing each other.

"Are you going to ride all the way to the top with your eyes closed?"

"That seems like a good plan." She had her inhaler with her, but she hoped she wouldn't have an asthma attack on this contraption.

"We're about to pass a support thing. It looks very sturdy."

"A support thing?" The gondola lurched and bounced, eliciting a gasp from Nadine and a giggle from Donna.

"We're going to die...and you're laughing."

"I'll warn you when we get to the next one."

"Thank you. I'll be here." She took another deep calming breath and peeked at her companion. "Isn't this bumping and swaying too much for the baby?"

"Maybe it is, maybe it isn't." Donna looked down at her protruding stomach. "In any case, I'm ready to deliver this bundle whenever he or she decides the time is right."

"Please don't let it be right now, not in this thing."

"Why? You've never delivered a baby before?"

"No. Have you?"

"I'm a lawyer. But how hard can it be? Besides, I've seen plenty of videos." She winced and squirmed slightly in her seat, taking deep breaths. "I can't do it alone, though."

Feeling somewhat worried, Nadine forced herself to glance behind them and then up the mountain. She couldn't see either the loading or unloading stations.

"I shouldn't have let you talk me into this. It's dangerous for you to be this far away from the hospital. Are you in labor? Are you having contractions?"

Nadine focused on her companion's face. There was an amused wrinkle forming in the corners of her eyes. They were up here because Donna needed to get a short break from her current stresses. But it was Nadine who was being needy, and her friend who was doing the distracting.

"Faking it, aren't you?"

"Yes, I'm faking it."

She sat back and took a deep breath. "You didn't call Ken and tell him we're having lunch up here, did you?"

"No, I didn't. He would have tried to talk me out of it. But I'll do it now." Donna reached inside her bag for her cell phone. She frowned. "No service. I'll call him when we get to the top."

The gondola bounced and swayed as they passed another support tower, and Nadine grabbed the seat. This time, she didn't voice any complaints. Here she was with a very pregnant woman who was waiting for potentially life-threatening news, and Nadine was allowing her own weakness to control her. She couldn't let that happen.

Now, keeping her eyes open, she turned again in her seat and looked down the mountain. Her stomach was knotted tight, but she took in the view. It was breathtaking.

Donna was right. The gondola was gliding along, skimming just above the tops of the trees. She couldn't get herself to peek straight down. Instead, she focused into the distance where Elkhorn looked like a toy town, nestled between two mountainous ridges that stretched far to the south. The wide, snow-covered valley had a river snaking through it, and on either side, deep green forests lay like a spiky blanket until the trees thinned out and then gave way to rocky peaks topped with snow. As she looked, thick grey clouds tumbled like a wave over the top of the ridge to the west, rolling downward and consuming the forested slope.

She turned in her seat to the east, wondering if she could see Xander's house. She thought of him working on his roof. Tonight and tomorrow were all they had left before she had to leave. He didn't complain, but she could tell that he'd been disappointed about her coming out with Donna today. Still, wasn't this better for them both? Regardless of how she felt, she couldn't let renewed intimacy creep into their relationship. Leaving was already painful. That would only make it worse.

When they pulled into the docking station at the top, an attendant opened the gondola door and helped Donna out. Nadine followed.

"Do you know Jared?" she asked the young man.

"Uh, yeah. We share an apartment."

"Well, you can tell him for me, he's a big fat liar. He said the trip was eight minutes."

"Uh, yeah? So?"

"We were on that thing for two and a half hours, at least."

"Don't pay any attention to her," Donna said with a laugh, turning to Nadine. "Now that you're back on *terra firma*, take a good look at that view."

From here at the summit, the view was even more amazing. She had to admit, it was unlike anything she'd ever seen. But they were also very high and standing on a platform on the edge of an abyss. The reality of it was too much for her, and Nadine's stomach flipped.

She took an involuntary step backward. "Almost on *terra firma*."

"Okay. Let's go." Donna laughed and linked her arm with Nadine's.

Leaving the gondola platform, the two made their way along a plowed and sanded path. The snow was deeper up here, and the air colder than it had been in town.

As Donna said, there was no sign of any vehicles up here, except for a few snowmobiles parked beneath a shed by the edge of a grove of fir trees that were twisted and bent from the mountain wind.

The restaurant was impressive. It was a huge log structure, also perched on the edge of a cliff. A wide timber deck jutted out over the precipice. Nadine winced, certain that people who enjoyed precarious seating would just love dining out there in the warmer months. Luckily, they wouldn't be serving food out there this afternoon.

The two women entered the restaurant, where an enthusiastic hostess greeted them and led them to a table by one of the large windows facing out onto the deck.

"I'll be right back. I have to use the bathroom."

Nadine watched Donna hurry off.

"How close is she?" the hostess asked.

"Thirty-six weeks," Nadine answered.

"Her first?"

"Yes."

"My first baby came at thirty-five weeks."

"Oh, great." Nadine shot a glance toward the restrooms. Even though one of her life's regrets was that she would never have a baby, she really didn't know much about delivery. At least, she didn't know much about how they handled it in 2022.

"That boy of mine gave me twenty hours of labor before he came kicking and screaming into this world," the hostess assured her. She handed her the menu. "First babies take their time."

Nadine certainly hoped so.

As the hostess moved away, Nadine surveyed the restaurant. The large open dining room gave off a vibe that was both formal and casual. Colossal log beams supported the roof, and chandeliers made from antlers hung over tables covered with snow-white cloths. A blazing log fire crackled on a wide hearth.

There were only five other parties scattered around the room. Nadine could see a portion of a walled-off bar area, but there appeared to be a few more people drinking there and watching a television.

Donna reappeared in a moment and stopped to take pictures of the interior of the restaurant.

As she reached their table, she gestured toward the chandeliers and the rack of elk antlers mounted over the fireplace. "I think Gaston did the decorating."

Nadine had no idea who Gaston was, but she smiled in agreement. "Are you okay?"

"I think so."

"Maybe we should head back down."

"We're here. Let's enjoy our lunch." She started to take a picture of the view beyond the huge plate glass windows, but the panorama had disappeared. "Oh, look. It's snowing again."

Nadine closed the menu with a snap and jumped to her feet. "We're leaving. We're not going to get stranded up here."

"We won't. It snows practically every day in the Rockies in April. Please sit." She smiled, shed her coat, and moved a chair to make room for herself. She settled in across from Nadine.

"Are you really okay? And don't tell me *I think so.*"

"*I think so* is about the best I can do, considering how this morning started."

Actually, Nadine marveled at how well Donna was handling everything.

"Are you going to send that picture to Ken and make him jealous?"

She glanced at her phone. "I still have no cell service. How about you?"

They'd already had a conversation about this. On their way to the doctor's office, Nadine told her that she didn't have a cell phone on her. Her excuse was that she didn't want her work and her boss to interfere when she was taking time off. "Mine is sitting in the guest bedroom at Xander's house."

"Oh, yeah. You told me that this morning. Pregnancy and brain fog. It's a real thing. I can attest to it."

"Won't Ken get worried if you don't call or text him?"

"I think he'd be more worried knowing how far away I am from him and the hospital." She picked up the menu. "I'll call him when we get back down to the car after lunch. Right now, I'm starving."

16

Xander's phone was dinging away like it was the end of a round and the boxers wouldn't stop slugging each other. When he was working, texts annoyed him. So many of them were just scams. And these were coming rapid-fire.

One of these days, he'd have to devise an app that punished scammers. Emptied their bank accounts. Hurt them where it counted.

He turned his collar up against the cold wind, which seemed to be blowing harder.

Perched on a slippery garage roof with a knee on a shingle a hammer in one hand and a nail in the other, he had no intention of checking messages. Nadine didn't have a phone on her, and his parents had their routines. They FaceTimed him every Saturday at noon, East Coast time. Constantly competing to get a word in, they cut in on each other's sentences as they relayed the news about everyone they knew. They were retired—and since he'd sold his company, Xander practically was as well—so there was only so much news. But still, it was a way for all of them to visit. To be honest, Xander enjoyed it as much as they did.

He'd never told them about Nadine. He doubted he'd mention it this week, either. After all, she'd be long gone by the time of their call. His mother still yearned for Xander to get married and give her grandchildren. She'd be happy to know he was in a steady relationship. Would three days in one year and three days this year count?

He brought down the hammer on the nail. *Not.*

A brief pause on the cell and then the calls started again. The first one went to voicemail. When the phone rang again, he started to get concerned. Sliding his hammer into his work belt, he peeled off his gloves and dug deep in his pocket for the phone.

He should have known. "Ken, I'm on the roof. This better be good."

"Have you heard from them?"

Xander checked his watch. "It's half past two in the afternoon. You weren't seriously expecting them to be back already?"

"Donna isn't answering her phone."

"Why should she? She's having fun."

"She said she'd check in after lunch."

"Maybe they aren't finished with lunch."

"I haven't heard from her since they left, this morning. She usually texts me and lets me know where she is every couple of hours."

Those two had too much togetherness. Xander rolled his eyes. "Are you done? Can I get back to work now?"

"Can you text or call Nadine? Find out where they're at?"

"She doesn't have a cell phone."

"Why? Where is it?"

"She never carries a cell phone." That's at least what she'd told him.

"Who doesn't carry a phone? Wait, is she one of those 5G conspiracy believers?"

"I doubt it, but I really don't know."

"How do people get hold of her?"

He wasn't going to mention her stories about coming from the future and traveling to the past. "I don't know. She manages somehow, I guess."

"How did she call you that first night from the airport?"

"She must have used a public phone."

"*Public* phone? Are there any of them left?"

"Look, pal, I don't have time for chitchat," Xander blasted him. "I'm trying to finish this damn roof because I have a baby shower, of all things, to attend this weekend. So why don't you go and work on whatever list Donna left you for today? They'll be back soon."

"Okay, but..."

"But what?"

"Did you check the weather today?"

"I did this morning."

"It's changed since then. The storm they were warning about for the weekend is gonna hit earlier than they thought. The wind is blowing like a bastard here. It's already snowing in town."

Xander squinted into the wind as he looked at the sky to the west. April was the second snowiest month of the year in Colorado. Last year, they'd had three good-sized storms dump about six feet of snow here. Mountain weather changed quickly, though, and the following days were often in the 60s or low 70s, so the snow didn't last. Only one of those April snows last year had been designated as a blizzard.

With Ken still on the phone, he checked the forecast. Shit. They had upgraded the storm, and they were calling it a potential 'bomb cyclone'. Heavy snow and winds over fifty miles per hour.

"Shit."

"Now you see why I'm worried?"

"I see it." Xander frowned. He figured Donna had her regular places for shopping and going out to eat. But being as late in her pregnancy as she was, she'd be aware of the weather and the condition of the roads. "Listen, if it's snowing in town, Donna is probably already driving home."

"Maybe. But I don't know why she doesn't answer her goddamn phone."

"Quit grousing. She's probably coming up your driveway right now."

"I hope so."

Damn it! If this storm turned into something serious, he didn't want Nadine getting stuck at Ken's house. This was her last night in Elkhorn.

"Will you call me when you hear from them? Or when they show up?"

"If they don't get home in a half hour, I'm going out looking for them."

Xander checked the radar on his phone again. The heaviest bands of snow were supposed to reach Elkhorn in two or three hours. But even as he looked at it, the prediction changed again. The dark blue bands suddenly got a lot wider. They were in for some serious snow.

"I'll call you in an hour. Whether you've heard from them or not at that point, I'll drive down to your house. Hell, they'll probably be sitting in your kitchen by then."

He hoped so, anyway, staring across the valley at the steel-grey sky.

ITALIAN FOOD as Nadine had never experienced it before. "This meal is amazing," she exclaimed as they waited for the main course—the *secondi*—to arrive. She and Donna had already spent the last hour or so taking their time to enjoy the *antipasto* and the *primi* courses.

The *antipasto* tray had been a meal in itself. Bite-sized portions of a variety of cheeses, smoked meats, sausages, olives, sardines, fresh and pickled vegetables, and peppers, along with stuffed mushrooms, and cold braised veal. The *primi* course had consisted of a selection of risotto, gnocchi, soup, lasagna, pasta, and a delicious broth.

She couldn't believe that her friend had insisted on ordering a main course too. Donna explained that even if she had to force down every last mouthful, she'd do it. This lunch was most likely the last elaborate meal she'd have before the chaotic days of motherhood started.

The menu was Italian and four pages long. Nadine had taken one look at it and asked Donna to order for them both while she escaped to the restroom.

Her jobs hadn't taken her to this decade too often, and the only Italian food she knew was pizza, spaghetti, and lasagna. She didn't have any idea what to order, and she didn't want to bring attention to that gap in her knowledge.

In 2078, the year she came from, going out to eat was not an experience like this. A diner rarely saw humans preparing and serving food. The personal nutrient monitor people wore tracked and customized the diner's order, based on their dietary needs, restrictions, and budget. For Nadine and others of her time, going out to eat was not the sensory pleasure overload that this experience offered.

The waitress explained the *secondi* course dishes—Gnocchi con Calamari and Cresta De Gallo Alla Bolognese—as she placed them on the table. Two smaller plates were also brought for them when Donna mentioned they were going to share the food.

"What do you think?" Donna asked when the young woman walked away. "Good choices?"

"Both of them are a first for me." Nadine stared at each dish. "But I don't think you should eat the calamari."

"Why?"

"These creatures are bottom feeders living in largely contaminated waters. I can give a half-hour lecture about the dangers and side effects of squid as food. In fact, all fish have their dangers." She stared at the scrunched-up tentacles in the dish. "Now that I think of it, I'm going to *insist* that you stay away from the calamari. No sharing. You can have the Cresta de Gallo."

"I want to at least try it."

As Donna reached, Nadine took the plate and put it in front of herself, out of her reach.

"You can't have it while you're pregnant. You must have been warned, no?"

"All right, Ms. Reference Librarian. Argue your case. Why is it bad for me."

Starting last night during dinner, testing Nadine's knowledge had proven to be a source of entertainment for Donna. She quizzed her constantly on random bits of knowledge on obscure topics.

"Really?"

"Really."

"Okay. Here goes. Bacterial contamination and toxic chemicals in the fish can cause cancer and brain degeneration and memory loss, liver damage, nervous system disorders, fetal damage, dioxins, and food poisoning. You could ingest radioactive substances like strontium 90 and other dangerous contaminants, along with cadmium, mercury, lead, chromium, and arsenic." She motioned to Donna's round belly. "This one dish could cause kidney damage in your baby, as well as impair his or her mental development. The high levels of mercury can lead to Alzheimer's, Parkinson's, and autism. Do you want me to go on?"

Donna sat back. "I just lost my appetite."

"Good. They can pack both dishes, and you can take them home to your starving husband."

Nadine glanced around her. The two of them were the only ones left in the dining room. And there was no sign of their waitress or the hostess who'd seated them.

Across the restaurant, Nadine could see the bartender, a few patrons, and a couple of the kitchen staff staring up at a TV screen behind the bar. She couldn't see the entire screen from where she was sitting, but it looked like there was a weather map with snowfall predictions on the screen. She hoped whatever they were watching was not local weather.

Donna broke into her thoughts "Are you much of a cook?"

Nadine turned her attention to her companion. "I'd like to be one, but I don't spend enough time in one place to hone my skills."

"Where are you going from here? When you leave tomorrow?"

She could be honest about it. "England."

Donna arched her eyebrows in surprise. "Where in England?"

"Hythe, a little village on the south coast of Kent."

"Have you been there before?"

"Yes."

"When?"

"Last week."

"So, you're going back."

"I have to. My job there wasn't finished."

Nadine glanced over her shoulder again, hoping to see someone working in the dining room. No one. She could get up and try to find their server. This morning, she'd borrowed some cash from Xander. The truth was, he'd insisted on giving her the money. She had enough to pay for lunch. And *borrowed* was inaccurate, considering she'd have no chance to repay him.

"Was this a vacation, coming to Colorado?"

"It feels like it, since you brought me up here." A strong gust of wind slammed snow against the plate glass window. The weather was deteriorating rapidly. "How about if I go and find our server?"

"Here she is." Donna motioned in the air, gesturing for the check. The young woman nodded and disappeared into the bar area.

"Please, let me pay for it."

"Definitely not. You did me a huge favor, coming today. You're my guest. But thank you for offering."

The etiquette of whether she should still insist on paying or not was another thing that she had to ponder. In the future, one didn't get a check after a meal. There were no checkout lines for groceries, or clothing, or anything. Surveillance systems kept track of what anyone bought, ate, and even tried to steal. Everything was automatically charged to a person's bank account.

Donna had a perplexed frown on her face.

"What's the matter?" Nadine asked.

"I guess...it's just that I've never run into someone like you before. You're unique, Nadine. Different."

"Thank you. I'll take that as a compliment."

"Yes, you should. Absolutely." Donna took a sip of her water, but her eyes stayed on Nadine. "We talked about this last night. It's not easy for me to trust people. I don't have any real friends here. But you...somehow you have moved right into my circle of trust. I feel comfortable with you, and we've only known each other less than twenty-four hours."

"Is that a bad thing?"

"No. It's not at all. That is, if I could understand you a little better."

"I thought you did. We're so much alike. That's why we get along."

"I understand you here." Donna pointed at her own heart. "You're extremely smart and have an incredible memory. But I'm having a little trouble connecting the dots about who you *say* you are."

Nadine looked at the wind-driven snow outside, wondering why it was taking their waitress so long to bring the check. She didn't want to get into this conversation.

"To be honest," Donna continued, "I don't believe what you say about what you do. And the few details you've shared about your life and where you've been—about how you have no base, no home and family, how you're always on the go—don't really add up. For example, I don't know—"

"My life is not normal," she broke in. "My job keeps me from settling down in one place. I don't have routines or stability like most people."

"Maybe that's true when you're right out of college. And I'm sure there are people older than that who fit the description. But there's more to you. I feel it. You're not who you say you are. What you've shared about your life is superficial. It sounds like you've scripted it. You've only let me see this...this veneer of who you are."

Before Nadine could say anything more in defense, Donna forged on.

"You *know* things. You're a walking encyclopedia. You're very well-read. It's like there's a computer chip in your brain that can spit out facts."

"It goes with the territory of the job I do."

"But there's something missing. Something about everyday life in the here and now."

"I don't know what you mean."

Nadine did know, of course. She hadn't been prepared to show up in 2022 and face this kind of interaction with people. A couple of years ago, she had some knowledge that was relevant at the time. But the job in Lake Tahoe was only supposed to take her less than a day to complete. After that, she merely had to lie low until she could make the quantum jump back to the future. Landing by mistake in Vegas had given her three unforgettable days in a hotel room with Xander, but she hadn't needed to know much in the way of current events.

"Wait, is this the lawyer in you asking these questions now?"

"Maybe it is. Our job choices and our personalities are connected. We can never separate the two, can we?"

"If we're lucky. If we have that choice."

Donna leaned toward her, the face serious, the gaze direct. "Are you saying you *didn't* choose your profession?"

No, she didn't. She had no option, really.

It was either accept the government's offer or die. There was no cure for her affliction, so she couldn't say *no* to the offer. Traveling into the past paused the disease's progression. So, she had to go back in time. Over and over. Of course, in doing so, she had the opportunity to meet people that she'd only read about. And she could live.

"My job *does* fit my personality. It matters to me where we came from, how we lived, and what we thought. The social history. The languages. The different versions of history, depending on who was recording it. That's why it's so important that we preserve it. I'm passionate about the written word. We should not forget or lose any of it. That's what I do."

"I hear the researcher speaking now. What about the real you?"

"What do you mean?"

"*Pop Music...Potent Potables...Sports...Food and Drink...Common Bonds...Fruits and Vegetables.*"

Nadine stared at the other woman in confusion. "Are you asking my preferences with these things?"

"Do you watch TV, Nadine?"

"I really don't have much time for it."

"And with all your traveling, you probably don't own a TV."

"Actually, I don't."

"And you've never heard of *Jeopardy*?"

"I assume it's a television show?"

Donna scoffed. "Do you read the newspapers?"

"Does anyone?"

"Probably not. Tell me where you get your entertainment news. Or any news, for that matter."

"The Internet. I'm not a Luddite." Nadine was bluffing, but she was treading on thin ice. Ask her about the prominent writers of this decade, the ones who had survived the test of time, and she could talk in depth about their work. But her knowledge of movies or politics or the rest of it was hit and miss.

And Donna was calling her bluff. "Who's in the headlines now?"

She shrugged. "I really don't know. I haven't been following the news...jeez, I don't know for how long."

"How about music? Do you listen to it?"

"Of course."

"Your favorite band?"

"The Beatles."

"They don't count. Name a current band you listen to. Or the artist who played the halftime show at the Superbowl this year. Or the past *five* years."

Nadine's mind raced to come up with a group that would be relevant for this time, but she was blanking. "Does it matter who I listen to?"

"Normally, no. But it does to me because I'm trying to prove something."

"Which is?"

"That you know nothing about *now*."

"Look, just because I've been buried in my work, you can't say—"

"What is this?" Donna interrupted. Taking a piece of paper and a pen out of her bag, she drew a large, rounded checkmark on it. "Do you know?"

"It's a checkmark."

"What if it's on your clothes...or on your shoes? What does it refer to?"

Trademarks. Donna was testing her on trademarks. Shit. Shit. Shit.

"Okay, how about this?" She drew a bullseye on the paper. "And it's red. And you shop there."

"I'm not much of a shopper. You heard me yesterday. I prefer to buy at thrift stores, rather than buy things new."

Shaking her head at Nadine's response, Donna drew a smile—or maybe it was a smirk—on the paper. "And this? It's on the side of every other truck in America."

"A smile?"

Donna leaned forward, tapping her pen on the table. Her eyes bored into Nadine's. "Who are you? I mean, who are you *really*? Or maybe I should ask, where did you come from?"

Damn it. The walls were closing in.

Luckily, at that very moment, the waitress hurried across the dining room.

"Can you box these dinners for us?" Nadine asked quickly before the server even arrived at the table.

"Yes, of course. But I'm really sorry, ladies," she replied, placing a leather folder on the table between them. "The manager has asked me to tell you that the gondola has shut down."

If Nadine was looking for a distraction, this announcement did it. Both stared in disbelief at the young woman.

"What do you mean, *shut down?*" Donna blurted out.

The waitress motioned toward the window. It was snowing so hard and the wind was blowing so fiercely that it was beginning to look like night had fallen.

"This isn't what they were expecting," she said apologetically. "But the wind is already too strong to operate the gondola. It's a full-fledged blizzard. And they're saying it might keep up all night."

"All night?" Nadine asked, unable to keep the note of dismay out of her voice.

The server nodded. "We're all stuck here, I'm afraid."

❧ 18 ❧

THE FORECAST and Ken's call worried Xander enough that he put away the ladder and his tools. He threw a few things for himself and Nadine in an overnight bag—just in case—and got on the road.

Whatever the snow predictions had been before, the forecasters had upgraded the storm even more. Now, they were calling for three to five inches *per hour* in Elkhorn with heavier snowfall in the foothills and increasing as the evening progressed. The totals looked to be staggering.

His plan was to get down to Ken and Donna's house, since that was where Nadine would be heading. Getting back to his house tonight would probably be a challenge. It didn't matter. His friends had plenty of room to put them up for the night.

Before leaving the house, he called Ken again. He still hadn't heard anything from his wife. No return texts or calls. He'd also checked in at some of Donna's regular stops. Nothing.

Xander had barely gotten his pickup out of the garage when the snow started falling. The wind was blowing hard too, forcing him to take his time.

The pickup was practically crawling down the treacherous mountain road. The fast-falling snow had reached him way ahead of the latest weather report. And the plows only came up here after the main roads were cleared.

"Well, Nadine," he said aloud as he passed the spot where he'd found her two nights ago. "Maybe this storm will change your plans."

A new pile of rock and dirt and snow had avalanched down since this morning. It was now encroaching on the roadway.

It occurred to him that he had no idea how she planned on leaving. She'd told him this morning that she didn't have any money or credit cards. Hell, he didn't even know if she could drive.

He thought about the two women out in this storm alone. Donna was a city driver and had always been vocal about her dislike for going out in bad weather. She was also thirty-six weeks pregnant. Wherever they were, he hoped she would call Ken to pick them up.

Xander was halfway down the mountain when his phone rang. He didn't recognize the number, but he still jumped to answer it.

"Hi."

His relief at hearing Nadine's voice was immense.

"Have you heard about the storm? They're already calling it a blizzard. Where are you? I'll come and get you."

"I think that would be a little difficult," she said. "In fact, I'd say it's impossible right now. It's the storm."

People were talking in the background, and he recognized Donna as one of them.

"We're all in the middle of it. But where are you exactly?"

"Tell him," Donna called out in the background. "Ana ask him to do that for me."

"Do what for her? Are you two in danger? Are you stranded somewhere? What's wrong?" He felt his blood pressure spiking.

"Xander, listen to me," Nadine said calmly. "Let me tell you what she wants so I can put her mind at ease."

Bits and pieces of conversation from Donna came through the line. She kept trying to interrupt.

"She wants you...Donna wants you to drive to their house and stay with Ken and make sure he doesn't do anything stupid."

Now, he was really getting worried. "What's considered stupid?"

Donna came on the line. "Xander? Where are you?"

"Half an hour, maybe an hour away from your house. The roads are a mess. Where are you?"

"Valley something. Oh...Valley View. No, that's not right. That was the old name. I'm having a mental block." Now Nadine was the one talking in the background. "That's right. The Eagle's Nest Lodge. The restaurant at the top of the gondola run. They've been renovating it."

It took him a second before their location registered. He glanced to the west, but he could barely see beyond the edge of the road. Xander's hands fisted on the wheel as the pickup truck went into a skid. He steered into it and negotiated the sharp bend.

That lodge was three thousand feet higher in elevation than he was. However bad the snow and wind were here, it had to be much worse where they were.

"What are you doing there? Did you drive? The service road...is it open? Does Ken know where you are?"

"Lunch...no...no...yes."

Leave it to Donna to answer him in code.

"You're saying there's no way to get to you?"

"Yes. Exactly! The gondola is shut down. The road is closed. We're stranded, and we don't know for how long. *Stranded.*"

Donna sounded more panicky than he'd ever heard her before. And he'd seen her in some pretty stressful situations. She was the queen of cool...normally.

"Xander, I'm begging you," she said in a rush. "Please get to Ken. Stay with him. Lock him in the house until the storm passes. When they restart the gondola, we'll come down. He almost lost it when I told him we came up here for lunch and got stuck. He was threatening to drive up, even though the road is closed."

Knowing what a nervous father-to-be Ken was, Xander wouldn't put it past him. But he'd be risking his life in doing it. The storms in the Rockies were deadly. They'd probably find him in a few weeks at the bottom of a gorge, frozen solid.

"I told him we're safe here. The lodge offered us a room, even though they're not actually ready. They're finding a place for everyone who's been stranded up here."

"Did you tell him that?"

"Yes, but you know him. He wasn't hearing me. Please, Xander. I just can't have him go crazy now. We have a baby coming. I need him. You understand. Don't you?"

"I do. I get it."

Ken was ferociously protective when it came to Donna. It would be the same with this baby.

"You'll stop him from going stupid on me?"

"I'll stop him," he promised. "But are you okay? Feeling okay?"

"I'm fine."

"Okay. Put Nadine on the line."

There was an exchange muffled by Donna's hand over the phone. Finally, Nadine came on.

"Is she really okay?"

"She's worried about Ken." Nadine lowered her voice. "From what I heard of their conversation, it wasn't pretty."

"I assume it wasn't your idea to go up there for lunch, considering your love of heights."

"No, it wasn't," she chuckled. "You remember."

He remembered everything, every word, every minute of their time together.

"She twisted my arm. She guilted me. I protested all the way. But I couldn't refuse her."

Why couldn't she just be stranded in *his* house during this storm?

"I didn't know those methods worked on you. Next time, I'll try harder."

"Maybe...maybe you should."

Her tone immediately threw a jolt into his spirit. He didn't want to hope, but he couldn't help himself. Maybe tomorrow wasn't the end of the road.

Donna's voice in the background became loud again.

"Is this a good number to call you back on?" Xander asked. "Any cell service up there?"

"We're using the restaurant's landline. They've only got one line. The lodge is still a couple of months from opening. The manager said the cell tower they had up here was knocked out during the ice storm this past week."

"So, there's no phone in the room where they're putting you two?"

"I don't know. But we haven't seen it yet. At least, we have a bed to sleep on. That's definite." She exchanged a few muffled words with Donna. "Yes, they're taking us through to the room right now."

"Will you call me after you're settled in?"

"I'll try. But what about Ken? Can you keep him from killing himself, trying to get up here?"

"Don't worry. Just take care of yourselves. I'll hold his hand until this storm passes."

19

THE ONLY PHONE connected to the outside world was in the restaurant office, next to the bar, and Nadine and Donna asked to have the closest room available.

The suite they were offered consisted of two rooms and a bathroom that had been used by the construction managers. In one room, twin beds, dark paneling, and shag carpet. In the other, a couch, a couple of folding chairs at a small table, a TV on the wall, and a kitchenette with a refrigerator, portable cooktop, microwave, and a battered coffeemaker.

From the musty smell, Nadine guessed this accommodation had not been used for a while. Beggars couldn't be choosers, but she got a sense that some of the other restaurant staff and patrons who'd been stranded were opting for chairs in the dining room.

The storm and their predicament had sidetracked Donna enough that there was no more of the earlier discussion they'd been having in the restaurant. Nadine was relieved about that. Her one wish right now was to get her new friend safely back to her husband and travel back to 1811 before it was too late.

They had no luggage. No change of clothes. No toiletries. Leaving their winter coats and bags in the room, Nadine and Donna headed back to the restaurant.

Almost everyone who was left was glued to the TV in the bar. A few others stood by the windows, watching the wind-whipped snow.

She and Donna were among the latter group. There was no sign of the storm letting up. They called Ken again around eight o'clock. Xander was with him, and Donna was relieved to learn he was planning to stay the night in Elkhorn.

Nadine was only able to exchange a few words with Xander, as there was a line of people waiting to use the phone.

Back in their room, Donna went immediately to bed. After some tossing and turning, Nadine fell asleep, listening to the rasping sound of snow against the window and the low pulsing drone of a generator.

The howling storm seemed to be intensifying, if anything, and Nadine found herself constantly startled awake by some random crash or bang outside. Looking out the window didn't help. There was nothing that she could see but shadows of the buildings and trees bending to the force of the wind.

Donna was restless too, but she showed no interest in what was going on outside. She constantly trekked back and forth to the bathroom. On one of her trips, she noticed Nadine by the window.

"I'm sorry I'm keeping you up," she said as she lowered herself onto the bed. "I read that the bladder is one of the most vulnerable organs during pregnancy. Tonight, I'm testing it to the max."

"You're not keeping me up. It's this weather." Nadine took two blankets out of the closet and put them at the foot of their beds. The room was cold. The heat wasn't keeping up with the freezing temperature outside. "Can I get you anything? Do anything?"

"No, go to bed. One of us should get some sleep. We're going to need it."

Nadine didn't know what that meant, but she crawled into bed herself. The next time she woke up, Donna's bed was empty. The bathroom door was open, but the light was off. Colorful flashes from the living room told her that the TV was on.

She checked the bedside clock. 5:40 a.m. The storm was still ferocious, rattling windows and pounding on the walls.

Padding to the window, she stared out in disbelief. Snow continued to come down hard, and the wind appeared to be creating a huge drift against the building. The window was half covered. Outside, dawn was making a futile attempt at brightening the landscape. She could see no more than a few feet beyond the glass. The other buildings, the trees, and the little else that had been identifiable before were all gone, curtained off by the driven snow. She'd never seen weather conditions like this.

Draping a blanket around her shoulders, she went to check on her friend.

Her stomach dipped at the sight that greeted her. In the kitchenette, Donna was leaning heavily on the counter, clutching it with both hands. Her head was down. She was making short, moaning sounds and struggling to catch her breath.

Nadine knew enough to recognize what was happening. This baby was coming.

She hurried to her side. "Hey, are you okay?"

It felt like hours before Nadine could answer.

"Okay. Okay." Donna straightened up. "Write the time down. Here, on this piece of paper."

Nadine stared at the sheet that had a half dozen times scrawled on it. "You're in labor."

"Write the time."

She checked the microwave clock and wrote the time down.

"How long since the last one?" Donna asked, holding her belly with one hand and clutching the counter with the other.

"Twenty-four minutes."

"That's good. The one before that?"

"Seven."

"And before that?"

Nadine did a quick calculation in her head. "Twenty-nine minutes."

"The contractions are irregular. And far apart. So, no reason to panic. We have...we have plenty of time."

"What's plenty?"

"Days, maybe."

Nadine didn't believe it. She'd seen her doubled over only a minute ago. "I'm going out to the restaurant. I'll call your house."

"No." Donna's hand gripped her arm. "Don't call Ken."

"Why?"

"Have you looked outside? He'll kill himself, trying to come up here."

"He's your husband. He should know."

Tears ran down Donna's flushed cheeks. "I'll never forgive myself if something happens to him. This baby can't lose us both."

"He...or she...isn't going to lose either of you. Give Ken credit to do the right thing," Nadine said calmly, rubbing Donna's back. "I did look outside. There's no way he can get up here. I don't believe he'd be crazy enough to try."

"Maybe you're right." She winced and let go of Nadine's arm.

"But there have to be other ways, besides the road and the gondola. Isn't there some kind of emergency service for a situation like this? There must be a way to get a doctor up here."

"Rescue helicopters don't fly in blizzards."

"What about jetpacks?"

Donna stared and then laughed. "Okay, Flash Gordon."

Nadine's mind raced, trying to remember what year individual jetpacks were approved for rescues. She was pretty sure the technology existed now. Still, there was no point in mentioning it again.

"If you're okay for a few minutes, I'm going to make that call to your husband. I'll be right back."

"Not until the sun comes up. Ken doesn't do well when half asleep."

"Listen to yourself," Nadine scolded. "You two have been together for what has to be more than a decade. But you don't trust him to know about the possible recurrence of breast cancer, and you don't trust him to know that you're about to deliver this baby. What's wrong with this picture?"

Donna's eyes closed and she sighed.

"Do you trust him as a partner or not?"

"I do. Of course, I do."

"Good. Then wait for me here."

Nadine hurried into the bedroom and began to throw on her clothes. A moment later, Donna appeared.

"I'm coming with you. He needs to hear my voice, or he'll think it's worse than it is."

Nadine couldn't imagine a scenario much worse than this. But as she pulled on her boots, she decided to keep that thought to herself.

A few minutes later, the two made their way along the chilly hallways of the lodge. They maneuvered around boxes of construction materials stacked up on the bare wood sub-flooring. Nadine had stuffed the list of contraction times into the pocket of her jeans, figuring it might be important information for Ken to know.

"Tell me about this jetpack thing," Donna said, giving her the side eye.

Nadine preferred not to get into that. "I must have been thinking of some movie or video—"

"I thought you don't watch movies," Donna said slyly.

"I don't know. Maybe I read about it somewhere. As a matter of fact, I think it was an article I found online."

"Whatever. I know it's a real thing. There've been a dozen sightings of them around the airport in Los Angeles alone. Of course, the government is quick to quash any news like that. The last time, there was a picture someone took out the window of an airliner. You could *see* the guy flying it. But the official report said it was a mylar balloon." She shook her head and nudged Nadine. "So, what do you know about it? Come on, I need a distraction right now."

"Let's see." Nadine thought about basic information she could share, hoping it wasn't too futuristic. "I seem to remember that they're a contraption with a small jet engine strapped onto a person's back. And there are two smaller jet engines worn on each forearm. They give direct thrust where the pilot feels it's needed. That way, the person can hover in the air or move in any direction and at any speed."

"Did it say if the public can get them now?" She took hold of Nadine's arm but kept talking. "Ken would love one of those. My guy has *more* toys than you can even imagine. He'd buy one of them in a heartbeat."

In Nadine's time, people did. "I really don't know. The article's focus was on emergency uses."

Donna stopped dead and then turned and planted both hands on the wall. Her face showed the strain she was feeling. Her breaths were once again coming in short, irregular bursts.

"Tell me what to do," Nadine asked, feeling helpless.

"Time," Donna gasped. "Record the time."

She scrambled to get Donna's phone out of her purse. Checking the time, she wrote it on the paper. "Seven minutes since the last one."

They stood together with Nadine supporting her until the

contraction eased. Seven minutes was worrisome, especially seeing how much pain she was in, this time.

"This contraction lasted longer," Donna said. Her face was still flushed from the exertion. "Next time, I want you to keep track of how long it lasts."

"Okay, what else."

"When we call Ken, we have to be calm. There's no rush. No emergency. False labor with first-time mothers is a thing. So is going beyond the due date. That's a thing too. I'm only at thirty-six weeks. Thirty-six weeks. This baby is still four weeks away."

"Okay. Calm. We stay calm."

"Neither of us says anything about the contractions getting stronger."

"Calm. Stay calm," Nadine repeated, wondering how the heck everyone could still be sleeping with this storm. Why hadn't they run into anyone?

What happened if the next contraction was two minutes from now? What if she was ready to deliver?

"And after the phone call, we're going back to our room," Donna said. "We'll stay there until the storm is over."

"Right. Back to the room." Bad idea. Really bad idea.

Nadine thought of the hostess who'd seated them at lunch yesterday. She said she'd had a baby. There were at least half a dozen women who had come back into the restaurant after the gondola shut down. Each of them surely must know more about childbirth than she did.

If Donna was ready to have this baby, they'd need some help.

"I'm not going to have this child in front of a bunch of strangers," Donna said as if reading her mind.

"Got it. We'll just take it one step at a time."

There was no one in the dining room. Through the large plate glass windows, the view of the storm was daunting, to say the least. The snow and wind continued unabated.

They were truly cut off from any outside aid. No one would be able to find their way through that.

Stay calm.

In the bar area, the bartender was asleep on a loveseat. Everyone else must have been situated in one of the unrenovated guest rooms.

Donna's pace increased as they approached their destination.

Nadine stayed close enough to lend a hand to steady her if another contraction seized her. The office door was open and the light was on.

Ken answered on the first ring, and Nadine stood close enough that she could hear his voice clearly.

"What's wrong, sweetheart? Are you okay?"

"No, I'm not," Donna announced as tears erupted and ran down her cheeks. "I'm in labor, honey. The contractions are coming fast, and they're strong. All night, I've been having a bloody show. And shit, shit, shit…"

She dropped the phone on the desk.

"What's wrong?" Nadine and Ken asked at the same time.

"My water just broke."

Nadine decided they were way past staying calm.

〄 20 〄

XANDER WAS STANDING at the island in the kitchen as his friend
ended the call. Right before hanging up, Donna was begging Nadine
to try to get someone on the phone who could help.

Ken buried his face in his hands and then looked up. His expression was of a man who'd had his insides ripped out.

"We've got to do something. I've got to go."

"You're not going anywhere. Not until the snow stops and the
plows come around."

There was nothing they could do. Nowhere they could go. The
wind had driven the snow into drifts of six feet or more. His truck was
buried up to the passenger windows. Even if they somehow managed
to get out of the driveway, they'd never get out of the neighborhood.
And getting stuck out there in the storm would help no one.

They were up shit's creek without a paddle.

Just then, the power went out.

"Don't you have a gener...?" Xander stopped as the built-in generator kicked on.

"I'm calling her obstetrician."

The answering service rang and rang and rang. No one was picking
up at the hospital, either. How was that possible?

The Elkhorn County 911 was busy for the first eight times. Finally,
a dispatcher answered but put them on hold. After twenty excruciating minutes, the harried-sounding woman came back on and took

the message. That's all she could do for now. Another few minutes of pacing back and forth in the kitchen and Ken called them again. This time a man's voice answered. The response was the same as the last time. They saw Ken's name on the list and knew that Donna was in labor, but there was nothing they could do until the storm eased up.

"Listen to me, sir. We're in full lifesaving mode," he told Ken. "The governor has already declared a state of emergency. We're telling everyone to shelter in place. This isn't your average Colorado storm."

"But my wife is having our baby *right fucking now*."

"You told us. But we can't get to her now, and we don't know when we will be able to get to her. It's not safe to fly a chopper. And even if we could, the hospital in Elkhorn has lost power, and their generators aren't supporting all the life-support machinery. Our priority right now is to evacuate some of those patients to other hospitals. And that is one slow process. Now, I need you to leave these lines open for other..."

With Ken still on the phone, Xander made coffee and then stalked to the window across the large great room, staring at the storm howling outside. He checked the latest weather report and news on his phone.

The April blizzard has dumped more than four feet of snow across Colorado, shutting down major highways, knocking out power, and leaving drivers stranded in life-threatening situations. State Police and the DOT are currently hamstrung by...

He thought of Nadine and wondered again how this storm would affect her plans. It was already Friday. She'd said she was leaving tonight, but he couldn't see that happening. There was no way the highways would be open or airports operating that fast.

He called back the number he had for the lodge. After about fifteen busy signals, the call went through. A woman answered and after hearing who he was and why he was calling, she put Nadine on the phone.

"How are you holding up?" he asked. He needed to hear her voice, to know that she was okay. Xander felt responsible for everything that was happening to Nadine.

"Much better, now that Donna agreed that going back to our room and locking ourselves in wasn't the best choice."

"Was she really going to do that?"

"She was quite adamant about privacy. Thankfully, common sense kicked in. Staying close to the phone is better."

"How did you get her to realize that?"

"It wasn't me. We just got off the phone with a midwife her doctor referred us to. That was the best thing that could have happened. They had a very positive conversation. Serious, but positive."

Xander had to tell Ken that Donna had gotten through to the doctor's office. Glancing over his shoulder, however, he found his friend blasting someone on the phone.

Venting his anger was one way to keep Ken here and not try to do something insane—like getting on the road.

"Did you know first-time mothers can be in labor for days?" Nadine asked.

"No, I didn't."

"It's barbaric."

He agreed.

"She goes along fine...fine...fine...and then the pain hits. And it *really* hits. She can't even talk. She's in real agony. I feel so helpless."

"How is she doing now? Is she still upset? The way she was while talking to Ken?"

"No. Not upset. She's...well, it's hard to describe. She has the midwife's direct phone number, just in case her contractions get stronger and closer together." Her voice turned lower. "Even with everything happening, she's so much calmer now. In control."

"That sounds more like Donna."

"It's pretty impressive. How is Ken?"

"If he can get the governor on the phone—and that might be who he's shouting at right now—they'll be sending the National Guard up that mountain to get to his wife."

"What's the National Guard?"

He smiled. She had a way of doing this, catching him off guard with her deadpan jokes. He glanced over his shoulder, looking for Ken and wondering if he wanted to talk to his wife again. There was no sign of him in the kitchen.

"Where's Donna now?"

"She's on her feet, pacing the floor of the restaurant. That's what the midwife recommended. Keep walking. Baths and showers are good too. But that means going back to the room, which we are absolutely *not* doing. It's freezing in there, and I'm not sure there's any hot water."

"Who's with her?"

"Some of the women who were stranded here."

"How many people are there?"

"I don't know. Maybe a dozen or more, including the restaurant staff," she said. "They're all starting to show up in the restaurant. A number of the women either have had a baby or know someone who's had a baby. They want to help, which is great, and the distraction of having others around is a good thing for Donna."

"I'm sorry I got you in the middle of this." If he'd only refused to go down to dinner at Ken and Donna's or made some excuse for not taking her down to their house again yesterday morning.

"You didn't. I volunteered to go out with her," she said. "And everything? All of this? What we are going through..."

Her voice wavered and there was a moment of silence. Xander wanted to wrap his arms around her and hold her. "Are you okay?"

"I'm better than okay. This is very special. In fact, amazing. To be here with Donna. Even to do the little I'm doing now. She's having a baby. A baby, Xander. I never thought...never imagined this would be something I'd experience in my life. Maybe I'll even get a chance to hold it." There was a sniffle, and she cleared her voice. "I have to go. She's having another contraction."

The call ended, and Xander stared at his reflection in the window. She got him. He felt choked up himself. He turned around and saw Ken coming down the stairs, a bunch of towels and blankets under his arm.

"I'm putting these in the car for when we can get on the road."

Xander told him about the phone call he'd just had with Nadine and how Donna was now in contact with a midwife.

"That's good. Better than nothing." Ken dropped the pile he was carrying on the counter. "Did she say how far apart are the contractions?"

"No."

"How long they were?"

Xander shook his head.

"Is the baby crowning?"

"I don't know what that means," he said. "I'm sure Donna will be happy to hear your voice if you call her."

"You're right. I will."

He called, but the woman who answered said Donna couldn't talk now. And they wanted the phone line open as the midwife was calling back.

Ken paced the room like a lion in a cage. He looked ready to burst out of his skin.

"Fuck this. I have to get to her."

"But you're no doctor. You can't go there and bring her back to a hospital in time, can you?"

"It doesn't matter. I need to get to her. Hold her. Be with her. I can't let her go through this alone...in some strange place with a bunch of strangers around her. She's part of me. All of me." His voice cracked as he struggled to get the words out. "What happens if something goes wrong? I can't let her be up there, going through this alone."

Xander always knew the relationship between these two was special. And after what they'd gone through, their other disappointments, he couldn't bring himself to offer empty promises that everything would turn out well. That Donna and their baby would be fine. He wasn't willing to offer false hope.

But Ken was right. They had to do something. The authorities were overwhelmed.

Suddenly, out of nowhere, an idea hit him. He'd read about a nonprofit search-and-rescue group when he first moved to the Rockies. They pitched in when hikers and climbers got lost or hurt in the wilderness. They supported firefighters. And they responded to calls to help drivers who were stranded in the storms like this.

They had their own snowplows. They were independent of the state, county, and township resources. He checked the Internet on his phone, searched out their number, and found it.

An answering machine was all he got. Of course. Still, he left a detailed message, explaining Donna's situation and asking if they could get them up the service road to the lodge. He also told them they could name their price.

The next few hours were unbearably slow. The storm continued full bore, but Xander couldn't stay inside any longer. Getting a shovel out of Ken's garage, he dug out his pickup as well as he could.

He was just making sure the truck would start when one of the rescue drivers called him back. He could help get them up there. Back inside, Ken was on the phone with someone at the lodge. The contractions were four minutes apart.

An hour earlier, Nadine had enlisted the restaurant staff to help get things ready.

The desk in the office had been cleared off and shoved against the wall. File cabinets were moved into one corner and extra chairs were taken out. A cot was brought in and set up with clean sheets. Pillows were stacked up at one end, and towels and blankets were ready on the desk. Every first aid kit available was brought in. The kitchen staff had pots of hot water on the stove.

Nadine sent a wish skyward that someone with medical experience would show up before this baby arrived.

Donna didn't want to talk to anyone on the phone anymore. Not even Ken. Her focus was on her breathing and moving as much as she could in between the contractions. Nadine took over speaking to the midwife and getting specific instructions about what to do.

The office had a door, but Donna had Nadine kick every man out of the bar area. Even though a couple of them wanted to help, they had no medical background. Being a father didn't count. Being in the delivery room with their own wives wasn't enough either.

Five women had offered to assist with the birth. As they stood by the office door, it immediately became clear that one of them was a dark cloud. She kept bringing up statistics about how dangerous delivering in a non-hospital setting was. Like they had a choice in any of this.

Seeing how the talk was adding stress to Donna, Nadine backed the woman out the door and told her to wait in the dining area. She wasn't helping.

For more than a decade, Nadine had traveled back in time to unfamiliar and sometimes extremely dangerous situations and settings. But never, before today, had she been this frightened. Not even when she stuffed manuscripts into an overcoat pocket and led Virginia Woolf to safety through the falling bombs of the London Blitz.

In the past, what was at stake most times was her own life, the danger that she'd fail in her mission and lose her place as a Scribe Guardian. The loss of a work of literature to the world was important, but failing meant certain death for her.

This was different.

Today, two lives were at stake. And Nadine was hardly an expert at childbirth. She wasn't given weeks of training. She had no knowledge, no tools, no means of bringing some of the medical advances of the future to bear on the crisis she and Donna were facing. Not even medications like the ones she'd given to Deirdre's asthmatic son.

She stared at the very basic tools and supplies the midwife had asked her to gather. It was beyond barbaric to think a child was going to come to this world with so little assistance.

Oh, yes. She was terrified.

Who was the dark cloud now? She should banish herself from the room.

She couldn't and wouldn't do that to Donna. Nadine shifted her attention and focused on the midwife's instructions.

The responsibilities were divided between the women who were left. Naturally, no one wanted to take charge and be the actual person to receive the baby. That was left to Nadine, the least knowledgeable of them all.

"A first time for everything," Donna said, moving awkwardly to her.

She suspected her friend had overheard the conversations. "For both of us."

"Nervous?"

"It's too late for jitters," Nadine said in what she hoped was a confident tone. "I did warn you that I've never delivered a baby before. Never even seen any videos."

"Yeah. You told me." Donna wiped a bead of sweat off her brow.

"I'm sorry this is all happening like this." She motioned to the makeshift delivery room. "Here, I mean. And not in the safety of—"

"Life isn't always about choices. Is it? We have to do what we can with what we've got. Don't we?"

"Yes. Absolutely." There were many things in her life that Nadine had no say about. Her past. Her future. Her health. Her relationships. She thought of Xander. "It could have been worse. You could have had this baby in that gondola."

"Exactly."

"With Jared at the end of the line."

They both shuddered.

"You're going to do great." Donna hugged her. "I trust you."

The two held each other tight until the next contraction caused Donna to double over.

Before the contraction was over, the midwife was back on the line, calmly telling them what to do, step-by-step.

"This is it," Donna panted.

And less than an hour later, Nadine was holding in her arms a content, round-faced baby girl.

THE PLOW ARRIVED at Ken's house two hours after the rescue group called. Xander drove, not trusting Ken behind the wheel, and they followed the truck through Elkhorn.

Traffic lights were out due to the power failure, and they swayed wildly overhead in the fierce wind. There wasn't a human being in sight. No sign of life anywhere. Snow drifts covered cars and pickups and formed hills against buildings all along the route. The residents of the town would remain hunkered down until it was over. Then, they'd dig out as they had so many times before. But for right now, Elkhorn looked more like the set of a post-apocalyptic survivor movie than the thriving community it was.

As they were leaving town, the snow began to ease slightly, and the wind only occasionally buffeted the side of the pickup. At about the same time, Xander noticed an Elkhorn rescue ambulance following them, lights flashing. He pointed out the vehicle to his friend.

"It's about time they sent help to that fucking lodge," Ken said, notes of frustration competing with hope in his voice.

"The guy in front of us probably let them know he was clearing the way."

His friend was silent for a moment.

"I hope it's not..." Ken's voice trailed off.

Not too late. Xander knew what he was thinking. There was no telling how long it would take to get up the side of this mountain. Right now, it was very slow going.

And as minutes ticked by, their travel didn't get any faster. With drops of hundreds and then thousands of feet on one side and sheer rock face and forest on the other, there wasn't much room for their three-vehicle caravan to maneuver. Several times, they had to stop and wait as the plow ahead of them worked back and forth to clear and navigate a dangerous section. Occasionally, the road led through heavy forest land.

"Jeez," Ken said once, looking at the tall pines. "I hope none of these monsters have fallen and blocked the road."

Xander nodded grimly, praying for the same thing.

As the evening approached, the temperature was dropping, and their pace slowed to a crawl. Thankfully, the last of the storm seemed to have passed. Patches of a star-studded sky began to appear through the clouds.

Xander's phone rang around seven. He answered it, surprised that a call had come through, considering the spotty service in the mountains.

It was Nadine. They hadn't talked to them since they'd left the house, keeping the phone line at the lodge open for communicating with the midwife. That alone had nearly killed Ken.

"Xander, is he with you?"

"I'm here," Ken said, his voice cracking.

Xander knew his friend. He was expecting the worst.

"Congratulations, Dad. Would you like to talk to your wife and your daughter?"

Ken's head sank into his hands. Xander saw the shoulders shake as he fought to control his sobs. He patted him on the back.

"Yes. Yes. Please."

Donna came on, sounding tired but happy. "Ken, she's right here. Lying on my stomach..." Static cut off the next words, but her voice came through erratically. "...both fine...midwife said help com...both fine..."

The line went dead before either of them could say anything else.

Xander stole another look at his friend. He was wiping his eyes. "Congratulations, pal. A baby girl. A daughter."

"They're fine. They're both fine," Ken repeated, looking over his shoulder.

Xander knew he was making sure the paramedics were still behind them. A safe distance back, the flashing lights reassured him.

"I'm a father, Xander." Ken smiled and slammed the dash with his hand. "I have a baby girl. Can't you make this fucking thing go faster?"

It was a few minutes past eight when they reached the lodge. The lights inside the restaurant were on. Outside, lights shone down on a small tractor laboring to clear the parking lot as they pulled in. No small feat, considering the depth of the snow up here. Some of the drifts had to be twelve feet high.

The rescue ambulance went around them and stopped at the front door of the restaurant.

A paramedic jumped out and disappeared inside, carrying a bag. Two others opened up the back, pulled out a gurney, and followed their partner.

Xander hadn't come to a full stop next to the emergency vehicle before the new father threw open the door and ran inside too.

He parked his pickup in a cleared area beyond the ambulance, grabbed his coat from behind the seat, and then sat for a moment, processing all that had happened.

Xander had paid the rescue organization up front, and the driver who'd led the way up here was technically done with the job. But the fellow had not even gotten out of the cab of his plow and was helping to finish clearing the lot.

Xander got out, stretched, and stood next to his pickup. The air was crisp and cold, but the breeze had shifted. The sturdy log structure blocked the wind, cutting it to almost nothing. Still, he pulled on his coat and stuffed his hands into his pockets.

Only a few scattered clouds scudded across the vast, moonless sky, and a million stars shone brightly on the midnight blue canvas. Vaguely aware of the pulsing hum of a generator, distant voices, and the scrape of the plows at the end of the lot, he breathed in the scent of pine and fresh snow.

As hard and fast as it had come in, the storm was now gone. But everything was changed.

He'd driven up here once before, during the summer. He hadn't eaten here; the restaurant had been closed due to the new ownership and renovation. There was a large oval of green grass in the center of the lot. Hikers were coming off the gondola, organizing their packs and gear, checking trail maps, and heading off into the wild.

It was all different now. The snowstorm had obliterated any trace of what he remembered. In the darkness, there was no sign of the trailhead. The grassy oval was now only an island of white covered by piles of snow. The lodge and restaurant were different too, almost unrecognizable beneath the coat of white.

Twice, Nadine had rolled into his life, and she too was a storm.

The first time, she left behind turbulence and chaos. She changed him. She revealed a life...a future...that he never even knew he was longing for. Before he met her, he thought he knew where his life was going. Long before, he'd formulated his plan, shouldered his pack, and gone off on his clearly marked trail.

During their three days in Las Vegas, however, that trail disappeared. Nadine was the only woman he'd ever felt so connected to. The only one he'd ever imagined a future with. She had set the bar high, and no one matched it...before her or since.

The truth was, his heart and mind wouldn't allow anyone to match it.

And then, she disappeared. Like melting snow, she evaporated into a cloudless sky.

What started as sex had turned into something deeply emotional. And when she was gone, he was left only with memories and the vaguest hope that she would return.

But what about now? Once again, she'd roared back into his world, appearing from nowhere. In a storm, no less. And she was going. Again.

A paramedic emerged from the building, took a blanket from the back and went inside again.

He wanted to go in, but he wasn't ready. He stared at the building but found his feet unwilling to get him there. Emotions tore at Xander's heart, and he was conflicted by them.

He tried to understand why.

Maybe it was because every aspect of life as he knew it had truly changed. A new era had arrived. His best friend, a man as close as a brother to him, was now a father. Fatherhood meant responsibility for someone other than yourself.

That was only part of it. He pinched the top of his nose, and his eyes were drawn to the front door of the building as it opened.

"Nadine," he murmured.

"Xander?" she called out to him. She was wearing no coat, no hat, nothing to protect her from the cold.

He started toward her, and she came across the snowy lot.

"You're going to freeze out here," he said as he reached her.

He quickly peeled off his coat, but before he could wrap it around her, she slid her arms around his waist and pressed her face against his chest. He wrapped his coat around her and gathered her tighter in his arms.

"Oh, my God, Xander. It was beautiful and scary and amazing. It was...it was miraculous. I've never believed in miracles. I've never understood how people can have faith in something that is beyond them. But it was there. What I witnessed was beyond science. It was beyond nature. It felt different. It *was* different."

She was different. She'd changed. The raw and honest outpouring of feelings told him how much she was moved by this experience. And how excited she was to talk about it.

"One moment, Donna was in excruciating pain. The next moment a sense of calm took over. A force outside of us, above us, spread a sense of peace over the room. I don't know how else to describe it." She took a deep breath. "And then Donna took charge. She *knew* what to do. Her body knew what to do. The baby knew what to do. The rest of us were just bystanders. Watching. She did all the work. And it was beautiful. It was the most beautiful thing I've ever seen in my life."

She lifted her face off his chest. Tears were running down her cheeks. Wisps of air crystallized as they escaped her quivering lips. *She* was the most beautiful thing he'd ever seen.

He kissed her eyebrows. Her cheeks. Her lips. And she kissed him back with more passion than they'd ever shared.

They held each other for a long time.

Somewhere, far away, a tree branch cracked beneath the strain of the cold and the snow. The raspy barks of a fox reached him.

Despite the mountain chill, Xander felt only one thing. And that was Nadine wrapped safely in his arms.

"I'll never forget this day," she whispered, drawing back and looking up at him. "Thank you for giving me this chance. For introducing me to Donna."

He shook his head, unwilling to take credit for a friendship that was destined to be.

"I will *always* love you, Xander...but I have to go back."

His heart soared and cracked at the same moment. He stared into her face.

"We need to talk." This wasn't the place for the conversation he wanted to have. "The keys are in the pickup. Turn up the heat." He kissed her lips again. "I'll tell Ken that we're leaving. I'll drive you back to my house."

"Xander—"

"I'll be right back."

Leaving her, he ran inside. An office next to the bar area was crowded with medics. They were arranging the gurney to take Donna, who was holding a small bundle.

Ken saw him by the door and came over. "They're getting Donna and the baby ready to move. We'll go down to the hospital in Elkhorn. They got power back there. They said I can ride with her."

"Good. Great. I'll see you back in Elkhorn. Tell Donna congratulations from me."

"Where's Nadine? I didn't get a chance to talk to her. She just ran out the door."

"She's waiting in the pickup for me."

"Please thank her. Thank her a million times for me."

Xander patted his friend on the back. "I will."

He spotted her coat and bag on the bar and grabbed them. Outside, the plow that had led them up the mountain was gone. The small tractor was still hard at work, clearing the paths to the gondola platform. Xander's pickup sat where he'd parked it. But he was shocked to find the engine wasn't running.

He pulled open the door. "You're going to freeze to death."

His coat lay on the driver's seat. But there was no sign of Nadine.

He looked around the parking lot.

"Nadine!" he shouted into the night.

The only response was the fading whisper of the wind in the trees.

22

So cold.

Nadine wondered if she was dreaming. It couldn't be. If this were a dream, how could she possibly be this cold?

And what was that low, rushing sound? Water? Wind? A crash, then a low gurgling rattle. Was it surf?

Consciousness began to return, little by little. Sensations began to penetrate her brain. The vile taste of brine and dead fish filled her nose and throat. Her joints were stiff and frozen.

The muscles in her arms and legs were dead, useless.

Rough, sandy rocks scratched and pressed into her face. She felt like she'd been dropped from a great height.

And chilly, wind-driven rain pummeling her.

This wasn't sleep. But it still felt like a nightmare. A sense of vague dread lay like a weight on her, seeping in and permeating her being.

Where was she?

Nadine tried to turn her head, only to feel the needles of rain stinging her cheek and neck, running into her ear. Her eyes burned when she tried to open them. They were filled with salt and grit.

The sound of the surf was close, and she tried to clear her head. Perhaps she'd washed up on some shore. Perhaps she had drowned.

Forcing her eyes to stay open, she saw through the blur that it was day, more or less. She tried again to move, but her limbs would not respond. She focused her bleared vision on a hand, lying near her on a mass of dark, wet stones. It must belong to her, she decided, since it was attached to the end of her unfeeling arm. But try as she might, she couldn't get the fingers to move.

A moment later, she found out how close the shoreline was as a wave crashed and frigid, salty water rushed up to her, surrounding her, rocking her immobile body. It splashed up over her face, filling her mouth.

She jerked her head clear, spat out the briny seawater, and pried her eyes open again. The water receded quickly, washing away with that rattling sound over the stones. But she knew another wave would be coming.

Nadine realized she'd made it. From a snowy mountaintop to a cold and rain-battered beach, she'd made the quantum leap. But had she landed at the right place? The right time?

It was all still a blur.

She remembered leaving Xander's coat in the driver's seat, sitting back, and closing her eyes. She'd needed to get back to 1811, to the village of Hythe.

But now, she'd lost track of time. The days merged. With her muddled senses, the hours were impossible to sort.

The next wave broke, and somehow her limbs remembered how to function. She managed to get herself up on her hands and knees before the sea washed up around her. As it did, the all too familiar nausea gripped her, and she retched a few times, spewing hot bile into the water beneath her.

God, she was so thirsty.

Water, water, everywhere, and not a drop to drink. Coleridge and his ancient mariner. The man had been so damned self-destructive, even for a poet.

She shook off the memory of the bygone mission. She needed to focus on the current one. Did she still have time to make a difference? Leaving Colorado, she didn't have time to go back to Xander's house to gather her things.

He'd be searching for her right now. Twice, she'd run away without saying goodbye. This was the end for them, she was sure. She'd never see him again, and the sadness made her heart ache.

She was still on all fours when another wave crashed. It washed up around her, foam gleaming in the dim gray light of day. She waited as the little stones tumbled back down, burying her hands, piling up against her knees. This wave had come up higher. The tide was coming up too fast. Unless she wanted to drown, she couldn't stay where she was.

A realization struck her hard. It was day. Not good. It should still be night. How long had she been unconscious?

Jane Austen was on her way, and Nadine needed to be there if she wanted to intervene. Every hour, every minute mattered.

She began to crawl up the slope of the beach. Her numbed fingers dug into the stony incline, seeking purchase. The piercingly cold rain continued to beat on her.

The question was...where was she? What day was it? How long has she been lying here in the rain?

The gusting wind stung her face as Nadine squinted around at her surroundings.

She'd landed on a beach, but she couldn't tell if it was the right beach. Hythe's strand was a stretch of small stones like this one, but so were a hundred such beaches along England's southern coast. She could be ten miles or fifty miles from her destination.

Mustering her strength, Nadine forced herself to sit. She wiped salty grit from her lips and face and blinked it out of her eyes. She was soaked through and chilled to the bone. She must have been lying here for quite a while.

All the familiar effects of a quantum jump were there. Her stomach felt ready to turn inside out, not remembering it had already emptied. Her legs felt weak and numb, as if they didn't belong to her.

"Damn it."

The cold windswept rain slapped at her again.

Nadine tried to collect her wits and gather the facts she had. If she'd landed in the right part of Britain, on the right date, then this storm would continue to intensify. There would be some of the worst downpours coastal England had experienced. And the raging waters of a swollen river would wash out the coach road toward Canterbury, forcing Jane Austen to spend Tuesday night in Hythe.

But had Nadine actually arrived on the right day?

The events in Colorado played back in her head. Donna delivered her baby girl on Friday night. At 6:39, to be exact. One of the women in the room had announced the time and mentioned the baby was born on April 15th. There had been a chuckle at the mention that it was Tax Day. Nadine left only a couple of hours later.

She knew the time in Hythe was ahead of Colorado. But how many hours? Six? Seven? If so, this *should* be Tuesday, April 16th, just before dawn. But it wasn't dawn. The pounding rain and swirling fog made it impossible to know if it was morning or afternoon. She'd been lying here unconscious, but for how long?

So even if she'd landed in the right place, Nadine had no idea how much time was left before the budding author arrived. Even worse, maybe Jane Austen was already here.

Nadine felt for her shoulder bag, hoping but knowing it wasn't there. She looked back at the water's edge. No sign of it. The last time she'd seen it was at the lodge. During Donna's labor, she'd gone back to their room, collected all their belongings, and brought them back to the restaurant.

Where was her period clothing? One of the two sets of clothes she'd brought back in time with her was at Xander's house. So was the coffin she'd traveled in.

She was wearing skinny jeans, cowboy boots, and a machine-made knit top. She wouldn't stand out at all in a village in Regency England. Not at all.

"Quite the professional, Nadine," she muttered. Showing up in Hythe wearing these clothes would be a disaster.

This was how so many anomalies came to be caught in historic photos or mentioned in ancient texts. What she'd done in shifting objects from one century to another—and then leaving them behind —might cause only minimal disturbance. But, on the other hand, *any* mistake had the potential to create a major tidal wave of disruption and result in a major impact on the future. Nadine was here because of another time traveler's error. Jane Austen and Captain Gordon would never have had a chance to meet today if a rippling effect had not been set in motion before.

Too late to worry about that now, she thought. She took a deep breath, a second, a third. Her lungs were behaving, at any rate. One thing she had to be conscious of was staying calm. Stress was the number one cause of her asthma attacks. Stress and a number of environmental triggers. She had no inhaler and no medication with her. They were in her bag back in Colorado.

A wave rolled in and tumbled against the shore before sliding up the stony beach. It almost reached her. The tide was indeed coming in. She looked behind her, but nothing was visible through the thick fog and rain.

Nadine struggled to her feet. Her first priority was to find out exactly where she was...and when.

Her joints were still stiff and aching from the time jump, and walking was painful. A little way down the beach, she spied a long, low shed. Boats had been pulled up from the sea and left in a row above the tide line. Nets hung from the walls of the shed.

As her legs began to right themselves, her stomach turned again. She fought down the nausea, taking deep breaths as she moved as quickly as she could toward the shed. Beyond it, long slatted tables extended for a hundred feet or so. Drying racks for the fish the men caught.

She turned her steps inland from the shed and managed to find the cart path leading up from the beach. If this was indeed Hythe, the 'Merfolk Gate'—as the locals called it—would soon come into view.

It took only a minute or two.

The path led directly through a pair of massive upright stones, twelve feet high and seven feet wide. A huge capstone lay across the top of them, forming an open doorway.

Nadine knew it had been erected in the Neolithic period, but local legend held that the gate had been built just after the Great Flood by Noah's sons, in gratitude for the sea people guiding the Ark to land here in England.

There wasn't another set of standing stones like this anywhere along Britain's coast, and Nadine's hopes rose. She was in Hythe.

The rain was easing a little, for the moment, but the fog grew thicker as she went inland. This cart path would soon widen to become the lane into the village. And it would pass close to Deirdre's cottage.

Grateful for small miracles, she plodded through the swirling fog and light rain. Not far beyond the Merfolk Gate, Nadine slipped on the muddy track as it passed through a shallow depression. She caught herself, landing on her hands, but the watery muck splashed up on her already wet clothes. When she managed to get herself upright, one of her boots stuck in the mud, and she nearly fell on her face again.

Pulling herself free, she trudged onward. The rain picked up again, and she was shivering badly. Her hair was plastered to her head, and water streamed down her face.

Feelings of doubt began to edge into the back of her mind. She was alone here, and for the first time in a long while, she wondered if she was up to the task. She'd made mistakes on this mission. It wasn't that Xander was a distraction, per se, but her feelings for him wouldn't fade. He was always there, tucked in her heart and lurking in the recesses of her brain.

Nadine shook off these thoughts.

This mission wasn't over. She might still complete her task successfully. But what time was it? That was the key.

Twice each day, a stagecoach came through Hythe, once in each direction. From her preparatory research, she knew Jane Austen's east-bound coach would be stopping at the Swan today around noon. Nadine prayed she'd have enough time to get back into her room at the inn, change her clothes, and go to Churchill House. How she might prevent Captain Gordon from meeting Austen was something she still needed to work out. She'd lost her advantage because of the three days in Colorado.

First, however, she'd need to get past the innkeeper.

She glanced down at her muddy knit top and jeans, and cringed.

What was she thinking? She'd never even get to the Swan. These clothes would draw unwanted attention. As soon as she reached the outskirts of the village, she'd be stopped and questioned. She'd probably be dragged before the authorities. How could she explain her presence, a woman dressed the way she was?

As the path widened, she passed a pair of cottages. The rain and fog hid any smoke issuing from the chimneys, and nothing stirred from either of them.

Suddenly, a shout came from behind her. Two coast guardsmen were coming up on her from the direction of the beach. They probably spotted her and imagined she'd just come ashore. No doubt a French agent, a harbinger of Napoleon's invading forces. Why else would someone be down there in this weather?

"Not again."

But this time, it was worse. She hadn't been here long enough to be able to make even a short jump through time. And she had nothing to protect herself with. One look at her, at the way she was dressed...

Nadine had only one choice.

Run.

With their shouts helping to propel her along, Nadine ran as hard as she could, hoping that the swirling mists would hide her.

The boots were heavy with muck, but at least the jeans gave her an advantage over a dress. Adrenaline pumped her blood.

She passed a few more cottages, and when she reached the tiny lane that led toward Deirdre's home, she glanced back to see if the guardsmen were in sight. Nothing. The rain was coming down hard again, and she could barely see twenty feet away through the fog. Grateful for it, she turned up the lane. Her friend's cottage emerged from the mists, and Nadine quickly went through the garden.

She knocked quietly, calling through the door in a low voice.

A moment later, the door opened, and Nadine was pulled inside.

Deirdre stared at her, wide-eyed.

"Bloody hell, miss! What in Janey Mac's happened to you?"

23

NADINE WAS GONE.

Xander couldn't believe this was happening to him a second time.

His eyes scanned the lot. There was no sign of her, but she wouldn't go off without her coat and bag. The wind still blowing in from the west was frigid. He didn't want to think of her out there in this.

Hurrying back into the restaurant, he stopped and questioned a young woman wearing a name tag saying, *Hostess*. He knew Nadine couldn't have gotten past him when he came in, but he asked anyway. Her only suggestion was that perhaps she'd gone back to the room they'd provided for her and Donna.

He went into the lodge, but the room was empty, and his questions to the staff back in the restaurant came up empty too. No one had seen her since she left the building after the emergency responders arrived.

Ken and Donna and their baby were already in the rescue vehicle when he went back outside. The team of paramedics was almost ready to go. Donna asked about Nadine. She wanted to talk to her.

"She's inside," he lied, not wanting to ruin their happiness with worry. "She'll be out soon, but we'll see you at the hospital."

The back doors closed, and he watched the emergency vehicle make its way to the end of the lot.

Worry ate away at him. The last time she disappeared, they were in Vegas. A city with airports, car rentals, and a dozen other ways to get around. But here? In the middle of nowhere?

The small tractor was pushing snow off a path at the far end of the lot. He searched for an answer.

The rescue group's snowplow was gone by the time Xander came back out to his pickup. The only logical answer was that Nadine *could* have asked for a ride. Calling the driver's number proved to be futile without cell service.

Still, it didn't make sense. The cold outside was brutal. She'd left his coat in the car. He had hers. She wouldn't just walk away from a mountaintop lodge in this weather in the middle of the night. No other cars had come up yet. And the gondola wouldn't be operating any time soon.

His mind kept going back to the plow. She had to have asked for a ride. But why? Xander would have driven her anywhere she wanted to go, and she knew that. What had he done to make her go away with a stranger? Was it him? Why wouldn't she tell him that she couldn't wait?

He no longer knew what to believe when it came to Nadine. One minute, she was a bundle of emotion, telling him she loved him. The next, she was gone. Didn't he deserve an explanation? Was everything she told him a lie?

A sharp pang of resentment edged into Xander's brain, but giving up wasn't in his nature. He forced the feeling back. He still wanted to believe that she had a good and logical reason for what she'd done. And that he could find her.

He talked himself into getting on the road. The only two people Nadine knew in Elkhorn were heading for the hospital. He guessed if there was any place she'd go, it would be to his house. If nothing else, she would want the things she'd left there.

By the time he'd gotten through Elkhorn and started up the mountain toward his house, a plow had cleared a single lane. That raised his hopes some. But seeing no tracks through the snow on his unplowed driveway killed his optimism.

Xander wasn't about to risk getting stuck in the deep snow leading to his house. It was a struggle just to pull in off the road. He'd stuffed his coat behind the seat when he left the lodge, and he didn't bother to grab it now. Zipping up his vest, he took her bag and slogged through the snow. The house was in darkness. As he drew near it, the motion sensors kicked the floodlights on. The snow around the doors was undisturbed.

He still wasn't ready to give up hope entirely, though.

He went in, calling out, "Nadine?"

Not bothering to take off his boots, Xander flipped on the lights and went up the stairs three at a time. There was no sign of her. The kitchen and the living room were dark. The fireplace was unlit. The curtains were closed, just as he'd left them the day before. In the guest bedroom, the bed was made. In the closet, the boots and the period dress Nadine had arrived in still hung there.

On the desk, he found a hand-drawn sketch of a calendar for the week. Today was circled repeatedly. Beneath the grid, other notes drew his attention.

Friday 15th April = Monday April 15th
Track time diff.

He had no clue what this meant. He checked the desk drawers for any other notes. Nothing. The book she'd borrowed last night sat on the bedside table.

Persuasion. By Jane Austen

He was glad when she'd chosen this particular book. It was a collector's item. A 1909 edition, with twenty-four color illustrations by C.E. Brock. Most of the editions in his bookcase, he'd bought from antique book dealers. This volume had cost him over a grand. The illustrations were works of art.

He wasn't a reader, but he did enjoy the idea of collecting. If he was going to spend the money, why not buy a volume with value, something that should be preserved?

Picking up the book, he opened it, hoping she might have left a note inside. Anything. Some clue about where she might have gone.

"What the hell?"

He paged through the volume. On some of the pages, the ink had faded. On others, the words were gone entirely.

It was the strangest thing. It was like someone had taken an eraser and wiped clean some of the words. The illustrations were all gone. Not one of them was left.

He looked at the cloth cover and binding. The same decorative gilt lettering on the spine. It was the same volume. The aged color and texture of the paper were unchanged. Even the musty smell of the paper was the same.

"No. There's something wrong here."

Xander tucked the volume under his arm as he went out of the guest room and down the stairs to the front door.

Outside, the temperature was dropping, and the wind was picking up again. The snow was still drifting, and his tracks by the door were starting to fill up.

He pulled his vest collar tighter around his throat, praying that Nadine was not out in this storm somewhere. Without good protective clothing, no one could survive this cold for very long.

Xander trudged through the high snow to get to the garage. Realizing his remote door opener was in the pickup, he worked his way around to the side door. It was unlocked, but frozen shut.

"Fuck this." Putting a shoulder to the door, he vented some of his growing frustration. The door popped open with a loud bang.

He switched on the light. The box was still there, sitting on the floor by the workbench, exactly where he'd left it.

As he crossed the cement floor to the coffin, Nadine's bag and the Austen book suddenly became heavy. Even stranger, something in his pocket was getting hot. So hot that it was beginning to burn his skin through several layers of material. Standing over the box, he dropped the bag and the book into it and searched in his pocket for whatever was burning him.

His fingers closed over the two small oddities he'd found in the coffin earlier. One of them—the thing that looked like a wooden whistle—was hot as hell.

At that moment, a peculiar wooziness hit him. It came out of nowhere, and then everything in the garage suddenly came into hyper-sharp focus before telescoping away from him. Xander leaned down and reached for the side of the box to steady himself.

"Nadine..."

As soon as he touched the wood, the lights went out entirely.

※ 24 ※

AT LEAST, one person in the cottage didn't ask questions. Sitting cross-legged on the floor with his back to the stove, little Andrew batted the column of wooden blocks they'd stacked up together, delighted when Nadine cheered as they went tumbling down.

"You want to play some more?"

The child nodded happily, gathering the blocks and starting again.

The wind continued to howl outside, and the rain battered the window by the door. The last time she'd looked, the lane beyond the garden gate had been transformed into a river of mud.

Wrapped from head to toe in a blanket, Nadine got up and went to the window for a third time in the half-hour that she'd been here. Thankfully, since arriving at Deirdre's door, she'd seen no sign of the coast guardsmen who'd been chasing after her, or anyone else.

She was soaked to the skin and shivering uncontrollably when Deirdre pulled her inside. The young woman had immediately ordered her out of those 'strange' clothes, handed her a blanket to wrap herself in, and stood her in front of the warm fire.

Deirdre also had a hundred questions that Nadine promised to answer later. Right now, she needed to borrow some clothes and get to the coaching inn.

As precious time slipped by, Deirdre searched for clothes that

Nadine could borrow. At least, this was what she claimed she was doing.

They both knew the young mother's clothes wouldn't fit her. The two women were built very differently. Deirdre had a slighter frame, and she was much shorter. The poor nutrition of this era limited childhood growth. And she had only one cloak. And no, Nadine couldn't borrow it.

Still, she had piles of clothing she'd taken in to mend. From villagers to men working on the military canal dropping off their garments, she had a steady business, hemming and fixing what needed fixing.

"These trousers you're wearing. They're not women's clothing, surely? And this material. I've never seen cotton twill so heavy."

Blue jeans, as they would come to be known, wouldn't make their appearance for another sixty years. Nadine saw her friend studying the wet pants like they were one of the wonders of the world. "Deirdre, please hurry. I need to be on my way."

"Wearing men's clothes will surely bring stares in the village, you know."

"I know! That's why you're looking for something I can borrow."

The other woman had shown no interest in the knit top or the cowboy boots. But the jeans had held her in thrall from the first moment she laid eyes on them.

"And the cloth certainly hasn't held its color any too well. They'll think you took them off a vagrant, I've no doubt."

"Please, never mind that now. I just need a dress to get back to my room at the Swan, *without* drawing attention. And a coat. I promise to return them to you tomorrow."

"I'm working on it." She held the jeans up. "Sure, these *are* a man's trousers. And quite a thin man, I'd say."

Nadine sighed. Deirdre was not giving this up, and there was no point in fighting her every step of the way. She was at the mercy of the young mother's trust and kindness...and curiosity. Perhaps the faster she gave her some answers, the sooner she would let her get out of here.

"Yes, a thin man."

"How did you get him to give you his trousers?"

"I bought them."

"Why? What was wrong with *your* clothes? And where are they, by the bye?"

Nadine looked around the cottage, searching for a clock. She didn't see any. The storm drowned out any chance of hearing the church bell toll the hour.

"I told you. I'll explain everything after I come back. But I've *got* to hurry now."

"Very well." Deirdre drew a heaping basket of mending closer, then picked up the jeans again. "But these metal rivets on the seams and the pockets. What purpose do they serve?"

"I don't know. Decoration?"

"Expensive. I always wonder why people waste their money on such nonsense." She ran her fingers over them, testing how they were fastened to the fabric. "They help hold the stitching. But this is the most curious thing. I've never seen anything like it."

She held the pants up for Nadine to see the zipper.

Oh, no.

"A zipper."

"What is a zipper?"

Now, they were talking about technology a century away. "They use them instead of buttons. It works like this." She showed her.

Wide-eyed, Deirdre opened and closed the front of the pants and looked up.

"Remarkable." She tested it again and again, smiling every time the zipper did its job. "It's astonishing. Where did you meet the man who sold you these trousers?"

"London." Nadine cringed inwardly. More lies.

"Did he have more like them?"

"He has a shop."

"I've never been to London, but I've heard talk of the garment makers there. In what street does he keep his shop?"

From her preparation about this period, she knew that the ladies of the ton frequented fashionable shops on Oxford Street or Bond Street in Mayfair, whereas the shops and clubs for gentlemen were clustered in the vicinity of St. James's Square.

"I don't recall the street. Wait, yes. I believe it was Ormond Yard."

The response met with a shrug from Deirdre. "Well, I'm surprised he'd sell trousers to a woman."

"London is a very different place from Hythe."

"I'm sure. But *why* did you buy them from him?"

There appeared to be no end to the questions. "Do you have a clock, by any chance? I need to know what time it is."

"You're avoiding the question, miss. What use would trousers be to you when you truly shouldn't be wearing them about?"

"I'm always cold. And like you, I was also so impressed by the zipper. I thought I could wear it...wear it under my frock."

"Did you have these trousers on, under your dress, when I saw you last week?"

"Absolutely." Another lie.

Deirdre eyed her skeptically. "Well, I know you weren't wearing those boots."

Observant. "No, I wasn't. But I *was* wearing the pants." Andrew knocked down the blocks again. Nadine cheered.

"Again?" he asked.

"Again," Nadine smiled and then turned to the mother. "About that dress you're lending me..."

Deirdre had a hard time tearing her eyes away from the jeans, but she laid them in her lap and nodded. "You need a frock. I've one in that pile that should fit. It has three buttons in the back, and you can ease it over your head. You also need a chemise, a corset—"

"The dress will suffice." At seeing the stunned expression on Deirdre's face, Nadine thought it wise to explain. "I have everything I need in my room at the Swan. I simply need something to wear to get me there. If you have a shawl, even, to keep me dry."

"I'll make a trade with you for a shawl."

"Of course." She thought Deirdre would ask for more medicine for Andrew. But Nadine had given her what she could. What she had left was the inhaler, and that was in her bag in the mountains of Colorado. "I can pay you...when I get back."

"Not money. I'll trade you a shawl for these trousers with the...what was it? Oh yes, the zipper."

The potential complication of giving those pants to Deirdre ran through her mind. The young mother would no doubt show the jeans to others in the village. She might even take it to market day. Word would get out. An engineer or an inventor might hear about it. It could be a disaster.

If Nadine managed to keep history on track, the zipper wouldn't debut until the 1893 World's Fair in Chicago. And even then, it wouldn't have much success. The early prototypes were bulky, expensive, and not considered suitable for clothing. That wouldn't happen until 1917 when Gideon Sundback, a Swedish-American design engineer, managed to develop a working zipper that used interlocking teeth that easily joined and released using an attached slider and pull.

Giving these jeans to Deirdre could create more than a ripple in history. In this period, they didn't have the technology advanced enough to duplicate the mechanism yet, but it could steer the industrial revolution in unexpected ways. That ripple could turn into a wave. And if the right person, or the wrong one, got hold of these jeans, the wave could become a tsunami.

"Don't you need to get out of here?" Deirdre gestured toward the door. "What happened to the rush, rush, rush?"

"I do need to hurry."

"A shawl for the trousers."

"I can't, Deirdre. I'll manage without a shawl."

"The trousers for the dress and a shawl. And you can keep them."

Nadine glared at the other woman. "Are you saying that you won't lend me a frock if I don't leave those trousers behind?"

The corner of Deirdre's lips turned up. "I'm a seamstress. I appreciate newfangled things. And haven't I protected your secrets?"

"I have no...secrets."

Deirdre laughed out loud. "Now, that's a fib, and we both know it. But haven't I opened the door and welcomed you inside my home even though you're running about in men's clothes?"

This was the only person in Hythe that Nadine could trust. She was her only ally. "It's true. You've done all of that."

"I know this is nothing more than a fashion novelty to you. But to me? It's a treasure." She worked the zipper up and down a couple of more times. "You want to stay warm and dry? I'll even let you borrow my cloak."

Deirdre was persistent, if nothing else. Perhaps Nadine could get her to promise not to show the jeans to anyone else. Fat chance of that, she thought.

Maybe, Nadine thought, she was worrying too much about it. Granted, there were no zippers or elastic or Velcro in this era, but people still had no trouble fastening their clothes with buttons, laces, hook and eye fasteners, brooches, pins, and buckles. And since the technology wasn't advanced enough to produce a zipper, perhaps no one would see any advantage to it.

"Very well. We'll trade. You can have the trousers. But only if you find me something else to wear right now."

The sun might as well have risen inside the cottage. Deirdre radiated joy. And immediately, everything Nadine needed in the way of clothes miraculously appeared before her.

She changed quickly. The dress was tight in the shoulders, but Nadine jammed her arms into the sleeves. Deirdre buttoned up the back. The cloak was too short, but it didn't matter. She found little Andrew sitting by the door, knocking dried mud off her boots. Nadine placed a kiss in the boy's hair and pulled them on.

"Are you still wondering about the time?" Deirdre asked.

"You have a clock in the cottage?"

Deirdre pulled a small timepiece the size of a locket from her dress. "It's five minutes before eleven. You'd best hurry."

Didn't she ask the time when she'd first been pulled inside the cottage? Nadine was certain she had, and the answer was to listen for the church bells. She shook her head clear of the other woman's cleverness.

Did she have time to go and change at the inn? That would be cutting it too close. She had to go directly to Churchill House and delay the captain.

"Do I look like a villager?" She stood straight.

"Ah, those secrets of yours," Deirdre tsked. "Mind your accent, don't say too much, and don't show off those boots of yours. You *might* fool them."

Nadine was hoping for just that. She had to fool a lot of people to accomplish what she had to do.

The rain was coming down even harder now than before, and the distant church bells faintly tolled eleven, confirming the time. The wind whipped at her, and the garden was a swampy morass. Muck sucked at her boot heels, and the cloak and the dress beneath it were spattered with mud up to her knees before she'd gone a few paces. She'd make quite the impression at Churchill House, asking to see the captain, but there was no helping it.

As she neared the gate to the lane, Nadine slipped on a flat stone and the hood of the cloak fell forward over her eyes. As she reached up to clear her vision, her foot banged into a solid block. She couldn't break her fall and tumbled, landing on her hands and elbows on a long box.

Not a box, a coffin.

"It can't be," she murmured.

There had been no coffin inside this gate when she arrived. It hadn't been there minutes earlier when she'd looked out the window.

"Oh, no."

From what she could see, it was the same one that transported her to Colorado. But how could it have come back here?

She pushed herself upright.

Could an object left behind in a time jump follow the traveler? This had never happened to her before.

She heard a noise, and the top moved. Someone was pushing it from the inside.

Her heart beating a mile a minute, she jumped up and stared. She had trouble believing what was happening,

Stunned, Nadine watched as the lid of the coffin was shoved aside and Xander sat up.

25

"XANDER?"

The voice came from the far end of a long tunnel.

He blinked into the light, dim and gray as it was. Where was he?

Up a slight hill, a thatched cottage sat in the middle of a vegetable garden. At least, it looked like a garden. Right now, it was a mud pit. The building was right off the set of a movie. Immediately, he gagged from the smell. The odor of animal shit competed with the smell of dead fish. The animal shit appeared to be winning.

What the hell? He was sitting in a box. It was the coffin that had been in his garage a minute ago. But it might as well have been a boat now, considering the way muddy water was rushing down the path around it. Rain pounded on his head and shoulders and legs, soaking him.

"Xander, what are you doing here?"

Nadine. He recognized the voice. Where was she? He could hear her, but he couldn't see her. And it was way too hard moving his head.

His skull had to weigh at least a hundred pounds. Her voice came from somewhere in the clouds. He tried to raise a hand to wipe the rain off his face, but his arms felt like overcooked noodles. A bulldozer must have run over him. And the pain didn't end there. His heart was racing, and a pounding headache suddenly had come on. And it was the mother of all headaches.

Was he having a heart attack? Maybe just a panic attack, he

thought hopefully. He couldn't be dead, or he wouldn't be in so much pain. What was happening to him?

"Fuck me," he mumbled, feeling his stomach flip. Jeez, he was going to throw up.

Xander turned and tried to climb over the edge of the box. A moment later, he was on all fours in the cold mud. His hands sank deep into the muck.

He took a deep breath to keep from vomiting, but it wasn't a very good idea. The smell of earth and manure filled his head, and whatever he had in his stomach spewed out. He retched a few times and tried to breathe as the muddy water streaming past carried his vomit away.

Head injury. Concussion. It had to be. He had all the signs. The last thing he remembered was falling in his garage. The floor must have been slippery. He didn't recall hitting the ground, but he must have. He had to have hit his head hard.

Nadine's voice sounded closer now. "I can't explain this, Xander. I don't know what's happening. You shouldn't be here."

"I belong here," he managed to mutter just for the sake of argument, even though he had no idea where *here* was. All he knew was that it was raining, a cold wind was blowing hard, and everything smelled bad. But at least, Nadine was here.

"We have to move you. You can't sit here. If someone sees you, we're in deep trouble."

"No, that's a good thing. I need a doctor. And I'm not sitting."

He could no longer see or feel his hands in the frigid muck. The ground was swallowing him up. In a few minutes, he'd be gone. Buried. Already, he could feel worms crawling up his arms.

"Fuck, get these things off of me." He pushed back until he was kneeling. Pulling his sleeves up to the elbow, he tried to get at the crawling creatures. "Get away."

"It's okay. It's okay. What you're feeling—that creepy, crawling sensation—it's not real. You're imagining it. It happens when you make a jump through time. The nerves in your body are still settling down, reconnecting the dots. Believe me, Xander. There's nothing there."

He looked at his bare arms, now stained with mud. Nadine always had an answer. Even though she hardly ever made sense.

"Maybe you're not here, either," he said. "Maybe I'm imagining your voice."

"Xander, look at me."

He wasn't going to make a fool of himself. He kept staring at his arms, wondering why he couldn't see the worms he still felt crawling on his skin. Only rain hitting him.

"You left. I hit my head. You promised to stay in the car and wait for me. But you couldn't even say goodbye. Twice, now. Twice, you've done it. And damn it, Nadine, it hurts."

"Xander, I tried to tell you."

"I'm dreaming that you're here. I *want* you to be here. But we don't get what we want, do we? Not with you. Never with you."

"We're both here. You followed me." Her face moved into his line of vision. Her beautiful face, framed by a hood. She was crouching in front of him. "I don't know what happened or how you did it, but you followed me through time, Xander. I don't think that's ever been done before. Not by someone from 2022."

She was weaving her crazy tales again. But it was her face that kept him entranced right now. Raindrops sparkled like jewels on her eyelashes and her cheeks. Her lips were wet. He blinked, waiting for her to disappear. Certain that she would. But her image only became clearer.

"Listen to me," she continued. "You're in danger. We're both in danger if someone finds you here, dressed like that."

He leaned back to get a look at what *she* was wearing. A gray dress under a hooded cloak, wet and muddy. "You left your clothes in my closet. How did you get them back? Is there a wardrobe department on this set? Do movie people dock your pay when you leave stuff behind?"

"You can't say things like that," she said quickly, looking around her. "Try to stand up. Take my hand. We're both too exposed here."

The mother of all headaches had turned into the mother of all dreams. He would take her hand and follow her to hell if she asked. Xander reached out a muddy hand, and she helped him stand up.

He was unsteady on his feet and almost fell, but she caught him by the elbow and pushed him to stay up straight.

The world around him tilted for a moment, but the stinging rain on his face helped to right things and he focused. His initial thought was correct. This had to be a movie set. Or one of those 'living muse-ums' like the Plimoth Patuxet Plantation or Old Williamsburg. She was definitely dressed for it.

The cottage they were closest to was right out of a TV movie about Salem witches. There was a beat-up shed with a low wooden fence around it and an outhouse at the far end of the garden. Outside of a gate, a muddy lane wound toward two other houses, some distance away. The buildings kept appearing and disappearing in the swirling mist and the driving rain. Everything had a gray look to it. It was like he was viewing the world through a filter.

All he could say was, they'd done a lot to make the smells realistic too. Though for the life of him, he couldn't understand why they'd go to the trouble for a movie. He was city-bred, but even to him this mud smelled like cow shit. There was another unpleasant, sickly-sweet stench in the air, and after a moment, he remembered what it was. Pigs. He'd driven past a few of them in Pennsylvania.

"Take a step, Xander."

The world started spinning again the moment he moved one foot forward. Nadine tried but couldn't hold his weight, and he went down hard onto his knees.

Funny, he thought. He didn't even feel it.

"Give me your hand. Let's try again."

"No, I'm fine here, thanks." He couldn't recall being this tired for ages, maybe ever. Maybe he was fighting the flu, and all of this was the product of fever and hallucination. It had to be. What happened to Colorado?

Xander settled his butt into the mud and pressed his back against the box. His pants were soaked. The wind was chilly, and the mud he was sitting in was pretty damn cold, but the temperature was still a lot better than he remembered, considering the blizzard they'd just had.

"That was a quick melt. What happened to all the snow?"

"We're not in 2022 anymore. You're not in Colorado. You traveled through time. We're in Hythe, England. You and I are trespassers here. Are you listening? We can't be found. The people here don't take kindly to strangers."

The sentences were clipped. Nadine's voice was rising in intensity, getting louder by the second.

"As much as I'd like to hang around the movie set and watch you work, right now I need a bed. I need a nap."

"You *can't* take a nap. Help me, Xander. I'm getting anxious. And when I get anxious, my asthma comes back. And that would be a disaster. There are no doctors and no hospitals with anyone who has a clue how to deal with it. Not here. Not in the year we're in. I left my medications back at the restaurant in Colorado."

He patted the pockets of the vest. He had something of hers on him, but he couldn't remember what it was.

An animal bleated somewhere far off. He could barely hear it with the wind blowing, but he thought it was a goat.

"I think I'm hearing things. I really want to sleep. Just a few minutes."

"Please, Xander. Get up. Somebody could come this way."

The sound of wheezing brought back an old memory. Was his mother here too? Xander glanced up and found Nadine bending over him. Her face was flushed, her breaths uneven.

Her bag wasn't at the restaurant. He'd had it with him in his garage. Did he still have it? Reaching behind him into the box, he put his hand on it immediately. He pulled it out.

"I have it. It's right here."

"Thank God." Nadine took it from him and searched inside, bringing out the thumb-sized device he'd seen her use before. He watched her take a couple of deep breaths. And the medication took effect almost instantly.

"Could we stop at a CVS or a Rite Aid? I want to pick up a couple of these things."

"Sure, we'll do it later." She opened the front of her cloak and looped the bag over her shoulder, pulling the cloak over it. "C'mon. Stand up."

"Do you need a prescription for it?"

"I'll get you a prescription."

He heard more strange things. The sound of a horse whinnying. Then a creaking noise of a wagon. And voices. Two men arguing. He couldn't place the accents.

Nadine pulled hard on his arm, and Xander cooperated, struggling to his feet. She urged him along, step by step.

"Where are we going? Can I be an extra?"

"You *are* extra," she whispered. "Extra trouble that I don't need right now. Keep your voice down."

He and Nadine plodded as quickly as they could through the mud. On either side of the path, rows of plants were sprouting up, but the young green leaves had been beaten down into the mud by the rain. Pools of water stood between the rows.

He thought Nadine was leading him to the cottage. Instead, she steered him toward the shed.

Over his shoulder, he spotted a rickety cart being pulled by a small horse. It was barely visible through the fog. Two men were walking the horse.

The lane went right by the gate at the bottom of the garden. They were in period costumes too. Xander realized the argument wasn't a serious one, for one of them laughed before breaking into a coughing fit.

Nadine climbed over the low fence and brought him into the enclosure with her. They slipped around the side of the shed. Two goats stared at them from beneath a low overhang.

Rain began to come down harder. Nadine pushed herself against him, pressing Xander's back against the wall. Her face turned up to his. Her voice was the softest of whispers.

"Time travel. Do you remember what I told you?"

Xander frowned at her. He'd never believed her stories. He simply gave her credit for being a good storyteller. He still didn't believe it.

"Refresh my memory."

"I'm repeating myself, but it's essential you remember these things. We're now in the year 1811. This is Hythe, England."

"Did I sleep through the flight?"

"Take this seriously, Xander. It's no joke. You and I could both get arrested. We could be executed." She paused. "Shh."

The cart was passing right outside the garden gate.

Xander looked into her eyes. The concern in them was real. He'd never seen her so wound up before. Not even when she was attacked by that killer chipmunk on his porch.

"We haven't done anything wrong," he whispered. "Why would they arrest us?"

"The laws in this time are different. We're different. We come from the future. But the locals won't believe it." She paused, listening.

The creaking cart and the voices were moving away.

Xander glanced around him, looking for cameras, people behind the scenes. Nothing. Only the miserable rain coming down in sheets and the stench.

She turned her attention back to him. "We've made a quantum leap into a time of unrest. There is serious uncertainty and distrust of strangers. The country is at war."

"War with who?"

"With the French. The people who live here are on the lookout for spies. They think Napoleon is ready to invade somewhere along this coast. And don't bother to say we're not French. They won't care."

He *was* going to say that. She stole his line.

One of the goats had come closer. The creature was nibbling on the leg of Xander's jeans. He shooed it away.

"Please pay attention. We look different, and we talk different. They *will* assume that we're spies, working for the French." She peered around the building. "They're gone...for now. "And you've got to remember. During this period in England, most crimes are punishable by hanging."

He scoffed. "Like what crimes?"

"Burglary. Sheep theft. Sodomy. Stealing letters. Counterfeiting documents." She pushed a wet lock of hair behind her ear and looked hard at him. "And being strangers."

"They'll hang us for being strangers?"

"They *love* hanging strangers. It's like the national pastime." She patted his pocket. "Do you have your wallet on you?"

He patted his pants pocket. "I do."

"Money in it?"

He nodded.

"They'll say it's forged. And the picture on your driver's license is the work of the devil."

"That's one way to describe the DMV."

Nadine expelled a long breath and shrugged. Her voice was a whisper. "Somehow, I got you into this, but I'm going to try to get you out. Send you back. But you have to trust me, Xander. You *must* trust me and do what I say."

"Okay." He was good at following orders...when it suited him.

"I'll be right back."

Xander leaned against the shed as she went over the fence back into the garden.

He felt steadier on his feet. The nausea had subsided. And the numbness in his arms and legs was better. The feeling of worms crawling on him was gone too.

Now, his stomach growled. He was starved. Thinking back, he couldn't remember the last time it was that he ate. Neither he nor Ken had eaten anything substantial after Donna went into labor. He'd brought along coffee and some protein bars in the car. But that was it.

Was that yesterday? Today? Had he really traveled to the other side of the world? And not just a different time zone...a different century? Reaching into his pocket, he took out his cell phone. The screen was black. He tried to reboot it, but nothing showed up. The thing was dead.

He thought about what Nadine said to him. She had no reason to lie. Not now. She was genuinely worried about their safety. And he hadn't been asking; she was offering information.

But it was all so hard to believe.

He had so many questions. But that was his history with Nadine. It was so hard to understand what she was about. Where she came from and where she disappeared to.

At least, he was with her. He'd found her. That was something. And wasn't that what he wanted? She'd said to trust her.

He heard a wet thud come from across the garden. When he looked around the corner of the shed, Nadine had slipped on the muddy path. She was heading toward the coffin.

He went after her and got to it right behind her.

"We have to hide this. It'll raise too many questions if we leave it where it is."

"Okay. Where?"

"Let's put it behind the shed."

Xander replaced the lid on top, and together they hauled the coffin along the garden path. The goats came out into the rain to watch them work. Nadine pointed to a nearby pile of heavy canvas, and they covered the box with it.

"That should work," she said. "I don't know if we're going to need this to get you back to Colorado, but at least we'll have it here if we do."

He tapped the box with his foot. "So, this is our DeLorean? That would make you Doc Brown and me Marty McFly."

"I have no idea who or what you're talking about."

"Of course, you don't. So, what's next?"

Nadine frowned and looked up at the cottage. "We've got to hurry, but we need to stop here first. I'm hoping my friend has some clothes that will fit you. She's the one who loaned me these."

"What's wrong with what I have on?"

"One look at you and a very nasty mob will form."

"Right."

They started toward the cottage, and Xander took her hand when her boot slipped on the mud. Her skin was warm and the grip strong.

"This woman is our only friend here. But let me do the talking. Less is more from you."

"Less is more," he repeated.

Before they reached the cottage, the door flew open.

"Quit ruining my garden, you two, and explain yourself. This instant."

Xander understood now what Nadine was saying about accents. These people talked differently.

The woman stood in the doorway with her hands planted firmly on her hips. Her dark blonde hair was twisted and pinned up on the back of her head. Her brown eyes were large and flashed fire. She was wearing a long gray dress with a white apron stained in spots. Her sleeves were pushed up to the elbows, and she looked worked up enough to fight both of them.

A little boy peered from behind her skirts with eyes the size of saucers. No wonder she was ready to do battle.

Nadine turned to Xander. "This is my friend Deirdre. She'll help us."

"Help you? Are you mad? What are you doing bringing a strange man to my door?" She pointed a finger at Xander. "Did he sprout in my garden when you were inside? Where did he come from? Who is he?"

"This is my husband." Nadine squeezed his hand and let go. "Mr. Finley. He's *just* arrived in Hythe."

Finley, Xander thought. She was giving him her last name, which was perfectly fine. He didn't know how his own last name Nouri, with its Persian and Arabic origin, would go down in the world of 1811 England.

Wait. Was he losing his mind? Was he actually starting to believe everything that was happening here? Time travel? He peered inside the dark cottage, hoping to see a camera crew. Nothing.

"The coach doesn't arrive 'til noon."

"Hired coach."

"Where did he come from? Why didn't he wait for you at the Swan?"

"He's come from London."

"Is that so? And I suppose he just *happened* to show up at my doorstep? Dressed like...like this?" Her eye traveled over him from head to toe. "And what is he wearing, anyway?"

"Well, the tailor I was telling you about—"

"Don't even, miss. I won't be listening to any fibs. You, I could handle. But the two of you?" The little boy's gaze was going from Nadine to him and back again. Deirdre pushed the child behind her out of sight. "You know my situation. I can't afford to get arrested for helping the likes of you two bringing danger to the village."

"I'm not...*we* are not dangerous. I can pay for whatever we borrow and explain everything."

"Let me guess. You'll explain later. Later. Always later. And that would be after you borrow some more clothes and traipse back here with two more such as yourself. I'm no charity, miss. And I'm tired of secrets. What reason have I to trust you?" She motioned to the road. "It's bad enough you're wearing my cloak. Now, be on your way, or I'll be shouting bloody murder and bringing the coast guardsmen down on you."

The coast guardsmen. Xander remembered Nadine telling him she was being chased by coast guardsmen when he found her on that road in Colorado. He didn't believe her.

Deirdre stepped back to close the door.

"Can I say something?" Xander put in. He imagined the two of them must present quite the picture. Like two muddy, half-drowned rats.

Deirdre held the door slightly ajar, staring distrustfully at him. Nadine shook her head.

"Miss Deirdre. It's a great pleasure to meet you." He felt like a solar panel salesman, going door-to-door. "Before we get on our way, I'd like to thank you. I'm Xander...Finley. And I'm so grateful to you for all your kindness to Nadine from the first moment you two encountered one another."

"How do you know about my kindness? You just arrived."

"It was...her letter." Xander was no historian, but he wasn't totally clueless. "She's been sending me letters, and my beloved wife has told me about you...and with great affection. You and your son..."

"Andrew," Nadine added.

"Yes. Andrew."

The door cracked open another inch or two, and Deirdre stole a look at Nadine.

"Where has she been sending letters? Where have you been?"

"I live in America."

"Well, that explains why you talk so funny." She tsked, and then suspicion again clouded her face. "But I've only known her for less than a fortnight. How could her letters reach you? And now you're here? None of this makes any sense."

"I am *from* America, but I have been to London." He smiled. From the time he was a little boy and making mischief in their apartment in Queens, his mother always said he could charm a crocodile with his smile. He also tried to enunciate his words, imagining that might be more like the way people spoke in 1811.

"And as my darling wife said, I arrived today and have come in search of her." When it came to locations and distances and how long it took to mail a letter to London or travel from there to here, Xander could only hope he was guessing correctly. He was winging it...big time. "Anyway, we will be on our way now. Thank you again for your kindness and hospitality."

He bowed again and reached for Nadine's hand.

"You are a gentleman, aren't you?" Deirdre commented, opening the door wide. "Well, why don't you come in, and I'll see what I can do."

✜ 26 ✜

FIFTEEN MINUTES.

Nadine had fifteen minutes to make it to Churchill House before the coach was due to arrive at the Swan. With any luck, the rains to the west will have slowed it down.

Deirdre was once again her best friend, thanks to Xander, her pretend husband. Nadine was surprised by the young mother's response. A married woman with a child and absent husband had a great deal at stake if she were to be accused of helping enemy spies. Still, Xander's handsome looks and charismatic presence won her over.

Without any hesitation, she'd offered him a greatcoat and a top hat, both of which Xander accepted with a show of gratitude. The hat belonged to her missing husband, the greatcoat to a customer, and she'd shown no inclination to barter. In fact, she'd given him no difficulty at all, and there had been no barrage of questions.

With flushed cheeks, Deirdre appeared to be hypnotized by Xander's charm and couldn't do enough for him. She didn't even seem to notice his vest, even though its zipper, snaps, and fabric with the synthetic insulation were unlike anything she'd ever seen or *would* see in her lifetime. There was no need to find a shirt, waistcoat, jacket, or breeches for him. Not yet. The greatcoat was large enough to cover Xander's jeans, vest, and sweater. His boots were already caked in mud and unlikely to draw attention.

Deirdre was visibly saddened when they had to go. They couldn't stay any longer, but Nadine did accept the half loaf of bread the woman slipped to her, wrapped in a cloth. She tucked it into her bag, knowing the additional side effects Xander would be facing very shortly.

Leaving Deirdre's house, it occurred to her that even though Xander's presence created serious complications, it would be far easier to move around the village with a man striding along at her side. The sight of a single woman who was a stranger in town had already caused her problems.

As they made their way through the lower end of the village, she considered her course of action. Her original plan was now clearly shot to hell. There would be no getting Charles Gordon out of Hythe before Jane Austen arrived. She suspected the rain had already washed out the road going toward Canterbury. With the onslaught of the storm, no one would be leaving the village in either direction.

She needed a new plan.

Even though she didn't know exactly how she was going to complete her mission, it only made sense to meet the captain before he and Austen reunited. An opportunity might then present itself, and Nadine could improvise as she went along.

Putting that thought aside for the moment, she focused on her immediate problems. When she was given the details of the assignment, there had been no way of knowing *when* today the two former lovebirds would meet. Would it be tonight? Tomorrow? The rain was supposed to keep falling, and the roads wouldn't be passable for a day or two. There was simply no record of the direction that the romance between Austen and Gordon would take.

"Good morning."

Shaken from her thoughts, Nadine looked up in surprise as Xander touched the brim of his hat and nodded to a woman who was passing them. The villager was pulling a child along beside her and eyeing him with interest, despite the driving rain.

"Don't talk to people," Nadine warned in a low voice. "Don't draw attention to us."

They were trudging along the muddy lane toward the canal bridge.

"She smiled at me."

"Of course, she did."

The man was over six feet tall, had a heavy beard, and was a stranger, but Xander's amiable manner and broad smile were bound to turn heads.

"Anyone smiles at me, I return the gesture."

"You're not running for mayor of Hythe."

"What's the city government like? Do they *have* a mayor? How many people live here?" He didn't wait for an answer. "It seems like a nice little town. A bit wet, but nice."

She scoffed. "We'll take a walk by the gallows later."

"Do they take American dollars here?"

"No, they…"

Xander didn't wait for an answer. Changing direction, he headed toward a couple of shops. One of them was a bakery. Nadine caught his arm and pulled him back to the right path.

"You'll be shocked to know they don't take money printed two hundred years in the future. Besides, we don't have time to stop."

"If we don't have any money, how are we going to buy food? We have to eat."

"Well, thanks to you bringing my bag, I have some period coins. And in my room at the Swan—the coaching inn where I'm staying—I also have some banknotes we can use."

"Can I borrow some money from you now?"

"No."

"You can go and do what you have to do."

"No."

"When you're done, you can come back and find me."

"Absolutely not. I can't let you out of my sight."

He looked wistfully over his shoulder at the bakery behind them. "I seriously can't remember ever being this hungry. And thirsty."

"Do you remember how sick I got the first night I arrived in Colorado?"

"How could I forget?"

"I ate and drank too much and too fast. When you make a quantum leap, it's best to wait and pace yourself."

"I'm all for pacing. But we have to start somewhere, don't we? I have yet to be offered anything to eat."

He was right. She felt for him. Reaching into her bag, she produced the wrapped bread and handed it to him.

"What's this?"

"Bread, but that's all you can have until later."

"How much later?"

"I'll let you know when I know myself."

Xander opened the napkin and took a bite as they walked.

He stopped dead. "Jeez, I thought you said it was bread. It tastes like plaster."

"Yes. Well, there are ingredients in there that they'll use in laundry detergent in the not-too-distant future."

"I believe it. How could people eat this?"

"Do you want to know the average life expectancy in this era?"

His eyes narrowed. "No, I'm good."

He wrapped up the bread and handed it back to her.

"And, for future reference, it's safer to drink the beer than the water."

"Why?"

"Cholera. Typhoid. The water quality is unsanitary, if not lethal."

She put the bread back in her bag, knowing it'd be only a matter of time before he'd give in and ask for it again. She'd eaten far less appetizing food in her years of travel.

"It'd be much easier if you let me know what's going on. Why am I here?"

"As far as why or how you got here, I have no clue."

Nothing made sense. Only Scribe Guardians were trained to jump time. After completing mission-specific tasks, the trainees spent the majority of their time exercising. Several times a day, for months, she had to do push-ups, pull-ups, sit-ups, and squats, in addition to weightlifting and running. Aside from the psychological conditioning, their bodies needed to become accustomed to having atomic particles dispersed into the universe during the leap across the time-space gyre loops, and then recover upon arrival. Strength and muscle helped this transition.

She stole a glance at Xander. She hadn't seen him naked for two years, but she hadn't forgotten the feel of his body against hers. She had a good idea he still had the same breathtaking brawn packed under those clothes. Clearly, he was fit enough.

But how could he initiate the jump? *And* pinpoint her location in time? Though she no longer used it, Nadine had a sub-molecular mobilizing device in her bag that helped jumpstart the quantum leap. But even with that, a novice would never be able to handle it.

It was a mystery that she had no time to solve now.

"I don't know how I got here." He was frowning at her. "But what brought *you* here?"

"I tried to tell you back in Colorado, but you wouldn't believe me."

They were nearing the bridge over the canal. With the incoming tide and the heavy rains, the water had risen beyond the stone walls of the channel and was climbing the muddy banks. People were hurrying as quickly as they could to get out from the deluge, but a pair of working men were standing on the bridge, watching the rising water below. Tool bags hung from their shoulders, and rain was running off their wide-brimmed hats and oilskin coats.

The two tradesmen turned and eyed them as they passed. Xander touched the brim of his hat, and the men nodded curtly before turning away.

Starting up the hill toward the town's main thoroughfare, Nadine was starting to think they might make it in time. Churchill House was beyond the High Street and up a lane west of the church.

"I had every reason to think you were making it up," Xander continued. "Time travel doesn't exist in 2022, other than what you see on some TV show or a movie. And you yourself knew what you were saying sounded farfetched. That's why you said nothing about it a couple of years ago when we were in Vegas. To be honest, it's still hard for me to get my head around."

He was right about Las Vegas. And she was certain he wouldn't believe her in Colorado, either, even though she'd tried her best to be honest about it. That's all her explanations were to him...farfetched stories.

"Most people in my time, in the future, don't understand it," she admitted. "It's difficult to believe that it's possible...until you jump time yourself."

Nadine's heart stopped at the sight of two armed guardsmen coming down the hill toward them. She fought the urge to turn and run. Their attention was focused on the flooding around the canal, though, and they barely glanced at them as they passed.

"Never talk to the likes of them," she warned once they were out of their hearing range.

"Why?"

"They're the reason I ended up in that coffin and made the quantum leap to Colorado. They were chasing me."

He stopped and turned to look at them. "Those two?"

"I don't know if it was specifically those two. It could have been them or another pair. It was nighttime, and I was running. Let's go." She pulled on his arm, but there was no moving him. "Xander, what are you doing?"

He fixed her with his dark gaze and took her hand in his. "I need to go back and thank them. Imagine how different my life would have been if you'd not shown up on that road in the middle of the storm."

"Yes. Different and better."

"No. Worse. I don't mind that the world is a little stormier since you arrived, Nadine. You *are* the storm. Twice, you've sailed into my life and turned it upside down."

Nadine couldn't believe he was doing this to her now. Making her go all soft inside.

"After you disappeared, I missed you. Missed you more than you could ever imagine." He pressed his lips to her palm. "In my mind, those men are miracle workers. I think I owe them a debt of gratitude...for you."

The words were romantic, but Xander's eyes said much more. She sensed that he would be all for the two of them tearing off their clothes and going at it right here. And any job she was supposed to do could damn well wait.

She knew how Deirdre felt. This man knew how to turn on the charm, how to be irresistible. Staring up into his face, she did not doubt that he meant every word he said. Absolutely fuckable. She hadn't had sex for two years. Two long years. Since they were last together in Vegas.

It was more than simply that physical pull, though. The fact was, she loved him. And she knew that no one in the universe, past or future, was as happy as Xander just being with her. Accepting her as she was. Wanting her.

A cart creaked and banged as a bedraggled horse struggled across the bridge, shaking her out of her musing. Common sense immediately kicked in.

"They're *hardly* miracle workers." She expelled a frustrated breath and pulled at his arm. "If you'll just do as I tell you and give me a couple of hours to get this mission back on track, I'll explain to you how time travel is all about the science of relativity, space-time geometries, and the expanding and contracting continuum of looping gyres. There's no magic or miracle or fate involved."

At her urging, he began to move again beside her.

"What year in the future are you from?"

"In my finite life, it's 2078."

"This makes sense. It only figures that technology and science must have progressed a lot in fifty-six years, no?" He didn't wait for her to answer. "If we looked *back* fifty-six years, imagine the disbelief someone living in 1966 would have if a person tried to explain iPhones, computer apps, email, selfies, Netflix, Costco, and Tesla roadsters."

She'd awakened the inquisitive mind of the engineer.

"Is he still around in 2078?"

"Who?"

"Elon Musk."

"I have no time for this now, Xander."

"How about Jeff Bezos?"

"Later. I'll answer your questions later. Right now, you have to act in a way that makes people believe we belong here in 1811."

"That's gonna be tough. I don't know anything about this time or this place."

"Just follow my lead."

A moment later, they reached the High Street.

In both directions, the cobblestones were generally invisible, submerged beneath deep, rain-splashed pools of water. Even the narrow, raised walkways that fronted the shops were covered in many places. The fog was not as heavy here, but she knew that when night fell, visibility on the narrow street would be almost non-existent. A few hardy people hurried along, ducking into shops. Far fewer were out and about than she remembered the last time she'd passed this intersection during the day. Up the way, by the White Hart Tavern, an oyster seller and a small boy were pushing a cart and calling out their wares.

Nadine breathed a sigh of relief. No coach stood in front of the

Swan, but a couple of grooms waited by the arched entry to the inner yard and stables.

She ushered Xander into a walkway that passed between two buildings and went up the hill between high walls and hedges.

"Where are we going? What do you want me to do or say when we get there?"

"You're to say nothing. I'll do all the talking." Thinking about it, she decided he'd be better off with a brief explanation. "We're going up to Churchill House, which is up that hill beyond the buildings along the High Street. Do you see the top of the square steeple of the church up there?"

"Yeah?"

"It's not far from there."

"Who lives there?"

"Sir Thomas Deedes and his wife—the former Margaret Gordon— live at Churchill House. Lady Deedes's brother, Captain Charles Gordon, is visiting right now. And my mission is to find a way to distract the captain and keep him from reconnecting with Jane Austen while she's stranded in Hythe."

"*The* Jane Austen."

"Yes, *the* Jane Austen."

Xander looked somewhat impressed.

"But why are you doing this?"

"Do you recall what I told you about *Moby Dick* and—"

"And *King Arthur* and how you're a Scribe Guardian and you protect literature."

"You were listening. You paid attention."

"I always pay attention. But tell me about Jane Austen again. What's the deal?"

"I just told you. I have to stop Captain Gordon from meeting her today."

"But why?"

"Because these two have a history. They met ten years ago, and the experience was more than friendly. There were real sparks between them. It could have become serious if he'd had prospects. But he was still a more or less penniless junior officer in the navy, and she was persuaded to move on."

"That's too bad."

"What I've just told you is only relevant to our...to my mission if they run into each other again today."

"Because...?"

"Because with this chance meeting, the old romance will fire up again. The hypothetical course change for history is that Austen and Gordon will eventually marry."

As the gates of Churchill House came into view, Xander again halted. "Your job is to break up their romance?"

From what she could see, no one was outside. No one was coming or going. She hoped Captain Gordon was happily entrenched indoors on such a miserable day.

"Nadine? Is that why you're here? To stop two people from finding a second chance at love?"

A second chance at love.

She knew what he was doing. He was drawing a parallel between Austen and Gordon's relationship and their own.

"They're not us, Xander," she said firmly. "They live in a different time. Their situation is unique."

"You and I live in different times, and I'd say our situation is unique."

"They are not *us*." She pressed her index finger into his chest, annunciating each word. "What do you know about her background? How it was that she became a writer?"

She took another look toward the house. Still, no one was coming out.

"Nothing."

"That's the point." She held his gaze. He needed to hear this. "Jane Austen turned down several opportunities for long-term relationships with men during her lifetime. Right now, she is a thirty-five-year-old spinster on the verge of greatness. There was never a Mr. Darcy or a romantic happily-ever-after for her. And that was why she became one of the greatest writers of the English language. *Sense and Sensibility*, *Pride and Prejudice*, *Emma*, *Persuasion*, among others. She believed that marriage could only be successful if certain criteria were met. Financial and social, as well as intellectual. Partners needed to have mutual respect. But even if those conditions were met, there were responsibilities that went along with the marital arrangement. Unfortunately, in this era, responsibilities and expectations exist that would prohibit her from becoming *the* Jane Austen."

"I understand what you're saying, but there are exceptions to everything. Maybe Gordon is different. Maybe he lets her be everything she wants to be. I still don't get how you would break up their relationship—"

"Look, I'm here to do a job." Nadine didn't want sentimentality to cloud the logic. She didn't operate in the world of *possible* exceptions. History couldn't be rewritten, not in her line of work. "You are someone who has nothing at stake here. I don't mean to be harsh, but your understanding of the matter is irrelevant. Now, come on. We've got to get this done."

Angry, she took a couple of steps toward the house and realized he wasn't coming. Turning around, she saw him standing where she'd left him. Rain dripped from the brim of the top hat. He was taking all of this personally. She couldn't leave him there.

At the same time, she couldn't explain that *her* life depended on completing this assignment. Failures weren't tolerated in the Scribe Guardian program. There were no three strikes. If you failed, you were out. And if she was out, her days of living were numbered.

"Xander, I have a reason for doing what I do." She held out her hand to him. "Please. You have to trust me."

With a frown, he closed the distance, and they approached the house together.

Beyond the open gates, a light-colored gravel drive encircled a large island of grass. Sheets of rain swept across broad puddles on the drive. Nadine had seen satellite photos before coming on her mission, and she knew Churchill House to be an impressive country seat. She'd also come here every day, asking for Captain Gordon before she'd jumped forward to Xander's time.

The rambling stone building rose a full three stories, with four high-pointed gables and a south wing that ran parallel to the line of hills. Rows of rectangular windows graced the front of the building, and a dozen chimneys were visible above the gleaming slate roof.

An arched walkway led to a stone terrace facing the sea, which was invisible now with the driving rain. On the right, the drive led to stables and eventually to fields and farms beyond.

Adrenaline quickened her pulse as they climbed the steps, and her mind pored over the fabrications she was about to deliver.

The connection she'd initially planned on using could still work. Her 'father' was an admiral who was actually known to the captain. From her preparatory research, Nadine knew that at this time 650 naval officers were Irish—well, Anglo-Irish—by birth. There were several who held the rank of admiral, and the man Captain Gordon knew in Portsmouth was an Admiral James Finley.

She glanced at Xander, her pretend husband. The complication that presented itself now was that she was introducing herself as *Mrs. Finley.* Even if she used the excuse that she and Xander were cousins and married and shared the same last name, why would she be needing Gordon's assistance for anything when she had a strapping husband at her side?

Think, Nadine. Think.

And what would happen if they *were* invited to come inside? Xander was wearing 21st-century clothes beneath the greatcoat. And her dress beneath the cloak was hardly fashionable or well fitting. It screamed of borrowed clothing, not the clothing of an admiral's daughter.

Damn. She was in trouble.

The time to come up with a strategy ended when the door opened and a footman appeared on the threshold. She recognized him. He was the same person she'd bribed for information last week. Only the slightest arch of an eyebrow showed that he recognized her. The footman glanced at Xander and then focused his gaze somewhere behind them.

She reached into her bag. Somewhere deep in its recesses, there was a case. Inside the case, she had calling cards. The cards were a necessary accessory for a lady who called upon friends or acquaintances. With the falling rain, opening her bag to search would be a disaster. Nadine decided to proceed without presenting a card.

"Captain Gordon, if you please," she said. "We are Mr. and Mrs. Finley. We're here on an urgent matter, and we need to see the captain."

"My apologies, ma'am. But the captain is not here, at present. Would you like me to announce you to Sir Thomas? Or to Lady Deedes?"

She'd avoided meeting the sister and brother-in-law on her visits last week, and she'd do the same now.

"Has the captain left Hythe already?" she asked hopefully.

She'd been gone more than three days. It was always possible that an error caused by another Guardian's jump may have occurred while she was in Colorado. Perhaps the situation had self-corrected, after all.

"No, ma'am. He's down in the village."

Nadine's stomach sank.

"Do you expect him back soon?"

"Aye, ma'am. He's waiting at the Swan for the noon coach. A good friend of the captain—another naval officer—is expected."

The noon coach. The same one that Jane Austen was on.

N ADINE WAS LIKE A WOMAN POSSESSED. Grabbing Xander's arm, she hurried out the gates and started back down the hill toward the High Street.

"What are we doing now?"

"Meeting Jane Austen at the coaching inn."

"And doing what?"

"Distracting her. I know enough about her family history and her current siblings' situations to come up with a connection."

"And you think that will work?"

"All we need to do is keep her preoccupied with us. If we can do that, perhaps she won't notice Captain Gordon."

A gust of wind knocked Xander's top hat off and pushed back the hood of Nadine's cloak. She waited impatiently, adjusting her hood.

She considered how many people would be on the coach coming from the direction of Plymouth and Brighton. Would Austen be the only woman arriving on it today? If not, would Nadine recognize her?

She had good visuals for many of the English writers of the eighteenth and nineteenth centuries. Images of George Eliot, Charles Dickens, Thomas Hardy, and a slew of others were known from extant portraits, and later from photographs. Jane Austen never sat for a formal portrait. In her lifetime, she never became as famous or wealthy as Fanny Burney, Maria Edgeworth, Mrs. Radcliffe, or Sir

Walter Scott; and her family never expected her to rise to such heights.

Even so, Nadine had several artifacts to help identify her. The most reliable likeness was a pencil-and-watercolor sketch made by Cassandra Austen, Jane's older sister, when Jane was around thirty-five years old. That informal portrait would be painted during the autumn of this year, and it still hung in London's National Portrait Gallery.

Cassandra depicted her sister with round, rosy cheeks and a long, pointed nose. Large, hazel eyes and dark brown curls. She wore one of her favored caps as opposed to a bonnet.

There was another picture as well, painted by Reverend James Daniel Clarke, the Prince Regent's librarian. He'd apparently done the painting for himself after the author visited Carlton House, the Prince's residence, in 1815. The future King George IV was a great admirer of Austen's work, and records showed that he kept multiple volumes of her work in all his residences. The painting was found in Clarke's personal 'friendship book' and showed Jane dressed in period finery for the visit. The painting did little to enhance Nadine's visual image of the writer, however, with the exception of confirming the shape of her face.

Beyond those two artifacts, what was available were descriptions given by people who knew Jane Austen.

One neighbor described her as being "fair and handsome, slight and elegant, but with cheeks a little too full." After her death, Jane's brother Henry wrote: "Her stature was that of true elegance. It could not have been increased without exceeding the middle height...Her features were separately good...her complexion was of the finest texture." Not entirely helpful.

According to Austen-Leigh, a grandnephew of Jane's, "in person she was very attractive; her figure was rather tall and slender, her step light and firm, and her whole appearance expressive of health and animation. In complexion she was a clear brunette with a rich color; she had full round cheeks, with mouth and nose small and well-formed, bright hazel eyes, and brown hair forming natural curls close round her face."

All of Nadine's research before arriving on this mission confirmed that Jane Austen was slim, and tall by the standards of her time, with a good posture, and a beautiful complexion. She was fairly optimistic that she would recognize her.

The path was slick and slowed them down, but she and Xander reached the High Street in a few minutes.

The coach, blocking most of the thoroughfare, stood in front of the coaching inn.

"Oh, no," she murmured.

A private company operated the coaches that ran through Hythe. They could carry six passengers inside, and more on top. Not a comfortable ride in weather like this, it was said, though Nadine had never experienced it. Normally, this stop would have been only about twenty minutes, giving the grooms time to change the horses and passengers to take care of personal business.

No fresh team of horses had been brought out from the stable yard, however. The dour-faced innkeeper was standing outside the Swan's front door, talking to the driver and the armed guard sitting up top. Passengers had already climbed from the coach, and from the looks on their faces, they'd just learned that the road to Canterbury was washed out.

"What are you going to do now?"

Nadine hurried toward the crowd gathered in the rain. "If I can find her, there's still time. Even if she's seen him, I'll try to get her attention and keep it. There's no such a thing as love at the first sight."

"I disagree," he scoffed.

He was doing it again. Comparing their relationship to that of Austen and Gordon. She had no time to argue this with him now.

Moving closer, Nadine saw her. Jane Austen, holding a travel bag, looked exactly as she'd envisioned her. Tall and composed, bright and alert to what was going on, she stood beneath the arched entry to the yard, out of the rain. She was smiling and listening to a tall, broad-shouldered gentleman in a naval uniform, who was speaking to her with his back to them. Another officer stood a discreet distance away, watching with interest.

"Is that her?" Xander asked, stopping beside Nadine, whose steps had faltered.

"Yes, that's her."

"And her Captain Gordon?"

"He's not *her* Captain Gordon. Not yet."

"I'd say they're almost there."

She didn't want to believe it. "What makes you say that?"

"Look at the way she's leaning toward him as he speaks. Look at her smile. Her eyes have not left his face."

Shit. Shit. Shit. Nadine's feet were nailed to the ground. She no longer felt the rain pounding down on her. There was nothing she could do now. Not at this moment. The one saving possibility pertained to the etiquette of this time. The captain couldn't and wouldn't carry Jane off to Churchill House. Even though they'd met before, the rules of social engagement were clear. If he cared to renew their acquaintance and take it further, inviting Austen to his sister's home would require that he come back with Lady Deedes or with a letter from her.

Jane laughed at something the captain said.

Damn it. Maybe Jane was open to having the captain spirit her away to his sister's house. As Xander said, her body language indicated that might be so.

She hoped that the Regency courtship protocol, in which men were counseled not to embark upon courtship lightly and women not to give affections too easily, was not bullshit.

Jane was laughing like a teenager as she chatted. And from behind, the captain appeared to be quite animated as they conversed.

Xander was right. The woman was flirting. Nadine would need time to drive a wedge into this.

"I'm fucked," she said under her breath as Jane gave a final nod and briefly took the captain's hand. Then, she turned and disappeared into the inn.

Captain Gordon watched her go and then joined his friend. The two men appeared to be in no hurry to get out of the rain. As they talked, they cast glances at the inn. From the captain's face, Nadine could see the man was pumped up by the chance meeting. Actually, *determined* might be the better word.

As the grooms and the driver maneuvered the coach into the inn's stable yard, Nadine took a moment to study Charles Gordon. Prior to taking this assignment, she'd watched every video adaptation of Austen's work that was ever made. And being this close to Mr. Almost-Right, she judged that the captain's looks in some ways resembled that of Rupert Penry-Jones, who'd played Wentworth in an old adaptation of *Persuasion*. Tall, handsome, confident, alert. Not the strapping and aloof young Colin Firth playing Mr. Darcy.

Nadine took Xander's arm and edged closer to Gordon and his friend. As they wandered by the two men, Nadine picked up some of the conversation over the shouts of the driver and the sounds of the horses.

"...Sidmouth...ten years past...unchanged, as beautiful and lively as I remember...retiring for the day...my sister...introductions tomorrow."

The two naval officers started along the High Street and a moment later turned up the walkway toward Churchill House.

The good news? The captain wouldn't be seeing Jane Austen until tomorrow. The bad news? His infatuation with her looked to be as strong as ever.

"Where to now?" Xander asked, totally unperturbed by the direness of the situation.

They stood by the front door of the inn as Nadine considered her next move. Because of the inclement weather, it was unlikely that Austen would be venturing out. She'd take a room at the Swan and rest after her travels. Looking in through one of the steamed-up windows facing the street, she could see that the public dining room was full. She couldn't tell if Jane was in there.

Nadine knew Xander needed to eat. They both did. Food and rest and some serious thinking were in order.

As she turned to him, her jaw dropped. In his arm, he was holding a dog. A squat, one-eyed dog.

Kai. The vicious little animal nestled against Xander's chest showed none of the snarling and snapping she'd experienced with him before. In fact, Kai paid no attention to Nadine at all.

"Where did you find this thing? Put him down."

She glanced around her in search of Elizabeth Hole, town busybody. No sign of her.

"The little guy just trotted over, sat down, and leaned against my boots. I think he was using me to block some of this rain. Look at him. He's shivering." Xander brought his face close to the dog's snout and got a kiss on the nose. "Cute little thing. Isn't he?"

"No, he's not cute at all. He's a nasty little rat. And don't trust that fake innocence. That beast has serious anger issues. The last time I saw him he tried to take a bite out of my ankle."

"What do you expect when you call him a rat?"

"Our mutual dislike started long before we got into name-calling." She searched around her again for the owner. Mrs. Hole was hurrying down the street, looking right and left and calling out for her dog.

"Oh, no! Here she comes." Nadine turned to Xander. "Please put him down. Let's go inside. We don't want to get into it with this woman. She's as bad as the dog. Worse, even."

The dog lay his head against Xander's shoulder and looked smugly at Nadine.

"You little—"

"Kai!" The cry of discovery came from across the High Street. "My Kai!"

"Oh, God. Too late."

Elizabeth Hole kept calling her dog as she frantically tried to maneuver around the puddles to get to them.

Nadine watched in disbelief as Xander, still holding the dog, stepped into the street to help her.

"That's it," she murmured. "It's over. We're done for."

There was no way around it. This mission was finished. He was like an extra on the set of a big production movie, the amateur who had no idea that he was supposed to blend in and not create a disturbance. He had no idea what was at stake. No idea how important it was for him to do exactly what she asked.

She raised her face briefly to the sky, allowing the raindrops to cool her rising panic. With the exception of those few precious moments in Deirdre's cottage, she'd been cold and wet all day. She was exhausted and hungry and needed a bath and a comfortable bed. None of which were in sight.

What *was* in sight was a short drop from the gallows, depending on how badly this went with Mrs. Hole. She sighed. That scenario was quite probable, in fact. The only positive thing they had going for them was that there were no coast guardsmen around.

As Nadine watched them, Kai crossed from Xander into the arms of the old busybody. Then, to her dismay, the two started toward her, arm in arm. She braced herself for what was to come.

"Why, my dear! We meet again. Why didn't you tell me that your husband was to join you here at Hythe?"

My dear! Seeing the smile on Elizabeth Hole's face, Nadine blinked to make sure this was the same person.

"I surprised her, Mrs. Hole."

"What a charming man you are, Mr. Finley. Such a pleasure."

"The pleasure is entirely mine, ma'am."

Nadine could find no words.

"And how extraordinary to meet someone from America who isn't a barbarian. So kind! It's no wonder my Kai took shelter with you, sir. He is a very good judge of character, I want you to know."

Xander told her that? They'd spent only a few seconds talking!

Elizabeth Hole sent Nadine a side look. Clearly, her opinion of her hadn't changed much...for all her 'my dears'.

"The moment I saw Kai across the way in your arms, I told myself, *that* fine-looking fellow is a gentleman, to be sure." She finally let go of Xander. "And I was correct. Now, if you please, tell me how long you're planning to stay in Hythe. I should very much like to have you in for tea and seedcake. This afternoon, if that suits you. Or come to dinner, if you'd prefer."

"Tea and seedcake would be great—"

"Thank you, Mrs. Hole, for your thoughtful invitation," Nadine interrupted, knowing that Xander was hungry enough to follow this woman home right now. "But as you know, my husband has just arrived, and I need to get him settled. Would it be all right if I called on you later in the week so that we can decide on a date?"

The old woman's face immediately clouded with suspicion. "Your husband was away, and yet you, yourself have been absent from Hythe for three days. Where were you?"

No 'my dear', Nadine noted. Clearly, Mrs. Hole's distrust of her had not faded. "I was—"

"She was with me," Xander broke in, turning on his charm. "In London. I surprised her there, and we traveled back here together."

The account they'd given Deirdre and Elizabeth Hole was quite different, but it was laughable to think the two would get together to compare notes.

"Very well. I'll expect you to call on me, Mrs. Finley," Mrs. Hole said curtly to Nadine before turning a bright smile on Xander. "Kai and I will be eagerly awaiting your visit, sir."

"I'll be looking forward to it, ma'am." He reached out and petted the little monster. "Be good, Kai."

Mrs. Hole sighed and looked like she was about to melt into the cobblestones.

Nadine waited until the woman and her dog were far enough up High Street before she turned to Xander.

"Twice now, you've saved the day. Thank you."

"You owe me a seedcake, whatever that is. And I hope it tastes better than the bread."

"Come on, we'll be able to find something for you inside."

"Does that mean there's a bed to sleep on in there too?"

She smiled and linked her arm with his, leading him through the archway toward a door that led from the inner yard into the inn. "Yes, but we still have one more obstacle before you can settle in for the afternoon."

"And that is?"

"The innkeeper. He's as suspicious and inhospitable as a hedgehog. And even though I paid for a week in advance, I wouldn't swear he hasn't given my room away while I was in Colorado."

"Okay. Well, tell me what I need to know about this place. Maybe I can do the talking inside."

On almost any other time, Nadine would have given him an earful about her ability to function without a male to speak for her. She'd completed plenty of her missions as a Scribe Guardian without the assistance of one. But her feeling at this moment was...whatever. Twice today, Xander had succeeded in charming a local. He was on a roll.

Under the protective covering of a gallery that overlooked the stable yard, she told him what he was facing.

"If I can mix up some terms, a coaching inn is a way station in a network of routes all over Great Britain. It's a livery for horses, a vehicle repair shop, a restaurant, a tavern, and a hotel. Most serve as post offices too."

She watched the activity near the coach. The horses had been unhitched and the guard had put his blunderbuss aside. He was in the process of handing down a lock box to the driver as a stable worker stood and chatted with them.

"Here at the Swan, the innkeeper generally works in the taproom, and his wife serves as the housekeeper. There's a boy who helps in the taproom, and he looks like a miniature version of the innkeeper. A couple of young fellows work as waiters, but I've seen them running errands. Two or three girls help the cook, who I haven't seen. Those girls also clean the rooms and do anything else they're asked to do."

"Most important...how is the food?"

"Good one day, horrible the next. There's no rhyme and reason to it that I could see."

"Is there another place around here where we could eat instead?"

"The White Hart is a tavern a few doors up, but I never checked it out. The Swan has two private sitting and dining rooms that customers can pay extra to eat in. At street level, there is a taproom and public dining parlor that they call the 'Coffee Room'. I've had most of my meals in the Coffee Room, but I also had a tray sent up."

The driver passed them on his way into the inn. He shot a curious look at Xander's boots but said nothing to them.

"I'm starting to shrivel like a prune in these clothes," Xander said. "Is there any chance of finding dry ones?"

She smiled, relieved that Xander was finally taking to heart everything she was saying. There was no teasing, no hint of disbelief about what she was telling him.

"There's no ready-made clothing available in the village that I'm aware of. Let's get up to the room. I'll send a message to Deirdre. Since you charmed her the way you did, she might be willing to help fix you up with appropriate attire."

"Charmed her? I was just being my usual agreeable self."

Inside, the Coffee Room was full of diners, but the taproom was steamy and crowded and smelled strongly of tobacco and men's bodies. Stranded travelers only made up a small part of the mob, and it appeared that the bad weather had brought out quite a few of the boisterous locals for an afternoon of dice, cards, draughts, and pots of ale.

Nadine worked her way through the crowd to the bar, and the innkeeper's perpetually dour expression brightened the moment he saw Xander standing at her shoulder. Before, she hadn't arrived on a coach, and she hadn't been accompanied by a family member or a chaperone. Now, having introduced Xander as her husband, she suddenly acquired legitimacy.

To Nadine's great relief, the room she'd paid for last week had been kept for her, despite her absence. It was ready for them, and food would be sent upstairs immediately.

Deciding it was safe enough to leave Xander to speak with the innkeeper for a few moments as he sampled the ale, Nadine poked her head into the Coffee Room, looking for Jane Austen. The dining room was more civilized than the taproom, but only slightly quieter since the loud voices and laughter in the next room were easily heard through the wall. Jane was not amongst the diners.

Collecting Xander from the taproom, they headed up the stairs. The two private dining rooms on the upper floor were empty, so the two of them went down a dark, narrow hallway to Nadine's room, which looked out over the High Street.

To her surprise and great relief, everything was just as she'd left it.

Her spare clothing still hung in a narrow wardrobe against one wall. Feeling on top of it, she found her packet of bank notes.

"Well, we have money to feed you with," she told Xander.

"You mean, we won't be *dining* with your dear friend Mrs. Hole?" he replied, a smile tugging at his lips.

She scoffed as he shrugged out of his greatcoat. Taking the cloak she'd borrowed from Deirdre, he hung them on pegs by the door. They put their boots beneath them.

Aside from the wardrobe and the window overlooking the street, the room had everything she needed. A small table and chair. A washstand. A mirror on the wall.

And a bed. One narrow bed.

Comfortable enough for a single occupant, but not quite wide enough for two people to lie on without full-body contact. And definitely not wide enough for two people with a history of not being able to keep their hands off each other.

Nadine glanced at Xander. His gaze was on the bed too, and he didn't exactly look unhappy about the situation. In fact, he looked delighted.

A knock came at the door, and Nadine opened it. Two of the serving girls were in the hallway.

"The bath your husband ordered, Mrs. Finley."

One of them carried a smallish tub and a large, steaming ewer. The other carried two more ewers.

"One moment." She closed the door and turned to Xander. "Asking for this to be sent up is unusual, you know. People in this era bathe every few weeks...or months."

"Months? They don't take a bath or a shower after they have sex?"

Her body caught fire. She looked into his eyes and saw the match was lit there too. It was two years since they'd had their time together in Vegas. Two years.

Right now, the literary world was about to turn upside down. Readers for centuries to come were about to lose Emma Woodhouse and Mr. Knightly and the Dashwood sisters and Fanny Price and Elizabeth Bennet and Darcy...and Anne Eliot.

But despite that, the thought of an afternoon and a night alone with Xander made Nadine's skin tingle all over.

She opened the door. "Bring it in."

❧ 28 ❧

NADINE DRAPED towels over the steaming tub and quickly ushered the serving women out the door.

The bath was obviously going to wait.

The moment they were alone, Xander drew her to him. He'd been waiting for this from the moment he'd opened his eyes a couple of hours ago and realized that he'd found her again.

To make it real, he needed to hold her, touch her, know that she was real. That this wasn't some wild dream he was caught in the middle of. 'I have to pinch myself' had run through his mind at least a dozen times.

She held him, kissed him, and whatever doubt he had in his mind as far as the reality of it all dispersed as a kiss turned to passion and sex. An hour later, they were both lying naked and breathless on the bed.

"Isn't this the way we started in Vegas?"

"We had dinner first," he answered.

"Room service. But I don't remember touching any of the food until after sex." She pressed her forehead against his, kissing him. "Remember?"

Oh, he remembered. The off-the-charts sparks had turned into a lot of sex, but also an instant bond. The idea of letting relationships simmer didn't apply to them. Nadine had known theirs wouldn't last.

Xander didn't feel that way. Still, they made every minute they had together count.

"I've been hoping for a replay since you showed up on that mountain road."

"I'm kicking myself for not letting it happen sooner." She smiled. "We missed out on some serious fun."

"We still have time."

"But we don't." She sat on the edge of the bed and wrapped a towel around her. "I have a job to do, Xander. I have to go and find Jane Austen. She's staying at this inn. It may be my only chance to talk to her."

"How insane would it be if you just showed up at her door and told her the truth?"

"Totally insane. She wouldn't believe me." Nadine crossed the room to the washstand, picked up a ball-shaped bar of soap, and walked to the tub.

Xander judged that Nadine might be able to fit into that tub, but there wouldn't be enough room for two. Not by a long shot.

She pulled the towels off the top of the tub, and steam rose in wisps around her.

"When I came on this mission, I was never going to deal with her directly. I didn't think I'd even see her. My intention was to get Gordon out of Hythe before she arrived."

Xander sat up against the sturdy wooden headboard and watched her. He had a million questions about her job and about the future that she lived in. But all of that faded in importance as he watched her get into the tub.

"I need a different approach now. A different story. One unique for her. She's only at the beginning of her publishing career, but she's already a master storyteller. She won't believe some half-baked tale told to her by a stranger."

"How long have you been doing this job? Being a Scribe Guardian, I mean."

"I was recruited when I was twenty-two. I'm thirty-five now."

"That's a long time. It gives a whole new meaning to all the stories you were telling me back in Colorado. You have a lot of experience. You'll figure it out."

"Yes, I'll figure it out. I have to." She looked up at the ceiling. "Stop being so wound up, Nadine."

"You need to de-stress to think?" He climbed out of the bed and started toward her.

She stared at his bare chest for a second before allowing her eyes to wander down his body.

"You're going to help me think, looking like that?"

"Sex relieves stress and anxiety by triggering the release of a feel-good hormone. Oxytocin."

"But we already had sex, and I'm no closer to finding an answer."

"That didn't count. It was far too quick."

"Are you saying having sex again will help me come up with a believable story?"

"That's exactly what I'm saying."

The corners of her lips lifted in a smile. "That's very convincing."

Suddenly awake, Xander lay in the dark, disoriented.

No glowing blue light from phones or clocks in the room. No soft buzz of electronics. No reflective illumination from the floodlights he'd installed outside of his house.

The sounds were foreign too. Rain pounded on panes of rattling glass, and the wind whistled through cracks in the walls and window frames.

He lifted his head and peered into the darkness. He remembered where he was.

His gaze immediately went to the warm body curled up next to him in the lumpy, narrow bed. Nadine. His relief was enormous.

None of this was a dream. He was with her.

The tub where they'd washed one another still sat in the corner. A low, dark hulk with the white smudges of towels hanging over the sides. The chair by the table was leaning against the wall where it had been knocked askew. He smiled at the memory.

A high-pitched squeak drew his eyes to the wardrobe. One of the doors was slightly ajar and being pushed back and forth by an unseen breeze. That was what had awakened him.

He believed her now. He believed everything she'd told him. She was a time traveler. A Scribe Guardian. And what did that make him? A cross-century stalker.

As crazy as it sounded, he'd traveled back in time. To 1811. To England. To a little village she called Hythe.

Getting stranded at Heathrow after missing a connecting flight was the only time Xander had ever been in England. If that even counted. He wished he'd been a better student of history. Nadine had said the English were at war with France, and that Hythe was perched on the shores of the English Channel. The only history courses he took in high school and college had been about American history. And when it came to literature? SparkNotes and swapping math and calculus homework for help with English papers had been enough to get him through the few mandatory courses.

Jane Austen, the woman at the center of Nadine's mission, was a mystery to him. He should have read the books he'd collected, rather than simply putting them up on those shelves.

His mind returned to the volume he'd found by Nadine's bed in the guest room. The book with the print missing from the pages. He hadn't had a chance to tell her about it. *Persuasion*.

What did he do with it? He had it with him when he went into his garage. And then the fall. Did he drop it? Or could it be that the book traveled back in time with him?

It was possible. Nadine's bag had been in the coffin. But he hadn't looked to see what else was in there. He frowned at the thin panes of glass in the window, smeared by the onslaught of rain and the wind. He'd like to go back to Deirdre's yard and check in the box. But he wouldn't go without Nadine.

She was snoring softly, her face half buried under the blanket. Even in the dark, she was so beautiful.

Xander's stomach growled loud enough to wake the dead, but she slept through it. It occurred to him that he had no idea what time it was.

Downstairs, he'd arranged for dinner to be sent up. Room service wasn't quite the same as it would be in the future, though. The food never arrived. But now that he thought about it, maybe it had. Maybe they were too preoccupied with each other to hear the knock.

Xander climbed out of bed as gently as he could, pulled on his boxers, and padded to the door. Opening it a few inches, he looked into the hallway. Sure enough, a wooden platter of food sat on the floor outside the door. When he leaned down to pick it up, a small dark creature jumped off a plate and scurried away.

A rat? A mouse? Growing up in New York, he'd seen plenty of rodents. But after Nadine's lecture on rats and the bubonic plague, he had a different feeling about the little varmints.

He shuddered in disgust and pushed the tray down the hall with his foot.

"It's all yours, pal," he muttered, closing the door.

His stomach growled again as he stood in the darkness. There was no denying his hunger, but he wasn't going to wake her up and complain. Before they'd fallen asleep, the two of them had finished off the bread Deirdre had given them. The fact that it hadn't tasted too bad said something about how hungry he was.

He considered the food out in the hall but realized he couldn't do it. There had to be something else available.

Xander decided that it couldn't be too late. He was never one to sleep long hours. Still, he had no idea if anyone was still working downstairs in the kitchen.

Hell, he'd never know unless he went down there. He started pulling on his clothes. If the kitchen was still open, maybe he could have a new tray sent up to them.

He paused, looking at his clothes. The pants and sweater were a lot different from what he'd seen the locals wearing. His down vest was out of the question too. He put a hand on the greatcoat. It was still wet.

Hell, he wasn't planning on leaving the inn. And how many people could be down there, no matter what time it was?

So far, saying he'd come from America seemed to be the perfect excuse for his speech and manners. Maybe it would work for the way he was dressed.

"Fuck it," he murmured. Pulling on his boots, Xander slipped out.

The hallway was only slightly less dark than their room. A candle in a sconce on the wall at the top of the stairs flickered dimly but lit the way.

Downstairs, there wasn't a soul around. The taproom where he'd spoken with the innkeeper was empty, and the bar itself was closed up tight with boards.

Xander looked into the large room that Nadine called the Coffee Room. She'd said that was where she had taken most of her meals.

The room had about a dozen tables and chairs. At first, he thought no one was there, but then a dying ember popped in the fireplace on one wall, drawing his eye. A woman sat near the hearth, a candle before her on the table. She had a pen in hand.

"Miss Austen? Miss Jane Austen?"

⟡ 29 ⟡

"Yes?" Her head tipped slightly in surprise, and she rose to her feet.

The candlelight was dim, but he could see that Jane Austen was wearing a dark shawl over a long dress that could have been gray or brown. Her hair was gathered up under a cap that looked like a floppy beret.

Her face was neither friendly nor unfriendly. Just attentive and cautious. Even in this light, he could see her eyes were sharply focused on him, a bit like a mountain lion he'd once startled crossing the road.

"I hope I'm not disturbing you. I'm Xander Finley." He gave a small bow as he'd seen others do this afternoon.

She returned the courtesy with a nod and a slight curtsy.

Too bad cell phones hadn't been invented yet. He'd text Nadine right now. What were the chances of catching the writer down here alone?

"Pleased to meet you, Mr. Finley."

Xander noticed that she gave his clothes the once over.

"Do we know each other?"

"Yes. Well, no. My wife knows you. Or knows *of* you. When you arrived on the coach this afternoon, she pointed you out to me."

"Your wife?"

"Yes, Nadine Finley," he said. "By any chance, do you know what time it is?"

She hid a smile and glanced around the room. "I don't know exactly. But I suspect it's close to midnight."

"Oh, that late." Xander leaned back inspecting the hallway. Not another soul was around.

Austen put a cork in a bottle of ink, hurriedly collecting up her papers and pens. Nervous. Hell, she had every right to be with a stranger showing up out of nowhere.

But he didn't want her to leave. Not until they'd made some kind of connection.

"Do you know the way to the kitchen, Miss Austen?"

"The kitchen?"

"Yes."

"May I ask why?"

"I can't remember the last time I ate anything substantial. My wife, either. I need to order some food to be sent up to our room."

She stopped packing up her things. "I don't know exactly where the kitchen is, but a serving lad comes in occasionally to check on me.

"Okay."

"*Okay?* That's a curious word, Mr. Finley. Are you a stranger here?"

"I'm an American. My wife and I are newly married. The innkeeper did have some dinner sent up, but it was left outside our door. By the time I found it, a creepy four-legged thief was sampling the dishes."

"You're from America?" she asked quickly.

From her frown, Xander guessed she was more disturbed by that than the fact that a rat had been into his food.

"I am. And I apologize for the way I talk and the way I'm dressed. We're newly arrived in England. Our luggage was lost, and I haven't had the opportunity to go to a...a tailor."

Did they have tailors in 1811? He had no idea, but it sounded right.

"This explains a great deal, sir. Though I must say I have never met anyone from America."

"I hope you don't have a bad opinion of them...of us."

Her frown was replaced by a look of caution. "Are you asking my opinion of Americans?"

He took a few steps into the room, giving her a clear run for the door if she felt the need to flee. "Of course. I'd love to hear your opinion."

"My honest opinion?"

"If you don't mind sharing it."

There was a slight pause as she studied him again from head to toe.

"I should warn you that a few persons of my acquaintance consider me a bit of a bluestocking."

"A bluestocking?"

The hint of a smile pulled at her lips. "You have no bluestockings in America?"

"I'm not sure. What are they?"

"It is a woman who dares to discuss controversial issues, such as war and politics. Shocking as this sounds, she even reads books. Philosophy. Science. And not only that, she *insists* on having an opinion."

"Then, I'm happy to say we've got them...in spades."

"*In spades?*"

"I mean, we have quite a few."

"I must say, I am surprised."

"Why?"

"Many men are appalled by the thought of educated women with opinions."

"I'm not. And I'd still love to know your opinion of America."

"Very well. If you insist." Her chin lifted. There was fire in her eyes. "I believe America is having a negative influence on the world. In my opinion, America is a dangerously radical, unreligious place where people of low birth and poor character can advance socially and materially, despite their unworthiness."

He suppressed the urge to laugh out loud, but smiled. "There are quite a few people in America who would agree with that."

It was fascinating to think that the American Revolution would still be considered recent history for people like Jane Austen. And the War of 1812 was coming up. It was only natural that, as a British citizen, she'd resent the loss of the colonies. He supposed she might have even lost someone in the fighting.

"But you mentioned you've never met an American before."

"My opinion is based on my reading, Mr. Finley." Her voice softened. "I have insulted you, have I not?"

"Not at all. You've expressed an opinion. And I respect other people's opinions. You have a right to them."

"You *respect* a woman's opinion." There was a doubtful, though amused look in her eyes.

"About your statement, however...from what I've seen, many people in America are deeply religious. But, as you say, many have gone there with the expressed hope of improving their lot in life. They don't see that as a bad thing."

"I see." Austen smiled and motioned to the chair across from her at the table. "If you'd care to join me for a few moments, I expect that serving lad will look in on me any time now. You can order your food from him, I believe."

"Thank you."

Did he dare run upstairs and get Nadine? Would Jane Austen be gone by the time he got back? He couldn't risk it. Xander motioned for her to sit down and then followed suit.

"I must say, hearing how amiably you received my slights—"

"Opinions," he cut in with a smile.

"Very well. Opinions." She paused and changed direction. "Tell me, would you consider your wife unexceptional in her views and manner of thinking?"

"Okay, here we go again. Is this unexceptional thing like being a bluestocking?"

Her hazel-colored eyes danced with mischief. "Just the opposite. Being considered an unexceptional woman is a high compliment amongst the ton."

"The ton?"

"Society's elite, Mr. Finley."

He laughed. "Well, I'd have to say my wife doesn't put much weight on those kinds of compliments. She's smart, well-read, and willing to speak her mind. She's exceptional in every way. And I'm very proud of her. But I'm intrigued. The things you're telling me about British society are sort of cringe-worthy."

"*Cringe-worthy*. Another delightful American word, I take it."

"Yes, sorry."

"Are you saying you've never spent any time amongst the British gentry?"

"No, ma'am. This is my first time in England."

"And you say you've recently arrived?"

"We have."

"If I may ask, what do you do, Mr. Finley?"

"You can ask anything you want, Miss Austen." Computer programming and app design were out of the question. "I'm an inventor."

"How interesting. Do you own a manufactory to produce the things you invent?"

Xander hesitated. He'd need to fudge his answer, but he didn't want to throw a monkey wrench into Nadine's mission. "I've recently sold my business."

"So then, what brings you to England?"

"I'm here to buy more, uh...manufactories."

"You're rich, then. I'm prying, I know, and being dreadfully personal. But you've piqued my curiosity about Americans."

"I'm happy to talk to you." Xander was not one to brag, and caution told him discretion might be the better course now. "My wife and I live comfortably."

"That means rich." She leaned forward, and her eyes reflected a hint of humor as she spoke. "No doubt you'll be invited to many balls while you are in England, so you shall get to experience the attitudes of the ton firsthand."

"That sounds a bit ominous. Have you had bad experiences with the ton, Miss Austen?"

"Not I." She laughed, but Xander sensed some seriousness behind the laugh. "But this goes back to our discussion of bluestockings. In our society, if a lady flirts with a baronet or a handsome viscount with the hope of finding a husband, she must disguise her intelligence. As I mentioned earlier, acumen in the female is viewed as a liability. Women who openly choose to use their brains are considered dangerous to society. Consequently, most of the brilliant women of our time live their entire lives unmarried."

Xander recalled the lecture Nadine had given him about Jane Austen's accomplishments and how none of that would be possible if she were to get married.

"You are unmarried?" he said, knowing the answer.

"Alas, yes." She grinned. "Thus far, secure in the ranks of spinsterhood."

"Thus far?"

She paused, growing pensive. "One never knows the future, does one?"

"I don't know about that. But if I can get personal too...no plans of marrying?"

"None at present, much to my mother's chagrin." The half-smile returned to her face. "Throwing her daughters in the paths of rich bachelors has been a lifelong vocation for her."

"Well, marriage is not for everyone, I guess."

She placed a hand vacantly on the leather folder she'd closed when he came into the room. "But you mentioned you are recently married."

"Yes."

"How recent?"

If he was going to lie and make up stories, it would be better to stay close to what had *almost* happened. "Two years."

"Two years is not recent."

"Time has a way of flying by." He thought of how they'd spent the afternoon. "We're still on our honeymoon."

"How romantic! And who is watching your children?"

"We have no children."

"Really? Isn't it the fashion in America that after a bride and groom exchange the sacred vows of marriage, the pitter-patter of little feet will soon follow? And then, more little feet? And then, more little feet?"

Xander chuckled. "Are you from a large family, Miss Austen?"

"My mother bore eight children and was fortunate to survive her ordeals. My brother Edward's dear wife did not fare so well. She died in childbirth with their eleventh child."

Xander thought of Ken and Donna and their daughter. His friend was scared when he couldn't be with his wife during labor.

"Yes, well, we have none."

"Don't tell me you have something *against* children, Mr. Finley."

"Me? No, not at all. My wife and I haven't discussed it."

"Discussed it?" She arched an eyebrow at him. "America continues to amaze me, sir. Discussion scarcely enters into the production of children in England, so far as I know."

"Yes...well..."

"But I believe I've embarrassed you. I must apologize."

"Nothing to apologize for, Miss Austen."

Marriage. Children. Hell, he didn't want to get into this stuff. He and Nadine hadn't decided on a story that involved any of this. But Jane Austen's quick wit and questions were giving him no room to breathe.

"How about you, ma'am? Are you for or against children?"

"I'm quite fond of my nieces and nephews. At the same time, I'm not so fond of them when they gather in large groups." She sat back and then frowned thoughtfully. "The act of bearing children is said to be a great blessing. At least, men say so. But I have no illusions about how a large family can sap the life of all but the wealthiest women. It is this toll on the body and spirit that is a bit undesirable. A large family is a comfort, I'm sure, but children tend to reveal, and mercilessly so, the character of the parents. Don't you agree?"

She was leaving him in the dust with this conversation. Xander hoped that Nadine would wake up, find him missing, and decide to come downstairs looking for him. Nothing would make him happier than if she took over.

"I really can't say. I was an only child, and so was my wife. Neither of us has much experience in this area. And neither of us feels any pressure to produce sons or daughters right now. You know, the pitter-patter of little feet that you mentioned."

Her smile came easy. "May I ask how old your wife is, Mr. Finley?"

"Thirty-five."

"My age." Her eyes rounded. "Was she a widow before you two married?"

"No, a first marriage for both of us."

"Was your union arranged by family?"

"No."

"Was it a business arrangement?" she asked. "Her father had some manufactories, and it suited both of you men to join forces."

He chuckled. "Nothing like that."

"A history then? Had you two met when you were very young? Was your coming together a reunion, of sorts?"

"No, we didn't have a history."

The way Xander was bending the facts to satisfy Jane Austen's curiosity was becoming complicated. But he also understood what the author was doing. She'd met her old boyfriend Gordon this afternoon, and the old flame was threatening to become a blaze.

Xander had suggested that it was intrusive and wrong to ruin Austen's chance at romance, but he was beginning to see things differently now. Talking to her about how a woman of talent and intelligence was viewed in 1811, he was getting a better understanding. In so many words, having both a family and a career would be hell for a woman in this society.

"You were rich when you met. You're a handsome man. And just from our conversation, I'd say you are intelligent and charming." She leaned forward, her questioning eyes looking directly into his. "If I am being far too personal, please decline to answer...but why *her*? Why did you ask Mrs. Finley to be your wife?"

Xander's mind jumped in time to Las Vegas, then forward to Colorado, and then he thought of the woman he'd left in the bed upstairs. He was no longer interested in finding satisfying answers to the game of twenty questions Jane Austen was playing. He only wanted to say out loud what was in his heart, and let the woman apply it to her own life as she pleased.

"To me, Nadine was...and is...beautiful. She is smart, passionate, kind...*exceptional*, as you say. There is an insane chemistry between us. But there is so much more too."

He'd come back through time to find her. Nadine said he'd done the impossible. Xander believed his feelings for her were responsible for it.

"But why *her*?" he continued. "Why did I ask Nadine to be my wife two years ago? I guess it was partly because I met her at the right time in my life. Career and ambition weren't pushing me in another direction."

"Is that it?"

"Oh, no. There's so much more," Xander admitted. "With Nadine, I don't need to play games."

"*Play games*," she cut in. "Americans have such delightful expressions."

"We get along...like best friends. I feel what she feels. We bring out the best in each other. We're two halves of one solid entity. And don't take me wrong. We all have flaws. We all make mistakes. But I'd like to think our combined strengths compensate. I know she makes me a better man."

The emotions rising in his chest were suddenly overwhelming. Xander never had to put his feelings into words like this before. Not even when he'd asked her to marry him.

"When I met Nadine, everything in me said she was the one. I felt...I knew that I'd found the person I was destined to love. And I do love her."

Austen sat back, silent and thoughtful. Xander's words had been spoken from his heart. He saw her gaze flick to the doorway behind him, and she rose to her feet.

Xander stood up and turned to see Nadine in the doorway.

When Nadine arrived in the doorway, Jane Austen was saying, "Why *her?*"

She heard every word that followed.

It was true, all that he said about the ways that they connected. And no one had ever come close to loving her like Xander. For her part, she'd never felt the love and affection for anyone that she felt for him. There was no denying it. No fighting it. If such a thing as soul-mates existed, Xander was hers. And that was where the tragedy lay.

After they saw her in the doorway, Nadine crossed the room to them. Xander introduced her, and then Jane Austen excused herself and fled the room as if a pack of wild boars were after her.

Nadine was glad she went. The emotions she was feeling were tender and raw. She was in no mood for chatting with Austen right now, regardless of her lifelong obsession with the author. Her mission as a Scribe Guardian was the last thing on her mind.

There was so much that she needed to explain to Xander. There was so little he knew about all the ways that their relationship was doomed.

Before they went back to their room, they found the kitchen and awakened a young man who was asleep in a chair. They waited in silence while he served up two bowls of warm stew. Carrying the stew, a small loaf of bread, and a pitcher of wine on a pewter tray, they climbed the stairs.

While they ate, Xander summarized what he and Jane Austen had spoken about. He told her about Austen's perception of America. About her observations regarding women, marriage, and children in her society. He told Nadine the stories he'd made up about his profession and wealth and how long they'd been married.

It was obvious that he'd made a profound impression on the author. They'd spoken on quite a few topics. Nothing about Xander surprised Nadine anymore. He was an extraordinary man. She told him so.

After they were done eating, Xander put the tray outside their door with the other one. He made some offhand comment about feeding his new best friend.

"What?"

"Nothing. You really don't want to know."

The rain continued to pound on the window. Nadine looked out at the High Street, wishing they could go out and walk. Her thoughts were always better organized when she moved. A lamp in a window across the way shed a little light on the flooded roadway. But between the storm and the late hour, her only option was to pace the room.

She'd had an introduction to Austen, thanks to Xander, and she'd try to pursue it tomorrow. But the assignment wasn't at the forefront of her thoughts. It was the discussion she'd overheard in the Coffee Room that consumed her right now.

Xander broke into her reflections.

"After talking to her, I have a better understanding of what you were saying about the expectations these people have for women. And the obstacles faced by a woman who wants to be a writer."

"Obstacles is an understatement."

He raised both hands. "I know. You tried to explain it to me. I should have believed you. But I was still shellshocked."

He started pulling his sweater off.

"Keep it on, my love. In fact, keep all your clothes on. I have to concentrate, and I don't want to be distracted by you while we talk."

He smiled. Kicking his boots off, he stretched out on the bed, his hands behind his head. "I won't be a pain in the ass anymore, Nadine. Tell me what to do. What's next?"

"You're never a pain in the ass. I've never called you a pain in the ass. And I never will."

"I'm going to remind you of that five years from now. Or fifteen. Or twenty."

Nadine stopped pacing and faced him. "That's just it, Xander. What we need to talk about. No matter what we feel at this moment, we won't have five years from now. Or fifteen. Or twenty. We belong in two different time periods."

"You could've said that to me in Colorado, and I might have believed you. But look at me. At us. We made the impossible happen. I don't know how. But we did it. And I'm certain we can do it again."

She shook her head and started pacing again. How could she get through to him?

"You're a Scribe Guardian. I get it. I finally understand what you do. But now that I've jumped through time, maybe I can become one too. Where do I send my resume?"

"You *can't* become one. My job is one that you can't have. I don't *want* you to have it."

He sat up in bed. "I was just joking. I'm sorry. I know I'm not a reader or a scholar, by any stretch of the imagination. I didn't mean to say I'm anywhere near qualified to—"

"The one requisite qualification for this job is that you must be terminally ill."

Xander stared at her, and she gave the words time to sink in.

"Yes. Terminally ill. That's why I don't want you to talk about it or joke about it...and why I would never want you to be part of it."

His face creased in a frown as he tried to understand.

She had never intended to tell him, but now she felt better for it. Now he knew.

Suddenly, he was standing in front of her and pulling her into his arms.

It took a moment, but she felt herself melt into his embrace. It warmed her to feel herself wrapped in his strength, in what she knew was his love.

Two years ago, when he'd first asked her to marry him, Nadine wished she'd been brave enough to tell him. Even though he wouldn't have believed the time travel aspect of her job, she could have told him the truth about her life-ending illness. But she'd chickened out, knowing she'd walk away at the last minute. After all, they would never see each other again.

In Colorado, she'd also omitted that part of the truth. But feeling as he did and going through everything he'd gone through, it was right that he should know.

She had accepted her fate years ago. Back then, Nadine had no family, no one who loved her, no one who would miss her when she was gone. It was better that way. Those who loved and were loved suffered more. It wasn't the fear of death; it was the fear of losing everyone you were leaving behind.

And because of Xander, her life was already changing. Her fears were taking on a new shape.

Nadine didn't know how long they stood in the middle of the room, holding each other. Finally, she pulled away and looked into his eyes. They were red. His face was wet with tears for her.

He wiped them away. "Explain this to me. How does it work? What is it that you're fighting? How is it that you look so healthy? You don't show any sign of being sick."

"We'll be here a thousand and one nights if I'm going to explain everything to you."

"That's okay with me. I want to know."

"And you have every right to know," she told him, leading him to the bed. He sat down next to her, holding her hand.

"What is it? Cancer?"

She nodded.

"Don't tell me they haven't cured it by 2078."

"They've cured so many types of cancer, but not what I have," she told him. "Mine is a rare type of lymphoma that doesn't respond to treatments."

"When..." He paused and took a breath. "When were you diagnosed with it?"

"Officially? When I was twenty-two." Sitting next to Xander, feeling him wrestling with his emotions, caused hers to surface.

After the first days of knowing, Nadine never let herself cry or be depressed about her illness. How many times had she made herself believe that she was at peace with it? Everyone died. Her end would come too, eventually—depending on her performance on the job— but it *would* happen.

She pushed to her feet and went to the window, absently watching the droplets stream down the panes of glass.

"My symptoms were there since my days at the youth home where I was sent after my parents died." She looked over her shoulder at him. "Sorry about telling you that stuff about my family. I haven't had any family since my parents both died in a highway accident when I was twelve."

"What about your illness."

"As a ward of the state, I wasn't a priority in the system. No doctor ever looked too closely at what was wrong with me. My enlarged lymph glands were blamed on viruses, fevers, night sweats, infections. For years. And then, I was always dealing with my asthma. In my records, they had me tagged with a weak immune system. They never dug deeper to see what the real culprit was."

Because of her age and shaky health, Nadine was never adopted. She stayed in the system until she went away to college.

"It was right after I started my first job out of college that I got very sick. This time, I had to be hospitalized, which is rare in my time."

"What were your symptoms?"

"I'd lost thirty pounds in six weeks. Neuropathy, numbness in my feet, legs, and hands. It got so bad that I couldn't walk. And all the old symptoms were back too, except that this time no medication would have any effect on them. Every day, I got weaker and weaker."

She stared at her hands, remembering the anguish of those long days and nights, waiting. Not feeling well enough to even hope.

"After a bunch of tests, they finally sorted it out. It just confirmed what I already knew. What I had was terminal. They gave me a month to live...maybe. A state social worker talked to me about euthanasia."

Nadine didn't want to dwell on those days. She didn't want to remember what she'd gone through, emotionally and physically.

"You were twenty-two."

"That was the worst part. I was supposed to be starting my life, but they were telling me I was at the end of the line."

She crossed her arms, leaning her back against the wall. It was cold and damp.

"Then, a hospital administrator came in to talk to me. Told me there was a new trial that might help me. I jumped at it. I wasn't actually hopeful, but I had no other option. I remember thinking, at the very least, I could replace one of the animal subjects they used for medical research. A couple of days later, a woman wearing a government badge visited me. I still had no clue who she was, or what the trial was, or how it would improve my chances of survival."

"She was a doctor?"

"No. That was the strangest thing. All she did was talk about a position she was offering me. It had something to do with books and preserving manuscripts. Here I was, dying, and she was offering me a job. I was sure the whole thing was a big misunderstanding. But I always loved books and reading. My degree was in library science. That was my passion. So, I decided to hear her out. She didn't mention anything about time travel. If she had, I would have been as skeptical as you were when I first told you. She explained, though, that it was a position in a prototype program they were starting, and it could keep me alive."

She moved back to the bed and sat down next to Xander.

"A twenty-two-year-old, given a chance at life. Even though I had no clue how books were connected to cancer research, my answer was, *Yes, sign me up!*"

"What happened next?"

"I was admitted to a new hospital that same week. Later, I learned that it wasn't a real hospital. It was a facility run by a top-secret arm of the government. It was called the QCD...Quantum Commute Division. Things moved pretty fast from the moment I got there since I didn't have much time left."

"How was it that they cured you?"

"They never cured me. The concept was that my cancer would go into remission when I jumped in time. They'd found that cell development was arrested through molecular dispersal and regeneration. They started slowly at first, jumping me backward only a few minutes at a time...then forward again. For a month we did this every day. And then another month. I started getting stronger. We kept it up month after month. Tests and scans showed it was working."

"That's unbelievable. Were you the only one?"

"I thought so, but then I realized there were others. Quite a few, in fact. But we were all facing the same situation. Everyone else who was recruited into the program was terminal. In all divisions."

"What do you mean...divisions?"

"The Quantum Commuters are organized into specific companies.

The Scribe Guardians. The Bodyguards. The Assassins. The Engineers. And others."

"You said that all these people...these agents...have a terminal disease?"

"As it stands now, yes. We all do. It makes a certain amount of sense because of the inherent dangers of the job. And none of us have family. No parents or siblings or partners. No one searching for us, poking questions at headquarters while we're on assignment. Maybe they'll open up the recruitment to others someday. But right now, that's it. A terminal illness, no family, no attachments. And a certain level of education, testing scores...and the ability to develop physically. Quantum leaps are hard on the body. And once you arrive on a mission, it doesn't get any easier."

"Let me understand this. You're fine when you travel back in time?"

"Absolutely. I feel great. None of the symptoms move in time...except my asthma. But the cancer will come back when I return for any extended period to the year 2078. That's why I have—why all the agents have—a limited time to receive additional training before we make the jump into the next mission. Time marches on into the future, but we're trapped in the past. Saved by it."

Xander shook his head. It was a lot to absorb.

"And the importance of what we do is written into our contracts. There are consequences if we fail. I must complete every mission. If I don't, I lose my position in the QCD."

"You mean—"

"I mean, I no longer travel. The agreement when I signed on was clear. One strike and I'm out of the program." She shrugged. "And I die. But at least I had a chance to live."

Xander stared at her. She knew where his next questions would lead.

"Why don't you get out?" He took her hand. "Why not stay in the past?"

Nadine looked into his eyes. "That's what the Assassins are for, among other things."

"They'll send someone to kill you?"

"They'll try to take me back to the future. If they're not successful, their job is to kill me."

"That's crazy."

"Think of it from their perspective. We're not allowed to change the past, but once someone goes rogue, there's no way to control them. With my training, I could show up anywhere in history. If I wanted to, I could profit from my knowledge. The agency's protocol states that I have to be terminated."

He pulled her into his arms. "That's grim."

"That's what I signed up for. I'm employed by them until I fail. And then it's over. It's the deal I made to stay alive. I could have said no, but I didn't."

Nadine had a restless night. Xander had even more questions after she'd explained the basics of whom she worked for and what she did. His questions were a reminder of how vulnerable her life was. Also, how hopeless and futile their relationship was.

Afterward, she took comfort in knowing that at least they had now, tonight, and maybe tomorrow. They had each other until the time came when she figured out a way to send him back to his life in Colorado.

Grey morning light was pouring in through the window when she heard footsteps in the hall. Other travelers were staying in rooms nearby, but this person stopped outside their door. A moment later, a letter slid in across the threshold.

She pushed the covers back, crossed the room, and picked up the letter. Breaking the seal, she opened it. She immediately recognized the handwriting.

Nadine had seen the manuscript of *Lady Susan* at the Morgan Library in New York. It was the only complete draft of an Austen novel known to have survived.

The artifact showed the author's own lovely handwriting, as well as other quirks that any bibliophile could appreciate. For instance, the way Austen filled her pages with text from top to bottom suggested that she was economical in her use of paper. Her idiosyncratic use of punctuation—commas and dashes, especially—made her something of a modern stylist in her day. It had reminded Nadine of the way Emily Dickinson would punctuate her poems almost fifty years later.

Two great writers, separated by time and an ocean.

She read the letter once and then read it again. Jane Austen was apologizing:

...and if you have the time—as this lovely Kentish weather continues unabated—would you do me the honor of joining me for a chat and some tea. I have engaged a private dining room and would very much like to make reparations for my abrupt departure, last night. Would you be available at, say, eleven o'clock this morning?

I have arranged for a luncheon to be served there at noon as well, and if Mr. Finley could join us then, Captain Gordon and his friend Captain Carville will be dining with us. I'm quite certain they would enjoy meeting your husband.

The skies do not look promising for a morning saunter about the village, but I am determined to brave the elements and climb to the old stone church on the hill. I have been informed by no less of an authority than our amiable innkeeper's wife—that the ancient Ossuary contains "skulls by the Thousands." A fine reminder of our mortality, perhaps...

AFTER DASHING off a note to Jane Austen, accepting the invitation, Nadine wrote another to Deirdre and took them both downstairs. Finding the innkeeper, she asked him if he could have her note sent up to Austen and have a letter delivered to a friend in town as well. After meeting Xander last night, the man's attitude had changed completely. He agreed to see to her requests right away and sent one of his boys running.

Deirdre was truly their salvation in Hythe. The only person she could trust. In the note she'd written, Nadine asked her friend to lend them whatever clothing she saw fit for Xander so that he could attend a luncheon with several naval officers. Her excuse was that her husband's trunks had yet to arrive from London. She had every intention of returning what they borrowed. She also included a five-pound note in the letter, hoping that would be enough to cover the expense.

The private dining room where Nadine was to meet the author was located above the taproom. Outside the door, before she knocked, Nadine took a deep breath and ran a hand down the front of her outfit. The white silk dress, with its subtle dots and fashionable design, was one that she'd brought back from the future. She'd intended to wear it on dressier occasions, should the need arise, while the travel dress she left at Xander's house was for day-to-day wear.

Well, this meeting with Austen was as formal a situation as she was likely to attend, and this was the only dress that didn't cry out that she was wearing borrowed clothes. Better to be overdressed, she decided.

Her hair was another matter. Because of the rain and humidity, her tangle of ringlets had been difficult to comb out, but she'd managed to gather them at the nape of her neck in a reasonably tidy knot.

This morning, she and Xander had again gone over his exchange with the author last night. She didn't want to make a mistake with any of the facts and thereby plant a seed of doubt in Jane Austen's mind. She wanted to come across as engaging enough company to be a welcome addition to Jane's circle of acquaintances while the woman remained in this village.

A serving lad held the door for Nadine, and she went in. The room was small and well-used. It was furnished only with what was necessary for it to function. A scarred sideboard ran along one wall, and a table with six ancient chairs sat on a worn Turkish rug. The innkeeper had at least seen fit to cover the table with a linen cloth.

Jane Austen was standing by the window, watching her intently.

The two women had met last night, but Austen was thinner than Nadine remembered. Wearing the same traveling dress, the author today sported a floppy lace cap. A few brunette curls spilled out, framing her face.

The cordial tone of her invitation didn't quite match the cool reception Nadine was sensing. The silence between them stretched on for what felt like minutes.

Perhaps it was her nerves, though. The expression on the host's face was quiet. Not hostile, by any means, but for a moment Nadine worried that her reply had not been worded suitably. Relief washed through her when Austen finally smiled slightly and crossed the room to greet her.

"Mrs. Finley."

"How do you do, Miss Austen?" she managed to get out.

To think, how easily Xander had spoken with the author. But for Nadine, the word 'starstruck' applied. She'd met and dealt with many of the world's literary greats, but Jane Austen was something else entirely.

Her eyes were bright. Her gaze was direct. "Thank you for coming, Mrs. Finley. Please, sit down. May I pour you a cup of tea?"

"Thank you. That would be lovely."

Austen's voice was husky, as if she were coming down with a cold. The sequence from *Pride and Prejudice* ran through Nadine's mind. When Lizzie's sister Jane got sick from her drenching, the Bingleys urged her to stay until she recovered. Would the same thing happen here at Hythe? Austen couldn't stay at the coaching inn with no one looking after her. The logical answer would be for her to go to Churchill House. Damn it. Love would bloom while she was under the care of Captain Gordon and his family.

As the author poured out the tea, Nadine sat down at the table. Austen took the chair beside her.

"Again, my apologies for running out when you came to the Coffee Room last night. I found I was in need of fresh air."

Rain and midnight air explained the hoarseness, and Nadine wondered if she'd gone up to that church this morning, after all.

"I had a very interesting conversation with your husband."

"Yes, he mentioned it."

"You two are from America."

"We are."

"And you've recently arrived in Hythe."

"Yes, London first...and then here."

Panic clawed at the edges of Nadine's memory. Had Xander mentioned how long they'd been here? How long since they'd arrived in England? She couldn't remember.

"Since last night, I have been trying to place you. I don't recall that we've met before. Have we?"

"No, I don't believe so."

"If I may ask then, how did you recognize me?"

"Pardon me?"

"Mr. Finley mentioned that you recognized me and pointed me out to him. That's how my conversation with your husband began in the Coffee Room."

Shit. Shit. Shit. Nadine's mind raced, trying to come up with a plausible story.

At this moment in history, Austen was an unpublished daughter of a former clergyman, now deceased. She lived quietly with her mother and sister in a small English village. And it wouldn't be until October the thirteenth of this year that *Sense and Sensibility* was published...anonymously. After that, aside from her immediate family and the publisher, only a small circle of people would know Austen's identity. Most of the British public would know only that the popular novel had been written "by a Lady." And a few skeptical reviewers would foolishly assert that a novel this accomplished could only have been written by a man.

The seconds ticked by.

"Oh, no. He was mistaken in what he told you. I...I saw you. My husband and I were outside the inn as you stepped from the carriage. A friend of yours addressed you by name. A tall gentleman."

"Indeed. Captain Gordon." She nodded. "I mentioned in my note that he'll be joining us today."

"Yes. Yes. Captain Gordon," Nadine repeated, relieved that she'd dodged a bullet. "With the rain coming down so hard, we'd been drenched by the storm and were in a hurry to get inside. Mr. Finley asked me a question, but with the coachman and the grooms shouting, there was some confusion about what he asked and what I heard. I believe I mentioned your name. I apologize if it caused any impropriety."

Nadine took a sip of her tea, hoping the explanation was sufficient. The trouble was that she knew too much about the author. Her habits, inclinations, and quirks. Her careful observations of everything she saw and heard. Nadine knew without a doubt that she was in the presence of formidable intelligence.

"Believe me, no apology is necessary. I am certainly delighted that such an informal introduction came about. I very much enjoyed speaking with Mr. Finley."

Nadine put down her cup, relieved. "What did the two of you speak about?"

"Marriage and matrimony, among other things." She leaned forward confidentially. "You and I are the same age."

"Are we?" Nadine hoped she captured enough surprise in her tone.

"Your husband told me you've been married two years."

"Yes, we have."

"Why so late in life?"

The abruptness of the question caused Nadine to pause as she searched for an appropriate response.

"Please excuse my impertinence," Austen continued, misinterpreting the hesitation. "But I wondered if the same social mores apply in America as in England. Here, in most cases, a woman is pressured to marry when she comes of age...for stability or financial benefit. If, of course, a suitable match can be made. Was it *your* choice to wait so long or were there other circumstances that caused the delay?"

Nadine tried to choose her words carefully. Here she was, once again, in a conversation where parallels were being drawn. Jane Austen had met Xander, liked him, and appreciated what she must have seen as a progressive attitude regarding women and marriage. In her eyes, Nadine and Xander had forged a satisfying relationship, despite her 'advanced' age. And now Austen was in a similar situation where, at an age when women didn't generally marry for the first time, she was on the cusp of renewing her own romance with Captain Gordon.

"For me, it was a choice," Nadine admitted. "Before Mr. Finley, I'd never been married. I'd never been engaged. I'd felt no love for any man. I was financially secure enough that I could have lived the rest of my life simply and comfortably."

"I see. Were you opposed to marriage?"

"In theory, no. In practice, yes. I liked my freedom a great deal more."

"This would truly be considered a radical position here, I must say." She held Nadine's gaze. "And yet, you changed your mind."

"Mr. Finley and I found we had a mutual attraction."

Austen smiled. "That came across quite clearly while he and I were speaking."

"What we have is quite unique." Nadine couldn't even begin to explain why. "And it doesn't change my firm belief that if a woman has a choice, she must choose the direction in which she wants her life to go. Freedom to follow one's passion is not always possible when marriage is the only choice we can make."

"Quite so," Austen said quietly. "Let me ask you this—"

"Before you do, may I ask you a question?" Within her social circle, the author would become famous for leading the course of conversations. Nadine decided to turn the questions back on the woman.

"Of course."

"Are you married, Miss Austen?"

"No. I have never taken that walk down the aisle."

"Are *you* opposed to marriage? Have you never been in love?"

"For a well-educated woman of small fortune here in England, only two motives exist for marriage. I mentioned them before. Social and financial security. Love plays almost no role for such a woman, I'm afraid."

"But, love aside, were you willing to sacrifice both of those things for *your* freedom?"

"Yes, I suppose so. To be honest, while the thought of poverty has never appealed to me, the mercenary motive for marrying has never appealed to me, either."

That exact dilemma would come up often in her novels, Nadine thought.

"I quite understand. Such choices are difficult, though."

"They are, indeed."

"You know, Miss Austen, this conversation brings to mind the works of Frances Burney. Have you read her?"

"Of course! She is one of my favorite authors."

"Mine too," Nadine replied, fully aware of the authors who influenced Austen. "My other favorite writers are Samuel Richardson...and William Cowper when I'm in the mood for poetry. And I loved Charlotte Turner Smith's *Emmeline, The Orphan of the Castle.* Have you read it?"

"I loved that novel!" Her face lit up. "Mrs. Finley, we have very similar literary tastes."

"Something told me that you would be a person drawn to literature." Nadine leaned forward, speaking confidentially. "Have you yourself ever considered writing."

"For publication, you mean?" A wary look crossed Jane's face.

"Yes, I do. An intelligent woman with literary interests. Why not?"

"Perhaps things are different for women in America, but here in England, a female member of the gentility would be greatly discouraged from following such pursuits."

"But aside from Fanny Burney and Charlotte Smith, Mrs. Radcliffe and Maria Edgeworth and Charlotte Lennox have certainly had considerable success. And others are publishing anonymously, I'm sure."

"There is good reason for anonymity." Austen looked around the room, as if afraid the walls might have ears. "But, I must admit, I do have such aspirations."

"I thought so."

"Am I so very obvious?"

"Hardly. What kind of writing do you do?"

Jane kept her voice low. "I enjoy creating comedies of manners. I like to lose myself in detailed portrayals of characters and their relationships."

Nadine nodded. "I'm impressed and intrigued. No wonder you have chosen to avoid wedlock. Even in America, a married woman would have little opportunity to indulge in such pursuits. I'm sure it must take a great deal of time to nurture and create a literary work."

"It's true." She smiled. "I have no husband and no children, but my novels *are* my darling children. And my mind is always occupied, thinking of my characters. I can no more forget them than a mother can forget her infant in the cradle."

"Your *novels*? More than one?"

"Yes. I have completed the drafts of several."

"But none published?"

Austen was coy in her reply. "Not as yet."

Nadine was on cloud nine hearing her admit so much already.

"You said, *comedies of manners*. Does marriage play a role in your writing?"

Austen's eyes widened. "You are quite astute, Mrs. Finley."

"Simply following our discussion."

The author nodded. "In my first attempt at a novel, which I wrote many years ago, I have a character, Charlotte Lucas, who marries a despicable fool of a man. I make it clear that Charlotte feels no affection whatsoever for the absurd, preening clergyman, yet she marries him to ensure food on her table, clothes on her back, and a roof over her head. And though the protagonist scorns Charlotte for her choice, the reasons for marrying are quite valid, given the Lucas family's financial situation."

"What do you call the novel?"

"*First Impressions.*"

Nadine knew it, of course. She'd read the book a dozen times. *First*

Impressions would become *Pride and Prejudice* when it was published two years from now.

"Are there other marriages in *First Impressions?*"

"Indeed. Several." Austen clasped her hands, her face animated with humor. She was clearly delighted to be able to talk about her work. "The first marriage the reader encounters is that of Mr. and Mrs. Bennet, the parents of my heroine. Including Elizabeth, the protagonist, they have five daughters, the others being Jane, Lydia, Kitty, and Mary; none of whom will inherit the estate. The novel is essentially the story of how Elizabeth finds happiness with a wealthy gentleman, Mr. Darcy. Now, because Mr. Bennet treats the nagging Mrs. Bennet like the fool she most assuredly is, Elizabeth will only marry a man she respects. The journey to conjugal felicity and domestic comfort is one fraught with peril for her."

Nadine watched the author stand up and begin pacing as she spoke.

"And there are other marriages as well, in this novel. The one between her sister Lydia and a charming villain is driven by lust and results in failure. Elizabeth's sister Jane eventually marries a gentleman with whom she shares great similarities of character. Jane and her future husband never in the course of the novel have a serious quarrel, but they have a serious obstacle to overcome. Both are easily influenced by the opinions and machinations of others..."

Austen's voice was hoarse, but she continued to talk. Nadine sat, thrilled to hear the author analyze her own story. It was a novel that Jane had drafted when she was only twenty. If the adage 'write what you know' applied to her, then Jane Austen *should* have had one of the happiest marriages in the history of matrimony prior to writing about it.

But Austen penned this story long before she arrived in Hythe and renewed her acquaintance with Captain Gordon. Regardless of how the hypothetical future played out, she'd already created a masterpiece of romantic love. What a loss it would be if she never pursued her passion and never had *any* of her works published.

"This story fascinates me," Nadine told her, encouraging her to continue. "But why the title, *First Impressions?*"

"A wonderful question. Our first impressions often form our permanent judgments, do they not? This is so, whether we consider our first meeting with people, or our first view of a place, or even the first lines of a book."

"That's very true."

"In my story, first impressions create havoc. When Elizabeth first encounters Darcy, he speaks and behaves in a rude and arrogant manner. She immediately develops an erroneous opinion of the man because she does not know the hidden motivation for his behavior. Ironically, Elizabeth's cool assessment of Mr. Darcy stems largely from her own pride; she has tremendous confidence in her quick wit and keen sense of discernment. For his part, Darcy's perception of the Bennet family creates a misunderstanding of the value of Elizabeth and her older sister. The rest of the story consists of the correction of those misreadings. Each must overcome the pride and prejudice that stand in the way of happiness."

"If I understand you, your novel is no blanket endorsement of marriage. The reader may end up with two happy marriages, but the story offers plenty of unhappy ones."

"Yes, you understand me perfectly."

Nadine shook her head admiringly. "What you have described to me is a perfect novel. One that will be timeless and universal in its appeal. I am certain your work *will* speak to readers across the centuries. It will become the supreme model for the romantic novel."

Jane turned to her, smiling. "Your praise is quite humbling. I thank you. But timeless? Centuries?" She shook her head. "The reality is that I am a woman. And society dictates that we are not to pursue fame or...heaven forbid, a literary career."

"Despite the success of Burney and others."

"Despite that. I am quite certain those women...and their families...pay a high price for their success."

Nadine didn't have weeks or days or even hours to convince her. Gordon was due to arrive momentarily. She was sure that this luncheon would be the event where the relationship between Austen and Gordon would shift gears. What started as a chance meeting in the rain yesterday would now spin out of her control.

It was now or never. She looked the author in the eye, holding her gaze.

"Trust me, Miss Austen. Your words, *It is a truth universally acknowledged, that a single man in possession of a good fortune must be in want of a wife* will become one the most cherished sentences in fiction for as long as people read."

Jane Austen's eyes grew wide as the color drained from her face. Before she could gather herself to respond, however, there was a knock at the door.

Captain Gordon and his friend had arrived.

CAPTAIN GORDON STRODE into the dining room with his friend, Captain Carville, who'd traveled in the carriage with Jane the day before. There was no sign of Xander, as yet.

Nadine knew she'd shocked the author with what she said. As introductions were made, Austen's gaze kept returning to her.

No stranger could have seen the first sentence of her unpublished novel, never mind have recited it back to her. She'd penned those words almost fifteen years earlier.

From about the age of twenty to twenty-five, Jane had worked diligently at her writing. Working with youthful vigor amid quiet goings on of rural Hampshire, she'd filled these years with tremendous productivity. The family was still living in Steventon, the farm village where she'd been born. The Austens knew of her efforts, but no one else did. Later, one close friend of the family would write that he "never suspected her of being an authoress."

Nadine knew that Jane had written at least three novels during this period: *First Impressions*—which would later become *Pride and Prejudice*—*Sense and Sensibility,* and *Northanger Abbey*.

When *Pride and Prejudice* was finished and shared within the immediate family, Jane's father was so impressed with the story that he made an effort to get it published. In November of 1797, he wrote to Thomas Cadell, a well-known London publisher. Without ever seeing even one line of the novel, he rejected the book with a five-word response: "declined by Return of Post." As a result, the brilliance of *Pride and Prejudice* would remain unknown to the public until sixteen years later.

Here in Hythe, Jane Austen knew there was no way Nadine could have seen the opening of that novel. Only members of her immediate family were even aware of its existence.

The luncheon guests were all still standing by the table when Xander arrived and was introduced to the other men.

Nadine could not take her eyes off him. The man was transformed. He was the very image of the Regency-era gentleman.

How Deirdre had possibly come up with these clothes, Nadine couldn't imagine. Xander was wearing a beautifully fitted hunter green, double-breasted tailcoat, a black waistcoat, faun-colored pants, and a white cravat. She had also somehow produced high, black Hessian boots.

And somehow in the last hour, Xander had managed to shave his beard, leaving only his sideburns. In a word, he looked gorgeous.

Catching Nadine staring at him, he smiled and winked at her.

As the meal was brought in, Captain Gordon and Jane sat on one side of the table. On the other side, Nadine was flanked by Xander and Captain Carville.

A question was asked if the Finleys, being Americans, had any connection to an Admiral James Finley of Portsmouth. Nadine was quick to deny any relation; she knew it was too late to use that association to their advantage.

The conversation flowed easily after that, and once again, she was impressed with how Xander was capable of handling any situation. Using the justification of where he was from, he plied Gordon with just enough questions to keep the captain talking, and his tone demonstrated confidence but not arrogance.

"I served with Admiral Nelson at Trafalgar in '05, bless the man," Gordon answered in response to a question about his service record. "I have been around the Cape of Good Hope to India and back. I have crossed the Atlantic four times, twice sailing to our islands in the West Indies."

Xander's general unfamiliarity with naval matters kept the conversation going with both Gordon and Carville, who had served with his friend since they were little more than boys. They talked of everything from the manner of life on board, daily routines, food, and far-off destinations. And whenever the others asked Xander questions, he entertained the room with his modified anecdotes of what he did to make his fortune, and what life in America was like.

Nadine forced herself to watch Captain Gordon carefully. Because of his connection to Jane, this was a man who had the power to reshape the future of the novel and literary history as a whole. She wanted to dislike him, wanted to find him haughty and belligerent. She looked to find some flaw in him that she could exploit. She had made this quantum leap with the preconceived notion that he was unworthy of this unique woman. He *had* to be.

Unfortunately, what she found in Gordon was that he was accomplished and amiable, with a quick wit and an understated sense of humor. Despite his responses to Xander, he remained attentive to Jane. He was eager to engage with anything she said. And once they started talking about books, it became evident that he was well-read, though his taste ran principally to poetry.

Nadine noticed that his gaze constantly returned to Jane as he spoke. There was affection in the way he looked at her. Clearly, he was happy to have found her again.

Lines from *Persuasion* played in her mind: *There could have been no two hearts so open, no tastes so similar, no feelings so in unison, no countenances so beloved. Now they were as strangers; nay, worse than strangers, for they could never become acquainted. It was a perpetual estrangement.*

But the ending of the passage didn't match this situation. Jane didn't behave with him as if they were strangers. She laughed at his lighthearted quips, argued happily with him, and leaned toward him as she spoke. There was definitely no personal estrangement between them. No hint of it.

Captain Gordon's friend was a soft-spoken man, and Nadine learned soon enough that he was quite knowledgeable about the history of the couple seated across from them.

"It was the summer of 1801 when they first met," Carville told her quietly as the conversation between the others continued. "Having no parent living, my friend here found a home for part of the year at Sidmouth. He was, as he is now, a remarkably fine man, with the same intelligence and spirit that you see today. He always spoke of Miss Austen in the most reverential terms, an extremely pretty young woman with qualities of gentleness, modesty, taste, and feeling like no one he'd ever known."

There was so much of their early romance that was never recorded, Nadine thought.

"Were you in Sidmouth then, Captain?" she asked.

He shook his head. "No, my duties confined me to Plymouth at the time, ma'am. My knowledge of her comes from Gordon himself."

"His feelings for her sound sincere."

"They were that, indeed. Hers too, I believe. Half the attraction on either side might have been enough," Carville explained. "Once they were acquainted, they fell rapidly and deeply in love. I couldn't say which one of them held the other in higher esteem, or which one was the happiest. Before the summer was gone, however, she had received his declarations of love and returned them."

"But they did not wed. What happened?"

"Her family immediately spoke against the match. Now, I don't know if it was the father, or mother, or sister, or brothers. All I know is that the family withheld their consent. My friend was met with great coldness, great silence. Miss Austen's family made it clear that they believed the match to be a degrading alliance."

Carville waited, as there was a pause in the others' conversation. A moment later, Xander was entertaining Gordon and Jane with a story of his own about the wild beasts of America.

"But why?" she asked. "They appear well matched."

"The family felt that Miss Austen should not involve herself in an engagement with a man who had nothing but himself to recommend him. At the time, Gordon was a young officer with little hope of affluence."

And Austen had by then done a great deal of writing, Nadine thought. Not that the family ever imagined the success she would attain.

"My friend had no fortune and no family of note," Carville continued. "He had been lucky in his profession, but he had saved nothing. Still, he was confident that he would soon be rich. Full of life, he knew that he should soon have a command of his own, and fortune would follow. He had always been blessed; he knew he would be still."

Jane laughed at something Captain Gordon said, and Nadine

watched their eyes lock. For a few seconds there was no one else in the room but the two of them. Carville noticed it too.

"Do you see? Nothing has changed."

Nadine had to agree. And that didn't make her situation any easier. "What happened after the family made their feelings known?"

"Gentle and kind as she was, she didn't want to stand against them. She was persuaded to believe the engagement was a wrong thing. Indiscreet, improper, hardly capable of success, and not deserving it. So, she put an end to it."

"That must have been hard on him."

"It was more than that. The man was gutted. Entirely. He made arrangements with the Admiralty and shipped out immediately. I don't know how the break affected her."

Nadine knew. Once again, words from *Persuasion* came back to her.

A few months had seen the beginning and the end of their acquaintance; but not with a few months ended her share of suffering from it. Her attachment and regrets, for a long time, clouded every enjoyment of youth, and an early loss of bloom and spirits had been their lasting effect.

Nadine now understood how much of that novel would be based on Jane Austen's life, on her own thwarted love affair with Captain Gordon. And at the end of that story, the heroine reunites with the hero and marries.

Damn it.

At that moment, two servants came into the room, and Nadine overheard Captain Gordon speaking to Jane.

"My sister and Sir Thomas asked me to invite you to dine with us tonight, Miss Austen. Would you do us the honor?"

Jane's gaze darted toward Nadine and then Xander.

Gordon immediately turned to them. "And I know Lady Deedes would be delighted to make the acquaintance of Mr. and Mrs. Finley as well. Would you be able to join us?"

This was exactly what Nadine had hoped for. She wanted to be present any time these two were in each other's company. She didn't have the opportunity today at lunch, but perhaps at Churchill House she could steer Gordon into revealing his opinions about family and travel…and about female authors.

It was a risk, but she'd like Jane to hear his opinions on having a wife who would be as much occupied in her mind with the characters in her novel as with her husband and her requisite domestic duties. She was knowledgeable enough about Austen's life and preferences. Now, she had to expose every prejudice the man might have about women. She only hoped he was not so different from other men of this era.

Even as she thought this, her eyes were drawn to Xander. She thought of their own renewed romance. Having him in her life was a precious gift, regardless of how much time they had left or what was to happen to them. They were living for today. For now. They were seizing an opportunity life had given them.

Nadine looked at Jane and Gordon.

Her attachment and regrets had, for a long time, clouded every enjoyment of youth...

Their heads were tilted toward the other. They were speaking softly, their faces reflecting hope for the future.

Across the table, Jane Austen was young again, sitting in the company of her own captain.

"Regretfully," Nadine announced, breaking into their moment, "we must decline, Captain. But thank you."

She couldn't...she *wouldn't* rob Jane of this opportunity to be happy.

𝕏 33 𝕏

XANDER WAITED until he and Nadine were back in their room before voicing his surprise.

"I thought it was your job to keep those two from getting together. You're giving them exactly what they don't need...time alone."

Nadine walked away from him to the window and stared out at the rain. It hadn't eased up at all. She pressed her fingers against the panes of glass.

"Why did you refuse Gordon's invitation?" he pressed.

"It won't make any difference if we go to Churchill House for dinner."

"Of course, it will. The more people in their company, the less romantic they can get."

His conversation with Nadine last night had been a revelation. How he felt about Austen and Gordon getting together—and about interfering with their romance—had flipped one hundred-eighty degrees. Nadine's life depended on completing the assignment, and Xander was ready to do whatever had to be done.

"They'll barely get a chance to look at each other if we're up there," he said. "I'm ready. I can be a one-man romance demolition team. I've got a million stupid questions I can ask about the navy and Gordon's travels."

Nadine was tracing a droplet of rain down the length of the glass.

At some point during the luncheon, Xander had seen the change in her. It happened when she was talking to Gordon's navy friend. Maybe it was something that Carville said. Or maybe it was a part of the conversation between Austen and Gordon that Xander had missed. Whatever it was, Nadine had become quiet. He didn't realize she was having a change of heart, though. And right now, she was lost in her own world as she stared at the wet street outside.

"Nadine. Don't leave me out. Please talk to me."

She turned and faced him. "The two of us going up there isn't right."

"I say it *is*! Your life depends on it." He motioned to the door. "I can still go after Gordon. I'll use some excuse and get us invited again. If that's bad manners, they'll just blame it on us being ignorant Americans. But I'm sure they'll have us."

Nadine shook her head, and Xander watched her cross the room to him. Her shoulders sagged, and her face was drawn. He could see she was on the verge of falling apart. He opened his arms, and she slipped into his embrace.

"What's wrong?"

She pressed her face against his chest. "Did you see her? And him? The way they were looking at each other? She glowed when she was talking to him. And he was hanging on her every word. The whispers that no one else could hear. The private smiles. They were in their own little world. Knowing what I know of her life, how she never found her 'Mr. Right', watching them was romantic and heartbreaking at the same time."

"I may have been preoccupied. I was trying to remember the year the first zoo in New York City opened. Do you know that, by the way?"

She lifted her chin to look into his face. "A menagerie was assembled in 1864. It was the first public zoo to open in New York."

"Damn it. I wasn't even close. Fifty-three years off. Well, I gave them a peek into the future." He caressed her back. "Good thing none of those three have been to New York City."

"Right now, most of Manhattan, beyond the southernmost tip, is little more than a handful of farm villages scattered over..." Her eyes narrowed. "Are you trying to distract me?"

"I'm trying to get you to do your job."

"I can't do it, Xander. I won't be a home wrecker."

The anguish in her voice was heartrending.

"For you to be a home wrecker, by definition they'd have to have a home. Or at least a relationship. They're not at that stage. Nowhere near it. They're still at the point of, 'Allow me to send my sister to ask your brother to check with your father if we can take a walk in the park two weeks from today.'"

"It's not like that." She backed away a step. "These two were ready to commit to each other ten years ago. Her family got in the way and shut it down. They're not strangers. They were in love with each other. They're meant for each other."

"Who says?"

"I do," she argued. "I saw it with my own eyes in that dining room. On top of that, I've read *Persuasion* five times. That novel is *their* story, Xander, and it ends with them together. Happily ever after. That's the way she wants it to happen."

"What you saw were two people who had a past. Like an old girl-friend who runs into an old boyfriend at a high school reunion."

She shook her head and started to say something, but he cut her off. He wasn't willing to give up. One of them had to fight, to remember that her life depended on it. This was the wrong time to be selfless.

"You misread what was going on in there. Today was like when a person sees that old friend and wonders how many surgeries went into keeping that face looking young. Or...was that old guy by the bar my classmate or my math teacher?" He was relieved to see a smile touch her lips. "Seriously, have you never gone to a reunion?"

"No."

"Why not?"

"I've been time traveling since I was twenty-two."

"Okay." He shrugged and reached out, taking her hands and drawing her back into his encircling arms. "But this lunch meeting wasn't about finding a lost soulmate. I'm pretty sure she was thinking, this guy's not married, he doesn't have a dozen kids, and he's still pretty good-looking. Maybe I'll check him out."

She scowled at him. "You're making fun of something serious."

"Who's being the romantic now?"

"Don't throw my own words back to me."

He expelled a long breath. "You're looking at their relationship and thinking of ours."

"You were doing the same thing yesterday."

"That's true. But what do I know? I come from 2022. Plus, you said in no uncertain terms that they're not us," Xander said. "And you were right, Nadine. They're *not* us."

"They still have a right to be happy."

"Happy?" he repeated. "Who says marrying an old boyfriend and becoming a navy wife will make her happy when she really wants to become a great and important writer? This is the one and only Jane Austen we're talking about. Tell me again how great she is."

She shook her head.

"Tell me, Nadine. Remind me how *important* she is."

"She's one of the greatest writers in English literature. Her books are read by people all over the world. And almost every year from the mid-twentieth century on, media adaptations of her stories are produced. You know this."

"My point exactly. Even I know it." He leaned down and looked into her eyes. "Why not let their history stay the way it was."

"But that's why I'm here. History has already been rewritten. And maybe there's a reason for it all. Maybe she's meant to experience her own romance and marry and—"

"Don't go there," he interrupted. "Outside of your group of quantum commuters, people live once. For good or bad, there's no 'redo' button. Right now, she's approaching a fork in the road. From what you say, she *already* made the choice to go with her family's wishes—and her own goals as a writer—rather than fight for this guy. That doesn't sound like love to me. Now, by pushing them into candlelight dinners at a country estate, you're not allowing that choice to stand. She decided what she wanted to do with her life a long time ago. She has a different destiny calling her now."

And you get to live, Xander finished silently.

Nadine looked up at the ceiling and let out a frustrated groan. "I agree with everything you say. We don't know if Captain Gordon will make a good husband. And we *do* know that if she marries him, she won't become one of the literary giants of the English language. I do want her to be the great writer that the world knows, but I just..."

Her voice trailed off, and she sat on the edge of the bed. Leaning forward, her elbows on her knees.

"I've never been faced with a dilemma like this before."

Xander wanted to help. More importantly, he wanted her to live.

He sat beside her. "As it stands, Austen has no clue about the phenomenon she will become, right? But she has dreams, doesn't she? Dreams that will never come about if she marries this guy?"

"Yes. But I don't know how to go about letting her know what she'll be giving up."

"Maybe by starting slow. Give her some subtle hints."

"I tried it this morning. And I wasn't so subtle. Before you and Gordon arrived, I quoted the first lines of *Pride and Prejudice* back to her. An unpublished work right now. She looked at me like I'd broken into her family's vault and stolen the manuscript."

"Maybe you should tell her who and what you are."

"That doesn't work, either." She stood up, obviously frustrated. "Did *you* believe anything I told you back in Colorado? Be honest now. Did you believe a word I said to you? Did you give it even a second thought?"

He hadn't. He didn't believe anything she said to him.

Xander's thoughts turned to the moment when he'd walked into the guest bedroom at his house. He was looking for her and trying to understand where she could have gone. Something had shifted in his thinking when she simply disappeared...again. And then he found the book she'd borrowed the night before on the bedside table.

"I'm not a magician," she continued. "I can't do some trick that will make her believe I come from the future. Whatever I say, she'll think I'm insane. There's nothing. Absolutely nothing that—"

"Wait. There might be something."

He got up and reached for her cloak and his greatcoat.

"Are we going somewhere?"

"To Deirdre's house."

"What for?"

"When I arrived—"

"Yesterday."

"Yeah. Did you look in the coffin? Was there anything in there?"

"No, I didn't." She put on the cloak and grabbed her bag. The two of them went out the door. "What are we looking for? What did you bring back with you?"

"When you disappeared from that mountain top—"

"Yesterday."

He shook his head. So much had happened since yesterday. They went down the stairs.

"Back at my house, I went looking for anything you might have left behind." They made their way toward the door. "Do you remember the volume you'd taken from the bookcase?"

As they stepped out into the inn's courtyard, he put his top hat on and helped her with her hood. The rain was beginning to ease up a little, and no one was close enough to hear their conversation. Grooms stood under the eaves of the stables, and one nodded to them.

"Of course. It was a rare 1909 edition of *Persuasion*, with the beautiful color illustrations by C.E. Brock. I left it on the little table next to the bed."

He shot a quick look at her, happy that she'd noticed the pictures. "Well, I picked that book up and thumbed through it. That was when I realized there had to be something to what you'd been telling me."

"What do you mean? I didn't leave anything in the book."

"Most of the pages were blank."

"I didn't read past the first chapter that night." She paused. "Blank? What do you mean, blank?"

"I mean blank. I might not be a big reader, but I loved the illustrations in that book. Several times, I've gone through it and looked at all of them. The pictures were gone. Every single one. So was the text. Well, most of it."

The High Street was still almost empty, and the mud-colored runoff from the hills flowed fast and deep in the road and up onto the walkways. They crossed where it looked passable and turned their steps down the hill toward the canal. It was even more slippery on the cobbled slope, and he took her hand.

"It surprised me," he continued. "I thumbed through the whole volume. On some of the pages, the ink had faded. On most of them, the words were gone entirely. It was the strangest thing. It was like someone had wiped words right off the pages."

"I know what happened," she said. "By the time you saw that volume, Jane and Captain Gordon's paths were about to intersect. Perhaps Captain Carville said something to her in the coach. Whatever it was, history was already being rewritten."

When they reached the bridge over the canal, water was high on the banks, but no higher than yesterday. They hurried across.

"Did you bring the book with you? Is that what's in the coffin?"

The slumping shoulders and teary, defeated look on her face were gone. Her eyes were lit with excitement. Xander felt a surge of hope; she was once again the energized Nadine that he knew and loved.

"I don't know. I hope so. The last thing I remember is that it was under my arm when I went into my garage."

"If that book did travel through time—and if it didn't get destroyed by the rain—I might be able to use it. After quoting *Pride and Prejudice*, I know Jane will want to talk to me."

"That's what I was thinking."

"I wonder how much of the novel text is left," she mused. "Considering today's lunch."

"When I found it in my house, the copy still had gilt lettering on the spine with 'Persuasion' and 'Jane Austen'. The pages with the title and the copyright print were there too."

"It still had her name on the title page?"

He nodded. "And her bio was in the back when I paged through it. Maybe that's still there. But even if it's gone, maybe just showing her the book...wouldn't that be enough?"

"It's the best chance we have right now."

Xander knew he was being hopeful, but this was better than sitting back and waiting for an invitation to Austen and Gordon's wedding.

As they made their way past shops and houses in the lower part of the town, it suddenly occurred to him that Nadine had said 'we'. The best chance *we* have.

They were a team.

She asked him a few more questions, but she was mostly focused on her thoughts until they turned up the lane toward Deirdre's cottage.

Xander smelled the salty tang in the air here. With the constant rain and clouds, he hadn't fully realized that the sea was so close. It was slow going through the deepening mud of the lane, and the odors of farm living again filled his senses.

Distant church bells tolled the hour, telling him it was late afternoon, though a person never would have known it from the gray murk. The rain had eased to little more than a cold drizzle. They slogged up the lane until they reached Deirdre's garden gate.

Smoke was rising from the chimney, but when Nadine knocked, no one answered.

"Not here," she said, peering in the window. "Let's look at the coffin."

It was just as they'd left it, covered by the goat shed. Xander pulled the wet canvas off, and Nadine lifted the lid. They both stared into the empty box.

"Nothing," she murmured, her disappointment evident in her voice.

The rain started falling harder again.

"I'm sorry. I thought it might have dropped in there when I reached down to catch myself."

She shook her head. "It's not your fault. We'll have to think of something else."

Xander pulled the lid back onto the coffin, and together they replaced the tarp. They were just finishing when a familiar voice called out to them from the lane.

Deirdre and her son Andrew were coming through the gate into the garden.

"What are you two doing out here?" she asked. "Let's get inside where we can warm ourselves."

Once inside, they shed their outer clothing, and Deirdre hung the greatcoat and the cloaks on pegs by the door. Andrew took Xander's top hat and placed it upside down on the floor.

Water ran off the coats onto a shiny piece of cloth Deirdre spread on the floor. She noticed Xander studying it.

"Don't tell me they have no oilcloth in America."

He shot a quick look at Nadine, who gave him a nod.

"Of course. I was just thinking how much use you must get out of...uh, oilcloth here."

Deirdre ignored his response. She'd already moved past that. She ogled him instead.

"You're looking quite fine today, Mr. Finley. Is it the clothes that I lent you or something else?"

Xander felt the color rising into his face. Subtlety was clearly not a strong point in the woman.

"Do you not agree, Mrs. Finley?"

"I do. It's your clothes...and he shaved as well," Nadine remarked with a glint in her eye.

"No sense hiding that handsome face, I'd say. The Good Book says something about not hiding your lamp under a bushel, don't it?"

"It certainly does." Nadine was gazing at him admiringly as well. He didn't mind that so much.

"I warrant you, miss, there's no finer-looking gentleman in all of England than your husband."

"All right, I'm starting to feel like a prize goat at the fair. Next, you'll be looking to tie a ribbon in my hair."

The women both laughed, and Deirdre herded them over to the fire, where she added a piece of dry driftwood. Blue-green flames flared, sending sparks up the flue.

Andrew came and stood beside Nadine. He was holding some wooden blocks.

"So then, what were you two doing in my garden just now?"

"Nothing, really..." he started, finding it difficult to explain a book published nearly a hundred years into the future that they'd hoped would be in a coffin in the woman's yard.

"A gift," Nadine said instead. "A gift Mr. Finley bought in London for me, but we must have misplaced it."

Deirdre reached up onto a shelf by the fireplace. "Was this the gift? I meant to bring it to you when I brought Mr. Finley's clothes up to the inn."

In her hand, she held out the book.

❧ 34 ❧

HOLDING the altered edition of *Persuasion* to her chest, Nadine stood before the window of their room at the Swan, watching for the author's return.

"Are you going to show it to her?"

She released a deep breath. "I don't know yet. I'll decide when I see her."

At Deirdre's house, they'd stayed for an early supper. There was no point in hurrying back since Jane would be dining up at Churchill House.

During the meal, Andrew quickly became enamored of Xander, dragging him afterward to the floor where they played the entire time Nadine and Deirdre spoke. He was as good at entertaining children as he was at charming adults.

The young mother had mostly given up trying to understand all the strange things about Nadine and Xander. Being too busy with her child and work and responsibilities, she had no time to page through the book or find anything unusual about it. What worried her most was their getting arrested and questioned by the authorities.

"You appeared out of nowhere. Both of you sprouted out of the ground or washed ashore, should I say. And your answers make no sense, miss. Believe me, the magistrate will hardly be as soft on you as I am. They'll hang you both for spies, I've no doubt." She frowned and motioned toward the window. "And here, you've added thievery to everything else. Last week, Mr. Clarke the coffin maker was crying bloody murder that one of his boxes was stolen. And then I find the thing out in my garden, covered by an old sail of my husband's. Do you want *me* to hang with you now?"

Nadine reached across the table and took Deirdre's hand. "Can I give you money to pay him?"

Deirdre snorted. "And what do I tell him...that my grandsire's ghost wanted a place in the garden, so I dragged the box down here?"

"He doesn't know the coffin is in your garden."

"But he will the moment I hand him the money."

She was right. This was the last thing Nadine wanted, to get her friend in trouble. She was already taking tremendous risks.

"Maybe there's some random boy I can give the money to. He can pass it on. Would that work?"

"Are you serious? I warrant you, every lad in this village would keep your money. And if he was found out, he'd point his dirty finger right at you. And then they'd be at my door." She shook her head. "This is Hythe, miss, not London. Here, everyone knows who belongs to who and what tomfoolery they're up to."

She was right. Nadine had raised Elizabeth Hole's suspicions without even trying. Outsiders stood out, and they were watched.

Elizabeth Hole. She looked over at Xander. Maybe the next time they saw the older woman—and no doubt they *would* see her—Xander could say something about having heard of the coffin maker's loss and give *her* some coins to pass on. That would only endear him to Mrs. Hole even more. But there was still the problem of the coffin sitting in Deirdre's yard. It was hidden, but it was still there.

"For now, can we leave the box behind the shed?"

"What box? I've seen nothing of any box by the shed," Deirdre replied, giving her a wink.

By the time they made their way back to the Swan a couple of hours later, the rain had finally stopped. A few stars were even beginning to poke through scattered breaks in the clouds.

As they passed through the arched entry to the inn's courtyard, Xander nodded across the open space. Grooms had pushed the coach out from beneath the stable overhang. By torchlight, they were drying the vehicle. Two men were applying grease to the wheel hubs under the watchful eye of the coach driver.

Nadine felt the clock in her head ticking even louder.

Inside, they were immediately approached by the innkeeper. He told them that a crew of men had been out working the roads all afternoon, and that word had come back that they would be passable by tomorrow morning. The coach, he said, would embark for London at noon, if they cared to be on it.

Nadine wondered about the chance of Jane Austen leaving on that coach.

And now, she and Xander were back in their room, watching and waiting.

He came and stood next to her. He took the book from her and began to page through it.

"No sign of her yet?" he said with a nod at the street below.

Nadine shook her head. The few lamps she could see up and down the High Street gleamed on the wet cobbles. The flooding water was largely gone, and there were a few people out and about.

"More of the print is missing. There's definitely less now than what I saw in Colorado." Xander paused, riffling to the end. "Huh. Her bio is still intact."

"A dry and academic biography. A lot of people were reading her in 1909, but the fame that followed after that would be unprecedented. That edition was published before the world *really* came to appreciate Austen."

"Still, even as it's written, the bio provides proof of what's yet to come for her novels...and for Austen herself."

Nadine agreed, but before she could reply, they both spotted the author and the captain coming down the walkway toward the Swan. Walking arm in arm with him, Jane was smiling and chatting away. A bit more reserved, he also appeared to be in good spirits. He was certainly attentive.

"I'd say dinner at Churchill House was a success," Xander noted.

"Will you wait for me here?" Nadine took the book from him and ran for the door.

"Where are you going?"

"I want to talk to her before she goes back to her room."

"Neutral ground. Good strategy," he called after her. "Remember, they're not us."

Nadine looked over her shoulder at him and smiled. "I know. And it's her life. I can't define happiness for her."

Hurrying down the hallway, she stopped at the top of the staircase. Below her, Austen was quietly saying goodbye to Gordon. The moment he went out the door, Nadine descended halfway down to the landing as Jane started up the stairs.

"Mrs. Finley." She looked up in surprise.

"Miss Austen. I hope you had a pleasant dinner at Churchill House."

"Very pleasant." She glanced over her shoulder and lowered her voice. "I must admit, however, that I wished several times in the course of the evening that you and your husband had dined with us. I know your presence would have helped to diminish some of the awkwardness."

"Oh?" Nadine could think of no better answer and settled for a question. "What awkwardness was that?"

"Captain Gordon's sister." She reached out and put a hand on Nadine's. "I know it's late, but would you have a few moments to chat?"

"Yes, absolutely."

"Will you give me enough time to shed my cloak? I can meet you—"

"I'll see if that private dining room is available."

"Perfect."

As Jane went up, Nadine descended to speak with the innkeeper, who was still in the taproom. He immediately dispatched a serving lad to prepare the room for them, and she hoped her discussion with the author would go as smoothly.

Nadine waited for her by the door to the dining room, and by the time they both entered, a cozy fire had been lit and two chairs had been arranged for them by the hearth.

Jane started in as soon as they sat down and were left to themselves.

"It was probably the wine," she said with a wry smile. "But for a moment I forgot myself on the stairs. Lady Deedes and Sir Thomas are the first family of this village. Even whispers conveyed in public will no doubt reach their ears."

"And do you care about their good opinion of you?"

"A little late for that, I suppose," she scoffed. "Her ladyship had an unalterably low opinion of me long before I crossed her threshold."

"This is the 'awkwardness' you referred to?"

"I was being generous. I should have said 'unpleasantness'."

Holding the book tightly on her lap, Nadine didn't know if this information was good news or not. It would be so much easier if Austen decided to leave Hythe of her own accord tomorrow. "And does Captain Gordon share his sister's opinion?"

Jane directed her gaze to the fire. "Not at all, happily."

The cheerful buoyancy Nadine had seen in the author as she chatted with the captain on the street only moments ago seemed to have disappeared. Either Lady Deedes's opinion did matter, or there was something else.

"I can see no reason for anyone to have a low opinion of you."

"That is very kind of you, but Lady Deedes is fully aware of the history between the captain and myself." She gave Nadine a knowing nod. "And you are as well. I overheard Captain Carville giving you a summary."

"I do hope you won't hold that against me. The information was not solicited."

"No, no. Not for a moment." Austen sighed and then fixed her eyes on Nadine's face. "But *you* don't fault me for turning him down all those years ago, do you?"

"Certainly not. Besides, who am I to judge? You had your reasons. That is sufficient."

Jane got up and stood beside the fireplace. "It is true, however, that I broke his heart. I did. But as cool and awkward as Lady Deedes was during dinner, as soon as she and I retired to the drawing room, she let me know her feelings regarding my relationship with her brother."

"That sounds a bit intrusive. I take it, her feelings were not...friendly."

"Not exactly! It was all claws and fangs on her part." She grinned at the memory. "And I may have been a little sharp myself."

A log popped, and glowing embers fell onto the stone hearth. She swept them back into the fire with her foot.

"The captain's sister is nothing if not loyal to her brother," Jane continued. "She informed me—as if I didn't know already—that ten years ago, my rejection pierced his heart and wounded his spirit. I almost broke the man, she said. She went on to tell me that contrary to her advice Captain Gordon is again quite serious in his intentions toward me. He is going to ask me to put off my journey to London."

"If she's correct, that does sound quite serious." Nadine ran her hand over the cover of the book.

"Lady Deedes told me in no uncertain terms that if I cared for him at all, I would not encourage his feelings. That *any* word of a possible union between us would diminish his station in society. She even said something about 'polluting the shades' of somewhere or other." Jane shook her head. "I must think carefully, she said, before I commit to him because any decision I make will have an adverse effect, not only on myself, but on others around me...including my family."

"That sounds threatening. Are you worried?"

"I would be...if I cared one whit for her opinion."

"And has the captain asked you to stay?"

Jane stared thoughtfully into the fire. "He has asked me to have my things moved up to Churchill House. He has offered to accompany me to London once the weather improves. He plans to speak with my brother Henry."

Nadine stood up, at the same time happy and sad. Rejoicing for Jane and mournful for herself. "He's asking you to marry him?"

"Indeed." Austen turned to her, but the smile on her lips didn't quite reach her eyes.

"And what was your answer?"

She drew a deep breath and then released it. "I like him a great deal. I loved him once, and I believe I can love him again. I can envision a life with him, a life as a navy wife. But I am somewhat alarmed at the requirements of domestic security at the expense of...well, that literary future that you and I discussed earlier. And of course, the dread thought of war with Napoleon dims my sunny imaginings of travel to all the places that I've never been."

Nadine held the volume of *Persuasion* tightly to her chest. If Jane said yes to Gordon, that would be the end of it. The decision would be made. She could never ruin this woman's romantic future, regardless of what that meant to her own life.

"Did you give him a final answer?"

"No. I told him we would speak of it tomorrow," Jane said. "He will join me here at the inn for breakfast to receive my answer."

❧ 35 ❧

Breakfast tomorrow. Nadine leaned back in her chair, trying to appear calm.

"That is not much time to think. You must have already made up your mind."

"No, not at all. Unfortunately." Jane rubbed her arms, despite the warmth of the fire. "I'm not generally indecisive, but I would very much like you to help me reason through the captain's offer. Normally, I would have my sister Cassandra to talk to, but—"

"I'm happy to help, if I can."

"Thank you."

Never in a million years would she have thought her mission would boil down to this moment, where she would be in the position of influencing the author directly.

"According to Lady Deedes, her brother needs a wife who has certain elegance of mind and sweetness of character." Jane began to pace as she spoke, her hands fluttering in the air, her tone dripping with mockery. "She must be, of course, a rational creature, agreeable and consistent. She must also possess a thorough knowledge of music, singing, drawing, dancing, and *all* the modern languages. And besides all this, she must possess a certain something in her air and manner of walking, in the tone of her voice, her address, her expressions."

Nadine heard echoes of *Pride and Prejudice* in the words.

"She was also quite clear about decorum and manners that uphold

252

the standards of good breeding." Jane stopped pacing and turned to her. "What do you think of all this?"

Nadine scoffed. "It's hard for me to believe that such a woman exists anywhere on the planet. But these are the requirements of Lady Deedes?"

"You mean my future *sister*?" Jane replied, sarcasm quite evident in her tone. "With the most condescending of words, she spoke to me like I was a fresh-faced, social-climbing chit of a girl, insidiously scheming to ensnare her brother in marriage."

"But these are not the opinions of Captain Gordon, I hope."

"No, they are not."

Nadine took a deep breath. "If I may say so, isn't the captain's opinion the only one that truly matters?"

"Yes. Yes. You're absolutely right," she said, the sarcasm gone and her voice turning much softer. "Gordon is an agreeable man with good understanding, correct opinions, a deep knowledge of the world, and a warm heart. He appears to live with the comfort of a man of fortune, but without ostentatious displays of wealth. Still, he has strong feelings of family attachment and family honor; marrying him would require that I develop an amicable relationship with his sister."

"That seems like a tall order."

"Indeed, for both parties."

"Before, you said you *could* love him. Do you care for him enough *now* to take such a risk?"

Austen hugged her arms around her middle and stood in front of the fire. "As I told you, I was in love with him once. Since then, I've encountered no man who is his equal. And seeing him again, spending time with him yesterday and today, has been such a gift." She looked over her shoulder at Nadine. "But his proposal came fast and it *was* unexpected. I was a bit overwhelmed tonight."

The directors of the Scribe Guardians had suspected that this romance would develop quickly, once the two of them were reunited. That was why Nadine had been instructed to take the captain far from Hythe before the author's arrival.

"You must still be everything that he is looking for in a wife. That's why he has again asked for your hand in marriage. To him, you're the same person he fell in love with *and* stayed in love with all these years."

"In some ways, I am the same person. I still value intelligence, sound judgment, responsible behavior, goodness, and kindness where I see it. But in other ways, I'm different," Jane asserted. "Far different from the woman I was ten years ago. Or even a year ago."

"In what way?"

"I am much freer in spirit than I once was. I like to dance more. I like my wine. Perhaps it is due to my writing, but I have developed a far more critical eye regarding those in my immediate social circle. I observe people, analyze them, and then write about them. And I must admit, I enjoy making fun of foolishness in others. I can be quite wicked."

"You haven't made fun of me."

"I've only known you for a day. Wait until we're better acquainted."

They both laughed. "I'll be on my guard."

"I also have come to enjoy the company and conversation of men more than women, present company excepted. A husband of mine might take offense at such behavior, thinking me a brazen flirt." Jane smiled. "And he wouldn't be far off."

Nadine knew Austen was all these things and more, regardless of the solemn, saintly image her family tried to portray her after death.

"So, my friend, it is not an exaggeration to say I have changed."

"Maybe we should say *improved*."

"That is very kind of you."

In Nadine's opinion, Austen's gifts were in many ways unique. She had a profound understanding of human nature. A clear and unsentimental perspective. Her satirical sense was incisive and often snarky. And she had a distinctive prose style that delivered the goods with grace and elegance.

"I will say, regardless of what Lady Deedes thinks of me—and despite my age—my existence is far from desperate. I do not seek charity, and the captain's proposal has not been made to me out of some misdirected sense of pity. Nor is it the result of any scheming."

"But do you think these changes—these improvements—would dampen Captain Gordon's affection once he became aware of them? Especially with regard to your writing?"

"This question goes to the heart of it, I suppose." Jane rubbed a blot of ink stain on her finger. "I was raised by encouraging parents, surrounded by well-read siblings. My literary inclinations were always supported and often applauded. The captain didn't know about my writing before, and he knows nothing of it now. I do not know if he would approve."

Nadine held her tongue, but she knew that if Jane Austen were to marry and at the same time pursue her literary endeavors, it would require a husband of very special qualities. Perhaps superhuman. Few men would ever be able to compete with the male characters she created. Men like Darcy, Knightly, and Captain Wentworth.

Based on the altered copy of *Persuasion* Nadine was holding, however, marriage to Captain Gordon would finish Austen as a novelist.

"In my stories, I know how limiting my female characters' situations are. I knowingly mock their circumstances...and sometimes the characters themselves. Will someone ever love them? Will they find happiness? And I suppose this is the same question I ask myself. Will someone ever love me? Will I find happiness?"

Austen pulled the chair a little closer to Nadine and sat down.

"But I need to ask you. How did you know those words?"

"What words?"

"The first sentence of *First Impressions.*"

"Oh. Yes." Nadine knew this was coming. "It is a truth universally acknowledged, that a single man in possession of a good fortune must be in want of a wife."

"How do you know this?"

Nadine tightened her grip on the volume on her lap. The time had come to tell Austen the truth. "I can recite more than those first words. I can repeat for you lines from the stories you've completed...and from those you have yet to write."

An eyebrow went up. Jane stared.

"Your novel *Sense and Sensibility,* which will be published this year, starts this way," Nadine continued. "The family of Dashwood had long been settled in Sussex. Their estate was large, and their residence was at Norland Park, in the center of their property, where, for many generations, they had lived in so respectable a manner as to engage the general good opinion of their surrounding acquaintance. The late owner—"

"Stop," Jane ordered. Her cheeks were flushed with confusion, and her eyes raked over Nadine's face. "Who are you?"

"I know you will find this alarming, but it is the truth." Nadine breathed in deeply. "I come from a time more than two centuries in the future. In my world, your popularity as a literary giant is rivaled only by Shakespeare. You are adored, Miss Austen. Your novels are studied in schools, acted out on...on stages. Your name is so well known that—"

"No," she interrupted. "I am the daughter of a clergyman. My father was a respected gentleman. My brothers are gentlemen. The author of *Sense and Sensibility* will simply be identified as 'A Lady'."

"That's true...for now. But the time will come—in part because of you—that women authors will be respected. And by the year 2078, the year I came from, you will have more than forty million copies of your novels in print. The heroines of your novels will serve as beacons for future women...and men. With a universal message of marrying for love and respect rather than for money, your stories provide examples of women making solid, reasoned marital choices. The satire in your work skewers those who do not choose wisely. And your name will be on every single copy."

Jane's perplexed gaze sank to the book on Nadine's lap.

"What is that volume you are holding?"

Nadine held it up. "Your novel *Persuasion*. It will be published in 1817. This is a 1909 edition of that book. You haven't written the final draft of this novel yet."

Shaking her head, Austen took the book being offered to her.

She ran her fingers over the binding, then opened to the book's title page and stared at her name.

Nadine had so much more explaining to do. Jane needed to be told why most of the pages were blank. She needed to be provided with answers to the questions she would surely have.

Austen fanned through the pages until she reached the biography at the end of the volume. She began to read aloud:

Persuasion is Jane Austen's last completed novel. She began it soon after she had finished Emma *and completed it in August 1816.*

Besides the theme of persuasion, the novel evokes other topics, such as the Royal Navy, in which two of Jane Austen's brothers ultimately rose to the rank of Admiral. As in Northanger Abbey, the superficial social life of Bath—well known to Austen, who spent several relatively unhappy and unproductive years there—is portrayed extensively and serves as a setting for the second half of the book. In many respects, Persuasion *marks a break with Austen's previous works, both in the more biting, even irritable satire directed at some of the novel's characters and in the regretful, resigned outlook of its otherwise admirable heroine, Anne Elliot, in the first part of the story. Against this is set the energy and appeal of the Royal Navy, which symbolizes for Anne and the reader the possibility of a more outgoing, engaged and fulfilling life, and it is this worldview that triumphs for the most part at the end of the novel.*

Jane Austen died, aged 41, July 18th of 1817; Persuasion *was published December 20th of that year.*

Jane was silent for a long time, staring down at the page.

Nadine prepared herself for the questions. It was brilliant that Xander brought this copy back in time with him. This was absolute proof of Austen's future place in history.

"This edition was published in 1909," Nadine repeated. "It's hardly the most impressive edition, but it is only one of a multitude. Also, in the 19th through the 21st centuries, you have had scores of biographies written about your life and work. Your letters—what could be collected of them—are kept in museums and considered treasures."

She wasn't about to mention that Cassandra burned nearly all the letters that passed between them.

Jane's eyes moved over the page again as if inscribing each word in her memory. She gave no indication that she'd heard anything Nadine said.

Finally, she handed the book back.

"I know this is a great deal to absorb. Anything you want to know, any question you have, I will answer."

Jane Austen sat in silence for a few moments more, her hands folded in her lap, her expression unreadable. Finally, she looked up at Nadine.

"The page I read says I will die five months shy of my 42nd birthday. That is indeed a great deal to absorb."

Without another word, she rose to her feet and walked out of the room.

36

NADINE TOSSED and turned restlessly all night.

Lying in the bed with Xander sleeping soundly beside her, she stared at the window and kicked herself for allowing Austen to read her own author's bio. She'd expected her to ask about the blank pages, but the author had said nothing about it.

What would be like to know when you die? The exact date? Everything else seemed to pale for Austen in the face of learning that information. Left alone in that private dining room, Nadine had no inkling whether Austen even cared that someday she'd become a phenomenally popular icon of literature.

Nadine knew that an incurable disease existed in her own body. She knew she was dying. But the exact date of her eventual passing was a blank. After the early days of her diagnosis, she'd suffered—mentally, physically, and emotionally—losing all motivation to accomplish even the simplest of tasks. She didn't want to get out of bed. Or eat. Or dress. Or see anyone. She'd been done with living, ready for the end.

Would she have done better or worse if she'd had an 'X' marked on the calendar? If she'd had a date that could not be changed, regardless of the efforts of science or faith? A date impervious to either plea or negotiation?

Nadine didn't have an answer. And yet, that was the burden she'd placed on Jane Austen...knowledge of the absolute, irreversible date for her rendezvous with death.

A sea breeze rattled the panes of glass, and she lay in the dark, her mind and heart heavy with the awareness that there was also nothing she could do to change it. She and her fellow quantum commuters worked constantly to correct aberrations in the landscape of the past. The unavoidable domino effect of errors needed continual attention.

Several of the earliest time travelers had screwed up. Because of their unintentional meddling, events changed. Since then, the rest of them traveled to correct, correct, correct. There were many things within their power to alter in history: jobs, marriages, divorces. There was one thing that they couldn't. The date a person died.

They could do nothing about the assassination of Abraham Lincoln. Or Martin Luther King, Jr. Nor could they do anything about the manmade, politically motivated chaos that followed such murders as that of Julius Caesar. Or Patrice Lumumba. Or Mohammad Mosaddegh.

They could also not heal Tchaikovsky's cholera or René Descartes's pneumonia. And they couldn't keep Austen from dying of either Addison's disease or Hodgkin's lymphoma. Whichever affliction would claim her, there was no altering the outcome.

A time traveler couldn't stop anyone from dying or getting killed when fate had already carved that date in stone. The medication she'd given Deirdre's son worked because Andrew wasn't destined to die of that sickness. She could ease the pain but not heal him if death waited in the wings.

Of course, because they were operating outside of their finite life-time, quantum commuters were exempt from these rules. The laws of fate didn't apply to them.

Jane Austen would die on July 18th, 1817. And Nadine couldn't do anything about it.

Now the question remained, would Austen accept Captain Gordon's offer? Would she decide to live in marital bliss for the six years she had left? Or would she walk away from him and pursue her literary destiny? Would she write? Would she weave her timeless fiction?

Their conversation last night gave Nadine no hint about which road she'd take.

To his credit, Xander had stayed up most of the night with her. After returning to their room, Nadine filled him in on what had passed between her and the author. He listened, and not once did he fault her for divulging what might be the determining factor in swaying Austen one way or the other. He was on Nadine's side, and they would handle whatever happened.

As the sky outside the window brightened with the dawn, the two of them dressed and went down to the Coffee Room.

Nadine knew Jane was to meet Gordon and give him her answer, but she didn't know where. Perhaps they would go out for a walk since the rain had stopped. Perhaps they would meet in one of the private dining rooms.

Nadine had said all she could. There was nothing else that she would do to influence her. The decision was now in the hands of the author herself. But if Austen wanted to meet with her again to ask questions, then Nadine would gladly accommodate her. She told the innkeeper where they were, in case someone was asking for them.

In the Coffee Room, Xander and Nadine sat side-by-side at a table. They had their backs to the wall and their eyes on the door. A server immediately showed up at their table, taking their order.

"If Austen decides to marry Gordon," Xander started, gathering her freezing fingers in one warm hand. "How much time will *we* have together?"

Nadine shook her head. "I don't know. A few days. Maybe a week or so. We have until my director realizes that I'm MIA and that Jane Austen has disappeared from the literary canon."

"That's when they'll send an assassin to kill us?"

She didn't say so now, but there was no 'us' when it came to her job and the contract she'd agreed to. Xander would be safe. She'd send him back to his own time before anyone showed up looking for her. She wasn't exactly sure how she'd do that yet, but she'd figure it out. The fact that he'd made the quantum leap by himself to get here made her feel more confident that it was possible.

Assassins. Liquidating her wasn't the only solution for the rogue Scribe Guardian. They could transport her back to 2078. There, they could let the illness run its course or wait until she requested euthanasia. The program directors were not monsters. And either way, her illness was a death sentence.

She realized she hadn't answered him. "I don't know when they'll come."

"Well, we won't go down without giving them a good goddamn fight. We've already broken a few rules regarding time travel. We'll do it again."

Nadine squeezed his hand. "Honestly, I can't think of anything right now, beyond Jane's decision."

He nodded, understanding. "If she marries Gordon, what would become of her novels? Of the influence she's had on literature. Does it all just fade away, like the volume we have upstairs?"

"I suspect *Sense and Sensibility* will still go forward through publication. The typesetting is finished. After stopping to see a brother near Canterbury, she's supposed to go to London to work through the page proofs. Even *Northanger Abbey* could have a chance. A different publisher, Crosby & Co., accepted that novel eight years ago. They've been sitting on it and have yet to publish it. Once she goes back home to Chawton, she needs to revise the novel *First Impressions* before it becomes *Pride and Prejudice*. If she marries Captain Gordon, I don't know if she would ever get back to it."

"I guess a lot depends on how Gordon feels about having an author for a wife."

"It's unlikely he'd approve. The Scribe Guardians' researchers believe that if she marries, Jane Austen becomes a forgotten entity in the world of literature," Nadine said. "And she wouldn't be the first. I can easily name a dozen authors and their novels who have disappeared because of..."

Nadine's words trailed off as Jane came into the Coffee Room. She scanned the room before her gaze settled on them. She crossed directly to their table.

At that moment, Nadine assumed that Jane may have come down to deny what she'd been told the night before. Denial was the first response of many people when they were told potentially devastating truths. Reacting with suspicion or anger, the human mind often used it as a common defense mechanism as it processed information a person wasn't prepared for. Human history was filled with the record of people who denied facts in order to wage war on science, to discount evidence of genocides, and finally to destroy their own environment.

The truth Nadine had revealed last night justifiably cried out for denial on so many levels.

She and Xander came to their feet as Jane reached their table, and the standard greeting passed between the three.

Jane Austen was dressed as she had been the day before, but she was not carrying her cloak. She had clearly been up most of the night crying. Her eyes were bloodshot. Her complexion was blotchy, and her nose red.

Feelings of guilt pierced Nadine's conscience. She'd done this to the woman. Never mind the issue of her possible marriage to Captain Gordon. Nadine had decimated any dream Jane had of getting old, of watching nieces and nephews grow tall, of finding contentment in what she thought would be the decades of life that lay ahead.

"May I join you?"

"Of course," they replied in unison.

Xander held a chair for her, and they sat down.

Austen's eyes were fixed on Xander. "Are you too from...?"

He nodded. "I go with Nadine. We're together."

It was a good answer. There was no reason to try to explain their own complicated situation right now.

The server appeared, and when Jane waved him away, Xander told him to hold their breakfast.

"Do you mind?" Austen asked.

"Not at all," Nadine replied.

The author looked around her before speaking.

"I've had all night to think." She inhaled deeply and released a shaky breath. "Can I change it? The end that is. The time when I will die?"

"There is no way to change that. I wish I could, but I can't rewrite history. No one can."

"But according to you, history will be rewritten if I do not become an authoress."

"That's true. But your end will still occur on that date."

Nadine realized there was no hint of denial in the other woman's words. She believed what she'd been told last night. She believed what she'd read in that edition of her own novel.

"I'm not godlike," Nadine continued. "I'm no magician. I can only travel through time because of the advances of science in the future. I cannot undo a person's fate. I cannot save someone from death."

"*If it be now, 'tis not to come. If it be not to come, it will be now. If it be not now, yet it will come. The readiness is all,*" Jane said softly. "Shakespeare never met you two, I take it."

"He still had it right," Nadine answered. "The readiness is all."

Austen stared at her hands for a short time before she spoke again. "It is somewhat daunting, don't you think? Knowing your life will soon end?"

"I wish you hadn't read your own biography. My intention was for you to see the brilliant future ahead for you and your work."

"And instead, my instinctive response was to see only my imminent demise." She laughed, but there was no amusement in it. "Six years."

There was no point in apologizing again. And discussing a woman's life expectancy in this era would certainly not help, either.

"How do I die?"

"A debilitating illness, but you have years before it afflicts you." Nadine wasn't going to tell her how the disease hung over Jane for two years, even as she continued to work on her novels.

"Who will be with me...at the end, I mean?"

"Your sister Cassandra."

A smile formed on her lips, and she nodded slightly, as if this was meant to be.

Nadine remembered a letter that the grieving Cassandra had written to Fanny Knight, Jane's beloved niece. Part of it went,

I have lost a treasure, such a sister, such a friend as never can have been surpassed. She was the sun of my life, the gilder of every pleasure, the soother of every sorrow; I had not a thought concealed from her, and it is as if I had lost a part of myself. I loved her only too well — not better than she deserved, but I am conscious that my affection for her made me sometimes unjust to and negligent of others; and I can acknowledge, more than as a general principle, the justice of the Hand which has struck this blow.

"Where will I be buried?"

"In the north aisle of Winchester Cathedral."

Her brows rose in surprise. "An honored place."

"A deserved place."

Over the years, historians had speculated how it came about that

Austen was buried there. After all, her late father was simply a country vicar. It was possible that a family friend who had influence with the bishop had secured special permission. No one really knew.

"Last night, I had so much time to think about that biography," Jane told them again. "Once I shook off my initial dismay, I tried to consider my life's goals. I see now that I have a very short time to accomplish what I hope to do. I should say rather, what I *had* hoped to do before fate complicated my plans by waylaying me here. In any case, six years is unexpectedly brief."

Nadine exchanged a look with Xander. If only *they* had the gift of six years together.

"As I considered this, I realized that knowing my death date should bring out the best in me." She paused as her voice trembled. After a moment, she continued. "This knowledge compels me to enjoy my family more. I must do all I can for them. I have two nieces, Anna and Fanny, who are particularly lovely. Anna even shows an inclination to write, heaven help her. And my brothers—scattered here, there, and everywhere—well, I must find a way to be closer to them all."

Nadine's emotions rose to the surface as she heard the love for family in Jane's words. She recalled the day when she'd been told she had so little time left. How lonely she'd felt. How purposeless.

Xander's hand slid across the table and took hers. Again, their eyes locked. He was reading her thoughts. Nadine didn't want to lose him. She thought of Cassandra's words again—*the sun of my life...the soother of my sorrows.* He was all she had. He was truly her love.

"I know it's only been hours since I learned the truth, but I already feel that I've changed in profound and positive ways. I feel stronger, more spiritual somehow. I now recognize with more resolve what I need to do. Because of you, I now know my scribblings will find an audience of readers. I will be recognized for my literary endeavors. That is a destiny that cannot be tossed off like a pair of old gloves."

"And what of the proposal?"

"Having this knowledge of my demise has also made me think long and hard about Captain Gordon," she said softly. "How fair would it be to him if I were to accept his proposal? He knows nothing of any of this. Nothing of my writing. I am too old to bear children, but he will surely expect that I travel with him, establish a home of our own, give up my family to some extent. When and how could I write my novels?"

Jane's eyes filled up, glistening as she looked at Nadine.

"And what happens if he is agreeable to everything I ask? What if he supports my literary endeavors? I shall be in love again, all the while knowing I cannot share with him the truth about...about..."

Nadine knew the thing that caused people to fear death the most —often more than their own death—was the loss of loved ones they would leave behind.

"I cannot do it. The unfairness of it chills me to the bone. I will meet with him this morning and reject him as I rejected him ten years ago. But what makes matters worse, I can give him no reasonable explanation that will console him. I cannot tell him the truth, and I cannot lie to him. This rejection will wound us both, perhaps irreparably, but it cannot be helped. I know he has not stopped loving me, but I cannot bring myself to conjure a falsehood to soften the blow."

The bells of the church on the hill were tolling the noon hour when Nadine and Xander stood beneath the archway of the inn and watched the passengers prepare to depart. Several travelers seated themselves on top of the coach while the others climbed inside.

A few bade tearful goodbyes to loved ones standing on the walkway. The driver and the guard were clearly in good spirits to be on their way after the rain.

The last passenger to enter the coach was Jane Austen.

"No sign of Captain Gordon," Xander said in a low voice.

"Perhaps that's for the best," Nadine replied.

In all of her travels, she had never faced a task so fraught with trouble. Hythe had unexpectedly turned out to be an emotional minefield. She knew there were two reasons for that. One was about to leave on this coach for London. The other was standing beside her.

For Austen, this unforeseen stop on the southern coast of England had been even harder. Jane knew that the thread of life was measured, and she now also knew when that thread would be severed. And she had chosen her truest passion over all else.

In Nadine's eyes, Austen had made her choice with the grace and with the inner strength of the greatest of her heroines. She had turned down a final chance for love, choosing instead the hard road that would lead to greatness. It was a choice that would result in a priceless legacy, a gift for all who would follow in the centuries to come. But the personal cost was heartbreaking.

The author hesitated on the step of the coach. Turning her head, she nodded to them and smiled. Then, as the sun broke through, Jane Austen climbed in and pulled the door shut behind her.

❦ 37 ❦

Nadine stood by the window of their room in the Swan and paged through Xander's copy of *Persuasion*, waiting for him to return from downstairs.

This morning, they'd dressed in their own clothes and gathered together the garments that had to go back to Deirdre, except for the cloak and greatcoat. A few minutes ago, Xander had gone down to commission one of the serving lads to run the bundle to their friend's cottage in the lower end of the village.

She closed the book and looked down at the busy main street below, trying to ignore a nagging feeling of emptiness. Yesterday, Jane Austen left the village for London. Since then, Nadine had been thinking about what would follow for the author.

In the years ahead, despite the scarcity of time allotted to her, she would not seek excitement. Or adventure. Or travel. She had already rejected the comfort and security of being the wife of a naval officer. She'd turned her back on the possibility of love.

Austen's decision to live the rest of her life in the same manner that she'd lived before was, in Nadine's eyes, an artist's expression of a greater love, a true and selfless love. She had a higher calling, and she answered that call.

There was so little that people living in the future would know about Austen. In so many ways, they'd be dead wrong about her. They would search for Jane in her words and her characters and in the unreliable testimony of family and people who'd never even met her. But they wouldn't find the real Jane Austen. In the end, they wouldn't know her.

All of Jane's biographers over the years would repeat a few scattered facts about her family. About her father. Her mother. Cassandra. The brothers. They would write about their careers, their marriages, and their children. They would color their erudite tomes with portraits of the brothers and the aunts and the men who *might* have wanted to marry her.

Those attempts at capturing the elusive Jane Austen—including the movies that would be made about her—would repeat romantic tales of a young Anglo-Irish rascal named Tom Lefroy, of a one-day engagement with a neighborhood friend of her brother's. None of those writers or filmmakers would mention Captain Charles Gordon. None would see how she captured the essence of her thwarted romance with him in her final novel, *Persuasion*.

In the end, the academics and critics and moviemakers would succeed in constructing little more than a roughly drawn silhouette of Jane Austen.

Nadine and Xander had seen the real woman, spoken to her, dined with her, suffered with her, and cried with her. Their acquaintance with her was brief, but it was crucial, and it was telling.

Jane Austen would now go on to write more of her novels. Critics and readers would love them and call them unique. The stories, the characters, and the settings would be recognizable to a degree that no other author in her time would achieve. Even in 2078—more than two centuries later—a reader like Nadine could follow Catherine Morland or Anne Elliot through the streets of Bath. She could still stand on the stone breakwater at Lyme and imagine the foolish, young Louisa Musgrove doing a swan dive just out of Captain Wentworth's reach. She could visit any of the great houses of England and feel Elizabeth Bennet's awakening and her admiration for Pemberley.

Austen's characters could have lived in any town or village in England. Their words were familiar echoes of conversations heard in streets and shops and homes everywhere. Her villains were not evil, virgin-hunting counts living in dark castles. Her heroines were not idealized versions of women who would swoon at the mere sight of a dominant male figure or a drop of blood. She didn't give her readers contrived plots where fairy godmothers or godfathers would appear at a final moment to save the day.

Instead, Jane Austen would give the world stories in which we could see our own lives, our loves, our frailties...and laugh at them. And in the end, we would see the undeniable miracle of our shared humanity.

Absently, Nadine ran her fingers over the cloth cover, the embossed title on the spine.

She didn't think her interaction with Jane could have ended with the same results if it weren't for this book. Saying she'd come from the future wouldn't have been enough. Reciting pages of Austen's unwritten or unpublished work wouldn't have been enough. Humans were skeptical by nature. Unless we saw proof—and often, not even then— we viewed seers as pretenders. Healers were charlatans unless there was something definite to measure. This book was Nadine's tangible proof that what she said wasn't simply smoke and mirrors.

"All the words show up again." Xander was back. He moved next to her at the window. "Every single page. And the illustrations are there too."

"Yes," she replied, forcing a smile.

"I never was much of a reader before, but I'm seeing things differently now."

Nadine woke up this morning to find him reading *Persuasion* next to her in bed. While they ate breakfast in their room, they'd spent a couple of hours talking about Anne Elliot and Captain Frederick Wentworth and all the similarities he'd already noted between the novel and what he'd learned of Austen's life. While Nadine dressed, she found him again reading. He only put the book down when it was time to get ready.

"It's as if she painted a picture of Anne Elliot's world with her words."

"I'll quote you when I make my mission report."

His gaze dropped away, and a look of sadness clouded his face. Since Austen's departure, they'd said very little about their own future.

"What will you say...in your report?"

"I'll say that Jane Austen was an artist with a vision. Clever and clear-sighted, she was a woman with her finger on the pulse of her world. As a writer, she knew that the novel could be a great art form.

Meeting us, seeing the copy of *Persuasion*, her opinion was reinforced." She paused for a few seconds and entwined her fingers with Xander's. "I'll say that she turned her back on love and marriage to follow the road she was destined for. She knew she couldn't have it all, so she chose her art. No meddling by other quantum commuters would change that."

"So, are we finally going to talk," he asked, "about our path? About our destiny?"

She conjured all her strength before speaking. "Today makes three days since we arrived. We can make the quantum leap."

"Together? To Colorado?"

"No. You have to go back to your time, Xander. And I do too."

"I don't agree."

"I know. But it's true."

"You'll have to explain that to me." Xander took a half step away and pointed at the street below. "She was Jane Austen. And I understand now that no man in this era would be prepared or maybe enlightened enough to give her the space she needed to do what she had to do."

"Very few would have done it."

"But I'm not one of those men." He took her hand. "I know who you are. You're a Scribe Guardian. Haven't I given you enough assurance to know that I won't interfere with that?"

"You think we can stay together, live together, and work together, but it doesn't work like that, my love. You're not able to jump into the future, just as I can't move beyond the date of my finite life. The quantum leap only goes *back* in time."

Xander was silent for a moment. "In 2078, I'll be ninety-four years old. Will I be dead then?"

"I've never checked." She didn't want to know. She'd been too afraid to know. And what was the point of it, anyway? Why would she want to torment herself with the life Xander had after she was gone from it?

"Do you have any say where and when they send you?"

She shook her head.

"Will we ever see each other?"

"I don't think we should plan on it." Nadine couldn't fight the emotions rising in her chest. Tears burned the backs of her eyes. "You need to go back to your time and live your life. Do what you do. Be the great person that you are."

"And all the while, I'll be looking for you at every turn in the road. In every hotel lobby. In crowds..." His voice broke as the words trailed off.

Yesterday, she'd refused to be anywhere near Jane Austen when she spoke to Captain Gordon and rejected his offer of marriage. Nadine knew then that she would have to do the same thing in a day's time.

Tears streamed down her face. Xander gathered her into his arms, and they held each other as she cried. He pressed kisses against her hair, and she lifted her lips to his, searching for some trace of comfort, some shred of solace that she could carry with her.

Something, anything, that could hold her broken heart together.

It was a long time before Nadine was able to pull herself from his embrace. He stayed by the window as she made her way to the bed. Sitting on the edge, she dumped out the contents of her bag.

"What are you looking for?"

Nadine had no idea about how Xander had traveled back to 1811. The coffin may have played a part, but beyond that, she was lost.

"I have a device in here that will help you make the leap back to your year."

She sorted through everything, feeling her anxiety begin to build. She couldn't find it. "It's not here."

"What are you looking for...exactly?"

"It's a sub-molecular, temporal mobilizing device. It's sort of GPS for time and space. It jumpstarts and directs the quantum leap for novice travelers."

He came and stood by the bed. "When was the last time you used it?"

"I don't use it. I don't need it. But I still have it in case of emergencies."

She stared down at the items spread out over the bedding. Her inhaler. The money she was going to leave for Deirdre. The remaining medicines.

It wasn't just the temporal mobilizer she was missing. Her defense stunner was missing too.

"I don't know what I could have done with them?"

"You mean these?"

Nadine looked up at the two devices in Xander's palm. "I found these in the coffin the day you went out for lunch with Donna."

She jumped off the bed and took the items from him.

"They must have fallen out of my bag the night I arrived in Colorado. You're a lifesaver, Xander. The book and now these. You're my hero."

The look on his face told her he didn't feel like a hero.

38

WHEN THEY STEPPED out of the inn, the sun was shining. The crowded High Street showed few remaining traces of the torrential rains.

The brightness didn't match Nadine's inner landscape, but her mind was at least clear about what she needed to do now.

Knowing that the temporal mobilizing device was responsible for Xander's accidental jump to 1811 had been a relief. Nadine didn't have to worry about how much trouble and danger he could get into if he were to suddenly develop the knowledge and skills to make quantum leaps at will.

They didn't settle the account at the Swan before leaving for Deirdre's. After sending Xander on to Colorado, she would be going back to the inn. Her excuse to him was that she needed to make another sweep through the room to make sure nothing had been left behind. The truth was, she needed a place later where she could cry her heart out.

Nadine still needed to clear her head of the frustration she was feeling about a world that wouldn't allow the two of them to stay together. She had to empty her mind of her anger...and her longing for him. She didn't want to make the same unintentional journey to 2022 that she made before.

She didn't think her heart could take it.

Her arm was linked with Xander's as they made their way down the cobbled lanes in the direction of Deirdre's cottage. She tried not to show it, but each step squeezed her insides a little more. Trying to keep things light, she pointed out items to Xander—brightly colored caricatures of Napoleon pasted up in a shop window, a pair of young boys chasing a carriage along the cobblestones, a kitten stalking an unruffled seagull by the military canal. She couldn't seem to convey the humor, though, and the polite smile on his face never seemed quite right.

"Do you have a neuralyzer in your bag?" he asked out of the blue after they'd crossed the bridge into the lower end of the village.

"What's that?" she asked.

"It's this gadget in the *Men in Black* movies. It makes a super bright flash and erases people's memories."

"I've never seen the movie, but I don't have one," she said. "Do you wish I did? Do you wish you could forget these past few days?"

He stopped right in the middle of the lane and gathered her in his arms. He kissed her hard, and she kissed him back with equal passion.

"No, Nadine. I don't want to forget a single thing about our third pass by the sun."

"Our what?" she smiled. "Our third pass by the sun?"

"Yeah. Vegas, Colorado, and Hythe. And I don't want to forget one second of it." He kissed her again, even more deeply this time.

A loud *harrumph* from a woman standing nearby brought a sudden end to their moment. For some reason, Nadine wasn't surprised in the least to find Elizabeth Hole and her one-eyed mutt glaring at them. Actually, Mrs. Hole was glaring; Kai was staring happily at Xander, tongue hanging out and tail wagging.

"Mrs. Finley," the village busybody barked. "I don't know how things are done in America, but this is Hythe. Here, anyone with any sense of decency would know that such a public display of...whatever that was...should be done in private. If it must be done at all."

Mrs. Hole shifted her gaze to Xander, and her cheeks flushed pink for an instant. Then, her focus swung back, and the icy darts flew again.

Nadine glanced down at Kai, who was now baring his teeth at her. The little beast was jealous. Clearly, the dog's owner was too.

"This is my husband," she protested, keeping her temper in check.

Her emotions were a little raw at the moment, and this woman was treading on dangerous ground.

"I don't associate with the hoity-toity, but even fishmongers' daughters know that here a lady will only allow a gentleman to kiss her *hand* upon meeting. But even that's too intimate, if you ask me. Far too intimate. I'm shocked. I had to hide my sweet Kai's eyes."

"The last thing we intended was to corrupt little Kai," Xander put in, turning on the charm.

"I know *you* wouldn't instigate such a public display, my dear. It was *her*. I saw it with my own two eyes." She patted him on the arm, now ignoring Nadine entirely. "But how are you today, Mr. Finley? Is this afternoon good for you to join me for a light supper? I'll have my cook make your favorite dish, if you'll just tell me what it is."

The shift in the woman's tone and demeanor was so drastic that Nadine almost snorted out loud. She stared in disbelief at Elizabeth Hole, now all soft words and sweetness. Even as she thought this, Kai rubbed himself against Xander's leg and then sat on his boots.

Xander, lifting the dog to his chest, was smiling like a politician on Election Day. "Actually, tomorrow would be better for us, if that doesn't inconvenience you."

"I'll send my servant to the inn in the morning. Just let him know what you'd like, and it will be waiting for you."

Nadine almost gagged.

"Thank you, Mrs. Hole."

"It's my pleasure, sir."

"You're so kind."

She was actually blushing. "Well, there are those in this village who say I have a heart of—"

"But more pressing than my dining preference," Xander cut in, "I have a matter of great importance that I was hoping you might help me with."

"Help you? Of course, Mr. Finley. Anything!"

The older woman was practically bouncing up and down.

"Well, I have some money I'd like to donate to a worthy cause that has come to our attention. I was hoping you'll be my...my ambassador of goodwill."

"A worthy cause? Ambassador? Say the word, good sir. I'm yours to command."

Nadine could only shake her head. Unbelievable.

Xander explained that they'd heard of the recent disappearance of a coffin.

"I realize this is a great deal to ask. But if I were to give you money enough to cover the coffin maker's loss, could you pass it on to him? Keeping my contribution anonymous, of course. I would be in your debt, Mrs. Hole. Deeply, deeply in your debt."

As Nadine had expected, the gesture endeared him to the older woman even more, if that were possible. She drew the money from her bag and handed it to Mrs. Hole, who took it without so much as a side glance. Nadine obviously didn't exist anymore. She may as well have been standing on Mars.

"Such a fine display of character, sir. Such manners. Such generosity," she said, raising her voice and drawing the attention of a few passersby. "Mr. Finley, you are freely giving aid to a valued village craftsman in his moment of hardship. Such a fine man, you are!"

"Anonymously, Mrs. Hole," Xander said quietly.

"Of course," the woman replied, pretending that she was buttoning her lips.

Little chance of that happening, Nadine thought.

"Until tomorrow, then?" Mrs. Hole said, eyelashes fluttering.

"Until tomorrow."

For a moment, Nadine thought he was going to kiss the woman's hand. She almost hoped he would, just to see her response. Oh, the irony!

Instead, Xander simply bid the old lady goodbye and handed Kai back.

Taking Nadine's arm, he led her away. "That was utterly embarrassing."

"Utterly," she agreed with a smile. "And it's *utterly* amazing to me how quickly you got the hang of this Regency-era language."

"It's a gift. One of many." With a glance back to make sure they were a safe distance away, he slid his arm around her waist and pulled her closer to his side. "I'm sorry about the way she treated you."

"I'm glad about how she treated *you*," she countered. "That busybody was a one-woman threat to my existence until you arrived."

"Then, maybe you should keep me around. At least for as long as you're staying here. I'm serious. I don't want to give up even one minute with you."

Nadine shook her head and rested it against his shoulder as they walked. She couldn't risk him being here, not when she couldn't trust her own heart. No, she had to create real distance between them...as much as that hurt her. She needed space to think. Her job, her very life depended on it.

As they turned up the lane, they saw Deirdre and her son coming down from her cottage. Andrew was the first to spot them. The mother's hands were full of bundled clothes, and the young boy toddled ahead to greet them.

Xander caught the child and swung him up over his head before settling the little fellow on his hip. It looked so natural, Nadine thought, feeling the ache in her heart deepening.

"Thank you for returning the lot you borrowed," Deirdre said. "I'm off to deliver this pile to my customer up near the churchyard. But if you don't mind waiting for me at the cottage, we'll be back before you know it."

"Yes. Absolutely. Take care of your business," Nadine replied, relieved that Deirdre wouldn't be there to witness Xander disappearing into thin air. "We'll be fine."

"And you, Mr. Finley," Deirdre said, turning to him with a wry smile. "I'd be obliged to you if there was nothing else left in my garden that'll put me before the magistrate."

"There'll be nothing, ma'am. Scout's honor."

"Whose honor? Scots?"

"Nothing. Just an American expression."

Deirdre nodded. "Well, I'll be out here tonight, breaking that thing up for firewood. And we can all just pray no one catches me doing it. Come on, Andrew lad."

Nadine watched the way Xander hugged the boy before putting him down. Unexpectedly, her eyes burned, and she fought back tears. This was goodbye.

As the mother and son went down the lane, Nadine and Xander turned once again toward the cottage.

"The greatcoat, the money, anything you have on you that belongs to 1811 should be left inside," she told him. "Did you grab your wallet? Your phone...?"

"I have everything I came with. But I'm leaving behind the most important thing. The most important thing in my life."

Nadine's throat closed tight, and more tears threatened to fall. She couldn't bring herself to look into his face. She didn't want to let him go. She *had* to.

He went into the cottage to leave the greatcoat, and she trudged toward the shed. The goats were eyeing her accusingly.

"Shut up, you," she said to them.

Pulling the cover off the coffin, she straightened up and looked at the cottage.

This was the moment Nadine would remember for as long as she lived. She gazed off into the distance. White puffs of clouds were scudding across a gauzy blue sky. The breeze was cool and carried the salty smells of the English Channel, mingled with the pungency of the farm and the nearby marshes. The sun was warm, but she still shivered.

She stared down at the temporal mobilizing device in her trembling hand. Wrapping her fingers around it, she synced her brain waves with the controls and programmed it to return Xander to his own time. As an afterthought, she also set it to disable the device after this jump. She couldn't risk having him—intentionally or unintentionally—using it again.

Xander came out and stood next to her.

"So, this is it?"

"Yes."

He frowned at the coffin. "It does feel like a funeral."

She faced him, looking up into his handsome face. She could no longer hold back the tears. His arms closed around her, and she pressed her body against his while her broken words tumbled out.

"I love you. And I'm sorry that this world doesn't allow us to be together. It's cruel and unfair. But I want you to go back and live your life. Live, Xander. And please don't look for me. Forget about me. Finding you once was an accident. Finding you twice was..." Nadine forced herself to finish. "The accident that threw us together has changed our lives, but it was still an accident...and you need to move on."

He cupped her face with his strong, warm hands, and she saw tears in his eyes too. "I love you, Nadine. We were never an accident. We were always meant to be together. And I'm telling you. I will never forget you. I will never, ever stop looking for you."

Her heart couldn't bear so much pain. She kissed him once more.

"Goodbye, my love," Nadine murmured against his lips as she dropped the device into his pocket.

And then, instantly, Xander vanished from her embrace.

❧ 39 ❧

BUZZING. What was that buzzing? Was it in his head?

No, the sound was coming from somewhere nearby. It was a phone. Suddenly, it stopped.

Xander's head was pounding. He was cold. Really cold. He was actually shivering. And something was stabbing him in the back. He tried to move but couldn't manage to make his muscles respond.

The fucking phone started buzzing again.

He tried to open his eyes, but everything around him twisted and shifted. Nothing would come into focus. Mercifully, the ringing stopped again.

Xander tasted bile rising into his throat, and he somehow rolled just in time. His stomach heaved, and he retched.

He was lying on a cold floor that smelled of oil and gasoline and sawdust. The stabbing in his back was the end of a two-by-four that he'd fallen on.

Fallen on? He didn't remember falling.

The air coming into his lungs was freezing. A whistling, howling sound reached his brain. It was wind, he realized, outside.

He cautiously tried to pry his eyes open again, but there was a weight pressing on his skull. Pushing himself onto all fours, his arms and legs struggled to hold his weight. The world was spinning.

He caught a glimpse of his truck parked beside him. His garage. He was in his garage.

And then it all came rushing back to him.

"*No!*"

He remembered everything, and physical pain cut through his body like a chainsaw. He was back. Back.

"Nadine!" A second ago, she was in his arms. "*NADINE!*"

Instantly, his emotions got the best of him. His throat shut tight. Hot tears scalded his eyes. Crawling to his workbench, he turned and sat with his back against the cabinet, his knees drawn up. A pins-and-needles numbness wracked every limb.

Nadine's tearful face was the last thing he'd seen, and it was now branded in his brain. He didn't get a chance to say goodbye.

He tried to recall what happened. They were standing in Deirdre's garden. Nadine put something in his vest pocket.

He plunged a hand inside, and his fingers wrapped around the device. The temporal mobilizer. It was still warm. He pulled it out and held it in front of his face.

"Take me back," he ordered. "Back to 1811. Hythe. Take me back to her. Now!"

The device sat, inert and cooling, in his palm.

"Fuck!"

He looked around him. There was no sign of the coffin. Maybe that was what made the jump possible the first time. How could he get back to her? How could he find her?

He had to.

Xander's head sank into his hands. He found her just to lose her again. It was too fucking brutal to know that she loved him as he loved her, but they couldn't be together.

There were so many things he'd wanted to tell her before he left. Things like, he'd wait for her to come back again. Days, months, years...it made no difference. He loved her. They'd done it before, and he had to believe that their paths would cross again. This time, he wouldn't waste time doubting her.

Valuable time. When he could be loving her.

The phone started buzzing again. He realized it was in his pocket. He took it out and peered at Ken's name on the display. He had service. His phone was fully charged. He pressed the off button. He couldn't talk to anybody. He wasn't ready.

He looked at his texts. More than a hundred. As many missed calls and voicemail messages. Missed FaceTime calls from his mother.

Opening the calendar app, Xander saw he'd only been gone for three days. Three incredible days. Why couldn't they have had an extra day? A week? A month? Why so short a time, he thought bitterly.

The cell rang again. Ken. His friend was not giving up.

He'd given himself away by sending the last call straight to voicemail. Xander knew if he didn't answer, Ken would be pulling into his driveway in an hour.

He cleared his throat and took the call.

"Ken."

"What the fuck, man? Where have you been?"

What did he say to that?

"Here and there."

"Here and there, *where*? Donna and I have been sick, worrying about you two. Where's Nadine? Where did you two go? And what was that stunt about, leaving your truck at the end of your driveway?"

Driveway. His truck.

When he came home from the lodge, his driveway wasn't plowed yet. He'd left it near the road. But now it was sitting in his garage.

"Thanks for moving it."

"You left the fucking thing running. With the keys in it. By the time I got to your house, the tank was empty, and your battery was dead."

"Yeah, it was stuck. The plows. You know."

"Yeah. Right. Where did you go?"

"Nadine had to get back to Denver. I went with her."

"How?"

"Uber."

"You were in Denver for three days?"

"Yeah, I was."

"Your parents called me. Your mom is fucking out of her head."

"I'll call them."

"Why didn't you answer your calls? The texts? All the messages I left?"

"How about more important stuff? How's Donna? The baby? Are they still in the hospital or are you home?"

"I'm not done with you."

"Okay. But what about Donna?"

"They came home yesterday," Ken huffed.

"How are they doing?" Xander knew the more questions he asked, the less explaining he'd have to do. Until he saw Donna, the prosecutor, anyway.

"She's perfect. They're both perfect. When are you going to come over so you can meet her?"

Xander ran a hand over his tired face. He wasn't ready to see them or anyone. He needed time to wallow in his misery for a while. "It won't be today. I'll text you before I come into town."

"When is Nadine coming back?"

Shit. He felt the knife go deep into his gut.

"Hey, listen. She's calling me right now," he lied. "I have to hang up."

Donna's voice rose in the background. "Have him tell Nadine that the biopsy was benign."

"What biopsy?" Xander asked.

"That was *my* first question when she told me yesterday. Tell Nadine. She'll know."

Xander hung up and stared at his phone. It must have been the day Nadine and Donna spent together, the one ending with the snowstorm and getting stranded. The biopsy must have happened then. She'd said nothing about it. But they didn't have much chance to talk about it once he landed in England.

What an ass he was! He'd barely asked Nadine about the birth or any of that.

They'd had so many other things to focus on. Never mind Jane Austen. All the stuff about her shit job. About her own life in the future.

He rubbed his neck. How well he understood her now. How much she'd struggled to make him understand the truth.

There were rational explanations for why and how she'd left him in Vegas and again in Colorado. There was science and purpose behind everything she did. Still, Xander wished he'd asked more questions about where their headquarters were located. He should have gotten the names of some of the scientists.

The reality of time travel couldn't have been developed overnight. Maybe there were physicists working on it right now. He had to learn more about it. Get involved with it. After all, he already had experience with quantum leaps.

Xander's stomach suddenly heaved, and he pushed to his feet. He didn't want to throw up in his garage. His legs wobbled, but he managed to stumble to the door.

As the opener pulled the door upward, he had to raise a hand to shade his eyes from the glare of the sun on the snow. His driveway was plowed, and a path had been cleared to the house.

Gulping down a few deep breaths of the crisp mountain air, he managed to fight off the nausea.

Food. Liquids. Sleep. In moderation. He recalled Nadine's advice.

"I'm not giving up, you know," he called out, the words carried away on the wind. "I'll find a way back to you."

The air was clear and nipped at his skin as Xander trudged across to the house.

He kicked the snow out of the treads of his boots and went in. Climbing the stairs to the great room, he knew no one was here. The shades were still closed, the temperature turned down, and an eerie silence filled the place.

In the kitchen, he yanked open the fridge door. His oldest friend had brought up his food delivery; the thing was stocked.

He took down a glass and filled it with water. He drank it as slowly as he could and put the glass on the counter.

"Fuck," he muttered, looking around at the sterile emptiness of his life.

He kicked off his boots by the door and wandered to the fireplace. He thought about lighting it, but his eye was drawn to the bookcase. His gaze scraped over the titles. There was a space where *Persuasion* had been. Next to it, another Austen novel beckoned to him.

He was reaching out for it when a knock on the kitchen door snapped Xander's head around.

His first thought was that some hungry creature was looking for a handout.

More knocking drew him over to the slider, and he opened the shades.

His heart stopped. Frozen in place, he blinked, not trusting his eyes.

"Are you going to open the door or not?" Nadine shouted from outside. "It's freezing out here."

Clumsily, his fingers fumbled with the lock, but he managed to open the sliding glass door. She tumbled in, bringing the smell of snow and fresh air.

He struggled to get the words out. "You...you're here."

Without waiting for her answer, he lifted her in his arms and twirled her around. She was laughing and crying, and her arms were wrapped tightly around his neck. "You're here. You're really here."

He set her down and kissed her face. Her mouth. She kissed him back.

"I can't believe it. You came after me. How?"

"I had to come." She smiled, her hands resting on his chest. "You left something behind."

"Yeah. You. I left you behind."

She kissed him on the lips again before pulling back. "Something else. You left something else behind."

For the life of him, he knew there was nothing else he needed. She was here, standing in his house. In his arms. She was here with *him*.

She reached into the bag hanging from her shoulder and pulled out *Persuasion*. "You left this behind."

"Really? You came back to return my book?"

"You weren't done reading it, were you?"

"No. Absolutely not." He took it out of her hand and dropped it on the floor. "I'm glad you brought it back. Now tell me you're staying."

Nadine stared at his chest. "Well, after our talk in Hythe, I realized I've been doing this job since I was twenty-two. And not once during that time have I taken a vacation."

"A vacation. You went to 2078, made your report, and asked for a vacation?"

"No, I couldn't do that." She smiled up at him. "What if they said no? What if they already had my next mission lined up?"

"So, you came here instead."

"Yeah. You know the old saying, it's better to ask forgiveness than permission."

Xander lifted her in his arms again and kissed her. He'd asked for extra days. They were going to have them.

Maybe, a lot of extra days.

EDITION NOTE

Dear Reader—

Thank you for reading *Jane Austen* Cannot *Marry!* If you enjoyed it, be sure to leave a review online.

If you like second-chance romance, we hope you will take a look at *Borrowed Dreams*, the first installment of the Pennington Family series. In that award-winning novel, a wonderful woman named Millicent Wentworth, who was introduced to readers in *The Promise*, has a chance at happiness with the notorious and badly wounded 'Lord of Scandal', Lyon Pennington, Earl of Aytoun. Reviewers have referred to this as a fresh twist on the Beauty and Beast tale.

AUTHOR'S NOTE

We hope you enjoyed reading the first book in our Quantum Commuters series, *Jane Austen* Cannot *Marry!* Many of you who have been following us might have questions about why we choose this path for our next project.

Earlier this year, I (Nikoo) was given the difficult diagnosis of metastatic breast cancer. My initial bout with breast cancer occurred nineteen years ago. Now, it's back. At the date of this publication, I've already started treatment.

Learning of my prognosis, I was thrown into a very difficult state of mind, trying to come to terms with the time that I have left in this world. We're all mortal, but sometimes it's more difficult to have the vague, hypothetical 'someday' replaced by a more finite window of time. During the early months, Jim and I had many conversations about what I would like to do with the time I have left. It was then that the idea of this novel was conceived and took shape.

In our novel, quantum commuters are people who have terminal illnesses. As time travelers, however, they can extend their lives and find personal fulfillment through journeys into the past. Sort of like writers do.

We chose the mountain town of Elkhorn as the setting for the Colorado portion of this story. For those of you who have read our Nik James Westerns, you're familiar with the place. We thought it would be fun to revisit this silver boomtown a century and a half after the gunslinger Caleb Marlowe strode along those streets.

Jane Austen is one of our all-time favorite authors. We don't have to tell anyone that she is one of the most important writers of her time. Her name is as well-known and her stories as familiar to us as any author writing in the English language. But it occurred to us that if Austen knew she would be dying at the age of 41, how might she have acted? Would she have written with the same passion? The same genius? And added to that knowledge, what if we gave her a chance to spend her last years in the arms of a man who loved her? We know that she never married, but what if she were given that opportunity? Would she choose security? Or a legacy of literary greatness?

We know that *we* choose to appreciate each day that is given to us, regardless of how many or how few we're destined to have. We were never guaranteed a *forever*.

Finally, I'd like you to know that I'm fully prepared for the challenge cancer presents, for as long as I can maintain my strength and my spirit and my hope. Through the stories Jim and I have created, I've tried to make this world a better place. I plan to continue doing so.

I love my husband and children and their families immeasurably. And I will always cherish you, my friends. I am extremely grateful for the trust you've placed in us in allowing us to entertain you and be even a small part of your lives.

Thank you.

Wishing you peace and health...always.

Note: As authors, we have always written our stories for you, our beloved readers. If you enjoyed *Jane Austen* Cannot *Marry!*, please leave a review online and tell a friend, tell two friends, tell many friends. And please visit us on our website - www.MayMcGoldrick.com for the complete list of our books and for the chance to keep up with our cancer journey on my blog.

Finally, if you haven't already done so, sign up for our newsletter and follow us on BookBub.

ABOUT THE AUTHOR

USA Today Bestselling Authors Nikoo and Jim McGoldrick have crafted over fifty fast-paced, conflict-filled novels, along with two works of nonfiction, under the pseudonyms May McGoldrick, Jan Coffey, and Nik James.

 These popular and prolific authors write historical romance, suspense, mystery, historical Westerns, and young adult novels. They are four-time Rita Award Finalists and the winners of numerous awards for their writing, including the Daphne DeMaurier Award for Excellence, the *Romantic Times Magazine* Reviewers' Choice Award, three NJRW Golden Leaf Awards, two Holt Medallions, and the Connecticut Press Club Award for Best Fiction. Their work is included in the Popular Culture Library collection of the National Museum of Scotland.

facebook.com/MayMcGoldrick

twitter.com/MayMcGoldrick

instagram.com/maymcgoldrick

bookbub.com/authors/may-mcgoldrick

Made in the USA
Columbia, SC
02 November 2022

70338848R00178